The Third Movement

The Third Movement

A Novel by

Gerald Buttrose

Nenge Books, Australia

The Third Movement
by Gerald Buttrose

Published by Nenge Books, Australia
ABN 26809396184
www.nengebooks.com
Email: nengebooks1@gmail.com

Book and cover design, desktop and editing by Nenge Books
Cover graphics: Music score - Michaelangeloop/Shutterstock.com
                Soldier - Rose Makin/Shutterstock.com

Nenge Books is a small Australian independent publisher assisting authors and writers to publish their stories using cost effective print-on-demand technology. Enquiries from authors and writers are welcomed at nengebooks1@gmail.com

Hardcover ISBN 978-0-6488206-5-9

Paperback ISBN 978-0-6488206-4-2

Ebook ISBN 978-0-6488206-6-6

Dedication

This book is humbly dedicated to those hundreds of Australians whose bodies lie in the Bomana War Cemetery in Papua New Guinea. They sacrificed their very young lives in the battle for Kokoda in 1942 and their victory prevented the invasion of our shores by a merciless enemy.

Contents

Foreword

*W*hen Gerald Buttrose completed his manuscript *The Third Movement*, he didn't put his name on it – but merely signed off as "An Australian story by an Australian author."

However, there's no cause for such modesty. Gerald spins a great yarn and *The Third Movement* is an engrossing Australian saga. When I first read the manuscript, I couldn't put it down. The life of Patrick Sheridan completely captured my imagination.

Gerald is my uncle. We met when I was about six months old during World War II. He had returned from New Guinea where he served with the Australian Army and came to visit his oldest brother, my father Charles, in Sydney. Gerald says there was an immediate connection between us. Today that connection is even stronger.

Of the seven original Buttrose siblings only Gerald, now 97, and his youngest sister Teresa 95, are alive. They are our family's super agers and we are all proud of them both.

After the War, Gerald had a successful career in business and became Managing Director of Fesq & Co, a leading wholesale wine and spirits company based in Sydney. He kept his story-telling ability under wraps, but not apparently from his wife, Colleen, and their four children.

According to Dominica, Bernadette, Geraldine and Michael, for as long as they can remember their father told them stories about growing up, family and the War. They loved hearing them and as Gerald told his stories with "humour and fanfare" he always had their complete attention.

He began writing down his stories when one of his brothers Phil, or "Apricot" as his siblings called him, had a major operation. Convalescence was slow and to give Phil and his wife, Josie, a laugh and something to read together, Gerald began writing his stories in weekly instalments.

Phil and Josie waited with excitement and anticipation for each instalment and not even Gerald knew where a story would go or end, until he put pen to paper. (This was in pre-computer days!)

These stories live on as they have been passed down to Gerald's grandchildren who love them as much as their parents did.

When Gerald's daughter, Geraldine, became a schoolteacher at Taree on the mid north coast of New South Wales, Gerald turned his hand to children's stories and created *Algernon the Donkey* for her to read to her class and for the children to draw illustrations.

And then along came Patrick, his appearance coincided with Gerald being diagnosed with wet age-related macular degeneration (AMD), a chronic eye disease that is the leading cause of vision loss and blindness in Australia. My father and two of the other siblings also had AMD. By the time Gerald was diagnosed, a drug treatment had been developed to stop the progression of wet AMD. It involves eye injections every four to six weeks.

At the time I was patron of Macular Disease Foundation Australia and knew the importance of Gerald having prompt treatment with a retina specialist, and made him come to Sydney from his home in Ballina for an appointment. As a result, his vision was saved. His older siblings were not so fortunate.

He has had more than 100 injections since beginning treatment 13 years ago and his doctor says his sight is better now than it was before he starting getting the sight-saving eye injections.

Patrick came into existence when Gerald began treatment. He was so grateful that his sight had been saved that he felt he had to do "something worthwhile."

Writing gives Gerald great enjoyment and building the characters in Patrick's story became a passion that kept him busy for hours every day. The story covers Patrick's decision to join up and do his part for Australia during World War II, tearing him from his family, his friends and his music – his musical talent is a driving force in his life as readers will discover.

For Gerald, *The Third Movement* carries an important message. He believes the sacrifices and courage shown by Australian troops who fought in Tobruk and North Africa, and Papua New Guinea have never been really understood or valued well enough by his fellow Australians. He hopes his book will correct that.

Originally Patrick's story was intended only for Gerald's immediate family but his extended family including his wife, his children, grandchildren, nieces, nephews and cousins thought otherwise.

Ita Buttrose
Sydney, May 2021

Historical Note

Between the years 1939 and 1945 there were four major conflicts fought throughout the world. These were the wars in Western Europe, The Middle East, Russia and the war in the Pacific against Japan. Each of these were major confrontations by any standard but were collectively known simply as World War II.

This story makes the point that the Australian Imperial Forces, known as the AIF, were the only ground troops from any of the Allied nations called upon to play a major role in two of those wars. This came about in 1942 when Australian Prime Minister Curtin had the 6th and 7th Divisions of the AIF recalled home from service in the Middle East to assist in repelling a Japanese invasion of Australia. Curtin had little other option at the time and probably did not realise his action would result in the deaths of thousands of young men who had already survived a long, bloody war on the other side of the world.

The majority of the soldiers in these Divisions had lived through great battles in the Western Desert, Greece, Crete, Lebanon and the special hellholes of Tobruk and Bardia. After enduring so much it was a tragic circumstance that their Country was compelled to ask them to do more but, to their eternal credit, they did so without demur. Upon their return to Australia from the Middle East, they were given brief home leave before being sent to jungle training camps in Queensland and then posted to fight the Japanese in New Guinea and other islands of the South Pacific.

Today, one can walk down rows and rows of grave sites in these places and learn the majority of these soldiers were still in their early twenties when they died for their country... veterans indeed!

Lest we forget? Of course they will be forgotten... the passing years and human nature will take care of that. Writing about those heroes can help delay that process and what follows here could be the story of some of those soon-to-be-forgotten young men who fought so valiantly for their country in two great theatres of war.

Though inspired from a range of actual experiences, the characters in this novel are ficticious. Any resemblance to actual persons, names or events is entirely unintentional and I apologise if any offence is created. At the same time I have sought to maintain historical accuracy when referring to actual places, people and key events.

Gerald Buttrose
Ballina, NSW
May 2010

Prologue

It was late on a Friday afternoon during the first week of September, 1939, when Julian Morrison burst into the Conservatorium studio.

"Quick, Pat, turn on the wireless," he stammered, quite out of breath, "my wife just rang to say Neville Chamberlain is about to make a statement on the BBC."

The British Prime Minister, in gravest of tone, gave a brief preamble concerning the German invasion of Poland and of how it had ignored the Allies' ultimatum to withdraw by the required time and date, "and, therefore, this Country is now in a state of war with Germany."

As Patrick stood there beside Julian, he was watching his mentor. When the Prime Minister uttered those final words, Julian appeared to droop. With shoulders sagged forward and a now haggard face, he became a figure of total despair.

As an Englishman he had lived through the 'War to end all Wars' when three million of his young British contemporaries were slain on the battlefields of France. He still had many close relatives and friends in the Old Country and dreaded the thought of what fate may now have in store for them.

As Julian left the studio without another word, Patrick was left to his own thoughts. He had enough Irish blood in his veins not to be too concerned for the British, but after reading and hearing of the speed at which the Nazis had swept through Poland, he had the awful thought that they could conquer the rest of Europe. That would have serious consequences for Australia, which was virtually unarmed. If it were cut off from the Mother Country and the rest of the Empire, Australia would be quite defenceless. Only last week he'd listened to the ABC when a panel of military experts discussed the possibility of war in Europe and what that could mean to our country. It gave emphasis to what the situation in the Middle East could become in the event of a conflict if, as was highly likely, Italy joined forces with Germany.

Apparently the Italians had over half a million troops stationed in Libya and Ethiopia, whereas the British only had a skeleton force for the entire Western Desert. The point they were making was that the Italians, using those forces, would be able to overrun Egypt and take the Suez Canal in the process. This would isolate the Sub-Continent, Singapore, Malaya, Hong Kong, and Australia and New Zealand. These places would just wither on the vine until the Axis Powers got around to occupying them. Such were the thoughts running at random through his mind after hearing the declaration. What he was endeavouring to determine for himself was whether or not the outbreak of war in Europe really constituted an armed threat to his own country.

If the answer to that had been "yes", he would have known where his duty lay and would have acted accordingly. But the opinion he reached was to wait and see how the war progressed in Europe before doing anything. Hopefully, by then there would prove to be no need to feel concern for Australia's security.

After leaving the studio he deliberately switched off from the war and turned his head to happier, lighter thoughts. He would shortly be meeting Cathy for dinner and afterwards, so as to honour a long standing promise, take her dancing at 'The Trocadero'. He'd declined at first and told her it was no place for young ladies from the Eastern Suburbs, and her mother would not approve anyway. She boohooed that and said many of her friends went to 'The Troc' on Friday nights - it was quite a respectable place of enjoyment for normal young people.

As they dined, they discussed more serious subjects than usual. The war, of course, and the immediate concern she had for her brothers and the possibility of them becoming involved. Patrick did not tell her then of how he felt about the matter as that would only add to her concern. Instead, he changed the subject to the recent confirmation of her appointment to the first violin section of the Sydney Symphony Orchestra. She was to commence early in the New Year and had begun a daily practise routine to make sure she remained on top of her instrument. He spoke warmly and encouragingly about all she had achieved, pointing out that she would be one of the youngest players in the important ensemble. Until she met Patrick, the violin was the only thing in life Cathy had taken seriously. She was looking forward to the role she would soon play in the profoundest way of performing classical music.

She knew of Patrick's changed career plans and of how he was waiting to hear what the ABC would come up with - and that this may be sooner than expected now that war had actually been declared.

"You're going to have a lot of time on your hands when you finish at the Con, my boy, what will you do?" she asked.

"With the piano around my neck I will never have a lot of spare time. It's like your violin - pretty demanding in its way," he replied. "So there will be the usual daily slog for a start. I'll only accept worthwhile engagements, Cath, and if these don't eventuate, I'll go back home to Magdalene and try to write some decent music. The war in Europe can't last forever!"

He didn't see the slightly shocked look on her face as he imparted his intentions but became aware she was staring quite forlornly at him.

"You mean you could take off for Bathurst and just leave me here?" she retorted.

Then he realised what he had just said. "Of course not, Cath, I'd thought about getting Dad to take you on as a jillaroo and then we could see each other now and then," he replied with light sarcasm, before adding more gently, "You belong to the SSO now, girl, and that demands you be down here. We'd just have to work something out if I do go back home."

There was a small tear on her cheek as she gazed across the table at him with a soulful look in her dark blue eyes.

"Let's get this straight, Pat Sheridan," she intoned rather wistfully. "A few weeks back I told you I had a crush on you but wanted to find out if I liked you. Well, I have found out, and I do like you but I'm afraid it is more than that, for I find myself in love with you in the worst possible way. So, if it became a choice between you and the SSO, you would win hands down."

He'd noticed she was upset and had reached over and taken her hand in his. It was occasions like this when his shyness returned and as she finished speaking he was staring down at the white tablecloth.

For a moment or two he stayed like that and then looked up at her serious face and said, "Well, I'm afraid we are in a hell of a mess, Cathy, because I feel exactly the same way."

I

Family

Chapter 1

Irene Sheridan woke early on that day in 1917 that was to change the rest of her life. She heard Bill, the property roustabout, enter the house as he did most mornings and put milk he had just taken from the cows, and perhaps a few eggs from the fowl run, into the cool room adjoining the kitchen.

She saw no point in getting up yet as there was little for her to do. The roustabout's wife would arrive shortly to clean out and light the big wood stove in the kitchen. After bringing in sufficient firewood to last the day, she would sweep and tidy up the kitchen and veranda areas before returning to her humpy on the other side of the creek which ran through the property. The rest of the interior homestead Irene maintained herself but as her husband was away again she saw no urgency about this.

As she lay there that morning, deep in the double bed, she was enveloped in a sense of melancholy as she reflected on her life since she married Tom Sheridan those eleven long years ago.

Irene had come from a happy and contented family background. She and her two older sisters had been educated at the Catholic Convent in Bathurst, a large country town in the midwest of New South Wales and about 130 miles from Sydney. Their father was the local Stock and Station Agent, Jack Brennan, a respected and popular figure in the community and a pillar of the local Catholic Church.

The Brennans were relatively well off and lived in a large, comfortable home on the outskirts of the town. Jack's wife, Catherine, was a good-looking, intelligent and hardworking soul who made their house a home and a source of security as well as a place of peaceful contentment for her husband and her children.

The Brennans liked entertaining and as the girls were growing up their home always seemed to be full of young people enjoying themselves. The whole family had a love of music and Catherine, a self-taught pianist, often accompanied Jack in entertaining guests with his uncommonly good tenor voice. The three girls learnt the piano at the Convent but it was Irene who showed most promise as the extent of her love for the instrument exceeded that of her older sisters.

Her siblings married quite young and moved away from home and she was 22 when she met Tom Sheridan at a dance night at the Bathurst Church Hall. They were attracted to each other despite the six year difference in their ages.

The mutual attraction quickly developed into a fine romance and she was ecstatic and excited when accepting his proposal of marriage less than six months after their first meeting.

She was in love, her parents and her friends seemed to approve of Tom. And so it was, before the year was out, the Bathurst Parish Priest, Fr. Ryan, was able, with due ceremony, to pronounce them man and wife. It was the years which followed that occupied her thoughts that morning.

After their honeymoon in Sydney and in the summer of 1906 Tom took her to live at Magdalene, his family's sheep property located 32 miles from Bathurst, out along the main track to Orange. The property was named after his grandmother who had raised seven children under difficult circumstances in County Limerick when Ireland was still under the British heel. The youngest of her brood was Tom's father, Denny, who came by himself to Australia whilst still in his late teenage years and after working for some years on various pastoral properties gratefully accepted a land grant from the Government New South Wales.

With endless of days of back-breaking work clearing the land, and despite difficult economic times, two years of drought and a devastating flood, within a few years Denny was able to transform Magdalene into a going concern. He found time to marry a good Australian girl who bore him two sons, Tom and his brother Ian. From an early age the boys were expected to help with running the property but their mother made certain sufficient time was put aside for her to give them a basic education.

When their parents died within a few months of each other, Ian decided to return to Ireland and assigned his half-share of Magdalene which they jointly-inherited from their father to Tom. Tom accepted the gift on the understanding, should Ian come back to Australia, all his rights to the property would be reinstated.

It was against this background of her early years at Magdalene that Irene reminisced this morning in bed. From the outset of their courtship she and Tom had discussed plans for the future many time. Tom was anxious to expand his holding by acquiring other property and she had grand ideas for making the Magdalene homestead into the type of family home in which she was raised. Fundamental to all their plans, however, was their great desire to raise a large family of happy, healthy Australian children.

To her great dismay and unending disappointment their wish was unfulfilled and, after four years of trying and seeking the best medical advice available, they remained childless. As time went by they ceased to try and Tom became colder and more distant and she was certain he blamed her for this calamity in their lives. She was aware it had not occurred to Tom the problem may lie with him, although her doctor advised he could find no reason why she should not conceive.

He started to spend more and more time away from the homestead. Whereas in the earlier years he left the mustering and droving of his sheep to the Aboriginal stockmen, Tom now did a lot of this work himself which meant he was absent from the homestead on occasions for weeks at a time. In the past few years he had been away more than he was at home.

During his earlier absences she contended with her isolation and extreme loneliness by spending long hours in the garden she had created at the side of the homestead. This gave her great satisfaction for a time but the recent droughts meant there was no water to spare for her flowers. Many were the times she watched in dismay as her plants died and withered away. She read voraciously when books and other reading material were available but the only true bastion against utter distraction was her piano. But even the solace of that escape was starting to wane as she yearned for somebody to share the enjoyment of the music she played so well.

When she finally arose and went to the kitchen her dark thoughts returned as she drank her morning cup of tea. Another long, pointless day lay ahead of her and gave her cause to compare her present existence with the happy and active life she led before she married Tom. Her resentment of him was now deeper than ever as her state of loneliness and isolation were compounded with an awareness of his deliberate neglect and near abandonment of her. At thirty three she was still young but life was passing her by. She experienced all the emotions and possessed all the passion of a healthy young woman. Her rising frustrations over the past five years were beginning to brim over. Recently she had entertained the idea of leaving Tom, but being raised in a good Catholic home, divorce was something she had not previously taken into the equation of her problem solving. The other question she had asked herself, of course, was, where would she go if she left Magdalene. She had no ready answer to this.

Burdened with these thoughts her mood had not improved as she set out in the late afternoon with the two homestead kelpies to walk the mile or so to the painted kerosene tin mail box at the front gate of the property, adjacent to the road, or rather track, leading to Orange. The mail bus came every second Wednesday and a letter from her parents, who had retired and moved to Wagga Wagga, or from one of her sisters, were now the highlights in her secluded life.

Chapter 2

There were only two letters, one from her mother, which she put in the pocket of apron as a deferred pleasure to be read by the light of the Tilley lamp when she got back to the drawing room. She opened and began to read the other from an old school friend who lived in Blainey and had just had her second child.

She had almost finished it when she heard an angry growl from the two dogs which made her look up to see the figure of a man walking down the track some hundred or so yards away. She called to the dogs, went back inside the homestead gate and started back towards the house. She had not gone far when the man reached the gate and called out to her in a light, cultured voice with a slight foreign accent.

"I say there" he said, "I am sorry to bother you but do you think you could let me have some water? I'm on my way to Orange and my bottle is just about empty. I would be most grateful."

She quietened the dogs, who had now started to bark, and turned around to look back at the caller. It was obvious he was not the type of sundowner common to this area. His voice alone gave testimony to that and now what she saw confirmed her initial surmise. A tallish fellow about forty, she guessed, reasonably well-built but because of the distance she was unable to fully discern the shape of his features. He wore a well-made grey business suit, which had seen better days, with an open-neck shirt and a short-brimmed felt hat pulled down over his eyes to protect them, no doubt, from the westering sun. A large sidepack hung from his shoulder to which was attached leather case of some description, which seemed unusual for someone on "shankses."

Feeling reasonably secure because of the dogs she decided to take a risk and help this stranger who appeared to have known better times.

"All right," she called to him, "you can come in if you like and get your water, but don't do anything to upset the dogs as they are just as likely as not to take your arm off."

After closing the gate after him, he caught up with her and the dogs and expressed his thanks. She could see now his face and smile were pleasant and there was a non-rugged masculinity about him which was more than noticeable. She was also somewhat surprised to see the item attached to his pack was after all a violin case, but thought no more of this as they reached the homestead gate.

"You will find the pump behind that barn over there," she told him pointing to a large out-building. "You can get your water and have a bit of a wash up if you like, we have enough water for that. Don't forget what I said about the dogs and whatever you do don't try to pat them. Find your own way out when you've finished and don't forget to close the gates." She knew that she sounded blunt but that was a accepted and proven attitude towards itinerants in this area. She went into the house and instead of opening and reading her mother's letter as she had intended, she went straight to the piano and soon commenced to play.

She thought she was in the mood for Bach but on finding a Schubert album on top of the sheet music in the piano seat, she looked through it instead and stopped at his Ständchen as for some reason she felt strangely drawn to this wistful and sombre piece she knew so well. She played it once and then again without being content she had done justice to the immortal Franz's *Serenade*. And now, as she played it for the third time, she was aware she had at last captured a true expression of the exquisite sense of sadness and yearning the composer intended to permeate this work. As she let the beauty of the music sweep over her, tears welled in her eyes as the pensive notes evoked the final realisation her precious girlhood dreams had gone forever.

She had barely concluded the last bars when she heard the unusual sound of a knock on the back door. She had forgotten all about the man from the track and dried her eyes before opening the door to find him standing there on the step. He looked very different somehow. He had shaved and washed and his coat had been replaced with a cleanish shirt he must have carried in his pack. The transformation was quite marked and she realised she was looking at a man who, in his day, had turned many a female head.

"What do you want?" she said.

"Oh, just to thank you for the use of the pump and say I appreciate the risk you took in admitting a stranger on to your property. I must also admit I've been standing out here listening to you play. It is such a long time since I heard any decent music and to be able to hear Schubert so beautifully played was a treat too good to walk away from. You do play remarkably well."

"Well, you obviously know something about music, so thanks for that," she said, maintaining the same abrupt tone of voice, "and you're welcome to the water."

As he smiled at her and turned to go on his way she realised what this very brief encounter had meant to her and, before she could stop herself, she inquired of him "What's with the violin case?"

He stopped and turned to face her. "I used to make my living with the fiddle but that was a long time ago. It would take too long to tell you the whole lousy story, but thanks again", and he turned to take his leave.

The tone of her voice had softened somewhat when she said, "Do you think you might play something for me?"

He turned again and looked at her from a different perspective and saw a fair-haired young woman with attractive features in need of cosmetic enhancement, and a good but slight figure ill-served by the drab clothes she wore. However, he learnt most about her from her moist, deep-set blue eyes which so clearly mirrored her heartbreaking loneliness and ever enduring sadness.

"I don't know why not," he said. "I will be sleeping rough tonight wherever I am so it doesn't matter much when I get away."

She opened the wire door to let him in to the kitchen. After detaching the violin case and putting it on the kitchen table, he dropped his pack on the floor

"I may play better for you if I could wash my hands in some warm water as my fingers are stiff and it would loosen them up a bit."

She pulled a chair out from the table and asked him to sit down and put before him a white enamel basin taken from the kitchen dresser. Taking the kettle from the stove, she proceeded to pour hot water into the basin.

"While you are doing that I will make you a cup of tea, if you like, and then perhaps we can get on with the violin."

She gave him a towel to dry his hands and put a cup of tea in front of him, together with some scones she had taken from the cool room. Telling him she would be back in a few minutes, she went to another part of the house.

Irene did not know what had come over her for she was in a state of excitement not experienced for many years. Not only was there somebody in the house she could actually talk to, but someone with whom she could possibly share for a short time her love of great music. The fact she found him slightly attractive gave her a sense of guilt at first and this was, no doubt, due to her Catholic upbringing. But this soon dissipated upon her reflecting how little residual loyalty she had left for Tom because of the neglectful and unfeeling way he had treated her for so long.

It turned out to be longer than a few minutes before she returned to the kitchen but he was still flexing the fingers of both hands trying to restore a degree of suppleness in them. He noticed she had changed into a light-blue cotton frock and had done sufficient touching-up to her hair and face to make her distinctly more attractive than when he first arrived.

He picked up his violin and followed her into the drawing room where she sat down at the piano. "You will probably need an A," she said. "It may not be spot on as the old Kapps is in need of a tune, but it will probably be near enough."

He took the violin and bow from the case and, after tightening the bow, lightly strummed the strings. There was no doubt the instrument was very much out of tune. She kept striking the A until he took the violin from under his chin and began to look through the music he also carried in the case.

"I really don't know what to play as I am not quite sure of your musical taste," he said looking straight at her. "There is this thing here of Saint-Saen's which is very pleasant and perhaps you would enjoy that? It is called *The Swan* and most fiddlers seem to have it in their repertoire these days. Let me know if you don't like it and we will try something else."

She was now sitting in one of the armchairs in the room and looking up at him. He propped the music up against the metronome on top of the piano and, after loosening his fingers once more with some very rapid scales, he turned towards her and commenced to play.

As the opening bars of this incredibly beautiful piece caressed her ears she closed her eyes, soon to find herself in a state of near ecstasy as the enchanting music began to plumb the very depths of her musical soul. Never had she expected to hear such exquisite music so magnificently played. She sat perfectly still but, at the risk of breaking the spell, opened her eyes briefly to look at the violinist who was bringing her such unbounded joy. The look on his face told her he was not in this world and seemed transcended to a place where only his music lived. The violin bore the appearance of age but the glorious timbre of its tone spoke eloquently of its undoubted classic origins. She resumed the delight of her musical reverie as the master and his instrument continued with their soulful and glorious harmony. It was some moments after the concluding bars before she opened her eyes again and without moving looked up at him.

He did not recognise the changed tone of voice she used when she asked softly, "What's your name?"

"Stefan Holst" he replied.

"Stefan, I cannot tell you just how much pleasure you have just given me. I will never forget the joy of these past few minutes as long as I live. I have waited so long to hear such music I had almost given up hope. Never have I heard anybody play any instrument with the beauty of the way you play your violin. I can never thank you enough."

He could see she had been really carried away and gracefully acknowledged her compliments, explaining his fingers were still not quite up to the task. When asked if he could possibly play something else for her, he replied, "Yes, why not. By the way, what is your name?"

When she replied he continued. "Well. Irene, I have this piece of Massenet's here which you may know. It's a bit hackneyed but as a violinist I still find *Meditation* somewhat uplifting."

She experienced very similar pleasure from this rendition and the emotional turbulence of her day of sad retrospection came to the fore as she tearfully thanked him once more for his music.

She dried her eyes and apologised for the tears, saying "I know I've kept you and you are probably anxious to be on your way," her tone now friendly and warm as she continued, "but there's a lamb's stew on the stove for my tea and you are welcome to share it before you go if you have the time."

"Thanks very much. I'm very peckish and that sounds great and, as I said, I am not in any great hurry."

It was, eventually, an enjoyable and entertaining meal for them both and after a shy and silent start they commenced to exchange all but the most intimate parts of their life stories.

Stefan Holst was the only son of Austrian parents who migrated to Australia from Vienna in 1895 when he was fifteen years old. His mother and father were musicians and he eventually became Professor for Violin at the Conservatorium. While incarcerated as an enemy alien in World War I, he lost his marriage and child. Unable to find work, an old student offered to 'put him up' and could give him a part-time position in his store with the added possibility of him finding work playing the violin evenings and weekends in the dining room of the Conobolas Hotel.

He accepted gratefully but found he only had enough money for the train fare as far as Bathurst and, therefore, would have to find his way by foot to his destination, which was over a hundred miles away. He had done a third of this trek when he found himself at Irene Sheridan's front gate.

She was able to thread parts of her own story into the conversation during the brief exposition of his life and despite his own desperate position she could see, from his sympathetic attitude, he felt strongly for her in her sad domestic plight.

After the meal they retired to the drawing room and she played some of her own favourite music for him before he raised his violin and began a selection of compositions he knew by heart. Her enjoyment of these was even greater, if that were possible, than his earlier rendition. Her enchantment was manifest in the expression on her attractive face. As he took the violin from his chin she came over and thanked him with all the sincerity of her being and reaching up, kissed him gently on the cheek.

Visibly and unbelievably struck by her unexpected affection he put down the violin, came over and took her in his arms, kissing her lips with a gentle passion which could not be misunderstood. At first she drew back as she realised what was happening. But then her own arousal, which she had not experienced for many years, took over and she drew herself back into his arms. It was many minutes before the first wave subsided and she freed herself from him. She left his side to turn down the gas lamp and lock the doors before returning and, as he kissed her once more, she took his hand and slowly led him down the long passageway to her bedroom and its large comfortable bed.

Upon entering the room she reached up again to put her arms around his neck and looked into his face seeking approval for what she was wordlessly proposing. What she saw there left no doubt of how he felt so she quietly closed the door and extinguished the bedside candle. In the pitch blackness which ensued, her loving arms sought her violinist as now she would attempt in one night to assuage all the sad frustration and bitterness which had been part of her young life for such a long time.

Chapter 3

*H*e was gone before the sun rose and Irene woke to find an empty space where he had slept beside her. However sad she was that he had departed she knew it was for the best but realised she could never forget this stranger who passed so briefly through her life and yet left her with memories to last a lifetime. He had satisfied her romantic yearnings to an extent she never dreamed possible. The exquisite sound of his violin was recorded forever in that special part of her soul she devoted to music.

And so this was a vastly different young woman from the one who had lain in this bed the previous morning. She felt an inexplicable sense of relief and lightness and a general underlying sense of happiness absolutely untrammelled by any sense of guilt. For the first time in many years her future did not seem bleak. Adultery was a matter of Confession but she could never tell the priest, in all honesty, that she was sorry for what had taken place. She would tell him she was sorry it was a mortal sin and hoped that would be sufficient to warrant his absolution. As for saying she would not commit that sin again, well, that depended on circumstances.

Tom Sheridan returned early one evening, a few days later from his nine week drove to a property on the other side of

Dubbo. For the first time in recent memory Irene came out of the house and down to the barn where he was feeding and watering his horse, the stockmen having taken the droving cart and horses to the outside stables where they also looked after the sheep dogs.

"How did it go?" she said.

"Oh, g'day Irene" He sounded tired. "Not too bad, I suppose. The bloody dingoes got a few head but other than that it was alright. Feeling a bit buggered though; it was bloody hot comin' back."

"I can see that," she said. "Look, there is some tucker on the stove and I'll run you a bath, so come up when you have finished with your horse."

He was surprised at this greeting and looked up at her retreating figure. She had been quite indifferent to him for some time now and their relationship had reached such an impersonal stage they were like two people who just happened to live the same house.

They no longer shared the master bedroom and he usually slept outside in a bed on the back veranda which was adjacent to the spare bedroom, where he kept his clothes and personal belongings. It was a nice change though, he thought, as he made his way up to the homestead and let himself into the kitchen.

He enjoyed the bath and sat down with her as they ate a satisfying meal she had prepared. They talked spasmodically about things in general but before the meal was quite over he started to droop from abject weariness and his constant yawning indicated the difficulty he had in keeping awake.

"You look like you have had it," she said, "better sleep in the big bed tonight as yours got wet with that rain we had the other day. I put your pyjamas on the pillow. I won't be in for a while as I will clean up here and then I want to play the piano before I turn in."

Though still surprised at this solicitude he offered no argument as he left the table and made his way up the passage to the bedroom. Within seconds of him falling into the large bed he was sound asleep.

It was some hours later before Irene joined him and he awoke as she gently rested her body against his. From then on, nature took its course and it seemed for a while like old times were back before eventually they fell in to a long and peaceful sleep.

It was about a month later when, without telling Tom why, she took the weekly mail bus to Bathurst and was dropped back two days later by the coach which ran between Bathurst to Dubbo. Tom, who had been a little more attentive of late, had heard the coach approaching and was waiting at the gate with the dogs when she got off the bus.

She was beaming as she made her way towards him and he asked, "What are you so bloody happy about?"

"None of your business, Tom Sheridan, and the only news I am prepared to give is to tell you your wife is pregnant and that Doctor Burton said to give you a 'well done'."

The Sheridan baby arrived at Magdalene on a mild, sunny morning in the early autumn of 1918. After attending to those items of procedure and care associated with the newborn, the midwife lowered a healthy baby boy into the arms of his waiting mother as she lay there on her bed, both tired out and overjoyed. Vapour shrouded Irene's eyes as she became enraptured by this wondrous moment in her life, a moment for which she had waited ever so long. Her tears of happiness were undiminished as she held her son up so that his face was close to hers and whispered, ever so gently, "Good morning Patrick Thomas Sheridan. Do have a wonderful life."

In due course Mrs. Slater, the midwife, opened the door to allow Tom Sheridan into the room to meet his son. "You better come in and have a look at this one, Mr. Sheridan," she said, "he is a dead ringer of you."

In true paternal fashion he had been pacing up and down the passageway for the two or three hours since Irene had gone into labour. As he came into the room he seemed overawed by the occasion. After looking down at the tiny face for some moments he leant over and kissed his wife before saying in a shy but affectionate way "Thanks, Ire, you've done a good job here, old girl."

Irene was grateful that her son had been born into, if nothing else, a reasonably united family household. She and Tom had made their peace very soon after her announcement and since that moment he had become a kind and attentive husband. He rarely left the property these days and would not remain away overnight unless it was most essential. He helped her with the housework, where appropriate, and renovated the second bedroom, which Irene had nominated for the nursery site, with new floor covering and a fresh coat of paint. By the time the new cot and mattress he had ordered from Bathurst had been installed, the baby's room was ready to go at least six months in advance of its required date.

Irene's attitude towards Tom also changed. Even though she could never forgive him for the way he had treated her, she never let the resentment she still felt show in any way. And, of course, her brief and loving episode with Stefan would always be a barrier to her resuming a loving relationship with Tom. He had returned now to sleep in their bedroom and she knew what his intentions would be after this baby was born - she even felt a little sad for him in the disappointment that would inevitably be his.

From the beginning the presence of the small child had an amazing effect on his parents as in less than a week the Magdalene homestead was transformed from a house into a home. The care and attention Tom extended to his wife and child were reciprocated by Irene to an acceptable extent and now a pleasant atmosphere prevailed throughout.

Mrs. Carter, the midwife, stayed on for another fortnight and by the time she said goodbye Irene was up and about and well versed in the essentials of raising a healthy infant child, as decreed by Mrs. Carter.

And so Patrick started life in what could be described as a happy home which seemed to be manifest in the child's demeanour of total contentment. Very rarely was he heard to cry and as the months went by his baby laughter and other cheerful gurgling noises could be heard coming from the nursery. This in itself was enough to add an extra dimension to the lives of the other two members of this formerly unhappy household.

Magdalene prospered as the price for wheat and wool rose considerably during the immediate postwar period. Tom was able to expand his holdings by acquiring some adjacent properties and thereby generated additional income from the land he owned.

In the early 1920s the advent of the motor car started to have an effect on the lives of people living in remote areas. Journeys which took hours by horse and trap could now be covered in a fraction of that time thus enabling residents in 'nearby' properties to call on each other from time to time. This helped to break down, to a greater extent, the utter isolation formerly endured by squatters and their families.

When Patrick was five years old Tom bought a new Model T from the Ford agent in Bathurst. In due course, Irene learnt to manage this new-fangled contraption and her days of perpetual loneliness were virtually gone forever. She planned on going to Sunday Mass in Bathurst at least once a month and meeting up again with her Catholic friends from the past, also insisting on Tom taking her shopping in town on a regular basis.

It was at about this time that Irene decided Patrick should learn to play the piano. In his infant years she took the opportunity of playing the piano whilst he was taking his afternoon sleep in the nursery. He was sometimes restless on these occasions and she found by bringing him into the room where she was playing he would lie in the pram quietly, seeming to listen to her music with his eyes wide open before dropping off to sleep. This apparent interest had continued up to the present time and now whenever she played in the daylight hours he would stop whatever he was doing and come and listen to her. Now, she decided, he was old enough to learn to play for himself.

By now Tom had come to the sad realisation that Patrick would never have brothers or sisters and that all his paternal ambitions would have to centre exclusively around his only child. He was, therefore, a little put out when he learnt of Irene's intention because he thought playing the piano was a bit "sissy" - he wanted his son to be raised as a real man. Besides, he had other plans for the boy and his future as eventual owner of Magdalene.

In the interests of continuing peace in the house, he did not voice his objection and surmised that the boy would drop the piano in favour of what he had in mind to offer him anyhow. He planned to give Patrick a pony of his own and teach him to ride so he could accompany him on some of the lighter jobs around the property. Getting him his own dog in due course would follow. That would help even more to get his thoughts out of doors and away from the drawing room and its musical environment. A gentle tug-of-war had started but it did not become a real issue between his parents as they realised their son would make up his own mind about these things just as soon as he was old enough to do so.

Patrick found he also had to find another hour or so in his carefree day for his mother to teach him the alphabet and the rudiments of reading and numbers, in preparation for enrolling him at the one-teacher school at Hedleys Gap when he reached the age of seven.

Chapter 4

The immediate years following Patrick's birth seemed to pass happily and quickly for the residents of Magdalene, and Irene was thankful there had been no real drama in their lives since he arrived. Therefore it was understandable Tom should read 'family upheaval' into the situation and was more than disturbed when, towards the end of the year 1930, Irene raised with him the matter of the boy's continuing education.

His primary school days at The Gap were just about over and it would mean a near-fulltime absence of at least three years in Bathurst if he were to pursue a secondary education to an acceptable standard. Tom thought one year of high school should be sufficient for a man who was to spend the rest of his life as owner-manager of a successful pastoral property.

"Why does he have to have so much learning?" Tom asked, raising the question some days later over the early breakfast table while Patrick was still in bed. "I only had Mum to teach me and I've done alright. I don't like it, Ire, the boy is far too young to be away from home for so long. If he is going to make his living from the land why can't we just let him learn what the land can teach him? Believe me that is more than enough for any man to learn."

Irene could see the question had been gnawing at him and he was having trouble retaining his composure, so she chose her words carefully,

"Look, Tom, I know how hard this is for you but have you thought he might like to do something else with his life. Times have changed and there are opportunities out there for people these days. They have started to move about more with steam trains, motor coaches and automobiles and there is no longer the need to be marooned in the Australian bush forever. All I want for him is a decent education so that he can become aware of what life can offer him, and then make up his own mind about how he wants to live it."

"That may be alright for you, Irene, but you know what I have always had in mind for Patrick. I'm past fifty now and getting on and won't be about the place for that much longer. I want him to be ready to take over here when I go. No! Three years is too long! Why don't we ask him how he feels about it?"

As she looked at him now, before replying she realised what he said about himself was true. He was getting old, not too many bush people lived beyond sixty these days. It was starting to show on him, the former dark curling main was now a thin tuft of grey and, between them, the passing years and hot Australian sun had left his brown face thin and wrinkled. She noticed the Irish eyes, which first attracted her to him, had receded somewhat and their wonderful shade of blue had started to fade. She could have felt a little sorry and somewhat sad for him now had he not destroyed the love and affection she felt for him during their courtship and the earlier years of their marriage.

"No, we will not ask him now. He is too young to make up his own mind and besides, it would be like asking him to choose between us, because he knows what I want him to do. But, I give you my firm promise, Tom, that when Patrick finishes high school the three of us will sit down together and decide what he should do with his future.

Irene had been adamant because the career she planned for Patrick required a well-informed mind and the required standard of education to qualify him to study for a Degree in Music when the time came. She was determined the ability she recognised in her son would be given every opportunity to blossom to its fullest extent, even if it meant a degree of confrontation with Tom.

She did not know if her son was a prodigy or not but had no doubt he was a most gifted child and, being at the same time aware of the source of that endowment, was determined such an astonishing legacy should not be wasted.

In less than three years of serious practical tuition, accompanied by an appropriate regimen of practise, and a thorough grounding in the theory of music, she found there was very little more she could teach Patrick about the piano. His ever increasing ability to read and understand the most difficult of scores had astounded her at first and then she accepted it as the natural progression of an extraordinary talent.

His mastery of the keyboard was plain to see but it was his gifted interpretation and intuition for difficult works for the piano, written by great composers, which took her breath away.

On a recent evening she had heard him play Brahms' *Wiegenlied,* a work he had learnt without her assistance. Technically it was a relatively simple piece but it left her in tears because of the sense of great serenity and peace it evoked in her by the exquisite tone and soft gentleness his playing brought to this most beguiling of lullabies.

No other music has moved her to that extent since she heard a very fine violinist play Massenet's *Meditation* in that same drawing room just a few short years back. It was not just admiration of the fine technique of those not yet fully grown hands, nor the actual joy she got from hearing that precious composition, which held that moment for her. No, it was more than that, for it was the moment which confirmed finally in her mind that Patrick had a potential for greatness.

Patrick had no such grand ideas about himself. His ability came to him without effort and he simply took it for granted. He certainly loved the piano and playing fine classical music and he did not mind the two or three hours of practise each day his mother insisted upon. In fact he mostly looked forward to it.

He did, though, feel like a slightly different person when sitting at the piano. But he had no trouble in immediately shedding that persona once he was away from it, for in all other respects Pat Sheridan was just a normal boy growing up in the bush, able to contend daily with the many joys, little problems and the great degree of aloneness such an existence entailed. He certainly had no 'airs' about himself and would have been surprised that anybody should think he should.

Patrick's life started to change from the time he was six years old. He went from being a child who spent much of his time at his mother's knee into a little boy who was able to help his father with his daily work on the property.

Early on the morning of his sixth birthday he was in the kitchen with his mother when his father called to him from the back veranda. He went out to find him standing by the stoop holding the reins of a small chestnut pony, fully saddled with adjusted stirrups and ready for riding.

"What did Mum give you for birthday?" Tom asked him. "I got a good game called Ludo and a big packet of lollies, Dad," he replied, staring at the most beautiful pony he had ever seen.

"All that! Well you're a lucky lad, aren't you? I'll give you a game of Ludo after dinner tonight if you like and perhaps you will give me some of your lollies then. Tell Mum I will see her a bit later on. I should be back in time for lunch"

He turned to go and started to walk away with the pony, then stopped and came back to the stoop.

"By the way, Son, this is yours" he said, handing Patrick the reins of the pony.

Patrick was speechless for a moment and then, throwing his arms around the little horse's neck, he said, "Gee whiz, thanks Dad. Is he really mine to ride and keep? I bet he is the best horse in the world."

"Yes, he's all yours Pat, and if you do look after him properly he will make a good mate for you."

As Tom was lifting him into the saddle, Irene came out on to the veranda because she knew what had been going on. She watched as Tom adjusted the stirrups further for Patrick's legs and with the boy holding the reins he took hold of the bridle and led the pony down the track which led to the barn. Irene called out to him as her son took his first ever ride on a horse

"Now, you be careful Patrick and don't fall off. And you tell him, Tom, he is not to gallop that thing until he is a lot older, and do be careful of his hands."

The little horse became the centre of Patrick's life. In no time at all Tom had taught him to ride sufficiently well so as not to require further supervision. He showed him how to unsaddle and resaddle and generally adjust straps and stirrups, as well as telling him how and when to feed the horse and how to rub him down after a long ride.

They all thought about a name at the dinner table that night and after turning down many suggestions settled for 'Old Mo'. This was Irene's nomination as she had noticed grey hairs at the junction of the horse's nostrils which was unusual for such a young colt. So 'Old Mo' it was and all agreed the name had a good ring to it.

Being satisfied, he could now ride well enough, Tom allowed Patrick to accompany him on jobs which were not too far from the homestead. Sometimes they mustered sheep from one paddock into another with the help of the station dogs. The boy got a lot of pleasure watching them work the flocks in response to his father's whistles, and he told Tom afterwards he wanted to learn how to do that. Quite often he had to help with the more mundane task of repairing fences which surrounded the property. There were mobs of kangaroos in the area and the fences were designed to keep them off the property. Many of the kangaroos were unsuccessful when attempting the leap in search of greener pastures and the speed at which they hit the top strands brought about a need for constant inspection and repair.

On other days he had ridden with his father when laying bait for dingoes, which were prevalent at certain times of the year. Patrick did not quite understand why his father did this because he had pointed out to him previously the bodies of these wild dogs which had taken these baits. They were such nice looking animals it made him sad to think his father had killed them.

"Look, boy," said Tom at the time, when he noticed the near tears, "you must understand once and for all these bloody dingoes are rotten mongrels which kill our sheep and baby lambs and we have to poison as many of the buggers as possible to stop them doing it. If you want to cry over something then cry over the lambs they've killed. You have to do this kind of thing when you live in the bush and you had better get used to the idea quick."

"Yes Dad. I understand," he responded quietly. But he still felt badly about those nice doggies he saw on lying dead on the ground.

This was the beginning of Patrick's apprenticeship as a sheep farmer and before he was finished he would be capable of managing the property on his own.

Being an only child and living in such isolation, Patrick has never played with or had hardly any contact with other children. He was, therefore, in for quite a shock when he started school at Hedleys Gap just prior to his seventh birthday.

For the first few days of the term his mother drove him to the school in the Model T but from then on he made the three and a half mile journey on Old Mo. It was an easy, flat ride which only required him to follow the main track to Orange, which ran past Magdalene's front gate. The school comprised one large classroom and an annexe where pupils left their coats, hats, lunchboxes and other paraphernalia not required in class. In the room were twelve desks in three orderly rows of four, each one capable of accommodating two pupils.

The present roll listed the names of nineteen children, eight girls and eleven boys, and their teacher was twenty-five year old Mr. Brady, who taught all grades from One to Six. After Grade Six the students either dropped out of education altogether or continued on to high school in Bathurst or Orange. This was a sore point with Ted Brady as there were many more of the former than the latter and he saw several potentially good minds go undeveloped because they were denied further education, mainly due to the family's poor financial circumstances.

Edward Barton Brady was a dedicated teacher who loved his job and enjoyed imparting knowledge to keen young minds from the bush. If he had one failing, it was his long standing love affair with the Land of the Southern Cross. No matter what subject he was teaching he always found a way to make reference to this golden land in seemingly relevant context.

It was the practise in most state public schools in New South Wales to start the day's work with the singing of God Save the King. This did not happen at Hedleys Gap and perhaps Brady's Irish background accounted for this, but his students did sing daily before being seated, and he sang loudest of all.

God Bless our lovely morning land, Australia.
On earth there is no other land,
Like our enchanting Southerland,
Our own dear home,
Our Mother Land.

Australia.

Patrick Sheridan had not yet come under the influence of Mr. Brady but in the years which lay ahead he would leave an indelible impression on the boy. Above all, the love of Country he instilled in him would last always and became the source of inspiration needed to make some of the most important decisions of his life.

Chapter 5

The pupils at Hedleys Gap were mainly a friendly lot and the young Sheridan had no trouble settling in there. A little shy at first he watched and heard how things were said and done in the classroom and school yard, and within a week or so he was well into the way of things. Because he enjoyed their company he was amiable and pleasant and most of the children, even the older ones, went out of their way to make him feel welcome. He liked Mr. Brady and had no trouble keeping up with the other three children doing Grade One with him because his mother had instructed him well.

He appeared to be a little brighter than the other boy and two girls in his grade as he often had his hand up first in response to teacher's questions. He soon realised instinctively this was wrong and he should sometimes give the others a chance to go first. Particularly the boy, Billy Tunstall, who walked slowly and wore a strange heavy boot on his left foot which made him a limp. This puzzled Patrick until Irene explained that Billy had a 'club foot' and could not walk and play like other boys. From then on Patrick would sit with Billy for part of every lunch hour when the other boys were playing those games which precluded Billy because of his foot. On the day he rode Old Mo to school for the first time, two of the older boys helped him unsaddle and showed him where to tether his horse under the shade of an old peppercorn tree. They got him the bucket used to get water to slake his mount's predictable thirst. There were only three other horses in the yard as the rest of students apparently walked to school.

Irene would see him off most mornings at the front gate before he started his long ride. He did not mind the trek except his mother told had him he could ride Old Mo no faster than a trot. He found the steady jogging monotonous and although normally an obedient boy he would wait until he was around the first bend of the track and out of his mother's sight before he gave Old Mo a kick in the ribs and sent him into a gallop. This not only made for a quicker journey but also a more enjoyable one. His mother would never know about it!

On one such occasion just before the end of the first term he noticed two riders come out of the scrub just up ahead and he rode even faster until he caught them. They turned out to be the Hinton boys, two brothers, Geoff and Noel, who were students at the school. Pat had not recognised them in the distance. Their family had a mixed farm a mile or so back in the scrub near a place called Mundina, which was little more than a clearing in the bush. Geoff was in Grade Three and his brother in Two. "Where did you come from?" asked Geoff.

"I come along here every day," said Pat, "but today I galloped pretty hard and that is how I caught up with you."

"You're a bit small to be galloping aren't you?" joined in Noel. "If you got bucked off out here there would be nobody to pick you up."

"I know," said Pat, "that's what Mum said but it takes too long if I just jog along."

"In any case," said Geoff, "from now on you can ride from here with us and we can look after you but don't go falling off just because of that, alright?"

This assurance came from a nine-year-old but he was 'one of the big boys' and therefore some kind of a hero to Pat, who was delighted with the arrangement.

Irene was pleased when Patrick gave her the news as she still had misgivings about this long ride for her seven-year-old son.

A strong boyhood friendship developed between Pat Sheridan and the Hintons and it would endure long after their days of school. None of the trio were plaster saints by any means. In their years together at The Gap many were the times they had to answer to Ted Brady or to their parents for varying degrees of misbehaviour. One particular incident stood out in the minds of all concerned.

It was just after Patrick had started in Grade Three. They arrived at school on a hot February morning to find Mr. Brady was sending everybody back home as the classroom was like a furnace and there was every prospect of continuing hot weather. So the three boys turned their horses around and started back home. They had only gone about half a mile when Geoff Hinton suggested they go out to Waddy's Creek and have a swim.

"Gee, I'd love to do that," said Pat, "but I can't swim."

"Doesn't matter, we can look after you. Besides it isn't very deep so you won't drown," said Geoff, "what about you, Noelly?"

"I don't mind but it's a fair way out there and we'll have to be sure we get home about the usual time otherwise we will cop it from Dad," said his brother. Patrick thought about the trouble he too would be in if he got home late but the temptation to have his first swim was overwhelming.

So the three boys tuned off the track and made their way through the bush towards the creek.

Waddy's Creek was more like a billabong, a circular, shallow stretch of water about fifty yards wide and surrounded by several old Weeping Willows. The Hintons tied their horses, whipped off all their clothes and were splashing around in the water almost before Patrick dismounted. Rather diffidently, he stood on the bank and watched them as he had never taken off his clothes before in the open.

"Come on Sherry, hurry up the water's good and not very deep so you be alright," yelled Geoff.

That was all the encouragement Pat needed and he was soon in the creek with them, in his birthday suit and enjoying the swim now that he found the water was cool and not very deep. They chased and splashed each other and the Hintons showed Patrick how well they could swim. They were not that good but Patrick was impressed and decided to ask his father to teach him some day. When they came out they pulled their underpants on over wet bodies and sat on a log, danglling their legs in the water whilst eating the school lunch their mothers had put in the saddlebags.

Geoff looked up at the sun and said it was after midday and there would only be time for a quick swim before taking Patrick back to the Orange track if they were all to get home on time. Noel suddenly raised his head and looked over towards the horses as something seemed to be spiking them.

"You better have a look, Noel," ordered Geoff. "We don't want them taking off."

He had walked the thirty or forty yards to where the horses were tethered and was holding his mount by the bridle and stroking its nose when he let out a wild yell. "I think I've been bitten by a snake, a big black bugger and it's taken off into the bush near you."

Geoff rushed to his side "Now sit down and don't move. Where did he get you?

Noel showed him a spot just above the ankle on his left leg and Geoff said, "Yeah. He got you. Now you sit still and don't move that leg while I get my pocket knife."

Noel started to cry because he knew Geoff would have to cut his leg the way their father had shown them. Patrick also wanted to cry because he was frightened. He did not know what was going on, but he held back his tears and instead tried to console Noel, who was in a near state of shock.

Patrick held on to Noel as Geoff tied very tightly a wide piece of twine, also brought from the saddlebag, around the leg just above bite which was now starting to inflame. The two younger boys watched in horror as Geoff took his pocket knife and cut into the skin over the bite until bled bleed freely and he then, leaning over began sucking the blood before quickly spitting it out onto the ground beside him.

Patrick took his legs and they carried him into the shade of a tree so that he could sit up and rest his back against the trunk. Geoff tore the tail off his shirt and made a light bandage on the wounded area before taking Pat to one side.

"Look, Pat, you will have to stay with him while I go and get Dad. We should be back in an hour or so and I can then take you out to the Orange track and you will be able to find your way home from there. Don't let him move but Dad also told us not to let him go to sleep."

Going back to Noel, he said. "You'll be alright. I think I got most of the poison and you were lucky it was a black bugger and not a brownie. I'm going to get Dad."

When Geoff had gone Pat sat beside him on the ground and kept asking, "How do you feel, Hinto? Does it hurt? Do you feel sleepy? Geoff says you are not to go to sleep."

Noel had had his eyes closed but finally opened them and replied to Patrick's barrage, "I feel alright now and it does not feel sore except where I was cut. I don't feel tired so I won't go to sleep on you. Ta for staying with me, Pat. It would not have been too good on my own. Give us a swig from that waterbag, will you?"

About an hour and a half later Geoff came galloping back with his father who looked most concerned and rushed over to Noel and felt his forehead and pulse before looking at the wound.

"I think he is alright, you probably got most of the venom. His pulse seems normal and he doesn't have a temperature. Let's get him on the horse and home to Mum, she'll know what to do."

He turned to look at Pat for the first time and said to Geoff "You get this boy out to the track and then come straight home. When his father finds out about this he will probably skin you alive… and serve you right."

Geoff took him to a point on the Orange track where they always met. Patrick arrived home nearly two hours later than usual to find a distracted mother at the front gate and his father about to get out the Model T to look for him.

His boots and socks and the rest of his clothes were spattered with mud and the dirty face and hair standing on end were evidence to his parents that their son had been up to no good.

Irene pulled him off the pony and hugged him tightly before delivering three sound whacks on his bottom for giving her so much worry.

He took Old Mo to the barn where he fed and watered him and gave him a rub down before going back to the house. His parents were in the kitchen awaiting an explanation of his behaviour. He told them the truth exactly as it happened and said he was sorry. Nevertheless he received a long combined lecture on obedience from them before being sent to bed without any dinner. However, his mother came to his room sometime later and he pretended to be asleep as she left a sandwich and a glass of milk on his bedside table.

When the school resumed after the heat wave Patrick was sent off from home with a letter to Mr. Brady detailing incidents surrounding the swim at Warbys Creek and, with Geoff Hinton, was on the end of another stern lecture about such behaviour from his teacher. The good news was that Noel suffered no ill-effects from his bite apart from a degree of shock and would be back at school soon.

There was one other standout incident in Pat's early schooling. After school he rode straight over to his father who was sorting lambs in the stockyard. Tom stopped what he was doing when he saw Patrick and his black eye but did not comment when handed the note from the school, which read:

Dear Mr. Sheridan,

As you will see, Patrick has been in a fist fight today and I would like you to know your boy was not to blame in any way. He did it to protect the smallest boy in the school, who is also handicapped, from an older and bigger boy who was bullying him. The fight was forced on Patrick who had to contend with a boy almost twice his size and gave a reasonable account of himself under the circumstances.

*I don't condone fighting in anyway but for what your son did
here today I feel you can be very proud of him. I certainly am.*
Respectfully,
Edward Brady.

When he finished reading Tom looked down at his son
again and said, "Better show this to your mother; she won't
be too happy but she may let you off if you have not hurt
your hands too much. When she has finished with you and
you've done your practise, come back here as I want to have
a yarn with you."

As Pat was about to leave, Tom put his hand on the boy's
shoulder and with some slight emotion said, "By the way
I think you did the right thing today and you can be proud
of what you did, but for Pete's sake don't tell your mother
I said so."

Pat gave his father a sad, wistful look because since the
fight he had carried the thought his parents would be angry
with him. In a relieved tone said, "Thanks, Dad but I really
did have to help Billy, didn't I?"

Tom watched as he walked away and realised his son was
no longer a little boy but a boy going on ten and growing
up fast. What he also observed was a boy broad of back for
his age, good shoulders and a tendency to be tall. An unruly
crop of dark wavy hair sat above a squarish Australian face
with a pair of dark blue eyes, a slightly aquiline nose, a good
normal mouth and a chin that had a tendency to jut.

All in all Tom was pleased with his son's physical
attributes to date even though they did not resemble his
own in any way. He had thought about this once or twice
before and accepted the fact that he must take after the
Brennan family. He was a little smug in noting the traits of
good character he son was showing at an early age and took

it for granted these were sourced exclusively from good Sheridan bloodlines.

When Pat came back to the barn an hour or two later, he and his father sat down on a couple of bags of chaff and faced each other.

"I want to talk to you about fighting," said Tom without any lead up. "You should never go looking for a fight but there could be times when you cannot reasonably avoid a stoush however hard you try so you should learn how to protect yourself. My father taught Ian and me to box and the bit of sparring I did with them helped me to defend myself on more than one occasion. These are the gloves we used and even though they are a bit old now they will be alright to start with, even though you might find them a bit big at first."

For the next half hour or so Tom taught his son the rudiments of boxing - the correct stance, leading with his left, keeping his right on guard of his head at all times. He told him of the advantages of being light on his feet, of balance and how to keep moving around his opponent, never being a stationary target easy to hit.

When they finished Tom showed him a full bag of chaff which was hanging by rope from a joist and suspended about three feet above the barn floor which he wanted him to use as a punching bag. Before they set off back to the house for the evening meal, Tom told him, "Come down here once or twice a week and punch that bag the way I showed you. Be sure to put on the gloves so that you don't hurt your hands otherwise your mother will come after me with a pitchfork. And perhaps we won't mention any of this to her, anyway?

In companionable silence they walked back to the house in the early evening light. It was times like this that Patrick realised just how much he enjoyed his father's company and how he was looking forward to the day when he would leave school and begin to work full time with him in the running of the family property.

He was not aware as yet his mother had other plans for his future or that only this week she had written to the Sydney Conservatorium of Music for the full syllabus for students studying for The Australian Diploma of Music (Piano).

She had noticed a remarkable maturity in his recent playing and, as he was now nearly ten, she decided it was time for his serious tuition to commence. She resolved again he would be given the opportunity for a career as a pianist if that is what he wanted.

Patrick was too young to understand what a career in music meant even if his mother had discussed it with him. But he had noticed how he now looked forward in his twice-daily visits to the piano. But he was unaware that it was because of this expanding interest that he quite often exceeded the number of hours his mother made him set aside for daily practise.

Chapter 6

When Patrick met up with the Hinton boys on his way to school the day following his confrontation with Brad Carlson, he was surprised at the extent of the praise and admiration they heaped on him. When they reached the school he found most of the other pupils felt the same way with everybody seeming to want to slap him on the back. He took this hero status with all due modesty indicating anyone would have done the same thing given the circumstances and made every effort to change the subject. His deed lingered on, however, and from then on it was not uncommon for one or other of them to come to him seeking help or advice with some of the lesser problems in their school life.

The girls in particular sought his council, though he was not old enough to realise how often their troubles were contrived and were only the means of achieving sole possession of his company for a few minutes. Patrick was a manly and pleasant enough looking boy but, unlike the girls, he did not yet realise it.

His last two years at The Gap School had been satisfying and happy ones for him both inside and outside the classroom but they seemed to him to pass very quickly. For the past three years his music had become central to his life as his mother demanded more of his time at the keyboard and greater concentration on his study of music. He had no trouble with this as it gave him almost as much pleasure as the rough and tumble games he sometimes played with his mates at school or helping his dad around the property at shearing time. In these other pastimes it was, thanks to his mother, almost instinctive for him to be careful of his hands.

Already his playing had achieved a standard far beyond that required by the syllabus for his Diploma of Music (piano) and he had mastered some of the most technically imposing works of well-known composers.

He had recently completed a study of an album devoted to the piano works of Fredric Chopin and his interpretation of these had delighted Irene who would interrupt what she was doing just to sit and listen as Patrick proceeded through the book. Once or twice when Tom happened to be in the house Irene noticed, to her amazement, that even he stopped to listen for a few minutes to some delightful passage before going on his way.

Irene was aware Chopin did not rank among the Great Composers but the insinuating, ever-haunting romanticism and incredible soul reaching beauty of his works had earned him a special place in her own musical firmament.

She was in awe still of the way Patrick contended so easily with the technical difficulties of these pieces but was affected more by the beauty and sublime tenderness of his unrehearsed rendition of some of the most delightful and beguiling piano music ever written.

His school work did not suffer as a consequence of his preoccupation and in fact Ted Brady considered him one of the better pupils to go through the school in his time. English was by far his best subject. In Pat's 6th year at The Gap, when Brady discovered he had an ear for poetry, he began to gently feed him a selection of light verse from the pens of Wordsworth, Browning, Masefield, R.L.Stevenson and some glorious others. Patrick was drawn to this charming verse in such a way that, without him realising it, it became ensconced in his memory. He was able to recall it, word perfect, for many years even though he was to be exposed later to more sophisticated and profound verse in his years at high school. Brady had discovered Patrick's poetic soul and he intended to nurture it in much the same way as Irene had done with his music.

At one of the school's rare Parents Meetings, and in Patrick's last year at The Gap, Irene told Ted Brady about Patrick's musical talent. But as the school did not possess a piano, he didn't hear him play until the Sheridan's invited him to lunch after one of the monthly Sunday Masses celebrated at the school. Almost as soon as the boy started to play Brady realised he was in the presence of a gifted artist and was quite amazed at the mantle of authority Patrick donned from the time he struck the first note. He was no longer a little school boy but an artist of mature ability and a posture that exuded the confidence of someone who was master of his chosen art.

After playing several of his favourite pieces, Patrick left the room for a few minutes and Brady took the opportunity to engage in an animated and excited conversation with Irene as to the boy's extraordinary gift, including the bright future which would undoubtedly lead him to halls of musical fame. Brady spoke of scholarships at one or other of Sydney's greater public schools and enrolment at the Sydney Conservatorium without delay. But this was the one point on which Irene disagreed with him and affirmed that Patrick would complete his secondary education in Bathurst. She would honour her undertaking to Tom to then decide whether Patrick should pursue a musical career or become a grazier, devoting his life to the management of Magdalene and their other nearby properties.

She told Ted Brady she had little doubt she could win Tom over to her way of thinking when the time came. But she had become aware, from many casual conversations of late, of Patrick's love for Magdalene and its surroundings in particular, and of the Australian bush in general. This had become for her a new and important factor in the determination of his future. She was also aware that, if he and Tom both voted for the bush, she would lose those wonderful dreams she held so long for her son's future.

When he was leaving, Irene and Tom walked Brady to his motor bike. He told them of Patrick's growing affinity for verse. This received a mixed reception. Tom was seen to wrinkle his nose and utter something like 'pansy stuff' whilst Irene said she was delighted but not surprised. Nobody could play the piano the way he did without having a poetic mind enjoined to his God-given gift. Before using the kick starter Ted Brady left them with a prophetic vision, that like daffodils which meant so much to Wordsworth's inward eye, the verse Patrick was absorbing now would haunt him in the most pleasant way for the rest of his life.

A warm summer's day in December, 1930 saw Patrick Sheridan attend his last day as a pupil of The Gap School.

Although at the age of 12, he was too young to be emotional about it, it was nevertheless one of those occasions he would remember for a long time.

He was the only pupil leaving that year as his friend, Billy Tunstall, was repeating Grade Six, and Shirley Hannah, who had started in his year, had left some time back when her family moved to Kelso.

After announcing exam results for the 1930 year, Ted Brady presented awards to the top student of each grade. He then reviewed the entire period, in and out of the classroom, with a mixture of serious comment and good humour which brought applause and lots of laughter from the school.

"Before closing I must make mention of Pat who is leaving us today," he said. "His time here has not been uneventful and earlier on there were occasions when he had me reaching for the strap. However, in the past two years he has set a fine example through a willingness to do all he could for our school and its pupils. Pat is what I call a decent Australian in that he seems to want everyone to have a fair go, and he made this obvious on a number of occasions. It appears instinctive for him to think of others before himself and that's a character trait we could all do well to emulate.

"He was no plaster saint mind you, and he still has his moments especially with his sport," Brady said with a big smile, "he even has been known to loudly question my lbw decisions in our games of cricket here. He also made it obvious on several occasions I had a lot to learn about the rules of Union.

"Next year he will attend Marist College in Bathurst and I think we will hear more of him one day. Not many of you know this but he is already a fine musician and plays the piano beautifully, and perhaps he will make his name in music. Patrick Sheridan has been a good student and a credit to The Gap School and I am sure all of us here are glad to call him 'friend'. We shall miss him but we wish him well."

As the school master finished speaking, Patrick, who had sat red-faced with his head down through the latter part of the speech, was surrounded by his school friends shouting their messages of good luck and goodbye. As Ted Brady ushered them from the classroom he stopped Pat, who was last. Putting his hand on his shoulder, he smiled broadly at him but his only words of farewell before closing the door behind his former pupil were, "Go to it, Pat."

He recalled those words as he rode home that afternoon and realised that final entreaty meant a lot to him. It was a clear message, however brief, that someone whom he liked and respected had confidence in him to do well. That was very satisfying to know right at this time.

He would miss the school he had attended for the past six years, particularly the master who had taught him so much more than what was contained in any syllabus. He had made many friends at The Gap and it might be some years before he met up with them again and that made him slightly pensive. However, in his own way, he realised it was time to move on and he was excited already at the prospect of attending a much bigger school early in the New Year.

Chapter 7

*A*fter completing primary school at The Gap, Patrick was able to take a break of several weeks prior to commencing high school in Bathurst. This turned out to be a glorious summer period in the Magdalene area, some very hot days and some very gentle, warm ones, all interspersed with sufficient rain to gladden the heart of those who made a living from the Land.

He enjoyed this unbroken time with his parents and the days were full. He spent the first waking hours at the piano each day, and then devoted the rest of the day to work on the property, sometimes with his father and sometimes alone.

The loneliness of life in the bush was not new to him but far from it being a matter of regret, the solitariness he felt at times was something he had come to cherish. It gave him time to think about this wonderful place in which he lived and enjoyed and of late these also had been periods when yet unwritten music began to penetrate his consciousness.

Often at the end of a working day when riding back alone from one of the far paddocks, he would stop and look at some of the many vistas the wide open country afforded. It filled him with a pleasure he could not quite understand. Looking east across the seemingly never-ending Bathurst Plains to the purple mists of the Blue Mountains rising in the distance was a scene which never failed to fill him with a sense of awe because of its incredible, uniquely Australian beauty.

Young as he was, Patrick could see what was happening. Soon now a decision would have to be made for him as to how he was to spend the rest his life. With his love for Magdalene growing with every passing day he could not foresee how it would be possible to forsake it in favour of a life, in the city, solely devoted to music. And yet there were other times when playing the piano he felt he was at the centre of his universe and this conviction was now reinforced by the urgent need he felt to create his own music.

It was quandary for a boy but it would be up to his parents to make a decision for the short-term. However, later on, when he was older, he could make such decisions for himself. He fervently hoped that then he would be able to devise ways to enjoy the best of those two worlds he loved so much.

After spending the day in Bathurst, it was the day after the Australia Day weekend that Irene Sheridan returned to Magdalene to say all arrangements were now in hand for Patrick to attend his new school.

His parents had chosen the Marist Brothers College which had a pleasant location near the bank of the river in South Bathurst. It was a day school for boys and had a good reputation as a place of learning, sound discipline, and sport. Its two hundred plus students were drawn from all over the Bathurst area with many of them travelling in by school buses from as far out as fifteen miles from the College.

The headmaster, Brother Bresnahan, attended to the enrolment formalities after interviewing Irene and reading her son's final school report from The Gap. He said he would like a meeting with Patrick prior to school commencement on 7th February and an arrangement was made for this to take place in his office after 10 am Mass at the Cathedral on the following Sunday.

All of this was the sole subject of conversation at the Sheridan tea table that night. Tom Sheridan did not say much but asked questions at times and, although he had accepted the idea of his son's education in Bathurst, it was quite clear he was not completely happy about it. One disappointment with the College was that its syllabus did not contain reference to music of any kind. There was a school choir which was conducted by a lay brother who could also play the piano, of which the college only had one and this, as Irene had observed on her visit, had seen better days.

Her concern was somewhat allayed after she mentioned the problem to the headmaster during her interview. She had told him of Patrick's musical talent and he undertook to speak to Sister Mary Annunciata, the music mistress at the nearby St. Mary's Convent Boarding School for girls, and felt she would be able to find a room at the convent with a piano for her son to practise.

Sister was getting on in years, he said, but had the reputation of being a fine teacher and had completed a degree (piano) at the Melbourne Conservatorium before taking her vows. He thought she and Patrick could have a lot in common and by bringing them together the boy's overall knowledge of music could benefit as a consequence.

A major concern was finding an appropriate place for Patrick to live and Irene had arranged this well beforehand. After considering some alternatives, she approached Kerry Beck who occupied a fine old home in Jerome Street which was fairly adjacent to the College, and an ideal location for her son.

Kerry Beck had not at any time contemplated taking a boarder, but after meeting Patrick she agreed to let him share her home as a guest and offered him all the benefits he would normally receive in his own home.

When all points had been covered to Tom's satisfaction, Patrick's parents cleared the table and washed the dishes whilst he went off to practise and think about what he had learnt during the meal. Laying in bed that night he realised that his immediate future away from Magdalene had been decided and there was nothing he could do to change it, even if he wanted to do so. He was a little sad at the prospect, slightly apprehensive also, but there was an underlying sense of excitement he felt in the immediacy of the many new experiences which lay now ahead of him.

The Sheridan family came in from Magdalene the following Sunday morning and attended the 10 o'clock Mass at the Bathurst Cathedral. Afterwards, as arranged, they drove around to the Marist College for Patrick's appointment with the headmaster. Brother Bresnahan met them at the College entrance door and Irene introduced him to Tom and Patrick. They stood there for a few minutes in conversation before he led them into the waiting room outside his office. He suggested he first have a few words with Patrick alone and then, perhaps, Irene and Tom would join them.

Inside his office he sat down at his desk and signalled Patrick to take the chair opposite. The headmaster, or Brother Superior, as he was known by his staff and pupils, was a tall, spare man in his mid-fifties, with a receding hairline and a pair of eyes which showed the general friendliness of his nature. Patrick felt at home with him and had no qualms about the upcoming interview. "I won't keep you long, Sheridan," he smiled, "but I like to have a few words with students before they join the College. I have heard good things about you from my friend Ted Brady at The Gap School and I am sure you will get on well here. This is a much bigger place, of course, but it won't take you long to settle in once you get used to having a lot more boys around you.

"What you must understand from the start is that we are a Catholic school and our faith is important to all of us here. Do you know anything about God?"

"My mother has told me about Him, Sir," replied Patrick, "and I have studied the Catechism and I say the prayers she taught me."

"That's fine Sheridan, your mother has done her job well. Now, after all she has taught you, do you believe in Almighty God?"

"I think so, Sir, but I don't have a very good idea of what He looks like. He made Australia, didn't he, so we must love Him for that."

"That is a patriotic answer to that question which I have not heard before but is nevertheless true. You will learn a lot more about God whilst here and I hope you will grow in His love.

"As for your general education, you do not appear to have any trouble with learning and our Brothers will teach you well. For the next three years you will be doing our basic course which comprises English, Arithmetic, Physics, Geography, English History and Religion. None of these subjects will be difficult for you, but do you have any questions?"

"No thank you, Sir, I understand what you have told me," he replied.

"Good. Then perhaps we can talk about sport which the boys, unfortunately, take a little more seriously than their lessons around here. Are you any good?"

"I don't know. I like Union and cricket and I can run a bit but I don't know if I am really good at any of them," Patrick answered.

"Well, we play a lot of rugby and cricket and have good coaches, so we will soon find out about that, but there is another consideration, of course. I understand you are a pianist and you, therefore, have to be careful of your hands so it may be necessary to get your parents' permission to play any sport in which you could injure your fingers or hands and that, of course, includes both rugby and cricket."

"Must you bring it up, Sir? Do the other boys have to get permission?" cut in Patrick.

"What!" exploded the surprised headmaster and then realising the innocence of the question said, "no, they don't but"... and he paused again... "Oh, I see what you are getting at. You had better let me think about this."

He leant forward on his desk and after a moment or two looked over at the boy and said, "Look, Sheridan, I feel a little guilty about this but I do understand your position in wanting to be treated like other boys.

"You are obviously very keen, whatever your sporting ability, and perhaps you should be given a chance and, at the risk of committing a sin of omission, I won't raise the matter with your parents now, but if they bring it up I will have to abide by their wishes. Do you understand?"

"Yes, Sir. Thank you very much, Sir, and I will look after my hands if you let me play," said Patrick.

"All right, then," said the Brother Superior "but heaven help us both if things go wrong... Now, I think I know enough about you, so we'll call your parents in and finalise your enrolment. Remember, if you wish to speak to me at any time you can do so by asking your class teacher to arrange an appointment. I wish you luck here, Patrick, and will watch your progress with interest."

As they stood up he looked down at the boy and liked what he saw. A thirteen-year-old, a little tall for his age, slim build and a shock of dark curly hair which had not seen a lot of the comb. A darkish complexion with good eyes, which were a little shy, wide and blue, that had looked directly at him during their interview, not deliberately, but in an innocent, open way which said much to a man who had seen so many boys pass his way.

The meeting with the parents was brief. The subject of school sport did not come up, much to the boy's relief. Subject to their agreement, the Brother had arranged an appointment with Sr. Annunciata at the Convent for 4 o'clock that day and, even though it would mean them getting back to Magdalene quite late, Irene jumped at the opportunity to clear up a matter which had been causing her some concern.

As they made their way back to the car, Tom thought they should have lunch at 'the Greeks' and afterwards he would visit an old Bathurst friend whilst they were at the convent. Then they could pick him up outside the Post Office at "say, half-past five… and don't be late." Irene did not know what to expect on meeting Sr. Annunciata and when she and Patrick sat down with her in the large room where she must have taught the piano, she found her to be polite, business-like and very much to the point. Irene liked what she could see of her features. The chin was firm and the visage somewhat stern, which gave a kind of warning she was not one to be crossed. Although she was said to be 'getting on in years', it was not apparent. She seemed to be very alert, and her short, slight figure moved quickly. After a brief time in her presence, one became aware of the sharpness of her mind. When the introductions were over she came right to the point.

"Bro. Bresnahan has been in touch with me about your son, Mrs. Sheridan," she said, "but I am not sure whether I am in a position to help. Brother says your boy is a good pianist and needs a place to practise but this would only be possible here at certain times of the day. We have a reasonably good piano in an annex in one of the outer class rooms, away from the dormitory, which he could use only between six and eight in the morning and five and eight in the evening. If this is of interest to you then I will take it up with Mother Superior and seek her permission."

"Oh! that would be an ideal arrangement, Sister," enthused Irene, "he will be staying just round the corner from here in Jerome Street and only a few minutes' walk away. It would be ideal for us and we would be most grateful to you and the convent if it could be arranged. Of course, we would be prepared to pay any fee you may care to charge."

"Don't worry about payment, Mrs. Sheridan, it will not be necessary and, if Mother agrees, we will be happy to have been of some service to Bro. Bresnahan… we owe him many favours."

"Thank you for that, Sister, and I will pray that Mother will let him have the room and, if that is to be the case, then I'm afraid I have another favour to ask. Should your time permit, do you think you could take Patrick once or twice a week to discuss music in its broadest sense with him? This could be in the form of lessons and again we would insist on paying the convent an appropriate fee.

"Technically he is a pianist already," Mrs Sheridan continued, "he has been sight reading since he was eight and is blessed with an astonishing musical memory. For the past four years we have been studying major piano works of great composers and having played a composition two or three times he no longer needs the score. When you hear him play you will see how strictly he follows the composers' instructions and at the same time seemingly entices a clarity and beauty of tone from the piano which is remarkable to hear. His interpretation and artistic sensitivity to this music seems to be almost instinctive and something I have never been able to understand."

Irene could see she had the Sister's interest and carried on without any change of expression when she said, "I know you will ask the obvious question, Sister, but all this talent comes naturally to him and my husband and I are at a loss to explain it. I am a reasonable pianist but other than that there is no real musical background in my family. As for the Sheridans, their taste does not run beyond a jig on an Irish fiddle."

Irene was now wound up as for years she had wanted to speak with somebody like this intelligent woman who would understand the enormous responsibility she carried for the proper nurturing of her son's great gift. And so she went on…

"Sister, despite his ability, there are some very wide gaps in the boy's musical knowledge. For instance, what he knows of the theory of music is limited to what I have been able to teach him. I know he has an urge to compose and I have had very little to pass on to him in that area. He has never heard a symphony orchestra and, therefore, has absolutely no knowledge of the wonderful instruments which go to make one up. I have told him of concerti for orchestra and piano and whilst his interest was profound, I was unable to enlighten him on the subject to any extent.

"So you can see there is a huge void there, Sister Annunciata, and I was hoping you would be prepared to help him fill a great deal of it. I am anxious he be reasonably well versed in all pertinent aspects of the profession I intend him to pursue and, if possible, before he enters the Conservatorium in three years' time."

Irene finally stopped and was a little red-faced as she thought she may have overdone the presentation of her son. The nun did not respond for a few moments and appeared to be considering what she had just heard.

"I admire your enthusiasm for your boy's talent, Mrs. Sheridan, and feel I was not listening just to an over-ambitious parent going on unduly about her offspring. Believe me, I do encounter a bit of that from time to time. I can see no reason why Mother will not agree to him using the room and I will see if there is any way in which I can work with the boy. I promise to let you know about both these matters as quickly as possible as you now have made me aware of how important these arrangements are to you."

She reached down into the large pocket of her habit and drew out her watch.

"Look, it is nearly five o'clock and I will soon have to hurry off to evening prayers but I would like to hear Patrick play something before I go."

"Of course, Sister," Irene said immediately. She turned to Patrick who gave her a quizzical look. "Play something short as we are all in a hurry. What about that Liszt *Consolation* you were playing before we left this morning?"

The nun raised her eyebrows at that choice as the boy walked over to the piano and raised the lid. It was an extraordinarily difficult piece and many a good pianist, including herself, avoided it because of its technical and aesthetic demands, and he was doing it without the score! Perhaps the Sheridan woman has bitten off more than her son could chew, she thought.

Patrick flexed his fingers and hands and ran a scale or two on the well-used keyboard before commencing. The nun's doubts were quickly and dramatically dispelled as the first notes of the delightful composition rang through the rather large music room.

She sat almost bolt upright as she observed that the little boy who went to the piano was no longer there. In his place sat someone with great presence who played this instrument like the great master he was. She realised his mother had not exaggerated in anything she had said, in fact to the contrary, and was in awe as she now closed her eyes to let the music take hold of her.

When Patrick finished there were tears in her eyes as she walked over and placed her hands on his shoulders and her voice shook slightly as she said.

"I am unable to tell you how much that meant to me, Patrick, and will forever be in your debt for an extraordinary musical experience. However reluctant your mother may be to use the word, you are indeed a prodigy and God has indeed been good just to let me hear you play. In my gratitude I will from this day pray for you and your career."

She stopped there as there was a knock on the door. Irene, who had heard what had taken place at the piano, was holding herself in check and opened the door as Sr. Annunciata walked back across the room to join her.

"Oh, Mother Camillus, come in. I want you to meet Mrs. Sheridan and her son, who were sent to us by Bro. Bresnahan." She told her Superior the reason for the visit and what had transpired.

"How do you do, Mrs. Sheridan. Please let me explain this rude interruption," she said laughingly. "Some of our senior girls returned from holidays early and I took them down to the park for a walk. When we came back we heard the music and stood outside the door here and listened. Was this young man the culprit? I have never heard such playing. Could he possibly do one more piece for me and the girls?"

"I don't think so Mother," said Sr. Annunciata, "we are almost due in chapel and Mrs. Sheridan has to meet her husband in town."

"The nuns won't mind waiting, I am sure, Sister," she replied, "and Mr. Sheridan would not begrudge me the pleasure of hearing his son play one small piece."

"Quickly, Patrick. Your father will kill us if we are much later than we are already," said Irene.

The boy sat down at the piano and there was mischief in his eye as he proceeded with a rendition of Chopin's *Minute Waltz*. Only sixty seconds elapsed before the nuns, the students and his mother were on their feet applauding what had been a bravura performance of another difficult work.

Patrick accepted the praise graciously as he and his mother made their way out with Mother Camillus.

"Of course Patrick can have the room," she said. "Just as soon as he is ready he can come around and collect his own key. However, I am afraid I cannot be as generous as Sister Annunciata and we will have to be reimbursed. Therefore, it will be necessary for Patrick to give a small recital each month for the nuns and our music students. Is that fair?

As for the other matter I am sure now that Sister will be delighted to help Patrick with his piano studies."

"Thank you Mother and thank you too Sister," Irene called out. "Of course, Patrick will play for you. We must run. Goodbye." They hurried off to the car with the time approaching half past six.

Tom was sitting on the long wooden seat in front of the post office as they drove up.

"Don't worry about me" he said coming up to the car, "I don't mind sitting an extra hour in the heat while you sip tea and biscuits with the nuns," he complained.

"Oh, do stop moaning Tom and get in the car and we'll tell you what happened," replied Irene.

When the explanation was complete, he turned to Patrick in the back seat and said, "So you laid them in the aisles! Good on you, Son."

And with that he pulled his hat down over his eyes and slept until they arrived at the Magdalene gates some two hours later.

Thinking about the day's events later that evening, Irene recalled Sr. Annunciata's astonishing reaction to Patrick's playing and how she likened it to her own emotional upheaval upon hearing his father play the violin that first time.

Chapter 8

Irene Sheridan had carried her secret with her now for nearly fifteen years. It was not a dark secret but it was one she shared only with God. She had not experienced any sense of residual guilt despite being fully aware of the eighth of those demands Moses brought down from the mount.

In the early years of her marriage to Tom she had offered prayer to her Maker to grant her the gift of children and reasoned He, in his infinite wisdom, had answered her entreaty in a most unusual way. Her recollection of that brief encounter with a very unusual and charming man had not been dimmed by passage of time. When she thought back, it was, strangely, those few hours of exquisite music in his company which had made the most lasting impression on her. At the same time she realised the music had been directly responsible for unleashing those human desires to which they finally had succumbed.

She quite deliberately avoided going to Orange since the fateful meeting for she was afraid if she found him there she would not have the strength to return to Magdalene and Tom. She tried not to dwell upon what happened that night too frequently but she had improvised the violin music of *The Swan* for the piano and occasionally, when the time of day and her mood were right, she would play it, indulging herself with gentle memories as they filtered back into that room where it had all started. Patrick was now her life. She had learned to tolerate Tom, perhaps, even like him a little, but the love she once bore him would never return. Fortunately their relationship in most other respects was amiable enough to ensure a reasonably happy domestic environment in which to raise her only child.

Now and again something occurred which brought back memories of Patrick's real father. None of these, so far, had been more dramatic or profound as the shock she received on that Sunday evening in Bathurst when saying goodbye to Patrick after installing him in the home of her friend, Kerry Beck.

She had started the car for the return journey to Magdalene and looked over towards the trio at the front gate to make a final wave. There, standing between the Becks, was Stefan Holst. She wiped the tears engendered by the farewell from her eyes before realising fully she was looking at Patrick standing there. It may have been a shorter and slighter version of Stefan but everything else about it bespoke his father. Patrick was in his school uniform and wearing his first pair of long trousers and it was probably this that had brought his likeness to his father into stark relief for her. Her hand she raised in a parting gesture had been frozen aloft and she now let it fall to her side and drove away.

Patrick's life away from his family and Magdalene began from that moment and the first pangs of homesickness set in almost immediately. He had anticipated these to some extent but had no intention of yielding to them and did not, even for a second, give any indication to the Becks of what he was going through. Beth and Harry had made him feel very much at home and he now was ensconced in the large, airy bedroom formerly used by their son.

It was the Becks' habit, when Harry was at home, to retire early and when he went to his room that first night Patrick was somewhat ashamed of himself as, for a short time there, he had almost resorted to tears. He forced off the mood and got into bed, picking up the copy of 'Treasure Island' which Kerry had obviously left for him by the bedside lamp. He read more avidly as he got into the yarn and only reluctantly turned off the lamp after falling asleep and waking up several times. His last thought before finally dropping off was that young Jim Hawkins would not let himself get upset with a bit of yearning for home and he resolved to do the same.

His first weeks in Bathurst in general, and at the Marist Brothers in particular, were full of 'for the first time' experiences for the boy from Magdalene. He enjoyed and was excited by most of them. There were thirty two boys in his class, a far cry from the three or four at The Gap. All were newly enrolled apart from three who were 'repeating'. He found most of the class friendly and easy going and before long became part of a group who, on most days, got together at lunch time and after school.

Sport became an increasingly important part of his school life. In his first term he was selected for the class cricket eleven after surviving a torrid session with the College's senior coach, Bro. Miller. Miller liked the way he kept his eye on the ball and how he moved his feet but was strongly critical of his 'cross-bat slogs' as he called them, and Patrick had to prove he could, and would, play straight bat shots in future.

In the first few matches he made only enough runs to keep his place in the team but his form had improved with each game. However, word had gone out to the staff about the safety of his hands and the coach told him in no uncertain terms he was never to bat without proper batting gloves nor should he field in any position other than on the boundary, thus keeping risk of fingers injury to a minimum.

It was during this cricket season that he lost his name. He had become a reasonably popular figure in class and his classmates must have found his full name too starchy and he became simply 'Pat' or 'Sherrie'. Pat did not mind this but thought his mother might have a word or two to say about the contractions.

When the football season started after the Easter break the procedure was pretty much the same. He tried out with the class fifteen and was greeted by Bro. Miller who was also rugby coach.

"Oh, not you again, Sheridan. How can I protect your hands in a game like this? Broken hands, fingers and thumbs are par for the course in these clashes. I don't think I can let you play."

"Sir, I would like to give it a go and will try to look after my hands and I don't think anything too bad could happen to them. It won't be fair if I can't have a game," implored Pat.

"That's alright about you, Son, but I've got Bro. Superior on my back about you and I understand your parents have not given permission for you to play any sport."

"I know that, Sir, but I would still like to play." The boy beseeched so earnestly that it impressed Miller.

The Brother's brow creased and he paused before replying. "Look, I'll tell you what I'll do Sheridan. You can try out on the wing, out of harm's way as much as possible, and if you are any good there, I'll give you a game." After a short trial match, in which he had not seen much of the ball, Pat approached the coach again for his decision.

"Alright, Sheridan, you're not bad and you can now consider yourself in the team. In any case that mob you are playing with won't give you a lot of ball as they don't seem to like passing out wide, so that will reduce the risk. I don't want you to come into the real field of play for any reason whatsoever and you are to avoid 'the pigs' like you would hell's fire. Play well, Sheridan and enjoy the game."

"Thank you very much, Sir," beamed Pat and made his way over to his classmates to say that he had made the side.

It would have been easy for these activities to affect his firm dedication to his music but he did not let that happen. In all other ways he was a boy but, when it came to the piano, he was most adult and knew instinctively what had to be done if he were to retain his art.

The arrangement with the Convent worked well for with his own key he could come and go as he pleased provided he used the room in those hours prescribed by the nuns. He was up early most mornings and would be at the Convent in time to practice for an hour or more before walking back home in time for the breakfast prepared for him by Kerry Beck. His morning practice was devoted to improving his technique and consisted of a vast array of scales, chords and other difficult exercises which, whilst he did not know it, were beyond the ability of most good pianists.

Dependent upon his after-class commitments at the College, he practised for two hours or more before or after the evening meal. This time was devoted to the works of the composer currently named on the schedule his mother had prepared for him. Prior to him going to Bathurst she had armed him with piano albums of the Three Bs, Mozart,

Schumann, Handel and one or two others, and given him a broad timetable of the order in which they should be studied. She had gone over with him those works which he previously had not played and referred him also to the copious information in front of each album.

She knew this was hardly necessary as Patrick, upon seeing the music for the first time, would become aware immediately of the composer's wishes and interpret the piece accordingly.

All along she had realised in these years of high school her son would be doing little more than marking time with his career. He should already be in the hands of a proven teacher at the Conservatorium but this would have meant him being deprived of full normal childhood. This interruption to the progress of his career was her decision but she was certain it was the right one and never wavered in that regard.

The regime she had laid down for Patrick was little more than an endeavour to ensure her son retained his ability and enthusiasm for the piano during this period of his formal schooling. The entry of Sr. Annunciata into the equation certainly leant strength to this overall strategy.

Sr. Annunciata had many calls upon her time but arranged to meet Patrick every second Thursday evening at 7 o'clock in her music room. At their first meetings the discussion covered a broad range of musical subjects and she learnt from these just how much this boy did and did not know. These talks disclosed obvious and expected gaps in his musical knowledge and she would set about remedying these. At these same sessions she also learnt there was little she could teach this boy when it came to performance and interpretation of major works composed for the piano. These meetings ended with Patrick playing something for her and no matter how many times she asked "...Do you know...?" he was usually able to oblige in a remarkably competent and artistic fashion.

Patrick enjoyed these early lessons as she took him on explorations of the majestic world of music she knew so well. She spoke of symphony orchestras comprising one hundred players in various sections performing under the baton of a single conductor. She told him of great concertos written for piano and orchestra and how it was the dream of every good pianist is to take part in such a performance.

Of all aspects of the music profession they discussed, none intrigued him more than the composition of new works. It was an involved first lesson for him on this subject in that he learnt composers, whilst having free rein of their creative talent, nevertheless had to conform with certain guidelines in order for a composition to be acceptable to those who ultimately would judge it in its technical entirety.

After two sessions on the subject she suggested Patrick write a piece and bring it to his next lesson. She would do no more than give him the key in which it should be written and the rest would be up to him.

He did not tell her he had composed already several pieces which he had committed to manuscript prior to leaving Magdalene, including etudes, studies, waltzes, nocturnes and one sonata. Like many pianists he had been under the spell of Chopin for a time and whilst this inspired his efforts, he in no way attempted to imitate the style or anything else he perceived in the great master's work.

His music had never been played, not even by himself, and his mother was not aware of its existence unless she had come across it in the top drawer of the wardrobe whilst cleaning his bedroom. If she had she had never referred to it.

His decision not to mention his work to the nun stemmed from the fact he was unaware, when writing, of the rules she just now imparted to him. He would now find to what extent these restrictions would, should he adhere to them, affect the outflow of unwritten music now coming into his mind and soul with increasing frequency.

As he left the Convent he decided to give a deal of thought to the composition he would prepare for his next lesson.

Something which had always amazed Irene was the immediate change in her son when he came away from the piano. Observing him at the keyboard one could sense the presence of a mature adult but as soon as he left the instrument he was just another young boy. This pleased her also for she realised her almost obsessive plan for him to enjoy a normal childhood was bearing fruit. Whilst his young mind never pondered the subject consciously, Pat found himself to be quite happy and content with life in this big country town. He still missed his parents and Magdalene, of course, but had learned to cope with that after a few weeks.

He was not cut off from Magdalene as much as he thought at first he would be, for he went home for term holidays, Easter, and the long summer breaks almost without fail. It also helped him maintain his ties with home by an arrangement, insisted upon by his parents, whereby he joined them for their monthly attendance at Sunday morning Mass at the Cathedral, then spending the rest of what was a very happy day in their company.

He also took advantage of the occasional long weekend when it was possible to get home for a few days during term. He caught the Mail-Bus to Orange outside the Oxford Hotel at 5 o'clock on Friday night and it dropped him at the family property some two or three hours later depending upon the state of the road. Irene and Tom could hear the bus coming from a far off and would be waiting at the gate, with the dogs, to greet t him on arrival. The three of them enjoyed these short breaks especially and things were a little quiet in the car when they drove back to the Beck household on the Monday evenings.

Life at the Becks was more than bearable for him as 'Aunty' Kerry was a cheery soul to be about and seemed genuinely fond of him, spoiling him in many ways, accordingly. Harry, when he was there, was caring and affable and let it be known he was pleased his wife's loneliness had been somewhat alleviated by Pat's presence in the house.

Kerry was a good cook and she fed him well. The evening routine was pleasant and unchanging when Harry was away. If Patrick had gone to the piano before the evening meal, they would stay at the table and talk long after it was finished, usually about their respective activities on that day, what was happening in the town and any idle gossip she happened to pick up from her many friends. He helped her with the dishes before going off to do his homework in his bedroom and looked forward to the friendly kiss and glass of warm milk Aunty Kerry would bring before she retired for the night.

Chapter 9

Patrick's first year at Marist College seemed to pass quickly but it was, nevertheless, an eventful one as he experienced so many things for the first time. He did well in most subjects and his teachers found no complaint with him other than he talked too much in class at times, usually about some upcoming sporting event or other in which he and his class were enthusiastically engaged.

He made friends in class and they frequently arranged to meet up outside of school hours. He saw more of two of them as they resided in Jerome Street. Brian Stiller lived almost opposite the Becks and he and Pat often dropped in on each other for no reason other than they enjoyed each other's company. Brian's father was a teller at the local Rural Bank and the family were quite 'well-to-do' on the standards of the day. The Stillers were made up of two older children and Mrs. Stiller, of course, who seemed to spend all her spare time in a very colourful garden she had created for their home. She was friendly enough but a little 'distant' and she and Kerry got on but were never close. However, Pat at no time felt unwelcome in the Stiller household.

Pat came out of Beck's gate each school morning at about half-past eight and Brian would be waiting and they'd set off for school together. Usually they had to wait a few minutes outside the home of their friend, Max Niven, who lived further down the street. This trio then made its way to the intended destination. They always had something to chat about and were never lost for a word. Their frequent natural laughter testified the friendly, boyish nature of their relationship.

There was another class mate, Eric Hanson, who made up the quartet of friends. He lived a mile or so on the other side of town and rode to the college each day on his bike. He was a shy, retiring kind of boy about their own age, famed in the class as a good fast-medium who was the backbone of bowling in the class eleven. His father worked in the maintenance section of the Bathurst rail yard and his mother was a regular helper in the College tuck shop. She was a second-generation Australian and part Tongan. This explained the light-tan shade of Eric's skin, about which he was somewhat sensitive and was responsible, to some extent, for his retiring nature.

The other two boys also had bikes and Patrick, after asking Harry, was allowed to take over the Beck family two-wheeler which formerly belonged to their son. He soon learned to ride and was able to join the other three on the weekends they went on long pushes around the wide, dusty streets of Bathurst and its surrounding countryside.

After these rides, when they had the money, they would leave their bikes outside Bathurst's new Milk Bar and have a malted milk. This American craze recently swept Australia, and its capital cities now were dotted with them. Most country towns, depending upon their size, boasted one or more of these pleasant establishments. To some it might not have been so important but to Pat Sheridan his first malted milk was a real occasion. His introduction to Coca Cola, which arrived in his town about a year later, was another first for him and proved to be something he liked and drank for some time afterwards. Pat derived a lot of pleasure from riding his bike both with his friends and on his own and would jump on it at the slightest excuse. When he came home from school his first question to Kerry was, "Do you want anything down the street, Aunty Kerry?" He would tear off immediately if the answer was "yes". He even rode it the short distance to the Convent for his daily practices. Whether they could hear him or not, the nuns and students would know he was 'in residence' because they would see his bike leaning against the classroom's outside wall. It was on one of the cycling trips with his three friends that Patrick had an experience he would have liked to have forgotten.

Since that fist fight he had at The Gap School, he had developed a strong dislike of violence of any kind. He was not afraid of it, he just did not like the idea of one person deliberately assaulting another. He had seen a few fights in the school yard at Marist Brothers but these were little more than scuffles and were quickly broken up. There were some which were a shade more serious and usually between boys in the senior classes, settled after school in a clearing in the wooded area just outside the school grounds. A lot of boys attended these bouts but Patrick could never bring himself to go.

His distaste for this kind of thing became more entrenched when he witnessed a brawl whilst doing a late afternoon message for Kerry Beck. The grocery shop where he had bought a pound of butter was next to the Royal Hotel which had, because of its clientele, a poor name in the town. It had just closed as it was after six o'clock and a group of drinkers were gathered around the pub door watching a fight which had broken out between two of their number. It went on for several minutes and Pat could see cuts and bruises appearing amongst the blood stains on the faces of the two combatants.

Finally one was knocked down and did not get up from the gutter in which he lay in pain and heaving for breath. The fellow who put him there simply turned his back and walked away without a word and the group dispersed without any of them offering to help the man who still lay on the ground.

The boy had watched all this in fascinated horror and could hardly believe the brutality he had just witnessed. As he rode home he recalled what his father had said about fighting, namely, "Dodge it at all costs but there may come a time when, for your own self-respect, it can't be avoided, so learn to defend yourself just in case".

He had taught Patrick how to do this. Right up to the time he left Magdalene he put on gloves and for about ten minutes most days punched the bag of chaff his father had hung in the barn for that purpose. He had done this for he, probably mistakenly, thought it would strengthen his fingers and hands, and because he enjoyed the exercise. He did not expect to use this skill in the area for which it was intended and could think of no circumstance which would warrant him inflicting pain on another person. Such a situation did arise, but it did not change the way he felt about the horror of gratuitous physical assault upon another human being.

It was some months later, on a warm Saturday afternoon in early autumn when the four friends, returning from a ride to the outskirts of the town, decided to go for a swim in a hole which was popular with boys of their age. It was situated at an isolated spot in a creek not far from the main river and was a deep but safe place for those who could swim reasonably well. Located behind a stand of gums there was a small pebbly beach leading into immediately deep water which was always cool and refreshing no matter the time of year.

Because it was so out of the way none of the swimmers worried about an appropriate costume and those who did not go 'starkers' left only their under briefs on for their dip. So, on a hot day, the place seemed to resemble a small, juvenile nudist camp - but for boys only. On arriving at the creek, the four riders leant their bikes against a tree, stripped off to their underpants and made their way towards the water. Under the trees out of the sun were a dozen or so lads who had been in the water and now stood about talking or skylarking in small groups.

Eric Hanson was impatient to get in and was already swimming strongly to the far side of the wide hole as his friends made their way through the trees. Just as they reached the edge a voice said:

"Hey, you"… and they turned to find themselves being addressed by a loutish looking boy about their own age who was sitting on the ground with three other youths.

"Yeah. What's your trouble," said Brian.

"Is that kid with you?" said the lout pointing across the water to Eric.

"Yes, he is. What about it?" responded Brian. "Well, he's a black and we don't like blacks in our swimming hole, so tell him to bugger off and if you don't I will."

It was here that Patrick put his hand on Brian's shoulder and interposed.

"No you won't," he said looking straight at the boy on the ground, "he's a friend and has as much right to be here as you, so leave him alone. Besides, he is not a black as you call him and even if he were it wouldn't make any difference, so you lay off."

"Yeah!" said the youth getting up off the ground, "and who's going to make me?"

Pat looked at the boy now standing up. He seemed slightly older than he was, not much taller, sturdier built but he could see some flab on the near-naked body. His mates were also standing but they had backed off a bit as they could see what was coming as Brian and Max moved in behind Pat.

"I will," said Pat, "and my mate is staying whether you like it or not."

The boy sneered at Pat. "Look, kid, if that black doesn't leave now I'll go and drag him out." And looking back as he said it he saw his mates had withdrawn even further and realised he could not count on their support.

"I suppose the three of you will try to stop me as a dill like you would be too yeller to try on his own," he said.

"No, this is just between me and you," replied Pat.

"Have a go, then," he said and started towards the water. Pat immediately blocked his path and as the boy stood back he threw a punch which took Pat on the chest and he toppled to the ground.

He was back on his feet instantly with his fists instinctively raised to protect his face and head and began to circle away from the boy to make himself a moving target as his father had told him. The lout came at him again with a flurry of blows most of which missed their mark as Pat fended them off the way he had been taught.

Then a blow which grazed the side of his face, and another which took him the pit of his stomach, really hurt and he realised he would have to do something to end the fight quickly, either way.

As the boy moved in again Pat waited for a chance and as he stopped circling he hit the boy on the side of his face with his right fist and followed it up with a hard left which took him on the point of the nose and Pat almost felt it buckle under his clenched fist.

The boy dropped to the ground and burst into tears as blood started to flow from his nose on to his naked chest. His mates had retreated further away as Pat, still rather breathless, helped him to his feet and took him down to the water's edge to wash away the blood. He stopped crying and whilst the nose was slightly bent, it soon stopped bleeding. He was able to put on his clothes and ride away slowly on his bike without uttering another word to anyone.

As they walked into the water for their swim Sheridan said to the other two, "I didn't like that but I had no option."

"Forget it, Pat," said Max Niven, "he had it coming and he deserved what he got. You did the right thing."

"And I didn't like all that talk about blacks and I hope it taught that kid a lesson. If you hadn't stopped him I would've and I still don't know why you butted in like that," added Brian.

They joined their friend on the other side of the pool where he was sitting on the bank but did not tarry long as they were all due home. Eric had not seen what had occurred under the trees and, as nobody was going to tell him, the incident was closed.

Irene Sheridan did not learn of this incident and, had she done so, would, undoubtedly, have been distressed by it. Be that as it may, the altercation, if nothing else, served to underline the fact her son was, indeed, continuing his journey through childhood in the very normal way she had craved for him.

Chapter 10

The Wireless came to Bathurst in the early weeks of 1933, about three years after the first transmission in Australia. The Beck's were among the first of the local families to have a receiver installed in their home. Harry thought it would be great company for Kerry during the day and anticipated the pleasure it could bring on those evenings when he and his wife could sit down and listen together. They enjoyed programmes broadcast by three Sydney commercial stations which included news, sports results, plays, quiz shows, situation comedies, variety shows, drama serials (listeners held in suspense pending next episode) interspersed often with recordings of popular music of the day.

Initially, Patrick was carried away by the incredible invention and listened in avidly each night with the Becks. But by the time he came to accept the miracle of wireless his interest in most of these programmes started to wane. After-school hours were busy and important to a fifteen-year-old. Class sport, piano practice, riding his bike, doing homework and reading books assumed priority over listening to programmes which did not interest him greatly. And so, it was only on rare occasions could he be seen with his ears glued to the set for any length of time and this usually had to do with a sporting event of some description. Patrick did not take it upon himself to touch or tune the Beck's set at any time so it was not until some weeks later he learned with surprise and great delight that a broad stream of the world's finest music was available night and day on the Beck's console if only it were tuned to the right station.

It was Sr. Mary Annunciata who alerted him to this at his fortnightly lesson with her. The Convent recently had installed two wireless sets, one in the nuns' parlour and one in her music studio for the use of her students. This set remained tuned permanently to Station 2FC, the classical music station of The Australian Broadcasting Commission, known as 'The ABC'.

Sr. Annunciata was brimming with excitement when her student entered her class room that evening as she wanted to let this boy know as quickly as she could form the words of just how important a part the wireless could play in his musical education.

"At long last, Patrick," she said, "you can hear the music you should have been hearing for years. I don't think you realise how far the wireless can expand your musical horizon and give you a fuller comprehension of our profession as a whole. That void in your music education, which so worried your mother, can now be filled so quickly and in such a way we never thought possible at the time."

"I don't understand, Sister," he said, "I listen to the wireless at times but I have never heard any 'good' music on it."

"You have been listening to the wrong stations," she replied, "you have to tune to 2FC which broadcasts our kind of music from mid morning until the station closes down about eleven o'clock. I have the schedule for this month and there are so many exciting programmes to be heard. Just look at this."

She spread the monthly tabloid Radio Call on the desk in front of her and pointed out the programmes she had underlined for him to listen to in the following weeks. Included were the recordings of Toscanini conducting the New York Symphony in a performance of Beethoven's *Fifth Symphony* and Sir Thomas Beecham with the London Philharmonic, Leopold Stokowski with the Philadelphia Symphony and Eugene Ormandy and the Chicago Symphonic, all performing major works.

She drew his attention to live broadcasts of concerts given by artists the ABC brought to Australia. Included during this period were the seventeen-year-old Jewish violinist, Yehudi Menuhin and Australia's foremost international concert pianist, Eileen Joyce. At different times and places they were giving solo recitals in four States as well doing a single performance of a concerto with the respective city's own orchestra. She added the words 'do not miss' to a live broadcast from the Adelaide Town Hall of Eileen Joyce doing the Tchaikovsky *Piano Concerto (No.1 in B flat minor)* with the Adelaide Symphony Orchestra. Apart from these, the paper listed a veritable banquet of music to be heard on this station throughout most days. Recordings of great singers such as Caruso, Gigli, and Melba were to be heard along with pianists Vladimir Horowitz, Solomon, Artur Schnabel, violinist Isaac Stern and other gifted instrumentalists.

Patrick left his lesson that night almost as excited as his mentor but there was a problem for, as he had pointed out to her, the Becks were not very fond of classical music and he could not ask them to sacrifice their own listening just for his benefit. The nun considered this and said he should speak with his parents and, perhaps, they might arrange to put a set in his bedroom. The nun said she felt certain his mother would recognise the importance of wireless in the furtherance to his career and do all she could to help him.

He spoke with his parents at their next monthly Mass and Irene wholeheartedly agreed immediately. If the Becks were agreeable, she would have a suitable set put in as soon as possible, but this on the clear understanding he would never play it in a way that would disturb the peace of the Beck household.

Kerry and Harry had no objection and, in a few days, he was able to listen to selected programmes in the privacy of his own room. His enjoyment was profound and whilst it was of immense interest to him to hear well-known pianists perform works he knew so well, it was symphonic music which claimed his mind and soul almost from the outset.

He could not understand how it was possible for a composer to create a single score of music for so many instruments to play at the same time. It was beyond his comprehension now, and he took a vow not to rest until he resolved that mystery, even if it took the rest of his musical life. Achieving a position of one day performing a great concerto with an orchestra was something else he would strive for with all the musical might with which he had been endowed.

Wireless added a huge dimension to his life of music and demanded the sacrifice of less time with his friends, fewer rambles on his beloved bike and fewer training hours for his chosen sports of rugby and cricket. Increasingly music was taking over his being but he hung on grimly to these diminished, and other, facets of his life which meant so much to him.

As his time at the College drew to a close Patrick began to realise it heralded that an important and very happy period of his life also was coming to an end.

He felt fortunate he had so many friends at the school and in the town. The close relationship he enjoyed with Brian, Eric and Max was something special to him. The four of them had been in the same class right through. But at the end of this year they would all go their separate, and as yet undetermined, ways. However that may be, he felt they would be friends for life.

Sr. Annunciata had been a true friend and mentor and he'd be ever grateful to her not only what she had taught him but for the way she had encouraged and inspired his will to succeed as a pianist and musician. She was plainly moved after their final lesson and when telling him he always would be in her prayers, she elicited the promise he would keep her informed of his progress at the Conservatorium. Big boys don't cry but young Sheridan had a small lump in his throat just after saying goodbye to his holy friend. He admired and respected the Marist brothers who had taught him but never became really close to any of them. The exception being Bro. Miller, the sports master, who had become a confidante over the years.

The Brothers were dedicated teachers and Patrick a good student who applied himself at lessons, and over the four years, in all subjects, he was never less than fifth of sixth in the class. He sat for the exam set by the State Government, known as 'The Intermediate' in the November of his final year and gained a level of marks consistent with the good standard he had achieved in class.

His best marks were for English, a lesson he always enjoyed, especially when it explored the essays and poetry of Australian authors like A.B. Paterson, Henry Lawson and such. The former's 'A Vision Splendid' had a permanent place on his bedside table and was often the choice for his final reading before turning off the light at night. The pure and simple Australianness of this man's work never failed to increase the boy's profound awareness of how blessed he was to be a citizen of a country he loved so much. He had developed a keenness for sport and often lamented his tie to the piano did not permit him sufficient time to train properly so as to become a better cricketer and footballer than he was.

In his final year he tried out for the school's first eleven and was disappointed when Brother Miller did not select him for the team.

"Look, Pat, you can't have it both ways," he told him, "it was a matter of whether you gave time to cricket or the piano and quite rightly the piano won. I would like to have had you in the 'firsts' but, like the piano, cricket requires practice if you are to be any good. I'm afraid you have fallen behind one or two other lads who have worked pretty hard on their game."

Despite his disappointment he said he understood why he was not picked and thanked the Brother for giving him the try-out. He had better luck with the football team. At the beginning of the season of his final year he was selected to play on the left wing for the College first fifteen. He had played good football during the opening weeks of that season and was in peak form for the annual grudge match against Bathurst High.

This was traditionally a knock-down, drag-out affair played on the Saturday of the June long weekend. It attracted five or six hundred spectators usually made up of teachers and pupils from both schools, parents and friends, ex-students and well-wishers for both sides. From the outset things did not go well for the Marists. It was a battering game with one or two flare-ups, in which Sheridan made himself prominent, and the coaches had to assist the referees to stop the mayhem on one occasion.

They were down 10-nil at half time and Patrick was irate as he sucked his lemon and told Brian Stiller, who was captain and five-eighth, he had been starved for the ball. It had only reached him half a dozen times in those first forty minutes. Although he had picked up many swear words at the school, he did not use them often but his passion for the game seemed to change his entire personality and he was unable to hold back.

"What the plurry hell is going on, Brian? These coots have never given me a lot of the ball but today it had been worse than ever. I made some good runs when I got the thing, but that does not seem to make any difference to these blighters."

"I know how you must feel, Mate," replied Brian, "but I can't help it as we have to follow the coach's new strategy for the game, but I wouldn't talk to 'Mill' about it at the moment if I were you. He's not happy! I'll see what I can do about getting you more ball in the second half."

"You better do something about it or I might as well go and have a shower now," replied the unhappy winger as he trudged back for the kick-off.

Things got a little better for his team as they scored a try which was unconverted but the fullback who missed the shot was reprieved when he kicked a penalty goal from a difficult position to make the score seven to ten with eight minutes to go. Sheridan had seen even less of the ball in the second half and on several occasion when it looked like it would come out to him the play was reversed and the ball went back to the other side of the field. He hurled boyish abuse at his nearest teammates and used some of those censored words to describe their stupidity and did not care whether the spectators heard him or not. He was only sixteen but his passion for this game was so intense it made the usual persona of Patrick Sheridan the musician, unrecognisable. By the closing few minutes of the game he had had enough. High had the ball and were raiding Marist territory when he ran infield, contrary to Brother Miller's instructions, and positioned himself behind the defenders. There was nothing to lose as he took himself up to the first line of defence and watched closely as High began passing the ball to his side of the field. He saw half an opportunity and burst through the attackers as he juggled but finally held the pass he had intercepted and strode out for his try line, which was no more than fifty yards away.

He knew he was too fast for any pursuer and, with only two players to beat, he could smell victory for his side. The first defender was easily avoided but required him to take a diagonal course towards the corner post because he could see the High fullback haring down the try-line at great speed. Patrick thought he had him covered as he stretched out for the dive to victory just as a blur which was the fullback in mid-air took him ball and all around the hips and bundled him into touch no less than a yard from home.

Patrick made his way back to his position on the wing, High won the line-out and within three minutes the match was all over. The Marists had lost by three points but they had made a game of it. The teams shook hands and started to leave the field as Pat looked up to see the High fullback, whom he knew, coming towards him.

"That was pretty close, Pat," he said. "I thought you were there."

"Yeah! Darn you, Jim, so did I for a minute. It was a great tackle I can tell you and it shook the hell out of me. Your mob played well and were just too good on the day, but you saved the game for them. Well done, mate."

Pat shook his hand again and they walked off the field together. His coach was waiting for him on the side line.

"What's wrong with your hand, Sheridan?" he said "I saw you flicking it as you got up from that tackle. Let me have a look at it."

"It's nothing" said Pat as he held up his right hand for inspection, "it hurt a bit when I landed on it at the end there. It still hurts but I can work it pretty well so it's not serious."

"You have some bruising there but it could have been a lot worse and that's what you get for grandstanding."

"I wasn't grandstanding," Pat snapped back. "I'd been stuck on the wing all day waiting to do something but the ball hardly ever came to me. It was as if they thought I would muck things up if they passed it to me. Look, our team was losing and we were running out of time so there was nothing to lose and perhaps something to gain in what I tried to do. And that is the reason I did it and it had nothing to do with grandstanding."

"Be that as it may," said Brother Miller, "you still didn't keep to our understanding to stay away from the main field of play and that is what I want to talk to you about. Go and have your shower and see me in my room in half an hour's time."

He did as he was told and when he arrived the coach was writing his report of the match for weekly assembly. He looked up as Patrick stood in front of his table and he told him to sit.

"Let's get this over, Sheridan," he said, "it's going to be painful for both of us and I want to get it out of the way as quickly as possible. For starters, you have played your last game of football for this college, so let us be quite clear about that."

He could see from the instant change of expression to concern and disbelief on the boy's face that he was about to explode, so went on quickly.

"Now, before you try to tear my head off, let me give you the reason for this, and it has nothing to do with what happened out there today. As a matter of fact your move was a great bit of rugby and under other circumstances I would have been the first to applaud, but what you did was absolutely contrary to our understanding and, therefore, involved something more important than just winning a football match."

Patrick started to say something but the coach cut him off and, in a slightly softer tone of voice, said "Don't interrupt me, son, listen to what I have to say; it's important. Some three weeks ago you played the piano at the Convent reception for the visit of their Order's Mother General and I was in the school auditorium with the students and clergy from the diocese. I'm no musician but I enjoy good music, as well as the other kind, and hearing you play that day is something I won't forget quickly. My mother played 'Claire de Lune' at home but never like that. You would not have noticed but during your entire performance there was not a single sound in that hall as nobody wanted to miss a note. Surely the applause made you realise how much pleasure you brought to those people."

He stopped there before going and looked more closely at the boy and saw the mantle of the tough footballer had started to fall away. He was listening now with a different expression on his face and so the coach continued.

"In spite of the enjoyment I just had from hearing you play that day all I came away with was a deep sense of guilt. You seem to take it for granted but I realise now God has given you an awesome gift and to think I placed it in jeopardy by giving you the okay to play sport was nothing short of gross negligence on my part.

"I decided to do something about it and the next morning I sent for Brian Stiller and told him to tell players the ball was not to be passed to your wing unless there was an opportunity for a certain try. That's why you have been starved for the ball; so blame me and not Brian and the others. I thought this would reduce the risk of injuring your hands and it seemed a better way than simply dropping you from the team. But, after today's episode with your hands, I am left with no alternative and am conscience bound to put an end to it here and now."

Silence followed for a few moments and as they both stood up, the coach came around the desk and attempted to console the boy with some kind words. However, it was not necessary for he had calmed down by now and understood what the Brother had been saying. He realised the piano was again demanding he surrender another real pleasure of his young life.

He started to leave the room and then turned back and in a shy boyish way faced Miller who was obviously upset by what had just transpired.

"Thanks for that, Sir. I didn't think it would end like this, but I know you're right and I just have to take it. The Marists, thanks to you, gave me a few years of good sport and now because of the rotten piano it's all over. In all the time I've been playing Union here it was only after that tackle today I realised I could really hurt my hands and I thought you should know that now. So it might all be for the best but I wish it wasn't because I liked being in the firsts and I hate the idea of missing the rest of the season.

"I really don't know how to thank you for what you have done for me over the years, Brother, but I am really grateful to you." And with that he left the room, collected his bike and slowly pushed home to the Becks. As he rode he pondered the aftermath of today's drama which had left him so disappointed. He was more concerned, however, with a new realisation the path to his career in music was narrowing to the extent that, eventually, there would be no room on it for any other interests in his life.

When he got home he found Aunty Kerry had not returned from doing the Altar at the Cathedral and, as Harry also was away, he took himself off to the convent for his evening practice. After returning about two hours later they were soon sitting down together at the evening meal and he confided in her the events of his day.

She did not comment immediately because she could still read the disappointment on his face. But then she said "I'm not surprised, Pat. I've never been happy about you playing rugby but it was none of my business even though I felt at times I should have told your mother. How it has gone on this long without her knowing is beyond me. Pat, your hands are precious and I am glad Brother Miller has finally seen the light. Suppose something did happen to your hands which prevented you from playing the piano. Your mother, Sister Annunciata and your other musical friends would be devastated but think what it would mean to you. It is so obvious to me since you have been with us that music is your life and I think part of you would die if you could not play the piano. I know you are disappointed but in time you will be grateful for the decision Brother Miller has made for you."

"I know, Aunt Kerry, but it is hard to accept just like that," and with that he got up and started to clear the dishes.

He had had many such warm and helpful conversations with Kerry and Harry since he came to live in their home nearly four years ago. They had become stand-in parents and his life in Bathurst could have been lonely had it not been for their affection and caring concern for him. In his own way, he had come to love them for this. As the end of his time in Bathurst approached he realised what a wrench it was going to be on leaving them.

He had come to the Marist Brothers as a little lad of twelve and would leave them as a well-grown boy of sixteen, well educated, fit and healthy, a little worldlier and, perhaps more importantly, with a better understanding of his Maker and an appreciation of the obligations this involved. There had been three or four sessions in his final year when priests from different religious Orders outlined to senior students the incredible satisfaction of a life devoted to the service of God. He did give a thought to this but it did not persevere. Nevertheless when he left the college he continued to carry a healthy fear of God with him.

In years to come, when reflecting on his time in this big town, his fondest memories would be of the Becks, Sister Annunciata, Brother Miller, his good companions Brian, Max and Eric, his teammates in the First Fifteen and many of the boys with whom he shared the same school class for four long years. They had played a significant part in his development and he felt indeed fortunate that so many very decent Australians has crossed his path at this important and impressionable time of his life.

The school year ended at noon on a very hot day in mid-December, 1934. All the final goodbyes were said together with the expressed intentions of keeping in touch. Patrick, Brian and Max walked home together and, because they were growing youths and having no truk with sentiment of any kind, there was no recognition of this final occasion. Max left them at his house with a simple, "see you later," and Brian told Pat he would see him before he left. And that was it.

Pat went home and completed the packing of his belongings. He and Aunty Kerry had a cup of tea whilst awaiting the arrival of his parents to pick him up and take him back to his still beloved Magdalene. School was over.

Chapter 11

Magdalene had prospered in recent times despite the financial difficulties of the day. Tom Sheridan had enjoyed reasonable prices for his enlarged wool-clip and at the same time had kept overheads to a minimum. Three good years in a row had enabled him to redeem mortgages on the properties he had acquired a few years back and there was now a healthy balance at the bank which would stand him in good stead for those more difficult times which inevitably lay in wait for the sheep farmer. However, at the moment, he could be considered well to do.

He put money back into the property with projects including new fencing, rebuilding the bunk house and kitchen for Aboriginal stockmen on the payroll, an extension to the shearing shed and renovation of a cottage on one of the acquired holdings. This latter had become the living quarters of the recently appointed Overseer who, under Tom's general supervision, had taken over much of the day to day running of the sheep station. An Overseer had been Irene's idea after she had noticed a change in Tom over some months. He was perpetually tired and his face had become lined and drawn and at times she thought he looked quite ill. He now was well into his fifties and the strain of forty years unrelenting hard work was starting to take its toll.

At her insistence he made an appointment with their family doctor in Bathurst and she was in the surgery the day he was examined by John Burton. Their worst fears were realised when the doctor told him his heart was not as good as it should be and it was time for him to take things easier or a now minor problem could become serious. He prescribed medication and a serious injunction to avoid becoming tired or exhausted, emphasising the importance of a short nap in the middle of every day.

Tom was run down to the extent he accepted the doctor's advice without question and fell in with Irene's suggestion to appoint an Overseer. He did not loosen the reins at once but waited until he was certain the man not only had the ability but also, just as importantly to him, the right attitude for the job. Ray Boundy was in his mid-forties and a very experienced sheepman. He had started out as a jackeroo and been on sheep properties in the far west of the State ever since so there was no reason for Tom to doubt the man's ability for the job. He reported to Tom most mornings for discussion prior to starting work and the way he carried out the decisions made at those meetings convinced Tom he had hired the right man for the job.

With the somewhat easier life his health started to improve but not to a sufficient extent to relieve Irene's concern altogether as he still had the face lining and pallor of a man who was not terribly well.

So this was the situation at Magdalene when Patrick's parents brought him back after completing his secondary education in Bathurst. They made light of it and did not go into the detail of Tom's condition but simply said the time had arrived for him to ease up and to get help in the detailed running the property.

The thought struck the boy then that, as he was now sixteen, there would have been no need to hire an Overseer if it had been his intention to take over from his father at some time in the near future. It disturbed him as he realised the tug-o'-war for his future could be very much alive in the minds of those concerned in the matter and that, of course, included himself.

Because of Tom's condition Irene decided not to raise immediately the question of Patrick's enrolment at the Conservatorium but to wait until things had settled down after the shock of his diagnosis, and Patrick's return from school.

She had taken it for granted he would agree in the long term but it was possible there would be some initial resistance and she did not want to put him through that at this time. There was no urgency about the enrolment as no time factor was involved and Patrick could start at any time of the year after passing his audition. She would wait for an appropriate occasion and then bring it up.

Patrick settled back into life at the homestead and for a time it seemed he had never been away. There were some changes to the daily routine brought about by modern science but this did not affect the boy's former preoccupations with his music and helping out on the property. A generator now supplied sufficient power to provide electric light in the kitchen and the lounge room of the homestead with enough left over to play the newly installed wireless set. The transmission through a relay station in Orange was not always good but it did pick up the vital 2FC which was so important to Irene and her son. This appliance, together with the installation of the telephone, even though it was a party line, finally brought to an end once and for all this family's sense of complete isolation which had been its lot for so many years.

Their Model T Ford after five years had started to show signs of its age and wear from the rough roads on which it travelled. Tom had traded it in on an Essex Sedan which virtually became Irene's car and was the pride of her life. He also purchased a Chrysler buckboard to do heavy cartage around the property and haul from Bathurst and other places the equipment and supplies increasingly required by his flourishing concern.

Tom and the Overseer used it constantly as, with a farmer's typical lack of respect for anything mechanical, they often drove it off the made dirt track and through sheep paddocks when it was quicker or more convenient than riding a horse. Much to the boy's delight, Tom taught Patrick how to drive it but it would be another five years before he could be licensed to use it other than within the boundaries of the property. To an untrained eye raising Australia's golden fleece just watching a mob of sheep grazing in a well-grassed paddock seemed a carefree and easy way to make a living. But that was far from being the case. Lambing and shearing seasons demanded long, hard hours of work, as did crutching, marking and drenching a few thousand head of sheep at regular intervals. Replacing and repairing fencing, laying wild dog bait, and culling 'roos were tasks which called for time and energy. It was, therefore, true to say the sheep farmer and his employees did, indeed, earn their respective incomes.

The tasks were endless and, as it was on all similar properties, there was never a time at Magdalene when there was not some job or work crying out to be done without delay.

Within a week or so of coming back Patrick had reverted to his previous daily routine of breakfast, practice and then work. He was now a capable sheepman in many respects, having been at it since childhood, and his father and Ray Boundy made good use of his abilities. He worked with Tom quite often and where possible relieved him of any strenuous aspect of the tasks they were performing, for now he too realised his father was not the man he was just a few years back.

His love affair with Magdalene had waned only slightly during his long sojourn in Bathurst but in these recent weeks it had been rekindled to the extent he was starting again to have doubts as to whether, when the time came, he would have the strength to leave this place which had become so much a part of him.

Despite these thoughts, music remained the dominant force in his life and thanks to Annunciata's encouragement his ambition had risen to an even greater level. She had been responsible for extending his repertoire to include important but lesser-known composers and had fostered his obvious and growing interest in writing his own music. He had never forgotten her remark after seeing one of his short works: "Patrick, there is no doubt you are already a fine pianist but I feel one day you'll be an even better composer."

He read the biographies of several of the great men of musical letters which she had loaned to him from her personal library. Each and every one of these masters amazed him for their prodigious output of music for ensembles and full orchestras and solo and concerto compositions for those instrument of which they comprised. What intrigued him most now was the knowledge that much of this great music was written some hundreds of years ago and yet today, still as fresh as ever, it was the essential mainstay of classical recitals and orchestral concerts being performed throughout the musical world.

During his last year or so in Bathurst he had not been altogether lax with his own composing efforts. Quite often when he was in his room at the convent the piano would be silent because he was busy committing to manuscript some musical structure which had come to mind during the day. He heard these works at what seemed very odd times, often when riding his bike in the late afternoon, walking home from school. On a few occasions in the middle of the night when he woke up for no reason he knew. Whatever the occasion, he realised through experience he could not force the issue by sitting down at the piano and endeavouring to compose. It either came to him of its own volition or not at all. In any event, that drawer in his wardrobe was starting to fill up and one of these days he intended to go through all these works and see if they made any sense.

It was five or six weeks after her son returned from school before Irene found what she thought was a good opportunity to raise the Conservatorium matter with Tom again. One evening in early February she had read in a recent copy of the 'Bathurst Weekly' of the large number of exhibits the town was to enter in several Sections at the upcoming Royal Easter Show in Sydney. It was normal for important matters to be discussed around the dining table at Magdalene and after breakfast the following morning she told Tom about the broad number of local entries and indicated she would like to go down for the big event and see how The Town got on.

"It might do you good, Tom," she said "we haven't been for years and, now that we can afford it, it'd be great for Patrick to go down for the Show and see Sydney for the first time, especially now that he is old enough to appreciate it all. Do you think you would be up to it?" Tom didn't say anything but just nodded his head slowly as though he was considering what she was saying. So she continued.

"We could make that appointment, for you to see a heart specialist in Macquarie Street, which Doctor Burton is always on about. I know you feel a bit better now but it wouldn't do any harm to have you checked out by a specialist and I want you to do that" she emphasised.

Tom nodded again. "Yeah. I suppose we could but I'll have to think about it," he said. It was here that Irene seized the moment.

"Also," she said, "I could make enquiries about Patrick starting at the Conservatorium and make arrangements for his audition. We could also look into places…" She was about to say "where he could board" when Tom cut her off sharply.

"Enough of that, Ire, you know we haven't talked about that yet and we haven't decided whether or not he'll be going to that place. You know I'm against it; the boy is only sixteen and too bloody young to be going off on his own. Let it go for a while. He's settling in now and likes this old place and he's a great help to me at the moment. Already he knows much about running a show like this, so he just might not want to leave here. Hold your horses and don't go rushing into it like this. Perhaps, in a couple of months' time the three of us can talk about it."

At times like this she felt an unrealistic, but quite understandable, sense of rage towards this man who was not the father of her son and, therefore, really had no say in any aspect of his upbringing, especially in matters like this. Fortunately for him, her common sense prevailed and she quickly calmed down and only paused a few moments before replying.

"Alright Tom, if that's the way you want it, but we can't delay this thing indefinitely. If he is going to enrol it will have to be before the middle of the year. Whether you can understand it or not, Patrick has an incredible talent, so please, start thinking about what is best for him and not what is best for you."

She was disappointed with the outcome of her planned approach but determined there and then they would go down to the Show. Tom would see the specialist and she would, most certainly, look into detail for Patrick's enrolment at the Conservatorium. As she tidied the kitchen that morning she watched her son through the window as he rode off towards a nearby paddock where he was helping the Magdalene stockmen crutch a large mob which had become flyblown. She gave a deep sigh for she was always concerned for his hands when he was away working like that.

At her insistence Tom had backed her up when she forbid Patrick to take part in any fencing work; an onerous chore which brought many a cut finger, hand or arm in its wake. She bought him a pair of leather gloves which he was told to wear at all times. He complied as far as possible but never when working with the stockmen. They had seen him grow up and enjoyed a friendly, easy-going relationship with him. But, as he told his father, they were cheeky young buggers and were always laughing at something and would give him merry hell had they caught him wearing gloves.

Irene had a routine for him after he had cleaned himself up after his working day. This required her to put on the kitchen table a bowl of warm water and vinegar in which he soaked his hands for several minutes before she examined and dried them. And then, for some minutes, she massaged the palms and the thumb and fingers of each hand before he went into his evening practice. He began to think this was a bit sissy but humoured his mother as she took it all so seriously. So far his hands and fingers had remained as flexible as ever and she listened carefully for confirmation of this from the scales and exercise he played at the beginning of each of these sessions.

A few days after their breakfast meeting Tom agreed they should go to the Show and Irene made a booking for them for ten days at Usher's Hotel in Castlereagh Street. She also made an appointment with the Macquarie Street specialist to whom Tom had been referred by Dr. Burton. Even though it was some weeks away, Irene and Patrick were quite excited at the prospect and even Tom perked up a little when they talked about what they would do and what they would see in the big city.

It had now become customary for Patrick to join his father and Ray Boundy in their discussions before the day's work began. It was a hot morning in early March when Ray reported hearing some distant noise coming from the eastern paddock. It sounded like dogs he said but could not be sure and thought somebody should check on it. The hands were away mustering and he was attending to some fencing which had been knocked down by mob of kangaroos so he suggested Patrick might ride out there and have a look at things.

"Righto, Ray, I'll go out as soon as we're finished here. Is that okay with you, Dad?"

"I think I will come with you. Haven't been out for a while and I wouldn't mind looking over the place," replied his father.

"Do you think you should? Mum said you were not to go out in this heat and I could go on my own and come back and tell you if anything has happened out there," replied his son.

"Don't try to mollycoddle me, boy, I'm alright. Your mother has always worried too much about everything. Saddle two horses while I get a couple of bottles of water and my rifle and let's get going. I think we've finished here Ray," he said as he turned to the Overseer, "see you tomorrow."

They eventually arrived at the area suggested by Boundy and he had indeed heard the noise of dogs last night. A whole pack of them, by the look of it, with part carcasses of stock strewn the length of the paddock. There were twenty or more in all and Patrick could see the dark look of anger and despair on his father's face as he surveyed the scene of destruction from his saddle.

"Just look at that," he grunted sadly, "these lousy animals kill for the sake of killing. I've battled these bastards of things ever since I got here and just when you think you've got 'em beat they come back at you like this. The dingo must be the filthiest thing God ever put on earth."

"I now know what you mean, Dad" said Patrick sympathetically, "and to think I once felt sorry for those rotten mongrels. Now I know why you hate them."

With ropes carried in their saddle bags they used the horses to drag the carcasses to a central point and made them into a pile ready for burning. They inspected the rest of the flock without finding any with serious injury before dismounting and taking a drink of the water Tom had brought along.

As he drank he turned to the boy and said, "When we get back, I want you to ride out to Ray and tell him one of the boys should camp here every night with a rifle for the next couple weeks. It's a rough deal and they can take it in turns if they like. He can tell them they are on an extra month's pay for every dog they shoot. That ought to make it worth their while. Also, you drive the ute out here tomorrow with some kero' and get them to burn this lot off before they start to stink and bring the flies."

"Right," was all the boy answered.

Overriding the boy's objection that he was trying to do too much on a hot day, Tom decided they should ride the paddock boundaries to check the fencing and over two hours elapsed before finally they started making their way back to the homestead. Tom had not said anything for some time and Patrick was keeping an anxious eye on him because he looked drawn and tired and appeared to be breathing quite heavily.

They were doing a light trot approaching a makeshift bridge which forded the property creek when Tom gave a short, sharp cry and bent right forward in the saddle. "We better stop, Pat, I've got a pain in the chest. I feel pretty crook," he gasped and then appeared to pass out all together.

Patrick leant over and grasped the reins of his father's horse and as both mounts came to a halt he leapt off and gently eased his father to the ground. He had regained consciousness and with the boy's help he walked a few yards to the shade of the nearby weeping willow. Patrick could see there was something seriously wrong with his father as he laid him on the grass and used his own hat to pillow his head. He did not like leaving him but he could see he needed medical help without delay. Wetting his handkerchief in the creek, he wiped his father's face which was now the colour of chalk.

Leaning over him he said, "I'm going to get help, Dad, and I'll be back as soon as I can. Just you take it easy and don't try to move."

He jumped on his horse and covered the near two miles to the homestead in under twenty minutes and was calling out to his mother as he rode into the station yard. Irene rushed out at once and he told her what had happened. The news shocked her and she didn't move. A look of great anxiety appeared on her face. Patrick knew he had to act quickly and instinctively took control of the situation.

"Don't worry, Mum, I think he will be alright if we are quick. You get on the phone to the doctor straight away and ask him what we should do because I don't think we have got a lot of time. I'll get a mattress and a couple of pillows off the veranda bed and put them on the buckboard. We should take a couple of towels, I think, more water, and his medicine."

Although still very anxious, Irene composed herself. By the time Patrick had loaded the vehicle and brought it to the back door she knew their course of action. She had picked up the medicine and as she got into buckboard she told the boy, "Dr. Burton has arranged for an ambulance and it will be here in about an hour. You drive me out to Tom and I'll stay with him until it comes. You'll have to drive to the gate to meet it and lead the driver to where we are."

"Okay, Mum. We can see what we will do after the ambulance people have had a look at him."

Tom had indeed had a serious heart attack and it was touch and go for several days before he started to pick up slightly and then be considered out of danger. He was in the Bathurst General Hospital for nearly six weeks and spent a further three in a private convalescent home before Dr. Burton allowed him to return to Magdalene. Irene was given strict instructions about his care and medication and for the first month he was to be allowed out of bed for only four hours a day. He was not to do work of any kind and was to be shielded from worry or concern where possible. Although he was improving slowly he was still a sick man and she had no problem in getting him to comply with the doctor's orders.

From the time of the owner's heart attack management of the property fell to Ray Boundy and, with Patrick's help, things had proceeded quite smoothly. When it became clear Tom would not be back home for some time, Irene and Patrick had a breakfast meeting with Ray to discuss the new situation.

Irene led the way by asking Ray if he would take over as acting manager of the property with the terms of his employment being adjusted appropriately from the date of Tom's absence. He agreed in his shy but definite manner and said he could do the job whilst Patrick's experienced help was available. But it would become difficult when he left to go to Sydney, and it was here that Patrick made his position clear.

"You're right, Ray. There is always a heck of a lot of work to be done around here and you need plenty of help. Mum and I have not discussed this yet but I know Dad isn't keen on me going to the Con. There is no way I'm going to bring that up with him until he is feeling a lot better. So there is no way I'll be starting down there until at least next year and that gives us eight or nine months to organise things here if I decide to go."

"What do you mean 'if I decide to go'?" snapped Irene. "Of course you're going and you'll start in July as I arranged and none of this next year business. What has happened doesn't change a thing and you will do as you're told."

Ray got up and went outside as he did not want to be part of this conversation.

"Mum, if I left when Dad was sick he wouldn't forgive me. You know he didn't want me to go even when he was well so you can imagine what he would think if I did that to him now. I won't disobey you but it needs his okay also and I don't think we should ask him about it until he is a lot better."

"You're going, Patrick, whether you like it or not. I'm prepared to wait a couple of weeks and see how your father is before I tell him but, take it from me, you are going. Now get Ray back and let's get on with it."

Ray said he had given a lot of thought to things for when Patrick left. He was already almost acting as an Overseer and would need to be replaced if Mr. Sheridan was unable to resume. He had looked at the old bunkhouse on the far side of the barn and thought it could be renovated to provide quarters for a new Overseer and, perhaps, one or two jackeroos. It was only a suggestion, he said, but he could see no other way out of it if Patrick and his father were off Magdalene's workforce.

Irene liked the idea from the outset because it meant Patrick would be free to leave. Of course, she would have to clear it with Tom when he was well enough and then discuss costs with their accountant, Harry Beck. She'd also have to raise the matter also with their pastoral agents, Dalgety & Company who would screen applicants for the jobs. She knew she could not handle these matters on her own and at her request, Ray agreed to take part in those discussions.

Patrick could see Ray's plan as a solution to the need for the more efficient running of the business but was not certain it freed him altogether of the obligations he owed to his father and Magdalene. Hired help was one thing but having a member of the family directly involved was another, and he knew the latter was what his father would want. In more difficult times his parent had toiled hard to provide for he and his mother and the arduous labour of those years was, undoubtedly, a major cause of his current ill-health.

Apart from the respect, loyalty and gratitude Patrick felt for his father, he was also fond of him. Whilst Tom Sheridan was not the type of man to extend or receive affection openly, the boy was aware they shared an unspoken bond which fully embraced the true meaning of a father/son relationship and all that that meant.

He always knew he had to grow up but now he knew he had to grow up quickly because of the new responsibility imposed on him by his father's infirmity. In spite of what his mother had said, he could not, and would not, leave his father under present circumstances. The only way he would change his mind about this would be to receive his father's unqualified blessing to do so, and this, he thought, was most unlikely.

During those few weeks his father was in hospital, Patrick worked long hours on the property and his attraction to the place was undiminished and perhaps even grew. But he was beginning to realise what he was doing in the fields was not altogether compatible with what he was trying to achieve in the music room. Drenching, marking and crutching were nearly at the opposite end of the cultural spectrum from the music of Mozart, Beethoven, Bach and friends, and he found he was not particularly inspired when returning to the piano after a working day spent on such activities. He was able to cope with it for now but if it went on too much longer he could see it would have a retrograde effect on his entire musical perspective. However, he knew where his duty lay and he would continue to work on the property until such time as his father gave his unqualified approval for him to leave.

Chapter 12

*I*t was some three months after being hospitalised that Tom Sheridan returned to Magdalene. He was still frail but his pallor had improved and there was a little life in his eyes now, the lines of a desperately sick man having disappeared from his face. Irene nursed him gently, but it was several weeks later before he began to show interest in anything other than his own illness.

She had taken over the task of bookkeeper during his absence, a job which he had always done himself because it 'kept him in touch with things'. After several weeks of him just sitting around and doing nothing, she suggested he resume that light clerical duty. When he agreed she knew it would not be long before she could raise with him the important matter that had lain in abeyance pending his recovery.

As it turned out she need not have been concerned as, much to her surprise and great relief, he brought up the subject himself. They were sitting in the small homestead office and she had finished bringing him up-to-date with the books when he leant back on his chair and, looking at her, started to speak.

"Ire, it's time we had a talk," and he paused for a few moments before going on. "First of all, I'm sorry you both missed out on the Show because of me. You were looking forward to it and I'll try to make up for it sometime.

"Now, Ire, I've had a chance to mull over about what you said to me about considering Pat and his music instead of just thinking about myself. You're quite right, of course, and if you think he is that good then pack him off to the Conservatorium whatever. I won't stand in his way and I'll look after the cost."

She felt a tear coming so she didn't interrupt. She did not know what had brought about this change of heart but there was no way she was going to question it.

"I'll miss him, that goes without saying, but also he has been a great help to Boundy in running this place. It'll probably be some time before I get back to hard yakka so we better think about getting some additional help around the place for when Pat goes," he said.

"There's no doubt about you Sheridan, you're full of surprises. Here I was thinking you'd give me a hard time about Patrick and you come out with something like this. I know how you feel about him leaving here and can't thank you enough for what you have offered to do," said his wife as she reached across the desk and gently touched him on the cheek.

"As for running the place, we have talked about it," she said, "and have come up with some ideas," and she told him of Ray Boundy's suggestions.

"That doesn't sound too bad," he said slowly after a moments thought. "I'd already decided to make Ray manager so we can get that fixed up as soon as I'm fit to have a yarn with him. As for doing-up the bunkhouse, that's another matter. It means we would have an overseer and two jackeroos on our doorstep here and would have to feed them and look after their quarters and that's a problem, I think. You've had enough on your plate since the roustabout and his missus went walkabout. You've had to look after this place on your own and that's a bit much, so I'm not having you taking on anything more."

"Ray's had a thought about that too," she said "but doesn't know how you will feel about it. He has a widowed sister living in Broken Hill whose kids have grown-up and gone. Now she wants to come out here to be with him but he said no because there'd be nothing for her to do all day.

"He could see I would need help with more people about the place here and thought, perhaps, we could give her a job as some kind of housekeeper. He says she can cook and always kept a tidy house so perhaps that would be a good idea. You think about it when you're pondering the bunkhouse and more hands questions."

"Leave it with me, Ire, I'll think it over and let you and Ray know later on."

"By the way, Tom, there is no tearing hurry. Pat can't start at the Con. now until next January so that gives us a few months to get things organised. You just take it easy and don't bust a boiler about the changes. Also, I have to tell you, Pat's insisted that he won't leave here unless he has your blessing. He's a good boy, our Pat, perhaps a bit too good for this tough old world we live in."

When Patrick got home from work that evening, Tom was back in bed and the boy stuck his head around the bedroom door.

"G'day, Dad," he said, "how's it going?"

"Not bad son. Come in for a minute, I want to talk to you."

Patrick went into the room and sat on the end of the bed and looked expectantly at his father as he began to speak.

"Your mother and I have been talking about you going to the Conservatorium. How do you feel about it?"he asked.

The subject and the question took the boy by surprise and for a moment he was lost for an answer.

"I think I want to go sometime," he said thoughtfully, "but there's no hurry and it can wait until you are up and about again. There's a lot of bloody work to be done on this place and Ray can't do it all by himself so I'll stick about until you are fit again. I know Mum wants me to go right away but that's not possible at the moment."

"Watch that swearing, Pat, your mother doesn't like it. She seems to think you should go down as soon as possible and I respect her opinion. I don't know when I will be able to pull my weight again but I'll arrange for Ray to get sufficient help when you leave, so don't you worry about that."

"Why the change, Dad? I thought you wanted me to stay on here and eventually take over the place."

"I still do. I like the idea of family being involved at Magdalene and you would be the third generation of Sheridan's to do that. But your mother and other people have different ideas and tell me you have a talent which would be a sin to waste and I don't want to be responsible for that. I don't know a lot about these things but apparently you are something special. You get yourself down there as soon as you can and I will do whatever I can to help"

It was an emotional moment for two people who could never be accused of wearing their heart on their sleeve.

"Thanks for that, Dad. I would like to give it a go for a couple of years and if it doesn't work out I'll be back here in a flash if you still feel the same way about things."

"Alright, Son, let it go at that. Get yourself organised and I will look after things here."

Dr. Charles Jermyn's brow knitted slightly as he read notes he had made concerning the student he was about to interview. As an applicant for enrolment to study piano at the Conservatorium of NSW, this young man had auditioned for him some six weeks' earlier, in mid-September to be exact. As senior fellow in the piano faculty it was Jermyn's appointed task to interview and audition such aspirants and it was his sole prerogative as to whether or not they were admitted to study piano at this august institution.

He remembered this seventeen-year-old young man, from country New South Wales, quite well. He was tallish, of slim but strong build, hair slightly tousled, good, intelligent eyes and likeable, open manner which made him easy to interview.

He had come to the audition with his mother who had outlined for him her son's musical background and, in her opinion, his extraordinary talent. This latter, he thought at the time, would be determined by himself because parents, he was aware from experience, tended to be carried away when espousing their offspring's capabilities. He had thanked her and suggested she wait in the reception area as the audition had to be conducted in private.

For some reason he had noticed that the applicant was not carrying music when he entered his room that day. When asked what he intended to play for the audition, he produced from his suit's inner pocket a paper which listed, in his own handwriting, more than twenty solo piano works of major composers.

Jermyn had perused the impressive list and told him to play, in the first instance, any of the listed works with which he felt comfortable, and then asked where was his music. On being advised by the young man that he had not thought it necessary to bring it as these compositions had been committed to memory, Jermyn remembered being both surprised and somewhat more than sceptical at the time.

Therefore, to get such doubts out of the way once and for all he told the student he had changed his mind and he now would select the first piece to be played.

He looked at the paper again and suggested the Beethoven *Appassionata* sonata. He knew this to be the grave yard of many a good pianist even when they had the music in front of them. It would be a telling test for this young fellow. He drew his chair up alongside the pianist's as he commenced to play this most difficult opus.

After the opening bars he sat back and watched the youth give a rendition that did not have a single flaw. When the final notes were played, he made no comment and just referred to the list once more.

He suggested he should now play the Bach *Goldberg Variations* and settled back again in his chair as the pianist began to play another very difficult piece. He did not move or take his eyes off the youth until the last note sounded. Again he made no comment other than to thank him, and after referring to this list again, requested he play the Chopin *G Minor Ballade*. Jermyn recalled the conversation between them which had taken place after the last notes of the work softly died away.

"That was excellent, Mr. Sheridan," he said with deliberate lack of over-enthusiasm, because he had not encountered such outstanding talent before. He restrained the praise he wanted to heap on this gifted young man because he did not know him and had no idea how he would you react to unstinted approbation. He was aware of instances where many a musical career had foundered on the rocks with a swollen head.

"I am impressed with what you do at the keyboard. You are precise, accurate and your attack is excellent and I do admire your touch which gives tonal elegance to your playing. Your interpretations were delightful and very much in accord with the composers' instructions. However, I have to tell you I am more intrigued with your memory for scores, which is quite remarkable. I understood such feats were peculiar to members of those families of olden Europe, with names like Bach, Brahms, Mozart, Strauss and so on and I can tell you, it is most unusual to find it in this day and age."

When he asked the obvious question he was informed his family had no musical background of any description, apart from his mother who was 'quite a good pianist'. This was the cause of his initial puzzlement when he began to read the audition notes; how could such talent come, virtually, out of nowhere?

He then told the youth the Conservatorium would be pleased to admit him as a student and all that remained now was to appoint a teacher for him.

"Before I select a mentor for you, Mr. Sheridan, I would like to try an exercise which would help make up my mind in that regard. The head of the piano faculty has a busy, year-long schedule and is unable to take on more than one or two students. Out of necessity, only those who show outstanding promise are considered. You are certainly in that category but I'd like you to carry out this assignment before we approach Professor Morrison."

"Of course," was Patrick's reply.

Jermyn had gone to his desk and had started to write and when he finished handed a slip of paper to the student on which was listed four, longish works for piano.

"Do you know these compositions, Mr. Sheridan?"

"I know of them, but I haven't seen the actual music or studied the pieces in any way," replied the student.

"Good," said Jermyn. "Take the list to our score library on the first floor and tell them you will want the music for six weeks and that you have my authority for this. I want you to take the scores away, learn them and come back and play them for me in six weeks' time and that is..." he said looking at a desk calendar "... November three, at say, eleven o'clock."

Jermyn had risen to his feet to indicate the audition was complete and extended his hand to the young man.

"Welcome to the Con, as the students unfortunately call it, Mr. Sheridan. In my opinion you are already a very good pianist and if you give us a couple of years, we will make you an even better one. I look forward to seeing you in a few weeks. Goodbye."

All this happened those weeks ago, thought Jermyn, and now the young man was back and, despite his normally quiet approach to these things, he was experiencing a slight degree of excitement. By what he showed today this student could confirm for him the strong first impression that he possessed an extraordinary talent.

Chapter 13

On that September afternoon after the first audition, Irene Sheridan sat with her Phillip Gibbs's novel in her lap on a comfortable chair in their room at Usher's Hotel in Castlereagh Street. After Patrick collected the music from the Conservatorium library that morning, they walked down Martin Place and after stopping for lunch, returned to the hotel where she completed the interrogation into her son's music examination.

With this over to her satisfaction, Patrick had gone off to explore more of this city which had fascinated him from the moment they got off the train from Bathurst three days earlier. Together they had walked miles and miles as she showed him some of the city's great sights which, of course, included first and foremost the comparatively new Sydney Harbour Bridge.

On the first full morning of their stay they took the train ride over The Bridge to Luna Park and in the afternoon the ferry to Manly. After walking the full length of The Corso, Patrick saw open sea for the first time in his life. The tram ride to Bondi Beach on the following day was a highlight of his holiday just for the sights on the journey itself. And then the incredible destination where he saw all those people surfing huge, white waves with others lying about in the sun on the golden beach.

They got back to the city in the early afternoon and had gone straight to Paling's Music Store where Irene had booked a piano studio so Patrick could do his final preparation for the audition the following morning.

The audition was over now and she thought of what Patrick had told her. Charles Jermyn must be a very silly man she thought, otherwise he would have been overcome by her son's genius and said as much, and not just used the same phrases he would utter to any very good applicant. But she was pleased to know Professor Julian Morrison could be involved for she was aware of his international reputation as master tutor of piano. Surely he would recognise Patrick for what, in her opinion, he undoubtedly was.

She was not surprised Jermyn had raised the question of Patrick's lineage. It was a most obvious question that had been asked before and undoubtedly would be asked many times again as her son's career progressed.

Only she, and she alone, knew of the generations of musicians in her son's paternal ancestry and no one would ever learn of this, not even her son. She would take the secret of it to the grave. Whenever she thought about it, as she was doing now, she found it almost unbelievable how those few short intimate hours with one man had transformed her life to such an incredible extent.

She dreaded to think what it would have been like had there been no Patrick. She knew her life would have been one of abject unhappiness and discontent as she and Tom's mutual dislike of each other would have, in time, turned to hate. There could have been no worthwhile future for her at Magdalene and their inevitable split when it came could only have led to an existence of utter loneliness for her in some other place.

Her fervent prayers, of former days, to be blessed with motherhood had been granted in an almost miraculous manner, for she had borne a child, and what a child it was, for it had filled her life from the moment of conception. For the last seventeen years her and Tom's life had meaning and purpose. Neither in their wildest dreams had thought a reconciliation between them was possible.

Now she was about to lose him, but not altogether, as his studies would not preclude him from coming home from time to time. She would most certainly be making visits to the city to see him. Looking beyond that she took it for granted he would grace the concert stages of the world in the not too distant future. It was her dream she would accompany him and witness firsthand the universal recognition and great acclaim which would be so rightfully his.

Still excited about all that he had seen and done these last four days, Patrick boarded the train with his mother for their return to Bathurst. Ray Boundy's sister and new housekeeper at Magdalene, Molly Read, met them at the station with the buckboard. They were home in time to share the evening meal with Tom, who was looking a lot better and seemed quite pleased to have them back.

After the meal had finished Patrick left his parents talking at the table and retired to the piano where he studied the score before commencing to play the first of the works Dr. Jermyn had set for him.

Somewhat satisfied, he closed the lid of the instrument and went out to the kitchen where his mother had just finished reading the mail which had come in during their absence.

"Now that you've finished," she said, "I'm going up to play, so now you can hear how a real pianist sounds."

"Oh, good on you, Mum. You know how I like the way you do Chopsticks," responded her son.

"Cheeky wretch," she laughed as she went into the lounge room and closed the door behind her, and then began to play. Patrick strolled out through the back door and onto the veranda where he found his father sitting in his favourite cane chair enjoying the cool of early evening.

"How's it going, Dad?" he said, more as a greeting than a question.

"Not bad, not bad. I'm feeling a lot better now and can get about a bit but I'll never be back to what I was before. Still, the place is ticking over and the new set-up is coming into place so I'm pretty happy about it, all things considered," Tom answered.

"Is the new Overseer coming along alright?" asked the boy.

"He's not bad, bit inexperienced but keen enough and Ray's got him well in hand. He'll do. Incidentally, Ray is doing a hell of a good job and the place is going well. He and his sister are a real part of Magdalene now and we're lucky to have them" said his father.

Pat sat down on the edge of the veranda near his father's chair and leant back against an adjacent post. As he looked out wistfully across the distant pastures he realised how much he was enjoying this quiet moment with his father. They had shared such times before but it was not the same for he was older now and understood his father a lot better. He was aware of a growing sense of respect and appreciation being added to the love he had always felt for his father.

"You know Dad, I'm going to miss you and this old place like hell and I hope I'm doing the right thing by going away for a while," he said.

And then as a wild thought struck him.

"Dad," he said leaning forward anxiously, "you'd never sell Magdalene would you?"

His father looked at him in the half-light and could see real concern on his son's face. Slowly but in a very definite tone he replied, "Never! One day it will be yours and you can do what you like with it. If you have kids I hope they might like to carry on the family tradition, but if you want to cash it up some time in the future that would be up to you, but I hope you don't.

"I've been thinking about the future a bit lately," he continued. "Ray Boundy is quite capable of handling things here now, and in a couple of years' time your mother and I might consider moving into town so we can be closer to things. Even though it has improved a bit, we are still relatively isolated out here and as we get older we'll need an easier way of life that only the town can offer. It's not definite yet, but we have talked about it. In any event, and to answer the question again, I will never sell this place so you can rest assured on that."

"Phew. That's a relief. I wondered what you were leading up to there for a while," said Patrick. "I will always want to come back here often, no matter where the piano makes me go. Look, Dad, you know that bit of high ground in the eastern paddock which you call 'Denny's Knoll' in honour of your father? Well, for a long time I have had a wish to one day build a house there and live in it for the rest of my life. If I make any money with the piano, that's the first thing I will do."

"You surprise me boy, I didn't know you felt so strongly about it. That is a great spot out there and my Dad and I always liked it. That's why I named it after him. I hope I live long enough to see the house you intend to build for yourself," commented a very happy Tom Sheridan who, from the size of his broad smile, seemed to be unable to contain his delight with what his son had just told him.

It was just before ten thirty on an overcast morning in early November when Patrick Sheridan found himself conveniently early for his appointment with Dr. Jermyn. He was standing in Macquarie Street looking at the building which housed the Conservatorium and, despite its different architectural style, found it quite pleasing to his eye. He was aware it had been the original mews for nearby Government House but also knew it was many a year since a horse had given a musical neigh within its precincts. With such lowly background he thought it unusual for it to be 'home' for an institution entirely devoted to the study of classical music but, he allowed, it did bring with it some sense of history.

He had come down on the train from Bathurst the night before with his mother's instructions still ringing in his ears. He had checked into Usher's, where he was well-known because of his previous extended stay and felt quite at home. He'd booked in for one night only as he was returning that day on the Western Mail which left Central Station at 4.45, by which time the purpose of his visit should have been fulfilled.

When he finally arrived outside Jermyn's door it was still ten minutes or so before the appointed time. As there was no answer to his knock he went into the room and after placing the scores set for him on top of the piano he paused for a few moments before opening the lid and, after adjusting the height of the stool, sat down and started to play.

Promptly on time Charles Jermyn breezed into his room. "Good morning, Mr. Sheridan," he said. "Glad you have made yourself at home and what was that you were playing when I came in?"

"Good morning, Dr. Jermyn," replied Patrick, "something I wrote awhile back which helps me to loosen up my hands a bit."

"I see," said Jermyn, "that's interesting. Now let's get down to it. I see you've brought music this time; do you need it?"

"No" said Patrick. "I intended to return it to the library when I came in this morning but then I thought you might want to refer to what you set for me."

"That won't be necessary. When you are ready you can start with the Mozart."

He drew his chair up alongside the pianist as Sheridan, who had now turned back to the keyboard, sat quite still for some moments as though collecting himself, before commencing to play the composer's *C major Sonata No.16.*

When he finished they both sat there without a word or comment until Patrick turned to look at his examiner. Eventually, when he started to speak, Jermyn still had an astonished look on his face.

"That was quite extraordinary! You've left me almost speechless I'm afraid, young man. I've heard that Sonata performed many times by important artists but never played to better effect than what you have just done. It was totally brilliant! To think you were able to do it from memory and be perfect in detail is almost beyond my comprehension. Are you sure your Christian names are not Wolfgang Amadeus? Where does such a faultless memory as yours come from?"

Patrick was starting to feel a little embarrassed but at the same time rather pleased. He'd had praise lavished upon his playing before but never by such an important music authority and to such an analytical extent.

"I don't know where it comes from but I suppose I'm very lucky to have the ability as it does make things a bit easier," he said in answer to the almost rhetorical question.

"Indeed it does and you can say that again. Now before we go on I want to make a call," said Jermyn as he picked up the house telephone on his desk and dialled a number. "Julian?" he said into the receiver, "Charles. Have you got a minute? I think you should hear this… That's right, young Sheridan, I spoke to you about him a few weeks ago after his audition… Fine, we'll see you in about ten minutes then." He turned back to the piano and was still somewhat excited as he addressed a seemingly, relaxed student. "Professor Morrison is coming down. I think it important he hear you before the academic year starts as I'm fairly certain he will want to be your sole mentor for your tenure in this place. He will be a few minutes yet, so let me hear the last half of the sonata once more, please."

The playing stopped as the Professor entered the room. When the introduction was over he asked Jermyn for the music he had set for this student. He looked at the titles only and returned them to the top of the piano. "You saw this music for the first time six weeks' ago, young man?" he asked Patrick.

"Yes, sir," he replied.

"This is all most interesting, Mr. Sheridan. I wish I had more time for pleasantries," said the Professor apologetically, "but you have caught me on the hop as I have appointments coming up very soon. So, perhaps we could begin and, may I suggest, with the Mozart you were playing as I came in."

There was no comment from either men when he had completed the sonata so he went on with the Rachmaninoff and had finished the Schumann before the Professor stood up and reached for Patrick's hand.

"You have just given me a great deal of pleasure, Mr. Sheridan. You already are a fine pianist by any standard and obviously blessed with a memory any musician would kill for. I would like to work with you whilst you are with us - just in case there are gaps in your musical education, but there is very little we could teach you about the playing of our great instrument," he said before turning to Jermyn.

'Thank you, Charles. What on earth have you come up with here? I've never heard the like of it and I'm getting a bit too long in the tooth to be set back on my heels like this, as enjoyable as it has been."

He then addressed them both.

"Our year opens on 28th January and I will put the morning of that day aside for you, Mr. Sheridan, so we can get to know each other better and enable me to see more clearly what you are about. If you have the time, Charles, it would be helpful if you could join us for half an hour or so at that time."

Before leaving he shook the student's hand again and looked at him quite keenly as he said, "I hope you enjoy your time with us, Patrick, isn't it?. We're very pleased to have you here and I feel working with you will prove to be interesting for all concerned."

When he got off the train at Bathurst that night, his mother was waiting. By the time they had driven back to Magdalene she had elicited from him every single detail of his interview at the Con. She was absolutely over-the-moon with what he told her but had to wait until they got out of the car to throw her arms around his broad shoulders and give him a resounding kiss on the cheek.

II

Music

Chapter 14

Patrick did not know what to expect from the morning he was to spend with Professor Julian Morrison on that opening day of the Conservatorium's year. After the 'lesson' he left the building and walked with his thoughts along Macquarie Street to Hyde Park where he sat on a bench near the Archibald Fountain and contemplated all that had been said and done in Julian Morrison's room over the past few hours.

Whether he realised it or not, it was a watershed in the young man's life for finally he had cut the painter and now seemed destined to spend his life upon a stream of never-ending music. From the outset the professor had been friendly and made his student feel at ease by amiably discussing mundane matters at some length before asking him for a list of works making up his present repertoire. Apart from remarking on the absence of concertos, he made no comment and suggested he commence by playing for him one of the works with which he felt quite comfortable. For the next hour or so he sat by the young man's side as he played, at his direction, extracts from several of the listed works which included compositions by the important composers and some others.

"That will do, son," he said at last. "Let us sit over here and talk for a while," and led the way to two comfortable chairs near the windows in this large office which overlooked the Botanic Gardens.

"Tell me about yourself. I would like to know more of your background, your ambitions, your interests outside music and so on. Is there anything about which you feel passionate, apart from the piano, that is?" He paused and looked directly at the youth for a moment and then continued gently. "Understand, I don't ask these questions just to make conversation, for, what you tell me now may have bearing on what I have to say to you about your future." Before responding, Patrick looked at his professor closely and there was an eye contact which, however momentary, gave mutual assurance of an honest concern in what was about to take place.

Reassured but somewhat self-conscious at first, Patrick told him of his contented life at Magdalene and how his mother had him playing the piano when he was five years old and that the instrument had demanded from him hours of daily practice ever since. He described his years at The Gap School and covered his time at the Marist Brothers and referred to his disappointment at being unable to continue playing contact sport, or virtually any sport for that matter, because of the need to safeguard his hands.

He made particular mention of Sister Annunciata and stressed how much he owed her for what she had taught him and how she had opened his eyes to a wider world of music. Finally, in answer to the particular question concerning his passions, he expressed in simple terms the affection he felt for the Australian countryside in general and his family's rural holding in particular. No matter where his music took him, he would one day return to his life at Magdalene.

"Thank you for that," said the professor, again looking closely at the young man before him, "it clears up many things for me and perhaps I should tell you my reasons for asking you about these things.

"In this place we have to be careful in what we say to our students with regard to their ability and the future it may afford them. We cannot mislead them by overstating the case nor discourage them when indicating lack of true talent. Some aspiring musicians are burdened with bigger than normal egos which can be accompanied by a lack of normal common sense. And so we have to tread warily if these same people also happen to be talented. Conceited students and conceited performing artists are a pain in the backside to all who have to deal with them but, more importantly, being overly self-absorbed can militate against a student's chances of becoming a successful artist, no matter how talented they may be.

"Mostly we are teaching and advising young people who are of an impressionable age and we are, therefore, most mindful of our responsibility towards them."

"Thank you, sir," said Patrick, "I know what you are getting at, but as I come from the bush you understand I haven't come up against these things before. I suppose early on my mother made me realise I had some talent for the piano and I just took it for granted. I don't see how I could be conceited about it as I looked upon it as some kind of gift and was just lucky enough to have a mother who made me realise that, unless I devoted a lot of time to it, it could be lost. As to whether I have a degree of talent, only you can decide."

"Well, that adds greatly to the picture you previously provided and gives me further assurance of what I have to say to you will be received and understood intelligently and in the way I intend it to be," said the professor. "Now, tell me," he continued, leaning closer to his student, "are you really certain you want to be what they call a concert pianist? It is not an easy life you know; at least six hours every day, and I mean every day, spent at the keyboard, constant travel, living in hotel rooms, no home life, with little or no time for anything, or anyone, outside your career. Does that appeal to you? Will it be worth the hours of back-breaking work you will need to do to be successful?"

The student was somewhat surprised by what he had just heard and paused some time before answering.

"I'm still a long way from that, aren't I?" he said, "and I must say I have not given it a lot of thought. I'm a little put-back by what you said but the hours of practise don't worry me as I have done that all my life, but the rest of it does not sound that good, especially to someone from the bush. Still, the piano is my life, Professor, and I would like to go as far as possible with it. Not only for my sake, but for my mother and people like Sister Annunciata and other friends who expect this of me. I don't want to let them, or myself, down. So, in answer to your question, my desire is strong and, were it ever possible, I would like to be a pianist and am prepared to accept the personal problems this may involve."

It was an adult response to a comprehensive set of unasked questions and the professor nodded his head approvingly, giving a smile as though he was expecting such answers.

"Well said, Patrick," he said, "in a way I was only testing your dedication and resolve but also letting you know it will not all be all beer and skittles. Believe me, adulation, rapturous applause and remuneration aside, the sheer joy and immense satisfaction of being a successful performing artist will far outweigh any of the inconveniences I have outlined.

"Charles Jermyn first alerted me to your obvious talent after an audition last year and I have given your future a lot of thought since I first heard you play several weeks ago. Upon hearing you again today and having this conversation, I can now tell you of the conclusions I have reached.

"This is an extraordinary fact but you are the first new student to come to our door and be already a better pianist than anybody else in the establishment, and I include teachers in that comment. You are a very good pianist and almost ready to 'concert' but, if you have the patience and desire, I think you can go further than being just 'a very good' pianist.

"There are a great number of these, Patrick, and perhaps ten or twenty outstanding ones as well, but there has never been more than three or four in the world at any one time who have been worthy to carry the title 'great' and I think you are good enough to aspire to such definition. Where your extraordinary talent came from we will never know, but it is there despite the absence of a serious musical background. I must say that is some kind of a first as I have never experienced the like of it.

"Nevertheless, and despite your ability, it won't be easy for it will take some years of unrelenting hard work, most of your waking hours and monk-like dedication, if you are to achieve such a magnificent goal."

Patrick, again feeling self-conscious, did not interrupt the professor's flow as he went on.

"Now, there is something I have to say about your playing which I consider vital and it is important you appreciate the point I wish to make, but I must warn you not everybody shares my point of view in this matter.

"It is obvious to those who understand such things, and have heard you play, that you follow impeccably the composers' directions for the performance of their work. This is most commendable practise and would gladden the heart of any good student's coach. But you are not just 'any good student', Patrick, and if you were I would not say this to you.

"Your memory for such detail is uncanny and your dedication to the composers' wishes, is pedantic. However, it is my contention, and I am not quite alone in this, is that the great players do not follow this line so strictly. I think writers of great music have left windows in their opuses which invite performers to express themselves in some way in interpreting their works. In parts their directions are not always explicit or seemingly as binding. This suggests there may be nuances there of which they were not quite certain themselves and seem to invite the performer to express themself in some way. I believe all the great pianists, both past and present, do this and so leave their personal stamp on many a great work."

He stopped there and looked at the boy.

"Is it possible for you to understand what I am getting at here, son?" he asked.

There was a slightly astonished look on the boy's face as he replied to the morning's second bombshell from the professor.

"I cannot believe what you have just told me. I don't have to think about it," he said, "I know exactly what you mean as it's something I have had to resist since the age of eight. Back then I did it once or twice only to attract my mother's ire and her firm instruction to 'do what the composer says, Patrick'. These words were repeated so often they still ring in my ear and have been the gospel which guided me in every work I do. Sister Annunciata also never wearied in reminding me to always do what the composer suggested.

"I cannot tell you the number of times I have wanted to stray from the given line, only slightly, of course, when I thought a change of emphasis, tempo, and expression or, even, time could make for a more artistic rendition of the work. My mother's training was too emphatic and I resisted such temptation."

The professor interjected there. "As much as I would like it to continue, this talk could go on and on and there is no need as we are on a parallel course. Initially, I want you to review your repertoire of important works and introduce a little Sheridan to any part of them whenever your artistic ear suggests it. This will take a lot of your time but it will tell us so much. My own studio is across the hallway from this office and I want you to use it at all times. It will be convenient should I wish to see you outside our usual tuition session. I must run now. See my secretary and she will give you dates for your lessons for this term."

He shook Patrick's hand, said goodbye and left the room. It had been an emotional and somewhat draining but nevertheless astoundingly exciting morning for him. His reverie complete, the young student got up from the park bench seemingly ten years older, and looked across to the Cathedral where people now were coming out from midday Mass. He made his way to Elizabeth Street where he caught the Randwick tram which would drop him off at his destination at Centennial Park

Number 17 Mitcham Crescent, Centennial Park was the address of 'Pine Trees' Guest House where Irene Sheridan

had arranged, after prior inspection, for Patrick to lodge whilst studying at 'The Con'.

It had been recommended by the Students' Assistance Office at the Conservatorium as it was a well-run establishment, located in a respectable suburb adjacent to the city and managed by an ex-student who had studied the flute there many years earlier. Although never married, Marion Cross was a motherly type in her mid-fifties who took an interest in her student-boarders, who were sourced only from 'out-of-town' undergraduates of the Conservatorium and Sydney University.

Pine Trees had been a large, comfortable, two storied family home set well back in its own grounds and had been bought by Miss Cross upon retiring after several years as flautist with the Sydney Symphony. The house was run down at the time and she had it renovated and converted into a guest home as a means of livelihood for herself in her retirement years.

Apart from the owner's downstairs quarters, there were four large bedrooms in the house; three upstairs and one down. When Patrick joined the household, six other boarders were in residence, comprising two eighteen/nineteen–year-old girls doing first year Arts at 'The Uni', who shared one of the large upstairs rooms, and two older female students from the Conservatorium who shared another on the same level. The large room on the ground floor was home to its sole-occupant, a young bass-baritone who was in his fourth and final year at the Conservatorium and the only original guest of Pine Trees still in residence. He was, as Patrick was to discover, Marion Cross's 'fair-haired boy.'

The third bedroom on the upper floor was occupied by a second-year Engineering student from Sydney University and he was about to share it with Pat Sheridan. It was a large area, light and airy with French windows opening, as did other rooms on that level, on to a wide veranda which overlooked a pleasant but rather unkempt English-style garden, affording a reasonably good view of Centennial Park.

Patrick was attracted to the place and its proprietor after being shown over it by her on his arrival late on that sunny Saturday afternoon. She informed him in a pleasant and matter-of-fact way that she required her house to be a place where students could eat, sleep and study so as to assist them to achieve their respective goals. Her simple rules-of–house were devised for that purpose… no alcohol, no visitors, no playing of any instruments, no loud playing of wireless sets and no unseemly noise or conduct which could disturb any other guest.

She also informed him lunch was not included in the tariff and breakfast was at 7.30 and dinner at 6.00, for which all were required to be on time. Apart from breakfast, no meals were served on weekends and food was not permitted in the bedrooms at any time.

The routine here would be so far removed from his life at Magdalene that he did not worry to contemplate it. He anticipated the long, busy period which lay ahead of him at the Conservatorium and did not expect to spend a lot of time at his lodgings . He was pleased to know he would have comfortable quarters and a somewhat congenial atmosphere to return to each night. When Marion Cross had finished introducing him to her establishment, he returned to his room and was completing his unpacking when the door opened and a tall, gangling young man came into the room and nonchalantly ambled over to where Pat was standing. After extending his hand, he said in a voice blessed with great Australian overtones, "G'day, Ken Sheppard! Crossie told me you were coming. Hope you like it here; it's not a bad joint," and then added, "but that depends upon what you are used to, I suppose."

Patrick returned the greeting in his own amiable way and looked at his roommate who had a pleasant visage complimented by a crop of straight black hair badly in need of a comb. On first impression, he felt he shouldn't have much trouble getting along with this apparently laid-back character. He was dressed in bathing shorts and an old singlet and a pair of sandals and had just come back from the beach where, he said, he was a member of the surf club.

"Look, mate," said Ken, "I don't know whether you know but they don't serve any tucker here on the weekend. I'm off for a shower first and then I'm going to walk those two kids from the Uni up for a meal at the cafe on the next street. You're welcome to join us, if you like. There's nowhere else to eat unless you go up to the Junction. It'll give you a chance to meet them anyway and, perhaps, have a bit of a yarn at the same time. You can tell us something about yourself then."

"That sounds good," said Patrick "I'm a bit peckish; I missed on lunch today." He looked at his watch. "It's a bit after five, I'll finish unpacking and then I'll be right. What do you say to six?"

"Done," Ken said. "Whilst I'm in the shower you might go along to room three and let the girls know what's going on so they will have no excuse for holding us up."

Whilst the meal was fairly ordinary, Patrick welcomed the opportunity to meet his fellow lodgers under relaxed circumstances. Like him, the girls were from 'the bush', fairly simple and unsophisticated but pleasant enough and seemingly interested in what he was doing. They were anxious to know when they could hear him play.

On the way back from the cafe the arts students hurried ahead as they wanted to catch the BBC show ITMA which was broadcast on ABC Wireless at seven fifteen on Saturday nights. This provided an opportunity for the young men to learn something about each other as they strolled back to the guest house.

For two young men meeting for the first time their exchange had been somewhat personal and this had come about because they seemed to establish good rapport from the moment of their self-introduction.

He left Patrick at the gate of Pine Trees as he was off to catch a tram to the city where he was going to the pictures with one of his girlfriends. He said he would be home about midnight and would try not to wake him when he came back to their room.

Patrick made his way upstairs and as he passed the girls' room he could hear the wireless even though it was playing softly. There was no sign of the other two students but perhaps he would meet them at breakfast. It had been a very long day for him since he had left Bathurst that morning and he was tired. Upon reaching his room he changed into pyjamas, climbed into bed and was soon fast asleep. He heard Ken come in but quickly went back to sleep.

He awoke very early the following morning, momentarily disorientated until he heard the sound of Sheppard's even breathing coming from the adjacent bed.

As he couldn't go back to sleep he lay there for some hours and contemplated his past, and his future, which was really his present. Realisation was now sinking in as to how his life would change from this point on. For here he was waking up in a strange house he shared with someone he barely knew, many miles for his parents and his beloved Magdalene homestead and the environment of rural Australian countryside which meant so much to him. He wrestled with these pangs of homesickness but quickly dismissed them as childish and unbecoming of someone approaching their twentieth year; he was now an adult, his boyhood years gone forever. But this did not stop him reflecting on them as he lay there in the early morning light.

He considered how the piano had dominated his existence for as long as he could remember and he had accepted this part of his personal world but was now aware the talent with which he had been endowed had not come cheaply for it had to be fostered diligently. This had meant sacrifice of those aspects of life that normal healthy boys and young men always cherished.

He had yearned to play sport, any sport – tennis, cricket, rugby and boxing. He loved the competitive nature of those pastimes and instinctively felt he would be good at them, but as each one constituted some risk of injury to his hands, the piano dictated he forego such pleasures. The instrument insisted it be the all and end all of his existence and such distractions were to be avoided at all costs.

He recalled fondly those all-too-brief years when, in defiance of the demanding instrument and without the knowledge of his parents, he played rugby for Marist College Bathurst. He had revelled in the camaraderie and sense of togetherness he felt with the team. The shared jubilation in the dressing shed after the match, if their side had won that day, were moments still very special in his memory. The pride in the relationship he had enjoyed with the other members of the team, on and off the field, after being selected to play in the college's first fifteen, was an experience he savoured to this very day. However, he recalled, the piano did catch up with him eventually and promptly brought his brief but promising sporting career to a very abrupt conclusion.

He was aware and accepted the fact that because of the isolation of the family home, he made no friends of his own age until he joined The Gap School. The comradeship he found there was therefore the more precious to him, and he earnestly wanted to maintain those friendships after leaving the one-teacher school.

This was particularly so with the two Hilton brothers with whom he rode to school most mornings and had so much fun with during their early boyhood years. There were a few others, including his teacher, Mr Brady, the young man who had enkindled his love of the Australian bush and laid open to him the beauty of the works of the great romantic poets of England, together with the emotionally evocative and raw stanzas of their gifted Australian counterparts.

As much as he had wanted to maintain contact with these companions of his youth he could not because the piano said 'you don't have time for that sort of thing'. The same applied to the many good friends and companions he had made at Marist College and he had even lost touch with his 'friends for life', Eric Hanson, Brian Stiller and Max Niven.

For no reason that he could think of, such thoughts continued to course through his mind as he lay there in a sombre mood. He now reflected on what Ken Sheppard had told him of his student life with his off-study hours spent on the rugby field or the beach or innocently chasing girls, taking them to the pictures or dancing with them at The Trocadero. None of these activities would be open to him as they were not only time consuming but also constituted a distraction to his vocation. Therefore just the mere thought of participating in such pastimes could not be entertained.

For some time now he had been aware of girls in a very normal masculine way and had enjoyed their company, even though he had experienced very little of it. It started when the Marist Brothers arranged for his class to be instructed in the art of ballroom dancing during their final year at the college. The purpose of this was to prepare these older boys to partner girls from the local parish when they made their debut (or 'coming out') and their presentation to the Bishop and the Grand Catholic Ball held in the Bathurst Town Hall at the end of every school year.

Girls! He considered them again. He enjoyed the dancing and found himself quite good at it. He was on the floor for every dance on that gala night and got to know some of the debs in the process. It was during one of these dances that we recognised the real intent of the Marist Brothers, and the occasional mission priest, giving such emphasis to their instruction on how to avoid 'sins of the flesh'.

He met up with a few of these girls again before he left the college; at Mass on Sundays, at the local milk bar, out on his bike or just passing on the streets of Bathurst and other places. They often stopped him to have a few words. It was without any conceit he recognised their obvious but innocent girl-like interest in him. But he declined to take matters any further, not only for the ecclesiastic warnings but also the realisation they could take up a lot of his time and the piano would never stand for that.

So, he realised girls were out for the present and he would try to forget about them as well as he could, though he knew it was only a matter of time before he would want to get to know them better. He even toyed with the idea that morning that, just for the experience and with or without Ken, he would try himself out at The Trocadero on at least one Friday night after his new life had settled into place.

That was his final thought before closing his eyes and drifting back to sleep again, only to wake a short time later in a totally different frame of mind. He now felt an immediate sense of excitement for what lay ahead of him tomorrow with his first lesson with the Professor and could not understand his gloomy thoughts of the previous hours. He quickly forgot them for, after all, he was in a win-win situation; music was his life above all other considerations and sacrifices, but if his career did not unfold the way he intended, he could return to Magdalene. There he essentially would still have his music together with the unending satisfaction of living in a place which was so much a part of him. He felt ashamed of the self-pity he had just experienced and vowed he would never again be other than eternally grateful for the gift with which he had been endowed. Nevertheless, a lot of hard work and seemingly never ending long hours lay ahead of him, and strangely he relished the thought.

In the context of all these deliberations, it was odd that just before getting out of bed that morning he should recall the final words his father had used on his departure from Magdalene to join the Conservatorium.

"You know I am proud of you," he said, "and even though I've never considered all this toffee music and piano playing a very masculine thing, I've no such ideas about you personally. You're a dinkum Sheridan and a good young bloke in my book and always will be. You have my blessing, for what it's worth, and I'll support anything you want to do, whether it be with your music or in the event of you deciding to come back and settle here where you belong."

It was a win-win situation he confirmed again to himself; but he hoped he could measure up to his father's opinion of him and live his life, whatever course it took, in a decent, manly way that would not disappoint his parent in any way.

Chapter 15

In the weeks prior coming to Sydney, Patrick had given a great deal of thought as to what life would be like at the Conservatorium. But he came nowhere near the mark in anticipating the work load he eventually would have to carry. It included self-imposed burdens which nevertheless had to be endured if he were to achieve the goals he had set for himself.

The first few weeks were relatively normal and included regular sessions with Professor Morrison, from which he gained so much knowledge and satisfaction. From the outset, on four days each week he attended Conservatorium classes in Harmony and Counterpoint, Composition, Basic Conducting (orchestral), Analysis of Music and History of Classical Music; subjects chosen for him by the Professor who thought it wise for him to have formal qualifications to compliment his performing talent. He had no difficulty with these subjects but they did require a deal of homework and exam preparation, both of which made demands of his precious time.

Added to these tasks was the self-requirement to practise at least four to five hours every day. This now involved mastering the initial repertoire set for him by Professor Morrison. It was an extensive list and whilst it contained many of the works he had memorised, the entire portfolio of works now required a more emotionally demanding approach because of an added dimension. Formerly, when he had learned an opus and no longer needed to use a score, he was able to practise it with a deal of enjoyable ease because he was aware of what the composer was asking for in each part of the work. Therefore, he played it without having to expend a great deal of thought other than that relating to the way he gave expression to each piece. The new dimension was Morrison's contention, with which Patrick strongly agreed, that pianists of calibre played passages of the work they were performing in a way dictated by their own musical soul. These were nuances which would not have disturbed the composer whilst allowing the performer to put a personal and recognisable stamp on a particular composition.

Eventually, his days became so full he was able to spend very little time at Pine Trees. He slept there each night in the room he shared with Ken Sheppard, had breakfast most mornings with the other guests and was usually away to the Con before eight thirty. Only rarely did he get back to the guest house in time for the evening meal.

This concerned Marion Cross somewhat for she thought he may be skipping meals. If he did eat elsewhere the food may not have been as nourishing as it should and his mother would not have liked that. Patrick had assured her he always had a meal of some sort in the evening and made a point of eating fruit during the day to compensate for any shortcoming in his overall diet.

He had long recognised the need to keep his body healthy as playing the piano for hours on end was physically demanding. The sedentary nature of his daily life was not conducive to this unless it was matched with a commensurate amount of physical exercise. As any sporting activity was 'not on' for him, he acquired the habit of walking home the four or so miles to Centennial Park two or three times a week, and this seemed to keep him reasonably fit.

The already busy tempo of his life of music picked up considerably when his mentor decided the void of concertos in his repertoire should be addressed forthwith. So late one afternoon, shortly after the Easter break, he came across from his office to his studio where Patrick was practising and placed a large score on top of the piano.

"Sorry to interrupt," he said, "but I keep forgetting to talk to you about this. It's the score of the Rachmaninoff *C Minor Concerto* which we will be doing with the Students' Orchestra at the end of May. You will be soloist. Intellectually it is a little light but it is a romantic and delightfully lyrical piece and, despite what the snobs say, I think it has considerable merit. He is by far the best of our more modern composers and, in turn, I think this his best work."

"I like him, too," said Patrick, "but the last time I played his work was at Bathurst with Annunciata and that was a year or two back."

"You won't have any trouble with it and I think you will enjoy this first experience, as it's an ideal opus to introduce you to the art of concerto performance. Mind you, we will only be twenty five instruments which is just enough for the purpose and I'll be conducting. The actual performance will be in our hall here and open to the public, which means there will be about two hundred or so people attending, made up mainly of students and their families. Read the score through so that you get a feeling for it and then run over it a few times and we will have a first rehearsal with the orchestra tomorrow week. Good luck with it," he concluded, and was off back to his office.

Patrick finished the Beethoven sonata he was working on before taking down the Rachmaninoff score and was perusing it when Julian Morrison strode into the room again - this time a little flushed and somewhat diffident, for him.

"Look, I'm sorry to burst in like this again but it was something I forgot to mention before and I do have a favour to ask. I know you have a tight schedule and will understand if you say 'no' although I'll be most grateful if you can help me out."

"I'll be pleased to do what I can," said Patrick, "what's it all about?"

"A good friend rang me at home last night to talk about his daughter who is doing her last term of violin study here. Apparently, she is having trouble finding a capable accompanist for some of the works she is doing for her final exam and asked if I could help. I am afraid yours was the only name which came to mind. Do you think you could fit it in? It would be an hour or so, say, three times a week for the next three weeks and then it would all be over. Graham Jordan is senior partner of that big legal crowd, Beldon and Phelps, and often thinks the whole world should be open to him and he appears to have blustered me in to saying 'of course, I can help!'"

The request put Patrick in a quite a bind as he really did not have time to spare. His daily classes and the study they involved, long sessions with the professor, hours of practice and the just imposed need to master the Rachmaninoff would leave very little of his working day available for anything else. But Patrick was aware his mentor had allocated him several hours of his own precious time each week and he could hardly refuse.

So after a few moments' thought, he replied, "The only time I could fit her in would be after the afternoon classes, in the evenings, perhaps from six o'clock. I couldn't do it any earlier than that, so if the time is suitable for her I will try to manage it."

"That's very good of you Patrick, thanks very much," said the professor. "Unless you hear from me she'll be here at six tomorrow night, and you can let me know if there are any problems. I've only met Cathy Jordan once or twice and she seemed a fairly normal girl of eighteen–or-so, so you shouldn't have much trouble working with her for this short period. Promise I won't interrupt again. I'll see you at tomorrow's lesson," he parted with.

As the door closed behind the Professor, Patrick went back to the Rachmaninoff as it had captured his interest from the time he opened the first page. He had not seen a full orchestral score before and, to read the individual musical lines for each of so many instruments to play at the same time, absolutely fascinated him. Strangely though, it also gave him a sense of unease.

Here he was embarking on a study of a concerto and many of the instruments involved in this were foreign to him. He could read and 'hear' the line for the piano and strings and even the flute, but this was not possible with others such as oboe, clarinet and other reeds, as well as those comprising the brass and wind sections written into the score. Totally unaware of the sound of these instruments, he could not write for them.

Rehearsing a concerto with an orchestra, small as it was, would be a start to his education in this area, he thought, but it would be that only, a beginning. He knew if he were to compose works of any substance not only would it be imperative to know intimately the sounds those instruments produced, but he would also have to be aware of what those sounds meant to him, personally. Whether or not their very individual sounding notes struck a chord, as it were, in the ear of his musical soul, would surely determine the extent of their inclusion in the compositions he, someday, hoped to write.

It was for this reason mainly that he made up his mind to attend the winter series of the ABC Symphony Concerts at the Sydney Town Hall, which started in a month or so. Also, he would try to get to the ABC's Youth (Orchestra's) Concerts when they commenced, but this could prove difficult as they started early-evening and could clash with items of his schedule at the Conservatorium.

Such part-remedies for his problem would not suffice. He determined to speak to Julian Morrison about it at the next lesson and see what he had to say about his ambition to compose, and his lack of knowledge of certain musical instruments, in particular. Having made up his mind on that subject, he returned to Rachmaninoff. The piece had gripped his interest to such an extent that, when he finished reading the score he could not resist playing the entire piano score of three movements there and then, despite the late hour. The music delighted him and he felt excited at the prospect of the first rehearsal with the orchestra.

When he finally looked up from the keyboard the light was starting to fail and he realised that once again he would miss the evening meal at Pine Trees.

Late the following afternoon Patrick was returning to his studio. After telephoning home to Magdalene from the public call box in the foyer of the Conservatorium he turned into the passageway and noticed somebody standing outside his door. He realised it must be the girl Julian Morrison had spoken about.

"Hello, I'm Patrick Sheridan," he said, as he came up to her and, in a more business-like tone, added "you must be the Miss Jordan Professor Morrison spoke about?" On opening the door for her, he continued, "Won't you come in?"

She put the violin case and the manuscripts she was carrying on an adjacent chair before turning to him. "How do you do?" she said, in rather a shy manner, "I'm Cathy Jordon and I'm very grateful for you helping me out like this."

"Not at all," said Patrick and, still with a firm tone, "I'm happy to help out even though I am, like you, a bit strapped for time. However, I'm sure we can work it out."

"I really am sorry to have bothered you but it's so hard to find an accompanist of any sort for my works, more so a decent one and Julian told my father how fortunate I was you had made yourself available. My finals are at the end of the month which leaves only a few weeks to get this part of them ready, so having your help is a big load off my mind. Julian says you probably can give me an hour or so three times a week for the next three weeks and that's more than generous of you."

"Don't mention it. Now, let's get down to it, shall we? What have you got there?" said Patrick as she handed him her music.

He sat at the piano and looked through the four manuscripts carefully before saying, "They seem okay, what would you like to start with?"

She put one of the manuscripts in front of him and after tuning her violin to the A natural he struck for her, they commenced to play.

By the time they had finished going through the four works it was well past the stipulated 'hour or so' but he did not seem to mind. He thought she played well and was impressed with the generous tonal qualities of the instrument she played, thinking that it must have cost her father a pretty penny. She seemed accurate, kept meticulous time and adhered to the writers' directions. She stopped him at various times and asked to go over passages with which she was not happy and he obliged without demur. There were one or two points he could have raised but refrained as he didn't wish to become involved with anything that might add to his daily commitments.

He got up from the piano as she put the violin, and music, into its case. When she turned to look at him there was now an expression of slight awe and respect in her eyes. It was as though she was seeing him for the first time.

"I can't thank you enough, Patrick,' she said. "Your accompaniment somehow has given me a fresh understanding of these works and I'm a lot happier about them now. Julian was certainly right about you and I'm lucky to have someone like you to help me out. He said you were an exceptional talent and that's more than obvious to me now."

"I don't know about that but thanks anyhow," replied Patrick, matter-of-factly. "I've a lot of work ahead of me as well as I am just starting out here but I'm glad to know I have been of some help. I'll see you Friday about the same time, Cathy. Practice hard!"

He let her out the door of the studio and watched as she walked down the passageway between the music studios. A nice kid, he thought, tallish, slim and, a little gawky, as Brian Stiller used to describe some of the Bathurst debs. She had an attractive face but did not seem to pay much attention to her appearance. Her medium length, dark hair was quite straight and she did not appear to use any makeup at all.

The light, short-sleeved, navy frock she was wearing, hung well below the knee and this, allied with her flat-heeled shoes, gave the overall appearance of what she probably was, a senior schoolgirl going through the awkward stage.

He closed the door and promptly forgot about her as he sat at the studio desk, coming to grips with the paper he had to prepare for tomorrow's class in Harmony. It was quite dark when he finally got up and realised his 'tea' again would consist of a meat pie and a cup of coffee at Reppins' Coffee Shop in Martin Place. He considered he must try to do something to arrest this harmful trend of missing the nutritious evening meal always provided by his landlady.

The first two orchestral rehearsals of the Rachmaninoff did not go well and Julian Morrison was almost driven to distraction by the string section, whose reading of tempo and expression were far below the standard he expected from them, even at that early stage. He took the orchestra through the work section by section and apparently had no problem with Patrick and the rest of the players. The following morning though he did confide to his pupil that judging by the first try-out, having the concerto ready by the performance date would take a lot more time and effort than he had originally anticipated. Towards the end of the second rehearsal the frown on his face left for a time as he led the now better performing strings through their work. At the conclusion of the session he told the entire ensemble he had called an additional rehearsal for ten-thirty the following Sunday morning. He thought it may be possible to play the three movements with the entire orchestra, without interruption, for the first time.

Breaking into their weekend would not go down well with the students, but he knew how important it was to every one of them to be part of the establishment's select playing group and, therefore, would be surprised if there were any absentees from the additional practice session he had imposed.

That Sunday morning was somewhat of a triumph for the young pianist from Bathurst as for the first time he was able to give his undivided attention to the piano's dominant role in the composition. Apart from the short intervals between the movements, the performance was uninterrupted despite one or two instrumental blips which would normally have disturbed the conductor.

When the final notes were played the Professor laid down his baton, and turned around to face Patrick. Making the slight gesture of half-raising his right hand, he nodded his head slowly several times, indicating by this, and the expression on his face, just how highly he regarded Patrick's playing of this significant work.

He then turned back to the orchestra and thanked them for their attendance, indicating the concerto was now coming along well and should be in good shape for the public performance in a few weeks time.

From that point on Patrick became an identity at the Con, and staff and students alike went out of their way to acknowledge him wherever they encountered him, both inside and outside the confines of their institution. All were aware he was tutored by the Professor for Piano and now knew the reason for him being extended that important privilege.

Musicians in general only perceive one star in their musical firmament and that is their own of course. But members of the orchestra had been more than impressed with Patrick's playing that Sunday morning to such an extent that his ability had become, for a time, a talking point wherever students and staff gathered at the Conservatorium.

Patrick took this newfound recognition in his stride and it did not turn his head in any manner but, in a way he could not describe, it gave him great satisfaction to know the extent of the goodwill he now enjoyed from his peers at this great seat of musical learning.

As they progressed he found the sessions with Cathy a welcome change from his normal routine and rather enjoyed them. He judged her to be a good violinist and easy to work with, still very grateful for what he was doing for her. Without kidding himself, he got the idea she had a slight crush on him. This was good for his ego and they usually chatted for a few minutes when the session was over. Her conversation was bright, humorous and well-informed for one so young and, he noted, despite her sometimes shy demeanour, she was not averse to expressing her opinion on a variety of subjects. This latter, he concluded, was probably something of her father coming out in her.

They had a longer exchange after one session when he decided he would walk home to Pine Trees that evening and strolled with her to Queen's Square, where she would catch the tram to Double Bay.

As they ambled along Macquarie Street she told him of her ambition to be an orchestral player and how she hoped to join the first violins of the Sydney Symphony one day. She also informed him, with a degree of restrained excitement, that as soon as her finals were complete she would be leaving for Paris to do several months of postgraduate study in the Strings Faculty of the French Academy of Music.

The trip was an eighteenth birthday present from her father but there was another sort of string attached to it. His gift was subject to her agreeing to attend a three months course at 'Ludea', an exclusive Swiss finishing school for 'young ladies' in Berne, where she would acquire some of the social graces she now appeared to lack.

Style, fashion, personal appearance, art of speech and all those kind of things had taken second place to her violin since she left school, and her father wished to remedy those shortcomings. She had two older brothers but no sister. She was, as the saying went, the apple of her father's eye, but he did want her to measure up. It would mean she would be away from Sydney longer than she wanted, but a deal was a deal and she would respect her father's wishes.

All this came out in idle conversation as they waited for her tram to arrive. As it approached The Loop from College Street, she put her hand on his arm and inquired, "And what about you, Patrick? My friend Erica, who is bassoonist in the Con orchestra, told me your playing at the last concerto rehearsal was absolutely breathtaking and everybody is talking about it. You must have an exciting and wonderful career ahead of you. Already you are the envy of many students and the word *virtuoso* has been freely bandied about by people who should know. But, I suppose, you are used to this kind of reaction by now. Do you have any firm plans at this stage"?

"No, I haven't any at all," he said dismissively. "I am just starting out really and it is up to Professor Morrison to say if and when regarding any career prospects I might have. I'm not in any hurry for I now realise I have a lot to learn yet and I am so lucky to have such a fine teacher. See you Monday, same time." He walked away as she boarded the 'toast rack' which would take her down William Street, through 'The Cross', and on to her destination of the rich man's suburb of Double Bay.

The sessions with Cathy came to an end and she sat for her finals. He understood from other students she had done well, but he had no word from her since their last practice together. It was another fortnight or so when he returned to the studio from lunch one day to find a small parcel and a written message from her on top of the piano.

The note expressed her deep sense of gratitude for the time and help he had given her and that he was responsible for the better-than-she–ever-expected results of her degree examination. She was sorry to have missed him but could not wait as she was rushing to make the last-minute arrangements for her trip abroad.

She was sailing for Southampton tomorrow on the SS Oronsay and there was so much to be done before she could get on the boat. She wished him luck with the concerto and said how sorry she was not to be at the public performance. A year or so was a long time to be away but she hoped he would still be here at the Conservatorium when she returned. She thanked him again and concluded the note with… "Love, Cathy."

He considered the word was a bit rich in light of their 'work only' relationship and pondered this as he opened the small parcel she had left. It contained an expensive tie and handkerchiefs from Peape's, the exclusive menswear store in George Street.

"Love!" He thought he had detected her slight crush on him but not to that extent. Then he realised it was just a word young girls used frequently about anything and everything, even their dog and cat, for instance. So, after putting the tie in the desk drawer he thought no more about the matter. If she did happen to have feelings for him, they would well and truly dissipate by the time she got back from her sojourn in Europe, so really, there was nothing for him to worry about at all.

Chapter 16

*A*fter the final rehearsal of the Rachmaninoff, Patrick sought a few words with the Professor. He told him he had been advised of the protocol attached to concerto performances and asked if it could be waived for this public playing. He explained it now was important to him to feel part of the orchestral team for he had got to know many of the members before, after and during breaks in rehearsals. For that reason, as soloist on the night, he would rather not make a separate entrance, but be seated with the ensemble when the Professor, as conductor, made his way to the podium. By the same token he would prefer not to leave the platform with him at the conclusion of the work but remain seated with the others until they all left the platform together. Patrick also volunteered his opinion that any applause which happened to come from the audience would be directed to the orchestra as a whole and should be acknowledged by it alone.

"Alright, if that's what you wish," said the Professor, after a few moments thought, "but I have to tell you it's an unusual request and it is the first time I have known a musician to steer away from the limelight. All soloists I've played with insisted on making the grand entrance with me and hogged any applause about the place whether it was intended for them or not. I hope there is nothing wrong with your ego, Son, but so be it."

"Thanks," said Patrick. "I am grateful but please understand this is not just false modesty on my part. Far from it, I appreciate applause in any form if it is warranted but I'm still a student and to carry on like a prima donna could be taken the wrong way by the other students, and I don't want that to happen."

The Professor gave his pupil a benign, tolerant but understanding glance and shrugged his shoulders before making his way back to his office.

Some weeks before, when Julian first indicated his intention to do the Rachmaninoff, Patrick mentioned it to his mother in the course of his weekly phone call to Magdalene and could not get over the extent of excitement the news generated in her. She was quite ecstatic as she fired question after question at him until she finally calmed down and told him she and Tom would be there, of course. He should make sure he got tickets for them as near as possible to the piano. Although she had heard it only two or three times, she said she absolutely adored the work for it was so wonderfully romantic while at the same time hauntingly plaintive and she was sure she would cry.

Irene subsequently wrote and told him Tom would not be quite up to it and would be unable to come. So when she contacted Sister Annunciata to tell her of the performance, she found the Sister's excitement akin to her own. She asked if it could be possible for her to come down with Irene to hear her former pupil play.

The good nun was doubtful about getting permission but would take it up immediately with Mother Superior. If she agreed she would then inquire if the Mother House at Potts Point could put her up for the two nights they would be in Sydney. Irene told Patrick she would let him know the outcome - and to get two tickets just in case.

As it turned out he had to find another ticket as the two other Con students at his guest house had mentioned the concert to Marion Cross, who promptly expressed her wish to attend also. Patrick then felt obliged to tell his roommate in case in he felt left out.

"What about you, Shep, do you think you could put up with it?" he put to him that same night after the evening meal.

"Bit bloody high-brow for a Newcastle boy, mate. In any event I've got an evening class at Uni that night and couldn't make it anyway. Good luck with it Sherry and if I get away from the session early enough I'll stick my head in and perhaps hear a bit of you at least."

It was some hours before Irene could contain herself upon hearing Patrick's news. She had waited so long for this day and felt justified in recognising it as the first significant step towards the glittering career that undoubtedly awaited her son. It was more than twenty years since she had seen his father for the first and last time, but the image of him in her mind had not dimmed in the least and she thought of how proud he surely would have been of the son of whose existence he was never aware.

Through those ensuing years she'd recounted often to herself how Patrick was of the fourth or fifth generation of an august musical family, but so far as she was aware, the word 'great' which described her son in her mind, had not been used in conjunction with the name of any of his forebears. What was the reason for her son's exceptional talent bursting forth here and now? Why in this still young, culturally harsh and distant land, so far removed from the classical traditions and marbled halls of European music and culture, where the seeds of his genius first were sown those ever so many years ago?

She had answered those questions to herself some years back by concluding it was just another example of the wonder of nature that such an incredible talent had been brought to life - a consequence of two lonely people sharing a few brief hours in each other's arms.

Since his talent had become manifest she had almost instinctively wanted to lay claim to some aspect of her son's extraordinary gift. She contended to herself that whilst she had no musical lineage to offer to that contention, she did possess a profound love of music. Therefore, perhaps, just perhaps, she thought, there was something in her genes which made her the trigger to create this astounding boy from the stored musicality of generations existent in the loins of his natural father.

As always, there was great demand for tickets for the Conservatorium orchestral concert. Family and friends of the orchestra, staff and other students of The Con and a limited number of the general public made up an appreciative and knowledgeable audience of nearly three hundred people for Patrick's debut concerto performance. Not that they had come just to hear him. They had heard about his playing but in the main they were there because their child, friend, pupil or relative was a member of the orchestra.

These were never long concerts, something under two hours. The first half saw the playing of Bach and Handel by a very good student string quartet which was well received. This was followed by a selection of Schubert Lieder sung by a rather nervous young tenor whose voice suggested he was still in a state of celibacy but nevertheless was accorded understanding and encouraging acclamation.

After a short break, not really an interval, the orchestra commenced taking their places on the platform and the atmosphere in the hall changed as it became charged with the air of expectation which had fallen over the gathering. For not only was this an important occasion for the players, it was equally so for those many in the audience to whom they were closely associated. This was 'for the first time' for many of the players and their anxiety to do well was shared by the many well-wishers who had gathered to hear them perform.

Patrick raised and propped the lid of the Steinway before adjusting his seat to a comfortable height. There was a smile on his face as he had just caught sight of his mother and Sr. Annunciata sitting near the aisle of the second row. He was calm and relaxed and quite at ease with what was going on around him and with what he was about to do. Irene, surely, would have thought him resplendent in the well-fitting dress-suit he was wearing for the first time and would have been pleased she had the foresight to equip him with the black-tie outfit prior to him leaving Bathurst.

The orchestra took a minute or so to tune their instruments before becoming quiet and still as Professor Julian Morrison made his way to the podium amidst a round of polite applause.

After a brief perusal of the score, he picked up his baton and turned to Patrick who was slightly to his rear-left and, upon receiving a smiling nod from him, turned to see that the players were ready. Then he led them into the delightful piece of orchestral music.

It was some forty-five minutes later he put his baton down, with a huge sigh and a satisfied smile on his face. It had been an outstanding performance by the students and they had played well above themselves. There was no doubt in his mind that young Sheridan was responsible, for his playing had been beyond anything he had expected. This had lifted the entire orchestra to a standard he never thought possible in their efforts to compliment his brilliant interpretation of the work.

These thoughts went through his mind as the players lowered their instruments and a great thunder clap of applause broke out behind him. This was a small, conservative audience but their cheers and acclamation was so loud and enthusiastic it was reminiscent of a football match. Again this was Sheridan's doing and the boy did not intend to acknowledge it. He held his arms out so as to embrace all the players and smiling broadly gave his nod of approval before turning on the podium to face the audience and bowing graciously for the continuing ovation.

When he turned back again and brought the orchestra and Patrick to their feet, there was a rising crescendo from the audience. After an acceptable time, he left the platform as the orchestra resumed their seats. He came back again with the entire gathering still on its feet and repeated the former procedure before leaving and returning once more to the unrestrained enthusiasm.

Mounting the podium, he faced the players and looked helplessly at the concert master. That was enough for him as he could see what was happening even though he did not know the reason why. He stood up, laying his violin and bow on his seat, and joined the conductor. Together they turned to face the piano and joined the audience in what was an unprecedented degree of acclaim, in this hall, in acknowledgement of what was, for many of them, an unforgettable musical experience.

Then in what was a profoundly emotional and tear-provoking moment, the entire ensemble spontaneously put down their own instruments and joined as one with their leaders, as they all turned and faced the pianist, applauding loudly. Their cries of "bravo, bravo" were quickly and avidly echoed by many in the audience.

And so Sheridan, finally, was forced to rise from his seat at the piano as the shouting and clapping became louder, for this was the moment the audience had been waiting. Indeed it had been a bravura performance by the young pianist and they were anxious he should be aware of the extent of their great admiration of it.

He walked to the open part of the concert stage and bowed very deliberately, several times, to the orchestra before smiling broadly but with a resigned air, taking and holding the conductor's extended hand for several moments before releasing it to take that of the concert master who had saved the day for his conductor.

It was only then that he turned to face the audience. He was beaming but now slightly overawed by the magnitude of the acclaim. He bowed several times to each part of the hall and in doing so noticed his mother's tear-stained face as she looked up at him. Sister Annunciata had tried to control her emotions too, with the evidence being there in her eyes for all to see that she had been quite unsuccessful.

He took one final bow and looked around to find his mentor behind him and together they left the concert platform. It was only then, some ten or so minutes since it began, the incredible applause began to subside.

The professor returned to the platform alone to conduct the national anthem and as the last chords of *God Save the King* rang out, Patrick made his way down to the hall to find his mother and her holy friend.

He led them out of the hall and down the passageway to the refectory where coffee and biscuits were being provided for the staff, orchestral players and friends. Before getting the refreshments he found chairs for them. They could do little more than look up at him, standing there drinking his coffee, for they were still in somewhat of a state of shock by what had just taken place in the hall. Irene did not want to embarrass him when he came up to her after the concert, so instead of throwing her arms around him as she dearly wanted to, she simply lingered a little too long with the kiss she put to his cheek, murmuring tearfully to his ear, "I knew this day would come."

In the midst of a lot of excited people, all laughing and chattering, he was also the centre of attention as teaching staff and players in the orchestra came over to congratulate him on his performance. Irene had a wish come true when Julian Morrison came to say a few words and Patrick introduced him to her and Sister Annunciata. He gave Irene a smile and said jokingly that it would be tough going but still he might be able to make a pianist of her son, one day.

It was when Patrick had started to think it about time to get Sister Annunciata back to her convent that he was approached by a member of the audience. She first apologised most graciously for the intrusion and then introduced herself as Marjorie Jordan, the mother of the girl he assisted with her violin exams. She was a tall, elegant looking woman who spoke in a gentle, well-modulated and unaffected way but with a tone which indicated she was probably a member of some echelon of polite society in this city.

"How do you do, this is a surprise. How is Cathy doing over there?" said Patrick.

"It's good of you to ask. She was a little home sick but that wore off and she is quite settled and well into her studies now. It's at her bequest I'm here. She spoke so much of you before she left that I feel I already know you. She was so enthusiastic about your playing she wanted to defer her trip just to be here tonight. We could not permit that of course, but she made me promise to come and then write to her about it. I now know she was not exaggerating in the slightest and I thought you played quite superbly with the orchestra. It was a most exciting evening, thanks to you, and I'm afraid my letter to Cathy will be a lot longer as a consequence."

"Those are kind words, Mrs. Jordan, thanks very much. Please give Cathy my best regards and I wish her well," said Patrick.

"I won't detain you any longer, Mr. Sheridan, and I'll let you get back to your friends," she said, before adding with a wide smile, "but I did want to meet you as much for my own as Cathy's sake. I did need to find out whether or not you wore a halo, for there were times when Cathy spoke of you that I began to wonder. Goodbye for now and I do hope we will meet some time in the future." Patrick gently held her extended hand for a moment before she turned and made her way out of the refectory.

Now what was that really all about? thought Patrick, as he watched her leave.

They eventually started to leave and slowly made their way towards the door through the small throng of people still wanting to pat him on the back and extend their congratulations and best wishes. The concert master, a young man in his final year of violin studies was also in the process of leaving and as he came up alongside Patrick and said, "It was a good night, wasn't it? I think old Morrison was well pleased. There is one thing I must say, Pat. I'm afraid you are way above the rest of us here and you did make us look better than we are. Something like the Don if he were to play in, say, a Randwick second eleven - so very, very much above his class."

"You're getting a bit wordy, Nigel, and rather over the top about this but thanks anyhow, I appreciate it," said Patrick as he led the two ladies into the foyer and then into one of the waiting taxi cabs.

He spent the night with Irene at Usher's, catching up with all that was happening with his father and at Magdalene and answering all of the many questions she levelled at him. After accompanying her to the Bathurst Mail train the following morning, they were joined on the platform by Sister Annunciata and the two nuns who had accompanied her from the convent.

He stood there for a few moments watching the train leave the station and started to think of immediate things to be done, as his normal routine had got a little out of kilter lately. With the concerto always in mind he had just come through a period which was even more hectic and busy than usual so perhaps he could take a break, he thought.

It was Friday and there were no classes today nor any arranged session with the Professor and, just for this once, by foregoing his long practice ritual for a couple of days he could afford himself the luxury of a free weekend.

So he took himself home to Pine Trees. At the front door he encountered Marion Cross who had seen him coming up the front path and was curious about him coming in at this time of day. She agreed heartily when he told her why, and then said how deeply impressed she had been with his playing the previous night. Last evening, when he was engaged with other people in the refectory, she'd had a few words with Irene, who wanted to know if he was behaving himself. So she told her about him missing meals and how this concerned her.

"I know, Marion, I wish you hadn't," said Patrick, "she told me about it in no uncertain terms and says she is going to check up on me through you in future."

"Serves you right, you should not neglect yourself like that. I don't want you getting run-down and that's a sure way to do it," replied Marion.

"Okay, I'll do better, I promise, but please keep her off my back," said Patrick.

Going upstairs to his room, he had a shower and changed into slacks and a shirt and the light-blue pullover Irene had knitted for him, before sitting down to read 'The Herald' which he had bought from the boy outside Central Station. He'd not felt freedom like this for months and had never realised how good it would feel.

When he finally looked up from the sports page he noticed Wendy, one of the Arts students from the room next to his, sitting out on the wide veranda and seemingly doing some study. He had always found her a quiet but friendly girl, not unattractive and always ready with a smile when she saw him. He opened the French windows and went out and spoke with her.

"Hi, Wendy," he said "how are things?" he said. She looked up in surprise.

"Hello, what are you doing home at this hour?"

"I'm taking the weekend off, so there," he replied. "Not a bad day, is it?" he said looking up at the sky and the near vista of Centennial Park.

Then, without realising why, unless it was an unexpressed need for feminine company, he said, "I'm thinking of going up to the Junction for some lunch as I like the idea of the walk through the park. Would you like to come or is it too far for you?"

"It's only a hop, skip and a jump for a country girl," Wendy responded. "You must be a bit lazy if you think that's a long way. It's a good idea though and I'd be glad to come. Give me half an hour or so to finish here and then I'll change and be right with you."

"Right. See you down stairs about half-past twelve," said Patrick after looking at his watch, and then went off to find Marion again to pay his weekly board.

They enjoyed the walk along one of the many wide pathways, shaded by generously leaved trees, as it wended its way through this fine public park. The girl seemed to him to have matured considerably in the few months she had been at the University as her conversation was a little more sophisticated than he expected and she had a good sense of humour to which it was easy to respond. Their conversation flowed quite freely, was light-hearted and topical for people of their age. It was a welcome change from the demands of his musical life and the usual conversations he had with people with whom he was involved at the Con.

There was seldom time for idle chatter in that august institution. There was a part of his makeup that still missed the chiacking and extreme language, not to mention the blasphemy of the shearing sheds at Magdalene. He often reminded himself of the companionship he had felt there for the young Aboriginal stockmen and being amused by their colourful eloquence. His peers and teachers at the Con would have been horrified at what was the normal repartee of those friends of this pupil.

They had their meal at the Junction fish cafe when they discovered they were both Catholics of a sort and, for some instinctive reason, still adhered to the rule of Friday abstinence from flesh meat.

It was whilst wandering back to their lodgings the subject of conversation became more serious. She had just told him how much she was looking-forward to taking an extended holiday in Europe when she completed her degree when he had interrupted her quietly and said,

"By that time you'll be lucky if it's still there."

"What do you mean?" she asked.

And he told her.

For some time now he had been buying 'The Herald' each morning at the tram stop on his way to the Conservatorium, initially to catch up with cricket scores and other sporting results but then he became interested in the news pages and the editorial comment. It was there he learnt of the serious political situation unfolding in Western Europe which had captured not only his interest but also his ongoing concern. He had his opinions about these matters but he'd never had an opportunity to express them in the way he did now.

"It is pretty obvious, Wendy, that Hitler has to be stopped, and when he is it will probably mean war. After his recent meeting with the Germans, the British Prime Minister flourished a piece of paper which proclaimed peace in our time. Nobody really believes that as the Poms and the French have started rearming now in a big way. I hope I'm wrong but I agree with those writers who know about foreign affairs who say war is inevitable. Let's hope it is a short one and will all be over by the time you want to make your trip.”

“Well, thanks for cheering me up like that. You have made my day. Do you really think it is a bad as that?” she asked.

“I’m afraid so,” said Pat, “but we shall see.”

As they approached the Pine Trees front gate, the subject then changed again when she told him, quite excitedly he thought, that she and Marion Cross were going to see ‘Naughty Marietta’ at the Paddington Orpheum tomorrow night. He was welcome to join them if he felt so inclined. He said he had not decided how he would spend his first free Saturday for so long and could he let her know. She thanked him for the lunch and the walk and said she would see him at dinner later on.

After shutting his bedroom door behind him he deliberately avoided taking out the notes he had written for a composition he was working on. Instead he picked up a paperback edition of Steinbeck’s ‘The Grapes of Wrath’ which was lying on Ken Sheppard’s bed. He found himself absorbed in the novel when Ken returned from the University.

“What’s going on here? Not playing the wag are we, Sheridan?” he said as he sat down heavily on his bed.

“No, just having a couple days off - like you do every weekend, although I won’t be able to indulge myself to the same extent. Now look here, Sheppard,” Patrick continued, “whether you like it or not, you’re taking me to the Troc tonight so I can see what attracts you so much to the place,” said Patrick.

“I tell you, I’ve had a rough week and I’m buggered and I’d thought I might have an early night for once. But if you’re intent on combing the flesh pots I suppose I can accommodate you. I expected more of you than this, Sheridan, so don't make a habit of it or I'll tell your Prof."

After dinner that night they sat around talking to Marion and the girls for a while before getting ready and taking themselves off to the big dance hall in the city.

Patrick was a little disappointed at first. He had several dances with attractive, well-groomed girls of his own age or slightly older. They were affable enough but seemed to have very little conversation and danced as though to entertain themselves only, with their partners simply an instrument to assist in that regard.

It could have been him or, perhaps, he had selected the wrong partners to dance. It all changed, however, when he had the last two dances of the night with the one girl who was somewhat different to the others he had encountered that evening. She was tall and slim but otherwise generously endowed and although somewhat his senior, still quite attractive. She danced very close which he found somewhat disconcerting and in a way that was physically new to him, but not really unpleasant. She really did want to talk and spoke of herself at length, also asking questions of him which bordered on the private and very personal. As the dance was ending she told him that the girl with whom she shared her Edgecliff flat was away for the weekend and she was feeling lonely. Relatively unsophisticated as he was, Patrick got the message and made his escape as gracefully as possible after the band ceased playing for the night. As they made their way home he told Ken about it. He said he must never go to that place without him if he didn't want to endanger his virginity.

Patrick liked to think it was a high moral standard and the teachings of his Faith that made him reject the blatant offer. But deep down he knew it was the possibility of involvement that really deterred him, as that was something he wanted to avoid at all costs. However, he had to admit, for a moment there he had been tempted and now was aware it was common sense and not a high moral code which told him to decline the 'come-on' from the girl.

What had that missionary priest said about 'avoiding the occasion of sin'? He now knew what that holy man was talking about.

His intention had been to make this a full and different weekend and the following morning at breakfast, when Ken told him of a first-grade rugby match between Randwick and Manly being played that afternoon at nearby Coogee Oval, he jumped at the invitation to go to the game with him.

He enjoyed it all as it was a close tussle and he quickly related to the Manly winger who was starved for the ball all afternoon. After the final whistle they paid a short visit to the Randwick dressing room as Shep knew several of the players. Like him, they were members of the local surf club and he wanted to congratulate them on their win.

It was almost six o'clock when they left the oval. At Sheppard's suggestion they walked over to the Coogee Bay shopping centre and bought fish and chips, eaten as only those with a young voracious appetites can, sitting at a bench overlooking a calm but cold-looking ocean.

Ken could not dally and when they finished their meal he hurried off to catch a tram as he was taking a girl to her local picture theatre at Strathfield, on the other side of the city.

Up to now Patrick had enjoyed his special Saturday and did not want it to end. He made his way quickly to his own tram when he recalled the invitation to go to the pictures with the people from the guest house. He arrived in time to change and join them on that short stroll to the tram stop, one which he had taken so often since becoming a resident of Pine Trees.

He enjoyed 'Naughty Marietta'. The singing and music was pleasant and tuneful but, whilst the voices were pretty good, he thought the acting by the principals to be quite hammy and Nelson Eddy only had two facial expressions, bland and blander. What he did enjoy during the picture was looking from time to time at Marion and Wendy, who were completely carried away with the romanticism of the story and with all the glamour they attached to the leading players.

He took them to a light supper in the milk bar attached to the theatre where they still carried on excitedly about the motion picture they had just seen. It was after midnight before he found himself climbing into bed; tired but content and with a complete absence of any sense of guilt about this stolen weekend.

He awoke in time for breakfast but his room-mate, who did not get in until the very wee hours and had tried not to disturb him, was still sound asleep. Afterwards he sat in the small parlour reading the Sunday papers and chatting intermittently with one or two of the other guests who were doing the same thing.

Back in the room Ken was still out to it, so he got ready as quietly as he could before heading for the tram and Sunday 11am *Missa cantata* at St. Mary's Cathedral in the city. For once the celebrant's voice matched the degree of excellence set by the choir and added greatly to the solemnity of this sung Sacrifice for the young music student.

It was getting well past midday when he came out of the Basilica to one of Sydney's sunny winter days which reminded one of spring. His appetite had resumed its call so he bought two 'doggies', hot dogs laced with hot mustard, from a street vendor before wandering down a side street to the Domain. Using his jacket as a pillow, he lay on the grass in the warm sun with a sense of freedom he'd seldom felt since leaving Magdalene.

When he finally woke up, later than intended, he strolled around among the many soap-box orators who gathered there on Sunday afternoons. He was surprised at the diversity of the many causes espoused, Communists and Fascists included, noting that while the latter attracted a big crowd, they were noticeably outnumbered by the many hecklers.

Patrick stayed and listened for a while and enjoyed the noisy outbursts from the throng as the dissidents, at regular intervals, interrupted the speakers and in general showed their unbridled disapproval of their obscene Movement in no uncertain manner.

He was in a light mood as he took the long walk along the harbour wall to the tram depot at Bennelong Point and then over to Circular Quay. A milk shake at the Manly Ferry Wharf and an ice cream cone added to his pleasures as he made his way to the tram stop for Centennial Park.

It was near dark when he came through the front door and heard voices coming from the kitchen. He found Wendy and her now-returned roommate having a pot of tea and eating corned-beef rolls they had bought at the local delicatessen which opened, illegally, for a few hours late on Sunday afternoons.

"Did you get me one?" asked Patrick as he took a chair at the table.

"No! I thought you would be out warmongering somewhere and wouldn't have time to eat," joked Wendy.

"Don't be flippant, girl. The advice I gave you about Europe yesterday was pertinent and accurate and I would like you to show some appreciation for me giving you the benefit on my sagacity in these matters and, also, for any advice I might happen to give you in future," said Patrick, feigning seriousness.

"Oh yes sir, of course I will. Would you like a cup of tea?" said Wendy, as she threw a nearby tea towel at him while getting up to put on the kettle.

"I thought you would never ask," said Patrick.

They stayed there for some time, talking about nothing in particular but savouring these moments of congenial company so important in the lives of people who are living away from home.

When he got up to his room it was after nine and Ken had still not returned. As he sat on his bed he began to ruminate on his great weekend, now over, and his mood started to change. He realised that his activities had been fairly mundane by any standard for most people but not for him as they were all something he had never experienced before.

Without any planning at all it had been a classically Australian few days for him. Taking a girl out for a bite, doing a bit of cheek to cheek at the Troc, seeing a good game of footie on Saturday 'arvo, eating fish and chips out of newspaper at the beach, pictures on Saturday night and finding time for God on Sunday morning. It would be a long time before he would forget this most pleasant, but brief interlude in his life.

Now he must return to that other life, the life with his piano and his music. It was an existence in which he was, for much of the time, very much alone, but never lonely. His music was a great companion, never dull and always beckoning him to greater heights of understanding of the reasons it brought so much joy to so many people in every part of the world.

He now knew of some of the simple but satisfying things the other world had to offer but those attractions, together with members of the opposite sex, would have to wait. For now, and in the foreseeable future, his mind and soul were spoken for - to the exclusion of all such possible distractions.

Chapter 17

In the opening months of his second year at the Conservatorium, Patrick imposed on himself even greater demands of time in pursuit of his career in music. The urge to compose his own symphonic work was becoming an obsession and so compelling it seemed to have taken priority over his initial objective of becoming a concert pianist.

Listening to the orchestral works of immortal composers was the only way he thought he could come to comprehend the basic structure of their music. So now, on two or three nights of each week, he stayed back to listen on the Professor's studio wireless to recordings of international symphony concerts broadcast by the ABC station 2FC on a regular basis.

Hearing the music of master composers played by orchestras such as the London Symphony, New York Philharmonic and the Philadelphia Symphony under the batons of renowned conductors, including Toscanini, Beecham, Barbirolli and Leopold Stokowski, were musical experiences he could not forsake even at the cost of much personal inconvenience. This listening not only improved his comprehension of the structure of music but also served as an added impetus to his need to write it.

Some months earlier he had spoken with Professor Morrison of this wish to compose and raised the problem of not knowing the exact musical sound of many of the instruments which go to make up a full symphony orchestra. He explained he could 'hear' the sounds they made but could not identify the instruments from which they came.

Morrison had no objection to this new ambition and thought it could compliment his playing. He offered his help and thought the best way for Patrick to overcome this lack of knowledge would be to attend orchestra rehearsals when conductors usually took each section of the ensemble separately through their particular parts of the composition being rehearsed.

The Concert Manager at the ABC was a friend and he obtained from him permission for Patrick to attend the regular rehearsals of the Sydney Symphony Orchestra, commonly known as the SSO, each Friday morning at its rehearsal hall in William Street close to Kings Cross. This was a rare privilege as conductors did not like 'others' to be present at these exercises - they could let their temperament show at such times, particularly when the orchestra was not complying with their directions in the way required. The need for privacy for some maestros was paramount - their language could become colourful and insulting at times and at complete variance with the *persona* normally presented to their musical public. Knowledge of tantrums displayed by esteemed musical figures had to be confined to those people properly entitled to be present at rehearsals and this did not include members of the general public, whatever their calling.

Professor Julian Morrison, however, was an exception, for the ABC never knew when it might need a returned favour from him and the Conservatorium and for that reason his pupil was given the green light to sit in at orchestra rehearsals.

By the time he had attended nine or ten of these Patrick's mind had identified the sound made by each orchestral instrument, to the extent he no longer needed to attend these sessions for that purpose. He continued to do so though as he felt there was much to be learnt from them by someone like himself who was vitally interested in composing instrumental music.

So as not to be the cause of any possible distraction he made a point of arriving well in advance of the scheduled starting time and usually sat in the hall with three or four members of the ABC staff who were responsible for all aspects of management of the orchestra apart from its actual playing.

Over the weeks he had been coming Patrick had become friendly with Cyril Burstone, the young assistant-manager. They usually sat together in silence whilst the orchestra was playing but always found time for a short yarn before or after the practise session. Patrick liked him and he was a fund of information about what was going on at the ABC in general and the SSO in particular.

As it turned out his attendance at one of these rehearsals proved to be somewhat of a turning point in his career and an occasion he would never forget.

On a winterish Friday in late June, he arrived as usual twenty-five minutes or so before the rehearsal was due to begin to find the players milling about in a state of agitation instead of being seated and ready to play. Patrick walked over to Burstone who was standing near the platform steps one of the violinists and asked what was going on. The assistant-manager gave him a seriously-toned summing-up of the situation.

It was intended for that morning to be given over to the rehearsal of the well known, but difficult, Tchaikovsky *Piano Concerto Number 1*. The orchestra was to perform this on the following Monday evening at the Sydney Town Hall with the ABC's German guest-artist, Karl Hauptman, as soloist.

Hauptman, who had just completed concerts in Melbourne was on his way to Sydney by train and should have arrived earlier that morning and in time for this rehearsal. However, thanks to a lightning rail strike by NSW Railway employees, he now was stranded some hundreds of miles away in Albury on the New South Wales - Victorian border. The ABC was endeavouring to arrange alternative transport but there was no possibility of him arriving in Sydney within the next twenty-four hours.

In the meantime the SSO's resident Conductor, William Lawson, and the ABC Concert Manager had been on the office telephone endeavouring to find a substitute pianist so that the orchestra could be properly prepared for the forthcoming concert. Lawson, who was an even-tempered Englishman in the second year of a three-year tenure with the SSO, was quite calm about it all, although somewhat concerned for this was to be the first and only rehearsal of the work and, therefore, it would necessarily be a long and detailed session. He was not concerned about rehearsing Hauptman who would be right up-to-date with the work as he had recently performed it in Melbourne.

Things were still up-in-the-air as they had no success in finding a replacement and now there was very little likelihood they could find someone suitable at such short notice. The Manager of the ABC himself was also making enquiries and they were waiting to hear from him as he was their last hope.

"That's where we are right now, Pat. We just have to wait on the big boss and hope he can come up with something. If he doesn't I don't know what we will do. They might have to cancel the concert because Lawson won't do it if it's not properly rehearsed," concluded Cyril Burstone.

"What rotten luck, Cyril," consoled Patrick resignedly, "I'll just stick about for a while and see what happens." He returned to a seat in the hall and sat there thinking for a few minutes before getting up again and walked over to where Burstone was still waiting with the concert master. After drawing him aside Patrick started to speak.

"Cyril, perhaps I can be of some help. I know the work well even though I've never played it with an orchestra as such. The orchestral section has been adapted for piano for ease of practise and I have done it several times with Professor Morison and other tutors at the Con. I've played both parts but spent more time on the soloist's work and I think I know it well enough to fill in here if there is no alternative."

"Bloody hell! Why didn't you say so, Pat! I'll be back in a minute," said Cyril as he mounted the stairs and dashed towards the little office.

A few minutes later he came to the edge of the platform and beckoned to Patrick to join him and together they went into the room where Cyril introduced him to the conductor.

"It's very good of you to offer, young man, but do you think you can do it?" asked Lawson. "I understand you are studying under Julian Morrison and that tells me a lot about your ability but you are still a student and this might be a bit much for you? Young Burstone tells me also that it is a few months back since you last did the work. Is that going to be a problem?"

"I don't think it is, so if there is no one else available I'm prepared to give it a try" replied Patrick. "As I told Cyril, I have not done the concerto with an orchestra but with another piano but I think I know it well enough for your purpose, otherwise I would not have made the offer."

The conductor ignored the bluntness of the young man's reply and looked thoughtfully at him for a while before speaking.

"Well, that's a fairly direct answer to my question and I appreciate your candour and so, like you, I think I am prepared to give it a try. What have we to lose? We'll get the score and let you look through it before we start. While you are doing that we'll find someone to turn page for you," offered Lawson.

"That won't be necessary," said Patrick in a less belligerent tone, "I remember the work quite well and I won't need the score except perhaps to know where you want to start if you find it necessary to recapitulate some sections of the work."

Lawson looked somewhat aghast and gave a doubtful kind of laugh.

"You mean to tell me you can recall the entire concerto even though its months since you've seen the score," he said. "I find that a little hard to believe. Are you really serious?"

"Quite," said Patrick with unfeigned assurance. Lawson started to look dubious but then took a deep breath, shook his head and said,

"Please understand, Sheridan, we are grateful for your offer but it was necessary for me to make those observations about your youth and inexperience and I hope you understand that. Now, if you're ready we'll get on with it," concluded Lawson as he led the way out to where the orchestra was waiting.

Patrick went to the piano and removed his jacket as it was quite warm in the hall and many in the orchestra were in shirtsleeves. He laid it on a nearby chair as William Lawson ascended the small podium and spoke to the orchestra.

"Good morning," he said. "You're all aware of the situation and we are indebted to this young pianist, who is a pupil at the Conservatorium, for offering to help us out. The General Manager himself is still looking but I've decided to proceed as it seems unlikely he'll be successful. Our young friend here has never done this work with a full ensemble but some months back he did it several times with the piano adaptation. Incredibly, he says he does not need the score as he remembers the work clearly and thinks it more important he watch me rather than the manuscript. We shall see! There's a possibility there will be 'incidents' and I suggest we play through these, if possible, and review at the end of the Movement. Please get on with the tuning, Concert Master, and when you and Mr. Sheridan are ready we will make a start."

As they matched their tunings to the Concert Master's 'A,' there were murmurs of surprise and disbelief from the players at what was proposed. As they waited for the conductor to raise his wand there was an air of resigned acceptance about the players which did not escape the notice of the conductor nor his stand-in soloist.

As Lawson raised his baton the brief but majestic opening bars from the horns rang out. Then the piano assumed its dominance of the first few pages of the long and melodious First Movement of the difficult, oft-played and extremely popular concerto by the great Russian composer. Because the opening passages belonged to the piano mainly, the conductor was looking almost constantly in the direction of the pianist and Patrick in turn was looking back at him whenever his playing permitted. There was an anxious look in Lawson's eyes as though he was hoping for the best but, to some extent, fearing the worst. Through the sensitive use of his baton he was trying to instil confidence into the boy and draw the very best out of him.

None of this was necessary, however, for the pianist was, mentally and emotionally, quite at ease, for he realised after the first few minutes he wouldn't have any problems playing with the orchestra provided he cleaved to Lawson's conducting. His great gift of being able always to recall every aspect of any work he had studied now stood him in great stead.

It was halfway through the movement when the Conductor once more turned towards the piano. By now all doubt had left his brow to be replaced by a look of total wonderment at what he was hearing. When he turned back to the orchestra he noticed the change which had come over it since it first commenced the work. There was an intensity about their playing which was not always present on such occasions and he then realised that he and the whole ensemble were endeavouring to match the high standard being set by a brilliant pianist. Both for him and his orchestra this was no longer a rehearsal but a full-blown performance in which they wanted to give their all to compliment the soloist's consummate pianism. It was a matter of routine for the conductor to take a break between movements to discuss anything he had noticed during the playing and where necessary take some sections of the orchestra through passages that he thought needed attention.

It did not happen on this occasion for as the final cords of the first stanza died away, Lawson put a finger to his lips and the players quickly and earnestly turned the pages of their manuscripts. Upon receiving a brief nod from Patrick, Lawson led them all into the Second Movement.

The same procedure followed the playing of the second segment and when William Lawson put down the baton at the conclusion of the work there was complete silence for several moments. It was as though all involved had just come through a great experience and were at a loss for words. It was broken finally when the Conductor spoke, quite emotionally for him, to the ensemble.

"I don't think I have heard you in better form and if you play like that on Monday night we are in for a great concert and," he said turning to beam at Patrick, "if Hauptman plays as well as you did this morning we are in for an even better one… and I didn't say that. Thank you so much for your help and I can assure you all here, whilst still a little flabbergasted, are most appreciative at what you have just done for us."

As he finished speaking Patrick started to put on his jacket and then became aware the entire ensemble, which had not moved since they finished playing, was looking in his direction. It started with the first violins and quickly joined by every section of the orchestra in a cacophony of tuneless sounds from their instruments in the traditional way orchestral players had of acknowledging what they considered at outstanding performance. They kept it up for two or three minutes intermingled with the usual "bravos" and similar expressions of praise and goodwill.

When it finally subsided, William Lawson, who had joined in by striking the front of the podium frequently and loudly with his baton, said, "Well, well, Mr. Sheridan, you can take that as a real compliment. It takes a lot to impress this crowd and there has been many a fine solo performance at the Sydney Town Hall which has failed to move them in such a way. I'm afraid I have to agree with their discernment on this occasion."

He told the players to take a ten minute break and then they would iron out a few minor points with the concerto before starting to rehearse the Sibelius which was to take up the first part of the Monday concert. He asked Patrick if he could spare a few minutes and they left the platform together, but not before Patrick had expressed his thanks, rather self-consciously, with silent words and gracious bows and arm gestures in thanking the players for their kindly reception of his playing.

Once in his room, the Conductor closed the door and then stood almost stood toe to toe with Patrick and looked searchingly into his eyes.

"Where in heaven's name did you come from Sheridan? I don't have to tell you how well you played out there, you know that yourself. As much as I admired and delighted in everything you did I am absolutely astounded by your memory. In all my years I've never seen the like of it. To think it was your first performance with a full orchestra, and I know you did not hit a single wrong note because I was listening for them. That is most incredible. If I had not been there to witness it I would never have believed it possible."

Patrick just continued looking at him, very embarrassed but smiling and brushing this hair back with his hand. He was about to reply but Lawson would not be interrupted. "What is your background and why is old Julian keeping you under wraps when you should be sharing your talent with the wide musical world? I refuse to be carried away by what you have just done but if there is a better pianist anywhere, please lead me to him."

The young man, understandably, was quite taken aback by the last comment from an eminent musician and he dropped his eyes and his face flushed as he absorbed the significance of the very forthright compliment.

"I really don't know what to say," said Patrick as he locked his eyes again into those of the Conductor. "I think you will find Professor Morrison is doing what he considers best for me. I've just turned twenty-one and I'm a boy from the bush who has been at the Conservatorium for less than a year and a half and he has taught me so much in that time. I have no musical background to speak of although my mother does play well and started to teach me the piano when I was about eight and, I do have to say, I have been at it ever since. I now have a fairly extensive repertoire although we are working to enlarge it even more."

Lawson was about to say something but could see Patrick had more on his mind and let him go on uninterrupted. "In view of my rustic background and age, Professor thinks I should complete this year at the Con and then review my progress with the idea I should then do a few months with one of the master coaches in Europe before contemplating a career."

"That's all well and good," said Lawson, "and please don't tell Morrison I said this, but you are as ready to start a concert career as you will ever be. I saw enough this morning to stake my reputation on that statement. In any event, and as you state you have a good repertoire, I intend to talk to the ABC management with a view to them approaching you to give recitals under their management, both stage and studio, next year. As I say, I would be grateful if you didn't tell Julian about this talk. He is a friend and I will raise the matter with him at an appropriate time. I have to tell you, young Sheridan, I was staggered at what you did this morning and felt compelled to let you know how I felt.

"They're waiting for me," he said, breaking away from the subject. "I better go but I intend to keep in close touch with you, so be warned," he concluded as he opened the door and the conductor and pianist went out of the little room and back into the hall.

Chapter 18

The pianist, Patrick Sheridan, often contemplated the other life he could have chosen for himself - the one away from music and the almost intolerable demands it made on him and his time.

He envisaged it would have included managing his beloved Magdalene in its fair, rural setting, whilst living with his parents who meant so much to him. He would have met and socialised with people from neighbouring properties and with the many friends he had made in Bathurst who were now less than an hour away from the homestead by car. He would have been part of the local sports scene and on weekends, perhaps, in season, would have played rugby, cricket or tennis, enjoying the after-match comradeship which was so important to young men. He would have joined his friends, the property's Aboriginal stockmen, in rounding-up and tending Magdalene's flocks and, at shearing time, would sit down on the shed floor and yarn with the shearers, drinking raw tea during their frequent breaks from taking the wool off the sheep's back. He would have met many girls and taken the one of his then current choice to weekly country dances and always the pictures on Saturday nights.

These were the pleasures he had forsaken and, simple as they were, it would have meant a lot to him, for Patrick Sheridan, divorced from music, was just a decent, ordinary young Australian who would have derived fulfilment in such a life comprised, as it was, of hard work and well-earned leisure.

He concluded these ruminations, as he usually did, with the realisation that he did not regret the role life had chosen for him. In fact, he had had very little option. His talent was a great gift, or "blessing" as his mother Irene insisted, and this was something, in all conscience, he could not have walked away from no matter the personal cost. Compensation for foregoing that other life had been immense at times and the exquisite pleasure he had just derived from performing a concerto with a symphony orchestra was just one illustration of this.

Such were the thoughts running through his mind as he left the rehearsal hall in William Street that morning and made his way towards the Sydney General Post Office where he would telephone his parents and tell them what had just transpired. It was not his intention to tell anyone else of the rehearsal but felt he should, at least, inform them, not only for the pleasure it would bring, but because they were entitled to know. For it were they, and they alone, who had made this minor triumph possible for him.

As he sat on the bench awaiting his telephone booth number to be called he realised the concerto had given him enormous satisfaction. But he was not overawed by the event for, without the benefit of any conceit, he was aware he was capable now of performing any work written for piano. There was no doubting today he had climbed another rung on his way to a musical career. But, at the same time, it had taken him further away from that other life upon which he had just reflected. This reflection certainly was triggered by the knowledge that today finally marked his point-of-no-return to that other, simpler existence.

It was as well he reversed the charges for his call because, after speaking to his father briefly, Irene came on the line and upon hearing his news, honed to the very basic facts. She plied him with question after question until she had the full picture, right down to the substance of the few minutes of his concluding conversation with the Conductor of the SSO.

She seized upon the opinion the maestro had expressed. "I agree with him, Patrick. You are ready and have been for some time. Make this point to Professor Morrison and see what he has to say. If he still thinks it important you receive a few months top-level mentoring in Europe then you should go immediately and not wait until next year. Your father would be more than happy to meet the expense and I think I should go with you as you are too young to go alone and would need someone to look after you. It would only be for a couple of months and Tom won't mind that as he does like a little space once in a while. Now, will you do as I say?"

"Yes, Mum," he replied patiently. "He is away for a few days giving a seminar in Newcastle and I'll talk with him when he gets back. I can't mention the conversation with William Lawson as I promised him I wouldn't. You must realise, Mum, a lot of prior planning and hard work goes into launching a musical career and we will need some good advice. A friend of mine at the ABC told me of some of the pitfalls and I'm having a yarn about it with him next week. I will let you know what he says."

It was well over half an hour before he hung up and started walking up Martin Place to the Conservatorium. He was somewhat keen to get back there as he wanted to resume work on the second movement of the initial symphonic composition he commenced a few weeks earlier when, for the first time, he was confident he had attained a sound knowledge of each musical instrument comprised in a full orchestra.

The writing was something he had not mentioned to anyone. It was music that had been welling up in him for a long time now and he had found relief and satisfaction in being able to commit it to manuscript.

Composing took up more and more of his time these days but not at the expense of time required to be spent at the keyboard. He had maintained this at the usual level of four to five hours every day, or longer, depending upon his mood. He was fully aware of the need for first things first and that he must strive to become a recognised pianist before anything else.

He had completed his formal studies at the Conservatorium and only had to undergo the Board's performance rating at the end of the year before gaining his Arts Degree in Music. The latter requirement was a mere formality, according to Julian Morrison.

The time formerly required for his formal studies was now directed to composing. But the hours slipped by so quickly when he was engaged in this that it often was some time into the night before he looked up from his work. He and the night-watchman at the Conservatorium had become very well-known to each other.

Professor Julian Morris was delayed for two days in Newcastle by the same rail strike that stranded the SSO's guest pianist, Karl Hauptman, in Albury. Because of the many matters which had come up during his extended absence, his secretary advised Patrick he had to cancel their usual Wednesday session and that he would see him at the same time the following day.

Patrick had completed his study of works by Schumann as suggested by the Professor at their previous meeting and now felt they could be included in his repertoire.

Morrison agreed after Patrick played a selection from them at the commencement of their delayed session. "That's good, that's good," he said, almost absently, "you can safely add that to the performance list," and noted the passages where Robert Schumann made way for young Sheridan to express himself in his work.

"Well done! Come and sit over here," he said drawing up two chairs away from the piano, "I'd like to talk for a while. Now tell me," he said, most intently, when Patrick was seated, "what happened at that rehearsal last week? I've had numerous notes and messages about it from several people at the ABC and, I understand, Tates and the J.C. Williamson people have been trying to get me on the telephone. So, whatever happened there has got out and I think you should bring me up to date. Bill Lawson also rang last night and told me he had a few words with you and he freed you to give me the essence of that conversation, if you are so inclined."

Patrick related a factual account of what transpired at the orchestra's rehearsal without elaboration and concluded with the gist of the few words he had in private with the conductor.

"You must have put on quite a show otherwise it would not have caused such a furore. I am quite astounded the players reacted in that way as that crowd usually reserve such approbation for great soloists, and only after a memorable performance, and it would need to be memorable. Every one of them is a knowledgeable musician and it's quite unheard off or them to applaud a 'new boy' like you. It makes me wonder just what was went on."

He paused and appeared to be simply thinking out loud rather than addressing Patrick when he said, "I suppose the very idea of Lawson comparing you with Hauptman just about says it all. The players, unknowingly, were agreeing with him that, despite your age, you were an accomplished and exciting pianist and you had, indeed, given them a memorable performance. Look, Patrick, I am fully aware you are a fine pianist but what you apparently did the other day is quite beyond anything I could have imagined."

"Well, that's the way it happened," said Patrick, "and it was simply that I was just in the right place at the right time. I knew the work and became excited at the possibility of playing with the orchestra and that is really why I offered to help out in the first place. The conductor, and the players, were anxious about me at first but when that wore off and we played the entire concerto without interruption, well, apparently that is a bit unusual for a rehearsal."

"Indeed it is," agreed Morrison. "Don't tell me anymore; I've heard enough, thank you! You have astounded and amazed a lot of musicians, including myself, with your playing which must have been of a standard I had failed to fully recognise.

"All of this has placed me in an awkward position. There are suggestions I'm holding you back and that you're ready for the concert platform now. I've no doubt at all about your ability but you are still young and I would like to have had you for another year or so before sending you off to my friend, Nienarber, at the Heidelberg University to conclude your preparation. How do you feel about it? Do you think you are ready?"

"I really don't know," replied Patrick. "I honestly feel I'm up to that standard but I like the idea of consulting a good European coach to round off my training for I feel there are side issues to this career business of which I am not yet aware. I spoke to my mother and she does think I'm ready and suggests, if you concur, that I go to Europe just as soon as it could be arranged, but insists you should have the final say in this matter. She said I should let you know she is prepared to go with me, and I suppose, that is a good idea," concluded Patrick somewhat doubtfully.

"Alright, I hear what she is saying but I want to think about it before asking her to come down to discuss it. In the meantime I'll get a cable away to Hans Nienarber and see how soon he could fit you in. Of all the mentors, I think he is the most highly regarded in our field and he, therefore, only has time for the most talented of pupils. I know he will accept my opinion of you in that regard."

They let things stand there but it was a thoughtful Julian Morrison who resumed the lesson with his pupil, who had resumed his seat at the piano.

It was an unsettled time for them both, and for Irene Sheridan too, until Hans Nienarber replied to Morrison's cable some three weeks later. He expressed pleasure in being able to agree to hearing a pupil who came so highly recommended but his schedule was such he would be unable to accept him until the beginning of next year's Spring term, which was 3rd March, 1940. He advised the tuition period would be restricted to a single term of ten weeks as he had prior commitments after that, but indicated it would be more than sufficient time for his purpose as Mr. Sheridan was, presumably, a most talented pianist already.

Irene arrived in Sydney the following week and an appointment was arranged in the Professor's office the day after she arrived, when it was agreed they should accept the offer from Heidelberg and that appropriate arrangements should be put in hand without delay.

She had made enquiries beforehand at the shipping offices and found the SS Orcades was sailing from Pyrmont for Southampton in mid-January. This would enable them to be in Germany by the end of February and give a day or two for Patrick to settle in before commencing study with his new coach.

Julian Morrison thought this was ideal timing and a booking should be made without delay. He would cable Nienarber and ask he arrange suitable accommodation for them in the scenic university township.

"This gives us less than six months to get other things in order, Mrs. Sheridan," said the Professor, "Patrick and I are almost satisfied with the extent and calibre of his repertoire although there is still some work to be done.

"You both understand, of course, that Patrick's formal association with me and the Conservatorium will conclude at the end of this academic year and I wish to say now I will be available to you to discuss and advise on any matters where you think I may be of help."

"You do not know how relieved I am to hear you say that, Professor," said Patrick almost eagerly. "I have not come to grips with the idea of being cut adrift from this wonderful place and I'm at a loss to know how to proceed after Heidelberg. I know through speaking with senior people here that getting a musical career underway is not easy. From day one it will take planning, organising and a great deal of preparation if it is to be done properly and people who know about these things have made that quite clear to me."

"Don't underestimate yourself, my boy," said Julian Morrison very evenly. "I'm quite satisfied you are, in so many ways, an exceptional talent which Nienarber and Heidelberg will be quick to recognise. Heidelberg University has been the source of many great artists and, if they are impressed, word will go out immediately and you could find yourself inundated with agents, impresarios and concert managers all vying for your signature on a contract document and the problems you now envisage may not eventuate at all.

"Are you happy to leave things like that, Mrs. Sheridan?" he said in a let's-wind-this-up tone of voice.

"Thank you," she replied. "I have not said very much but I've listened to what you have both had to say. I think the arrangements as they stand are fine but I'd like to make a point. The Australian Broadcasting Commission seems rather interested in Patrick at the moment and I'm wondering if we should not capitalise on that. Should we give their concert and music department people a complete audition after telling them of the Heidelberg intention?

"Then, on the understanding Patrick gets a favourable report from Doctor Nienbarber with interest in his services coming from overseas impresarios, we would be prepared to launch his career here subject to receiving a contract for a full season of ABC orchestral concerts and recitals. We would still be feeling our way and it would give us more control to start here rather than in some foreign capital where we would not know a single soul and have a language problem to boot."

"I hope you realise you have a very astute mother, Patrick," said the professor. "Quite honestly, Mrs. Sheridan, I was going to suggest something along those same lines but your approach is excellent and a very commonsense solution to what could be a difficult problem. If you're agreeable I will approach the ABC on your behalf and try to get something in motion."

Patrick leant over and touched his mother on the armwhilst nodding in agreement and the trio broke up for the time being. Young Sheridan was relieved and somewhat excited now that he knew what lay in the immediate future. It was no longer when, where and who but January 1940, Heidelberg and a Doctor Hans Nienarber.

His mind was clearer as there was nothing else to bind his days apart from his acceptable practise regimen and working on his repertoire with Julian Morrison. This meant more time could be devoted to completing his symphonic work which had absorbed him to the extent it had become imperative to the needs of his artistic being.

To attempt such a task may have seemed precocious and, perhaps, pretentious, for one of his years but he knew this was not so. He was writing this work because he just had to do it and it was a matter of indifference to him as to whether it would ever be performed or not. Selfishly, he thought at times, he was writing this opus for himself and himself alone.

This music was inspired by the land of his birth which the young man from the bush loved deeply and the first two movements had simply flowed to the manuscript for they concerned past and present times of the island Continent. The third movement, however, which was to express in musical terms what lay ahead of the young country, was not that easy for he only could speculate and surmise as to what the portending years held for his Land of the Southern Cross.

He was enjoying this challenge and a stream of music was starting to flow again at long last. He knew he could finish the full score prior to his departure for Heidelberg.

In recent weeks he had felt the atmosphere of the studio and its surrounds were not conducive for the writing of his music. Much the same applied to his lodgings for, despite the fact he liked the place and all its inhabitants, it was not right for his purpose. He had intended to speak with his parents about getting a garden flat in an inner suburb and installing a piano which would be then at his disposal day and night, enabling him to work as and when the muse compelled him. The necessity of being totally isolated when composing had become increasingly apparent to him.

However he decided now to put off such a move until he returned from Heidelberg but in any event, when he said "goodbye" to Pine Trees in January it would be, however reluctantly, for the last time.

It was on those frequent walks home to Centennial Park that he allowed himself to think about the career that possibly lay ahead. Now that matters were en train he was starting to experience a slight sense of urgency and impatience about it.

The real prospect of giving recitals in the foremost musical capitals of the world and performing with name orchestras under renowned conductors was, naturally, exhilarating and exciting for him, and all this could not come soon enough. He knew he would have to hold in check the persistent urge to compose until such time as he had established himself as a recitalist. But he knew that one day his need to write music would overwhelm any residual desire he may have to continuing on as concert pianist. Still thinking about his career, he recalled his conversation with Cyril Burstone when he finally caught up with him in his office at the ABC.

Burstone was older than he looked and had spent several years working mainly with artists, for theatrical companies and agencies in Australia and Europe and he knew a lot about the concert business.

He told Patrick how he thought he should progress his career and emphasised he should never contemplate starting anywhere but at the highest level for an artist. He had found in the music world that artists who commenced from a lower strata were, almost invariably, unable to make it up the first rung to an important career. Should the ABC approach him initially with a contract to play a season of studio recitals and performances in provincial cities, he should reject it out of hand.

He lengthened their conversation by telling Patrick he had come back from Europe with the idea of setting up his own concert business but had misread the depth of the Great Depression in Australia. He was now biding his time at the ABC pending better days.

"Look here, Pat," he said in conclusion, "with your youth, good looks and extraordinary talent you are already an impresario's gold mine, so never settle for anything other than the top line. You carry my best wishes, my friend, and, if I can help you in any way, you know where to find me."

These were reassuring and encouraging words from someone whose opinion Patrick respected. The sound advice he had proffered would be stored away and used at some appropriate time in the future.

Chapter 19

It was some ten days after the Sydney meeting that Irene was able to tell Patrick on the phone that their passports had arrived from Canberra and their travel arrangements for Europe were now complete: The SS Orcades to Southampton and, after a two-day stopover in London, by boat and train to Paris and from there, German rail and bus to Heidelberg, all booked and confirmed.

Patrick had made his call to tell her Heidelberg University had advised Professor Morrison that suitable accommodation had been arranged for the period of their stay. It was a relief for Irene to know all their travel arrangements had been now finalised.

Apart from the excitement she felt about this important step in Patrick's career, she was looking forward to her own first trip abroad and the prospect of seeing London and Paris had given her a real sense of anticipation. She felt a little guilty about being away from Tom for so long, but his health was much better and he did not seem to mind her going. He got on well with the housekeeper, Molly Read, the manager's sister, who had become more of a family friend than an employee.

He'll cope, she concluded.

Patrick had made that telephone call to his mother rather late in the day after spending most of the afternoon with Charles Jermyn, the man who had inducted him into the Con and maintained an interest in him ever since. Jermyn had just received a recording of the great Australian pianist, Eileen Joyce, playing the great Beethoven piano concerto with the London Philharmonic under Sir Thomas Beecham and he thought he and Patrick should listen to it together. Afterwards, they had discussed what had been an exciting performance at The Albert Hall in London. They replayed some of the more engaging passages of the opus until it was time for Jermyn to leave for the usual Friday staff meeting.

It was getting on for five o'clock when he made his way down the long passageway to his studio. It was Friday and for once this week he was determined to get back to Pine Trees in time for the evening meal. He would pick up the manuscript of 'his work-in-progress' and would continue on with it in his room after dinner when in all probability his roommate, Ken, would be out on his usual weekend gallivant.

He had left the studio door open and was putting the music into his brief case when he heard the noise of someone wearing high-heeled shoes coming down the hallway. When they stopped outside his door and he heard a gentle knock, he thought it must have been one of the girls from the Con office with a message for Julian Morrison and without looking up said, "Yes?"

"Hello, Patrick," a female voice came back softly, "I thought I would find you here."

He recognised the voice immediately but, when he turned his head and looked at its owner, he thought he must have been mistaken.

"Blow me down, is that you, Cathy?" he said in a very surprised tone of voice. "I'd never have recognised you. What have you done to yourself? Welcome home, it's good to see you," he said in greeting her warmly.

"It's wonderful to see you too, Patrick," she replied with feeling as she came into the room whilst removing a glove and extending a well-manicured right hand to the young man. He took it in both of his, held it a moment before letting it go.

"You know, Patrick Sheridan, a young Frenchman would have kissed it in this situation," she said with a mock reproach.

"Is that so? Well we Aussies can do better than that," he replied enthusiastically and leant over and kissed her on the cheek.

She reeled back in mock surprise putting her fingers to her face where his lips had touched.

"I cannot believe it. A gesture like that from you, Patrick! Will wonders never cease? Thank you, anyhow; but will that be the first of many, please?"

"Enough of that nonsense," said Patrick. "Remember you are very young, so please behave yourself and tell me how you got on over there."

But before she could answer, he went on.

"Just look at you. I've never seen such a change in a girl. Before you usually looked ruffled and unkempt, as though you had just got out of bed and today you look like you've just got out of a band box. Wonderful dress, high heel shoes and that little hat, and gloves of all things. I like it, I like it. You learnt more in Paris than just how to play the violin, apparently. You must have won a heart or two over there looking like that."

"I'm glad you're impressed but I didn't know I was that awful before. Why didn't you say something?" she responded. "Paris was quite wonderful and I was there over a year. We had to work hard at the Conservatoire because quite quickly you would be asked to leave if you didn't shape up, for there was such a long list of kids waiting to get in who would be prepared to work. The teaching was superb and I learnt so much more than I expected. I think I'm a good player now and, perhaps, you can hear me some time and see what you think."

Their talk continued as she told him how easy it had been to get on with her fellow students, mainly young Parisians, at the Conservatoire once her schoolgirl French had improved. They had a strong work ethic but whilst they studied and practised hard at their particular instrument, they still found time to relax and enjoy the company of their own group. This usually meant eating together occasionally at good but reasonably priced restaurants and bistro-type cafes which abounded on the Left Bank. She had never thought food and wine could be so interesting and entertaining, apart from being so enjoyable to partake.

There were parties; birthdays, engagements, important public holidays and the like, to which she was invited and these provided lots of lively and topical conversation which was both thought-provoking and somewhat frightening when it got around to events in Italy and Germany. She herself had noted the growing anxiety among the outspoken intelligentsia which gathered on the Left Bank about the inevitability of war with the Nazis and that was a bit frightening," she observed before going on with a change of subject.

"You raised a question of 'winning a heart'," she recalled. "Well, there were one or two or more in Paris and another rather serious one - not me, him - in Berne, but I was able to fob them all off before any harm was done by saying I had 'someone' waiting for me back home. Hope you didn't mind me using you like that, Patrick?" she laughed, perhaps, a little shyly.

He didn't reply to what was virtually a question but let it pass and allowed her to proceed uninterrupted as she related intelligently, but with youthful animation, some of the more memorable episodes of her sojourn at the Conservatoire, and then of the very worthwhile period she spent at the exclusive Swiss finishing school in Berne. She concluded this part of her narrative by saying quite seriously.

"All that was just light backdrop to what I was doing over there which was to learn. I gave it my best try and, as I said before, I think I came away from Paris a better musician and that is important to me. After all, the violin is the most important thing in my life." Then a smile broke across her face as she added almost as an afterthought, "but after you, Patrick, of course."

Once again he let the leading remark pass but at the same time he realised it gave him no great displeasure to hear it. Normally, such conversation wouldn't have interested him in the least. There were always too many other things on his mind for it to tolerate what previously he would have considered as girlish prattle. But, for some reason which he could not quite fathom, he was intrigued by the great change he saw in this girl and it must be that which captured his whole-hearted attention. Or so he thought.

Neither of them appeared to notice time slipping away, for when the daylight started to fail there was no thought given to turning on the switch, even though it was in easy reach of his chair.

She leant forward with anticipation as she turned the conversation on to him and told of the glowing report she received from her mother of the concerto with the Con orchestra. She was keen to know about the rehearsal with the SSO of which a friend had written her but without detail.

That was enough for him to break the mood of their exchange by switching on the light. He did not know what was happening to him and needed to pull himself together as he was becoming far too interested in the charming and attractive female sitting in front of him.

"Look at the time," he said, with real surprise. "You better get on home. It's well after six and the family will be wondering where you are."

"No they won't," she came back, "I told them I would be staying in town for dinner."

"Oh! That's alright then. What time is that?" he asked.

"Well, that's up to you; you're taking me, Patrick?" she replied.

"I'm what?" he said with his eyes wide open staring at her in disbelief.

"Look, Sheridan," she said quietly but firmly, "whether you like it or not, I've got a crush on you which has lasted for a long time and a girl could grow old waiting for a response from a cold-hearted piano player like you. Apart from the crush I want to know if I like you and you taking me to dinner would be a start to me finding out." He pretended to be shocked into silence and looked at her with a stern, stony glare but exploded into laughter when she added with a little girl's plaintive voice, "Please."

"You're a bit of a nuisance, you know," he said. "I was going home early tonight to work. I have a long job to complete before I go away and haven't time to socialise with anyone, even if they are slightly attractive."

"What job? Where are you going?" she asked with a note of real concern in her voice.

"Not now. I'll tell you over dinner," he said as he reached into his pocket and produced some change. Selecting two pennies, he said to her, "Here's tuppence. Telephone your mother from the foyer and tell her I'm taking you to dinner and you will be home by nine o'clock. I'll join you at the front door when I've cleared away here."

"She knows you are taking me," she informed him, "I told her before I left home, but I will call and say I'll be in by nine." And before he could respond she contrived a smug grin, picked up her bag and gloves and left the studio with high heels clicking again as she made her way up the hallway.

He took her to the elegant dining room at Usher's Hotel where he and Irene ate meals when she was in town. It was a little crowded tonight but the *maître de* found them a good table near a window and at a pleasant distance from the piano in the centre of the room, which was being softly played by a motherly-looking older woman.

They ordered from a comprehensive menu and she told him how she missed the good table wines she'd enjoyed when dining out in Paris. That's not done here, he told her. Nobody drinks wine with meals although there is nothing wrong with an occasional after-dinner port or a sherry. When the meal arrived she leant forward and touched him on the arm and inquired.

"Now, tell me quickly about this work you are doing and what is this about you going away?"

He looked across the white, glistening table at her and found it a harmonious sight. He was inwardly pleased she should show such interest in him and he noticed how her face fell when he told her he was leaving in a few months to study in Europe.

"How long will you be away? Do you intend to come back at all?" she asked a little incredulously.

"I really don't know, Cath. My coach at Heidelberg is Hans Nienarber who's also some kind of an unofficial talent indicator for the international concert set.

"Should he give me the nod, I am told, I could pick up worthwhile engagements in Europe almost immediately. I'm looking to Julian Morrison for advice and he thinks I should come back here after Heidelberg and do a full season of recitals for the ABC as a start to a career. They've made a tentative offer, whether I go or not to Heidelberg, but if I should receive an attractive approach over there it would be hard to refuse because if I'm to succeed, that's where my future would lie as a pianist."

All this and much more came out during the meal. He had her undivided attention as he continued to talk about his ambitions. During a brief silence as they ate, he considered he had never done this before, not even with his mother or his mentor. So why, he asked himself, did he find it so important to share these things with this girl whom he had known, really, only briefly.

It half-occurred to him he might be smitten for he had read of such things, but that could never happen. He would not allow it. She may have beguiled him but it would only be a quickly passing thing and would not constitute a threat to the regimented life he had chosen for himself of necessity.

He was becoming embarrassed and turned the subject by asking, "What do you plan to do with your fiddle now?"

"I think I've got into the SSO and should commence rehearsing with its First Violins at the beginning of the next year. Until then I'll just practice and work in Daddy's office to earn some pocket-money. It is not quite final. I have another interview to attend with the Concert-Master but have been given to understand it is just a formality."

"That's great, Jordan. You have achieved your goal and congratulations are truly in order - well done!" and, as if to emphasise his words, he did a most un-Patrick-like thing by reaching across and gently touching her hand, which happened to be resting on the edge of their table.

"Well," she said, "that just one of nicest things you have ever said and done and makes all the hard work seem worthwhile," was her wistful comment on his gesture. "The trouble is, my good Irish friend, I had a wonderful dream about you attending all 'my' SSO concerts and then taking me to supper afterwards and we would find out where such trysts would lead us. Now, you are taking off and leaving me alone and the prospect makes me very sad, Patrick. I've thought such a lot about you over the past two years and I know I never even crossed your mind in that time, but I did not think the infatuation I had for my pianist would have to end in such a way."

"I'm afraid that's the way things are, Cath. Perhaps when I come back?" he offered.

"You won't come back," she said a little sadly. "Those sophisticated Continentals will seduce you. I know, I've been there and the things they have to offer talent like yours cannot be refused. No! I will probably never see you again."

"Don't be too sure about that," he replied "I'm coming back whatever happens. If I'm to be a recitalist it will only be for a few years; that will be enough for me and after that it's back to Magdalene. My real yen is to write music not just to play it and I can't think of a better place to do it than in the heart of the Australian bush. So that's for me; then it will be 'Mozart, look out'," he added lightly.

"You know," he went on, "there's an elevation on our property, well away from the homestead, that commands beaut distant views and I intend to build a house there one day, with wide verandas surrounding it and enormous windows looking out in every direction. It is something I have dreamed about since I was a kid and I don't know why I'm telling you these things, girl."

"You tell me because you know I'm interested and that's all there is to it. Tell me, do you plan to live alone in your house or will it just be some kind of monastery?" she asked.

"Composing is a pretty monk-like occupation but we will have to see about that," he said with a tender smile. "You better finish up your coffee if I'm to get you home by nine."

On their way up to the Loop after leaving the hotel he took her hand in his and held it lightly as they walked along in rather companionable silence.

"How far do you have to walk when you get off the tram?" he asked.

"About a quarter of a mile, a hop, skip and a jump," she answered.

"That's too far on your own at this time of night, I'll put you in a cab," he advised, "you can't be too careful, you know?"

"If you say so, Patrick, that would be nice as I have had a long day. But it has been a wonderful day for me, especially this last part. I am sorry I was so forward with you but you have been on my mind for a long time and I had to do something about it. I hope you understand that what I did was not like me and I certainly won't do it again. If ever we go out again it will be because you asked me."

"You are absolutely right about that. Miss Jordan, I could not agree with you more," he said dismissively. "By the way, what is your telephone number at home? I feel responsible for you tonight and want to make sure you get home safely."

She reached into her handbag before handing him her father's business card which bore both his home and business number.

As they approached the cab rank near Museum Station they stopped and he looked down at her. "I have to tell you, Cathy, you are a delight in so many ways but so full of surprises and, in case you are interested, for some strange reason I enjoyed being with you. You say you have been waiting a long time to see me and I can tell you I've been wanting to do this all night," and he took her lightly in his arms, kissed her gently on the lips, then put her into the waiting cab and watched it drive away.

He decided to walk home as he thought the hour and a half or so it took would be a good time to mull over the stage he had reached with the fourth movement of his symphony. I enjoyed this evening, he thought, and it was a great break from the normal routine. She's a nice kid and quite good company and it was a pity he did not have any spare time to spend with her in the immediate future. He would give her a call in a couple of weeks' time and see how she got on with her SSO interview. As he continued to walk he turned his mind to his opus.

He was battling with a passage for the brass when she rudely interrupted him with that first apparition in the doorway of the studio. He shrugged her off quickly and got his mind back to his music when she blocked him again with the sad look she had on her face when he told her he was going away. She kept the intermittent disruptions up for the rest of the journey and he found when he reached Pine Trees his work had not progressed a single note. It was nearly midnight when he finally got to bed and the 'darn woman' was still dominating his thoughts. I must be a bit tired, he concluded. All this nonsense will go when I get up in the morning and I can get back to work without interruption. It was a positive thought but very wide of the mark as he would find out in the weeks to come. Before he dozed off it was with a slight sense of guilt he realised he had not called to see if she got home safely.

Chapter 20

On a cold morning in August, 1939, it was a slightly disconsolate Patrick Sheridan who got off the tram and walked along College Street on his way to attend Mass at St. Mary's Cathedral. It was the 15th, the Feast of the Assumption, and the date upon which he made his first holy communion at the little church hall at The Gap all those years ago. The flame of his Catholic faith, flickering but not extinguished, was still sufficient for him to recall the occasion as a very happy day in his life. His attendance at Mass on this 'Holy Day of Obligation' was his way of doing so.

He was feeling despondent as he had been unable to overcome the preoccupation he appeared to have for Catherine Jordan. It was as though she had cast a spell over him for she was so frequently on his mind in waking hours and, try as he might, he could not shake it off. It had become a distraction to his music, particularly when composing, and this concerned him greatly - he was at a loss to know what to do about it.

It was nearly a week now since their night at Usher's and he had resisted an insistent urge to contact her since, for he felt to do so could lead to a relationship far too binding and demanding for him to accept. He would never admit to himself it was something like love at first sight for the new Cathy. That was the root of his dilemma or that, eventually, he would have to yield and make his way to her side.

After Mass he headed to his studio at the Conservatorium and, on arriving, slumped into one of the chairs and began to think. There was now something else occupying his senses which was so important it relegated Cathy, albeit briefly, to the back of his mind. This new problem had to do with his immediate future and the possible fate of his career as a pianist.

For several months now he had kept up with the political situation in Europe through the columns of The Herald, mostly read during the tram ride to the city each morning. He had seen Germany's road to war progress through The Ruhr, Austria, Czechoslovakia and now the Danzig Corridor and confrontation with Poland.

But the Allies, England and France, had already drawn a line in the sand which insisted they could not and would not tolerate this, or any future territorial demand, made by Nazi Germany

When he stepped off the tram this morning, he was convinced in his own mind that Hitler would never give way and war was, therefore, inevitable. He reflected briefly what an unspeakable calamity this would be for Europe and the World but then, quite humanly, became concerned as to how it would affect him, personally. No Heidelberg and a lost opportunity for commencing a concert career in great cities of Europe.

He was devastated and his disappointment was manifest as he sat there and contemplated where he would go from here. Even if war was not declared before their intended departure date, Germany was so dangerous a country right now he would not even consider taking his mother there. No, Heidelberg for him was dead and buried!

He would talk with Julian Morrison and seek his advice. Perhaps something could be done with the ABC, but what? How long would the war last, anyhow? His career could be 'marking time' for years if the last great conflict was any guide. He had the not-altogether-unpleasant thought of returning to Magdalene to write music and wait out the hostilities there, but this would mean abandoning all the great plans he and Irene had for his future as a pianist.

It did not cross his mind, just then, that Australia could be involved in this conflict as it seemed too far from where the fighting would actually take place.

When he approached Julian Morrison in his room later that afternoon, he found him in agreement with his assessment of the situation in Europe, not to the extent that a war was imminent but that Germany was no place to visit at the present time. He would cable Dr Nienarber accordingly.

"As to your career, son," he said, "there would be offers, undoubtedly, from the Australian Broadcasting Commission which would have to be considered and, if acceptable, could take care of the whole of 1940 for you. Then you would just have to wait and see what happens after that.

"Mind you," he said, "if the war does come there is no way overseas artists could get here in safety, so you could see yourself very much in demand, and not only by the ABC. Tates and Williamsons would have to be interested also but that could put you on a long-running Australian roundabout which may not be the best way to start your career. I suggest you just wait and see what happens over there and then play it by ear. I'll let you know what the ABC says just as soon as I hear," he concluded.

"Thanks for that," said Patrick. "I'll heed your advice, Professor. I had thought I might go home to Magdalene and wait the war out there. I could keep up the piano and it would give me an opportunity to attempt writing some serious music."

"I wouldn't do that, Patrick," said Julian Morrison quite sharply, "I think it imperative you stay around the music heart of things in Sydney as it would be too easy to drop out of sight of the people who could play an important part in your career in such changed circumstances. As I said before, just play it by ear.

"I'm sorry all this has happened as I know how bitterly disappointed you must be. I do hope everything turns out well in the long run and that, eventually, you will have the career you so certainly deserve. You should tell your mother of our talk and pass on my regrets that things turned out this way. One thing I would like you to know, Patrick, is that I am always here to help you in any way I can."

Patrick thanked him again and left his room, not much clearer in his mind about things, but somewhat relieved he had cleared the air with his professor.

He decided he should let his mother know his decision straight away and when he left his studio that evening went to the GPO and booked a trunk call. Irene was quite dismayed but not altogether surprised as the European news had been on the radio and the recent happenings there had been alarming enough to receive front page coverage in the Bathurst Times.

"We'll see what happens, Mum. It may settle down but it's not likely. The problem then would be whether or not Nienarber could take me. I read in the paper there's been lots of cancellations of bookings for England so there shouldn't be a problem getting a refund of our fares."

They continued to talk for some time, with him, as usual, answering Irene's many questions about himself and his work. She agreed they should wait to see what the immediate future held before making any decision about the future direction of his career. After a few words with Tom, who said what a 'crook deal' it was about Heidelberg but agreed with the cancellation, he hung up and left the Post Office, just as the clock in its tower struck six. He would not walk home tonight and would instead take the tram as he intended to be back at Pine Trees in time for the evening meal.

As soon as he took his seat in the tram his thoughts turned to Cathy Jordan when he realised she would be the one person who'd be happy with the abandonment of his proposed European sojourn. He kept thinking about her, intermittently, for the rest of the journey and by the time he got off the tram at Centennial Park he knew what he must do.

He walked to a public telephone booth which was adjacent to the tram stop and taking her father's card from his wallet, inserted two pennies and dialled the home number. He recognised her voice from just the 'hello' at the other end.

"Hello yourself there, Cathy," he said casually, "it's Pat Sheridan. How are you going?"

There was quite a pause before she replied in a half-broken and somewhat subdued voice.

"Is that really you, Pat? I didn't think I'd ever hear from you again."

"And why not?" he asked with forced emphasis.

"I made such a fool of myself the other night and I knew how you would have resented it and thought I'd be the last person in the world you'd want to see," she said as tears began to appear.

"Oh, not at all, Cathy?" he said, in a kind, sympathetic voice, "I enjoyed every minute of it and, in fact, I'd like to see you again."

Once more there was a pause before she answered in a voice which seemed to have shaken off the tears,

"Are you really serious about wanting to see me again?"

"Of course I am! That's what I've rung about. In the canteen today some of the kids were raving about a picture called 'Intermezzo' which is on at Hoyts. Apparently, it's about an acclaimed violinist who leaves his wife to take up with his accompanist. Sound interesting? The music is supposed to be good and played by somebody named Kreisler. Would you like to see it with me?"

"I don't know about you, Sheridan," she responded cheekily. "You take me out and then I don't hear from you for a week and I start preparing for spinsterhood and here you are out of the blue. Of course, yes, I would love to go with you, but please promise to hold my hand through the picture."

"That's great, I'm glad you can come. I don't know about that hand holding business though - next thing you will be wanting me to kiss you and we can't have any of that, can we? Being Friday, there is a five o'clock shoppers' session and perhaps we could have a bite to eat afterwards. What do you think?"

"About the kissing, you mean?" she asked in her old cheeky voice. "I'm teasing. I know what you mean, my dear young man. I'll be outside Hoyts about ten to as it's near Daddy's office and I'm working there tomorrow afternoon."

"See you then Jordan, and do try to behave," he said laughingly. "Oh, by the way, I forgot to tell you. Heidelberg is off. It would be too dangerous there for my mother with that ratbag Hitler on the loose. I would like to go on my own but she won't hear of it, so the whole thing's cancelled. Now, it looks as though I will be about the place for some time yet."

There was a pause and she replied, "Oh, Pat, personal feelings aside, I'm so sad to hear that. I know how much it meant to you," she said seriously sincere. "It will probably mean some delay to the start of your career, but that's all it will be, just a delay, because nothing and nobody can stop you, my Mr. Sheridan. You must be so disappointed and I wish I was there now to give you a big hug. I'm so sorry, Pat."

"You do go on a bit, Cath, but I'll talk to you about it tomorrow." He hung up and began the short walk home to Pine Trees.

Well, I've done it, he thought to himself. Talk about the best laid plans of mice and men. Yesterday, my future was secure, everything was in place with no commitments other than to my future with music and the piano. Today, I don't know where I'm going and I think I've just taken a major distraction on board.

He smiled when he thought about that. The life he had led since leaving Magdalene was of necessity devoid of any real emotional warmth such as he had experienced with his parents at the family homestead, with the Becks and his friends at school in Bathurst, and from the wise and friendly Sister Annunciata. He had just decided while on the tram that he was the kind of person who needed such contact and it was something he had not experienced in Sydney until that recent evening with Cathy Jordan. Her presence seemed to spread over him that evening and, despite the distraction it could cause to his work, he could not let her go. He just seemed to need her and that's all there was to it.

"So be it!" was his final thought before entering the gate to the guest house and, going inside, he sat down with his fellow boarders and enjoyed the meal and their company as never before.

Chapter 21

There was such upheaval to his regulated life in so short a time, the young musician from Bathurst was left quite bemused. Until recently, there had been a void in his life which he had felt rather than recognised. This now had been filled and to an extent he was a different person since the return of Catherine Jordan.

They had seen each other on occasions in the fortnight that had elapsed since he had taken her to 'Intermezzo' and there were telephone calls originating from him. Strangely, it had not unduly affected his music, rather, perhaps, to the contrary. Professor Morrison was moved to say to him recently, with a twinkle in his eye, that his playing had taken on an added dimension, especially when those romantic fellows, Johannes Brahms or Fredric Chopin, were about the place.

A looming problem for him had been the requirement to quit the Conservatorium before the end of the year, which meant, amongst other things, he would have no place to practise unless he made other arrangements.

When this first dawned upon him he mentioned it to Charles Jermyn who had told him some days later that, quite fortuitously, he had learnt of a friend's flat at Elizabeth Bay which was to become vacant early in the New Year. It was a ground floor, two bedroom unit with its own small courtyard, fully furnished in a solid, old fashioned style but, most importantly, included a piano. Jermyn did not know the make or the condition it was in but, at least, it was a piano.

Patrick jumped at the opportunity as for some time he had recognised the need of a place of his own which would enable him to practise and write music in an appropriate surrounding. He asked Jermyn if he could have a day or two to decide and, before looking at the place, rang Magdalene and spoke to his father to discuss the additional expense involved.

After outlining things to his father, he said, "I hate asking, Dad, but I intend to repay you for all it has cost down here."

He started to explain and was about to go on when his father interrupted. "Forget it, son," said Tom Sheridan laconically, "that's what money's for. Of course, it's okay and I'll get the bank on to it right away. Pay it back if you like but it's not important as I am glad to have been of some help.

"Your mother says you're coming home for a while in December and I'll look forward to that, son. You better talk to her now and tell her about your flat idea." Irene had misgivings about the move. Who would do his cooking, cleaning and laundry?

"You certainly don't know about those things, Patrick..." she lamented.

But he told her not to worry as he would cope. She wanted to come down to look the place over but again he told her he would have to decide no later than today after inspecting the unit. When he hung up he knew she was not happy about him leaving Pine Trees and he also knew she would have a lot more to say about the move before it took place.

It was every bit as good as Jermyn had indicated and eminently suitable for his needs. The piano was a well-known German make with a solid iron frame and fairly good tone but was in need of tuning, which was not a problem. The timing was perfect - the flat would be available from mid-January which meant he could move in after leaving Pine Trees in December and then spending the intervening weeks at home at Magdalene.

His concerns were becoming fewer now except for the major item of how to establish his career as a concert pianist without the Heidelberg launching pad. He was waiting to hear, through Julian Morrison, from the Australian Broadcasting Commission as to what they could offer him for next year.

An understanding between the mentor and the student had also undergone a change. When they discussed the matter of the ABC earlier in the week, Morrison told him whilst he was still quite prepared to continue handling the discussions with the broadcaster, he thought it time Patrick took these matters into his own hands. He had developed a mature approach in such matters and knew exactly what he wanted and he, therefore, would make the final decision when it was reached anyhow.

"You'll know where you stand with them then," he said. "I expect they'll contact me sometime soon about their plans for you and I'll then inform them that you personally will handle all future discussions. I think you're in the box seat as they should be concerned about getting overseas guest artists in light of the state of things in Europe. You are more than capable of handling these things yourself but I want to reiterate, I'm more than interested in what you decide to do, so please understand I'm here to help in any way I can. Is that alright with you?"

"I don't have any problem with that, Professor. I'm fully aware of the way I have imposed on your time and I'm happy to lighten that load in this way. Certainly I can take it from here knowing you're not far away. If the ABC offer is worthwhile I can start thinking about engaging some kind of impresario to handle things, if and when it seems appropriate." That is the way things stood and Patrick was reasonably optimistic about his future

However, he was unable to take into consideration a coming event which would dominate the lives of people throughout the world for years to come.

It was late on a Friday afternoon during the first week of September, 1939, when Julian Morrison burst into the studio.

"Quick, Pat, turn on the wireless," he stammered, quite out of breath, "my wife just rang to say Neville Chamberlain is about to make a statement on the BBC."

The British Prime Minister, in gravest of tone, gave a brief preamble concerning the German invasion of Poland and of how it had ignored the Allies' ultimatum to withdraw by the required time and date, "and, therefore, this Country is now in a state of war with Germany."

As Patrick stood there beside Julian, he was watching his mentor. As the Prime Minister uttered those final words, he appeared to droop and, with shoulders sagged forward and a now haggard face, he became a figure of total despair.

As an Englishman he had lived through the 'War to end all Wars' when three million of his young British contemporaries were slain on the battlefields of France. He still had many close relatives and friends in the Old Country and dreaded the thought of what fate may now have in store for them.

Julian left the studio without another word and Patrick was left to his own thoughts. He had enough Irish blood in his veins not to be too concerned for the British, but after reading and hearing of the speed at which the Nazis had swept through Poland he had the awful thought that they could conquer the rest of Europe. That would have serious consequences for Australia, which was virtually unarmed, and if it were cut off from the Mother Country and the rest of the Empire, would be quite defenceless. Only last week he had listened to the ABC when a panel of military experts discussed the possibility of war in Europe and what that could mean to our country. It gave emphasis to what the situation in the Middle East could be if, as was highly likely, Italy joined forces with Germany in the event of a conflict.

Apparently, the Italians had over half a million troops stationed in Libya and Ethiopia, whereas the British only had a skeleton force for the entire Western Desert. The point they were making was that the Italians, using those forces, would be able to overrun Egypt and take the Suez Canal in the process. This would isolate the Sub-Continent, Singapore, Malaya, Hong Kong and Australia and New Zealand and these places would just wither on the vine until the Axis Powers got around to occupying them. Such were the thoughts running at random through his mind after hearing the declaration. What he was endeavouring to determine for himself was whether or not the outbreak of war in Europe really constituted an armed threat to his own country.

If the answer to that had been 'yes', he would have known where his duty lay and would have acted accordingly. But the opinion he reached was to wait and see how the war progressed in Europe before doing anything. Hopefully, by then there would prove to be no need to feel concern for Australia's security.

After leaving the studio he deliberately switched off from the war and turned his head to happier, lighter thoughts. Shortly, he would be meeting Cathy for dinner and afterwards, so as to honour a long standing promise, take her dancing at The Trocadero. He had declined at first and told her it was no place for young ladies from the Eastern Suburbs and her mother would not approve. She boohooed that and said many of her friends went to The Troc on Friday nights, and it was quite a respectable place of enjoyment for normal young people.

As they dined, they discussed more serious subjects than usual. The war, of course, and the immediate concern she had for her brothers and the possibility of them becoming involved. Patrick did not tell her then of how he felt about the matter as that would only add to her concern. Instead, he changed the subject to the recent confirmation of her appointment to the first violin section of the Sydney Symphony Orchestra. She was to commence early in the New Year and had begun a daily practise routine to make sure she remained on top of her instrument. He spoke warmly and encouragingly about all she had achieved and pointed out she would be one of the youngest players in the important ensemble. Until she met Patrick, the violin was the only thing in life Cathy had taken seriously. She was looking forward to the role she would soon play in the profoundest way of performing classical music.

She knew of Patrick's changed career plans and of how he was waiting to hear what the ABC would come up with - and that this may be sooner than expected now that war had actually been declared.

"You're going to have a lot of time on your hands when you finish at the Con, my boy, what will you do?"

"With the piano around my neck I will never have a lot of spare time. It's like your violin - pretty demanding in its way," he replied, "so there will be the usual daily slog for a start. I'll only accept worthwhile engagements, Cath, and if these don't eventuate, I'll go back to Magdalene and try to write some decent music The war in Europe can't last forever!"

He did not see the slightly shocked look on her face as he imparted his intentions but became aware she was staring quite forlornly at him.

"You mean you could take off for Bathurst and just leave me here," she retorted, and he then realised what he had said.

"Of course not, Cath," he replied, "I'd thought about getting Dad to take you on as a jillaroo and we could then see each other now and then," he replied with light sarcasm and then more gently added, "you belong to the SSO now, girl, and that demands you be down here. We would just have to work something out if I do go back home"

There was a small tear on her cheek as she gazed across the table at him with a soulful look in her dark blue eyes.

"Let's get this straight, Pat Sheridan," she intoned rather wistfully. "A few weeks back I told you I had a crush on you but wanted to find out if I liked you. Well, I have found out, and I do like you but I'm afraid it is more than that, for I find myself in love with you in the worst possible way. So, if it became a choice between you and the SSO, you would win hands down."

He had noticed she was upset and had reached over and taken her hand in his. It was occasions like this when his shyness returned. As she finished speaking, he was staring down at the white tablecloth.

For a moment or two he stayed like that and then looked up at her serious face and said, "Well, I'm afraid we are in a hell of a mess, Cathy, because I feel exactly the same way."

He stood up quickly and went across to the cashier and settled the bill. Coming back to the table, he took her by the arm and left the restaurant. He walked her briskly down the street until they came to a darkened doorway, where they stood whilst he took her in his arms and kissed her long and gently through moments of ecstasy the like of which neither of them had previously experienced. They danced some dream like hours away at The Trocadero where they blended into one. For them, there was no one else on the crowded floor and the artistry of her dancing learnt at the school in Switzerland was complimented by his unerring ability to take the right step in full harmony with the band. They did not talk much as she danced entranced, with her eyes closed, whilst he was unable to look elsewhere than at what he considered to be the very beautiful features of his beloved partner.

He accompanied her home in a taxi cab and, whilst still holding her hand, gently placed her to the other side of back seat before telling her with a smirk that he was avoiding the occasion of sin.

Her only response to that had been... "Meany."

He dismissed the cab and they walked to the wide front gate of the Jordan home where, after another long, lingering kiss he watched her go up the paved pathway and, after a final, long wave of her gloved hand, disappear through the front door of the near-darkened house.

As he made his way home to Pine Trees, by foot and public transport, his music for once did not occupy his mind.

It was fully taken up with thoughts of the beautiful girl with whom he had just spent several innocent, tender and intoxicating hours. The joint declaration of their feelings for each other had been an unexpected and emotional bombshell - an experience he would never forget. Their dancing together had been like a long pleasant dream and the sublime togetherness and closeness of their bodies was something he could still feel.

Before reaching his lodgings he had the realisation there now was a new dimension to their relationship and one which could cause all kinds of problems unless it was handled with caution. The intimacy of the dance had made manifest the physical attraction they held for each other and to the extent they had not found it necessary to put it into words, they both just knew.

He thought he had the natural instincts and desires common to most young men of his age but he had also been carefully taught by the Marist Brothers and his Confessors that such feelings must be curbed and repressed until one was in a wedded state. In his senior years at school he had been told time and again that Catholic religious were called upon to practise celibacy for their entire lifetimes whilst the laity were required to do it only for a few short years. Surely, this law was not asking too much of them and, besides, it was a serious mortal sin not to comply with the Church's interpretation of God's Eighth Commandment given to Moses, "Thou shalt not commit adultery."

He believed the teachings but nevertheless realised it would take all the power of his will to repress his inclinations under circumstances which would certainly arise during their courtship. And, even then, he thought, he might not be strong enough to withstand the temptation.

His need to restrain himself was assisted by the knowledge that, despite the slight touch of sophistication she acquired in France, she was young and vulnerable and to make love to her, and compromise her purity, would be an act of desecration in his opinion. He knew he could not abide that despite now being aware of her willingness to give herself to him.

Marriage was out of the question for it would mean abandoning both their careers and render years of hard work to being worthless. He could not earn a living as a pianist at the present time and the alternative would be, if he married, to return to Bathurst and manage the family property - which would mean depriving her of her ambition to play with the SSO.

No. Marriage was out of the question, he concluded as he opened the front gate and ended another long, thought laden walk. In any event her long term interests were paramount to him and if it meant making emotional sacrifices and she being disappointed in the short term, then that's the way it would have to be.

Chapter 22

*P*erhaps it was the realisation that only a few months of his student tenure remained at the Conservatorium that drove Patrick and Professor Morrison to accomplish as much as possible in their final sessions together. Morrison now was introducing him to a wider range of the more modern composers, not only to extend his repertoire but also to expose him to the structural changes which had occurred in the composition of classical music.

At some sessions, Morrison would simply listen as Patrick played major works and would, when he thought necessary, interrupt to ask why certain passages had been interpreted in such a way. Patrick usually had sound reasons but if the Professor did not agree, they would discuss it before proceeding.

The young pianist found these pauses enlightening for a lot more came out of them than just a resolution of the passage under discussion, with the gifted teacher giving points of view which reflected his total mastery of the art of the pianoforte. It was on such occasions Patrick realised just how much he owed this man for all he had taught him in two short years. He knew he would be ever grateful.

It was a morning in late November when Patrick came to the Professor's room to show him a letter he had just received from the ABC asking him to make an appointment to meet with the General Manager at a convenient time during the following week. The Concert Manager and the Director of Music would be present also, with a view to discussing the possibility of a performance agreement.

"Congratulations, Patrick!" said his mentor after reading the missive, "this is wonderful. They did not presume to ask for an audition and have obviously accepted what Bill Lawson and I have been telling them. You are more than ready for this, son, and they are, indeed, fortunate to have you available at this particular time. I'm sure they realise this and will make you an offer which you will find acceptable. They are very decent people to deal with and won't muck you about."

They stood there discussing this turn of events and Patrick thanked him for the considerable part he had played bringing it about, and said he would be in touch with him as soon as possible after the interview.

It turned out the offer was everything he had hoped for and more than he expected. He was able to restrain himself and instead of giving, as he wanted to, an excited and immediate 'yes', he raised minor points and appeared to ponder, at times, the salient points of the proposal. The remuneration, which was not important to him at this stage, would be sufficient to repay his father and also provide a financial cushion until his next professional engagement, provided that was not too far in the future. But it was the programme schedule and itinerary which excited the young pianist.

He was to be the principal performer for the ABC's 'Winter Series of Concerts', with two recitals in Sydney and two in Melbourne, and one in Brisbane, Adelaide, Perth and Hobart. In addition there would be two concerto performances with each of the ABC's Sydney, Brisbane and Melbourne symphony orchestras. The General Manager made a point of advising him all his performances would be broadcast live throughout Australia through the ABC's wireless network and took it for granted Patrick would appreciate how much that wide exposure could benefit him in this early part of his career.

It was arranged he would discuss the works he would play for the recitals with the Musical Director at an early date, at which time he would be advised of the concertos to be performed with the state orchestras. The only other requirement of the very simple agreement, yet to be drawn up, was that the Commission would have an option on his services for the following year with the stipulation such option be exercised, or otherwise, prior to the expiration of this contact.

The Commission undertook to send to him a binding letter of intent within a day or so, in accordance with their discussions. But for budgetary and administrative reasons a formal contract would not be available for his signature until the beginning of February next year. His first performance would be the concerto with the Melbourne Symphony Orchestra scheduled for early May next year in the Melbourne Town Hall.

With all this on the table, Patrick thanked the GM and his two colleagues and confirmed he would be pleased to accept their offer and that he would look forward to working with them in the New Year. They shook hands before Patrick left the meeting with the understanding they would get together again just as soon as the Christmas and New Year festive season was out of the way.

Just to get it over with, he phoned his mother before returning to the Con and told her of the turn of events. As usual she elicited every detail from him, with her pleasure and excitement mounting with every detail. Before they hung up she stated firmly she would go to Melbourne for the first performance and perhaps Tom would come too as he was in a much better state of health these days. It crossed his mind just then that he had not yet told his mother about Cathy and thought it might be an idea if he brought them together on that significant occasion - and then shuddered to think how she would react upon learning there was another woman in his life. Cathy, when he rang her immediately after his mother, was, of course, highly delighted.

"That's wonderful news, darling," she enthused "as I know this is just a beginning to a great career and, whether you like it or not, I'll always be there to help you on your way. Never forget how good you are, Pat, and that one day you will have the whole musical world at your feet. I'm very proud of you my good man and can't wait to give you a 'well done' kiss. I hope those bods at the ABC know how lucky they are to have you for next year."

He thanked her for letting him get a word in edge ways and, before saying goodbye, told her of tickets he had been given for '*Maid of the Mountains*', featuring Our Glad at the Theatre Royal. They are for tomorrow night, he said, and asked if she would like to go.

"Would I ever," she replied "how wonderful, it's a great musical. She sings what is now my favourite song, Love will find a way and, my dear boy, you better believe that."

Julian Morrison was out at a meeting at the time Patrick got back to the Conservatorium and later that afternoon came into the studio and asked, "Well, how did it go?" and his young pupil told him.

"Your talent has been recognised, Patrick," he said. "It was inevitable, of course, and just a matter of time, but the day has arrived and I'm delighted for you. You are not only the best student I have ever had the pleasure of coaching, but also the hardest-working, and you are starting to reap your just reward.

"It is unfortunate about the war," he went on, "I know you had set your heart on starting a career on the larger European stage and that's been disappointing for you. Nevertheless, this is a wonderful opportunity and Australia is not such a backwater as to prevent parts of the international music world learning of your exploits with the Commission next year. It is almost certain the BBC will take some of the broadcasts, particularly those from Melbourne and Sydney. You are well and truly on your way."

The student just stood there calmly looking at his mentor as he uttered those words, accepting the generous praise. Such accolades coming from anyone else would have been mildly pleasing but when they were obviously the heartfelt opinion of such an eminent and scholarly musician, Patrick realised he had the right to assume that one day he could become an important international pianist.

With the Professor back in his rooms, Patrick went to the piano to complete an adequate practise period for the day and then spent what were always fleeting hours with his symphony, the final movement of which was giving him trouble. There was something elusive about this part of the opus which demanded constant rewriting and had prevented him bringing the entire work to conclusion.

He would not compromise. The first three movements had simply flowed from him and he was satisfied with them, but it was not so with what he had written so far of the final stanza and he would persist until he was. He did not accept the reason for the problem could be his mind had been elsewhere because of several distractions including

Cathy Jordan, Heidelberg, the ABC, leaving Pine Trees and how and where was he going to spend the six months between leaving the Conservatorium and commencing his engagements with the ABC. He had long contended that a composer must be capable of dismissing everything else from his mind if he was to write music to which people would wish to listen and, unless he could do that, he would be wasting his time. There was no room for any excuse what so ever.

It was in the late afternoon when he finally let himself out of the studio and was walking along the hallway when he noticed the light still burning in Charles Jermyn's office. He knocked and went in to find the Doctor sitting at a desk littered with papers and files and realised he must be reviewing the applications of the many students who wanted to enrol at the Conservatorium next year.

Immediately he saw Patrick he got up and, smiling broadly, extended his arm as he came over to the student. Taking his hand, he pumped it with great warmth.

"Congratulations, I've heard your news. Apparently it caused a buzz at the ABC and a friend in their Music Department just rang and wanted to know who this boy genius was the Commission had signed up for next year. How do you feel about it?" he asked. "Pretty good, I guess."

"Pretty good is right" said Patrick. "I thought I would be a little apprehensive at the prospect but I find I am rather looking forward to it all."

"That's because you are good and you know it and without the burden of conceit. This is a big step for you, Pat, and, whether you realise it or not, you are going to need a degree of support until your career gets under way. When I heard the news I decided I would speak to Julian in that regard to see what the Conservatorium could do to help you. After all, there is reflected glory in this for us and the least we can do is to express our gratitude in some material manner."

"Well, thanks a lot for that, Charles. I realise already I'm going to need some help before this is all over. I will no longer be a student here but I'll be able to practise and rehearse at the Elizabeth Bay flat when I move in there. However, I think I will need a little more than that if I am to keep in touch with the essential requirements of what lies ahead of me."

"Say no more. I know what you mean. Leave it to me and I can assure you all our people and our facilities will be available to you at any time you want to use them.

"I do want to add to that, Pat, because I've been giving it a bit of thought since I realised some time back the ABC would be sure to chase you. Now, you are going to be pretty much on your own down here and I'm of the opinion you will need some ongoing support during these early days of your career.

"We should think about a group of your friends including Julian and me, your mother, that orchestra manager fellow you mentioned, your violinist friend and, perhaps, her father as you never know when you will need legal advice. We could be there for you at all times to discuss anything which may come up, personal or otherwise, to interfere with your preparation. Don't consider this another obligation and just think of it as a group who have your interests at heart and want to help in any way they can.

"This is only a suggestion on my part and you don't have to take it up unless you want to. Give it some thought and let me know what you think," he concluded.

"All I can say to that, Charles, is, firstly, it is darn good of you to give me so much consideration, particularly as you always have such a lot on your own plate. And, secondly, I think it a great and very thoughtful idea and I'd be delighted and reassured to know I'd have such a group behind me."

Patrick broke off there before saying, "Look, I can see how busy you are here and I'll get out of your hair and, perhaps, we can speak again when you have more time. I'm very grateful, Charles, and thanks again," he said. After shaking the doctor's hand again in appreciation, he turned and left the office.

All in all it had been another momentous and emotional day in his life and the excitement of it was still with him as he hailed a cab in Macquarie Street to get him to Pine Trees in time for the evening meal. He wanted to share his news with his fellow boarders, who were now his good friends as well. Also, he needed to give formal notice to Marion Cross of his intention to leave her guest house in mid-December, which was only two or three weeks away. It had been a place where he had found peace and contentment.

When he got to the lodgings the meal was not yet on the table, so he went up to his room where another shock was added to his eventful day.

Ken Sheppard had just come out from a shower and was drying himself in front of the wardrobe mirror. He greeted his roommate as he came through the door. "Hello, mate," he said, "you're a bit of a bloody stranger. What brings you home at this hour? Are you feeling alright?"

"Sure, I'm fine, Ken," said Pat. "How are you, son? No, I've got a bit of news and I wanted to tell you lot about it before it got cold," and then informed his friend of what had transpired at the ABC.

"Gee, that's great Sherry. Good on you, mate. You are one of those blokes who work bloody hard at their job and you deserve all you get. I reckon it's great," was the student engineer's response

Patrick then told him he would soon have the room to himself as he would be moving out in a couple of weeks' time.

"It won't be like that, mate. I'll be gone before you. I've joined up, the AIF, and report for induction at Victoria Barracks next week. So how about that?"

"You've what?" said a shocked Patrick. "What about your degree, you have less than a year to go. Are you just going to chuck it in? After all, this war is none of our business despite what R.G. Menzies says. Do you think it important enough to toss away your career and all the work you have done already? After all, our country is not in any danger, is it?"

"You've got it all ballsed up, Pat, but we won't talk about it now. I'm as hungry as a horse so we'll come up here and have a yarn about it after dinner."

Patrick, whilst still in a state of shock, agreed and they went down stairs to the dining room where the others were gathering for their evening meal. Without further ado, Patrick gave them his news, which was greeted with cheers and words of congratulation. Marion Cross came in from the kitchen to see what all the fuss was about. She, more than the others, perhaps, realised what a great achievement this was for the boy and came over and gave him a light hug and a kiss on the cheek. He noticed there was a tear in her eye as she did so.

When the meal was over he spent some time with Marion after giving her his notice. She had been expecting it for some time as she was aware he was coming to the end of his time at the Conservatorium. She told him that whilst she saw very little of him during his stay, it had been a pleasure having him in her house and she wished him well for the future. She asked if he would get in touch with her from time to time to let her know how his career was progressing.

Back in their room Ken was packing and sorting his clothes as he was going home to Newcastle for the weekend and would not be returning to Pine Trees.

"Now tell me where I'm wrong about this war thing," said Patrick. Ken came over and sat on the edge of the bed opposite him.

"First of all, I'm not giving up my career as I'll be able to resume the course where I left off as soon as the army is done with me. As for the war, they talk a lot about it at Uni and it is very much our business. Staff blokes who have studied these things for years reckon the phoney war is nearly over and, once Hitler and Uncle Joe Stalin have finished carving up Poland, the Nazis will go through the rest of Europe like a packet of salts. Musso is just waiting to get the nod from Adolph before joining in and he has strong forces in the Middle East which could mean us losing the Suez Canal and you know what that would mean to us here."

"I've heard of that," said Patrick, "but do you think it likely?"

"You better believe it," he replied. "The Poms have got very little with which to stop them, according to these experts, and what weapons and manpower they have will be concentrated in Europe. They're also of the opinion the Poms are up to a bit of no good so far as we are concerned.

"Australia has been asked by John Bull to raise three full divisions of infantry as quickly as possible. After their initial training here they'll be shipped to Egypt where they'll undergo final training with the British prior to being posted to join the British Expeditionary Force in France. In reality, what the Poms want is some kind of additional force on the ground in the Western Desert, trained or untrained, to try to stop the Italians if they decide to break out. That's how dangerous the situation is there according to these people.

"When you consider that, mate, together with the real possibility of Germany occupying all of Western Europe, including England, you will realise Australia faces a bloody uncertain future."

It was like a bucket of cold water being tossed over him as the young pianist ingested what his friend had just told him. He had been too preoccupied of late with his own affairs to appreciate the parlous state his defenceless country was in, and it created an immediate sense of guilt.

He had seen the long queues outside the Australian Army recruiting depot in Martin Place and elsewhere. The roving recruiting buses were doing fire sale business in the major suburbs, but he had been given to understand this was just an initial surge from legions of unemployed young men, victims of the great depression, seeking a source of income for themselves and their families.

He left Ken Sheppard to his packing and went walking in the night, as he thought more clearly when he was doing so. He dismissed everybody, and everything else, from his mind bar the war. His career, the Conservatorium, the ABC and even Cathy Jordan and Magdalene were relegated as he pondered the new and serious question he had to ask himself.

He considered himself a patriot who had developed a special love of country as soon as he had been of an age to do so. An illustration of continuing affection was his very first, but as yet unfinished, orchestral composition. It was based on his homeland and reflected everything this vast southern land meant to him. The most memorable piece of poetry he had read, even though Rupert Brooke had another country in mind, included the words the sentiments of which he embraced so strongly… 'Breathes there a man with soul so dead?'… And, for him, that said it all.

By the time he got back to the house, some two or so hours later, he had made his decision. He would not act upon it immediately, but soon, for his intended course of action would have consequence for people near and dear to him. It would require both sensitive consideration and timing if he were to soften the impact of it by any possible degree.

He retired for the night and fell into an uneasy sleep but woke in the early hours to be confronted by the prospect of what his intended course of action would mean to him personally. The enormity of it was frightening at first but he forced himself to take a positive view of it. He would not be abandoning his career, he was merely putting it on hold until the war was over when, all being well, he would resume where he had left off - in much the same way as Ken Sheppard and his Engineering Degree.

His quickly dismissed thinking about what could happen to his hands during army service in wartime and, with the typical attitude of most young servicemen, contended to himself, "it won't happen to me."

They had breakfast together the following morning and back in the room again after his friend had finished his packing and was about to leave, they shook hands with the other hand holding each other's shoulder. They said the usual things with slight embarrassment, exchanged home addresses and promised to keep in touch.

"Good luck, Shep," said Patrick as he opened the bedroom door for him, "and by the way, I won't be far behind you so perhaps we will meet up in the desert one day."

"You!" said the Engineer, quite aghast as he dropped his bag to the floor and looking his friend straight in the eye said with anxious concern, "Don't be a bloody fool, Pat, the war is not for blokes like you. You are something special and we can't afford to risk losing a talent like yours. Now don't you muck about, and just tell me you will keep on with the piano."

"You can go to buggery, Sheppard," said Patrick with a laugh, "what do you mean the war is not for blokes like me? Do you think I'm a suede shoe or something? I don't expect anybody to do my fighting for me. The only job I've ever held down was that of stockman and when the Army asks 'what was my civilian occupation?' that's what I'll tell them. Look, mate, I don't want to appear noble but you told me the country is in trouble and I realise that now and nothing is going to stop me doing my bit. I've been half thinking about it for some time and tonight I have made up my mind." He paused before concluding, "By the way, don't mention this when you go down stairs as nobody else knows and I don't want it to get out before I've had a chance to tell my parents and a few other people. I hope all go well for you, Shep, good luck!"

"You're hopeless Sheridan and there is nothing I can do about it, apparently," he replied as, resignedly, he picked his case again and started down the stairs with his final words. "See you, mate!"

He closed the door and sat down on the edge of the bed. With the bravado displayed to his roommate no longer necessary, he unintentionally lapsed into his own Gethsemane.

His situation was quite hopeless and his despair palpable as he sat there alone contemplating what lay ahead. No music, no piano, nor career for, perhaps, some years and these were things that had comprised his entire life for as long as he could remember.

It would be so easy to forget the war and just carry on with his true vocation in life. Because of his special talent nobody would think the less of him and, in fact, many would be shocked if he did join up for, like Ken, they would probably think "the war is not for blokes like you."

Be that as it may, he had thrashed it out with himself on his night walk and knew what he must do. There was no other way for him. He was not happy about it but had no sense of self-pity for it was his own decision. He was of the opinion all men had their obligations in life, both to themselves and to others, and these had to be met if they were to have enduring peace of mind. The die was now cast so far as he was concerned and as soon as possible he would embark on a plan to clear the way for his eventual induction into the AIF.

His parents, particularly Irene, and Cathy were his chief concerns and he decided not tell them until after the Christmas season. He would go back to Magdalene a week or so beforehand and would ask Cathy to come up to the property for a few days and meet Tom and Irene. He would arrive on Boxing Day or the day after when he could, perhaps, tell them all at the same time, thinking that might make it a little easier all round.

He would then get himself back to Sydney on the first working day of the New Year with a list of items for attention. The most urgent of these being the need to advise the people at the ABC so they should not proceed with advertising or publicity of the scheduled performances he was about to cancel. Professor Morrison would be next on his list and then Charles Jermyn and, at the same time, arrange with him the cancellation of his plans to take the flat in Elizabeth Bay.

He cleared all the things in his mind as he sat there in his room that morning. When he finally got up he felt an urgent need to be with his Cathy. Despite his preoccupation with so many other matters she was never far from his mind and the thought struck him at that very moment that above other considerations, including the piano, leaving her would be the greatest sacrifice of all.

Chapter 23

Pat Sheridan was determined his final two weeks at the Conservatorium would be very much 'business as usual'. He arrived early each morning and began the long hours of practise he enjoyed so much. It was only now he was beginning to realise the extent to which he would miss these precious hours he spent alone with beloved composers who wrote beautiful and profound music for the piano.

He was also intent on completing the writing of his Australian symphony before he departed the hallowed walls of this place of musical learning. The end was in sight as the creative block which had frustrated him for some weeks had dispersed. Now that his way ahead had been determined, albeit in a violently different direction, he was able to approach his work in a clearer frame of mind and when he took up pen and manuscript there were no distractions to stem the tide of music which now began to surge effortlessly from his soul and mind.

The final movement was finished on the third day of the first week and the fourth day he spent reading through the entire score several times, when he was able to hear in his mind every note he had composed for every instrument as though it was actually being performed by a full orchestra.

He sat there at the piano for some time after the final reading and thought it was good, although just how good would be determined by musicians better qualified to make such judgment. It was important to him, however, that he himself be satisfied with it. Whatever other's opinions turned out to be, he would always treasure the opus, for it embraced in music every aspect he held dear of the land of his birth.

He put the full manuscript into his briefcase, ready to be taken back to Magdalene, where it would join the great pile of music he had composed over the last fifteen years or so - in the top drawer of the wardrobe of his bedroom there. Apart from himself, no one had heard these works and he now thought it a good idea if he were to bring it all to light when he came home from the war and so discover then if he had a gift for composing worthwhile classical music.

Whilst dreading, to some extent, the actual day when he would shelve the piano and his career and leave Cathy, his parents and Magdalene behind, he still set about his plan for enlistment. The decision had been made and he saw no point in delaying the process any longer than necessary.

He thought he could clear his Sydney obligations early in the New Year and then go back home to Bathurst to be with Irene and Tom for a week or so before taking the final step into uniform. He hoped Cathy would be able to join him for part of that time but it was unlikely as her duties with the SSO would have commenced by then. This meant he would need to spend extra days in Sydney for he could not leave without spending extended time with her, especially as they would have so much to say to each other.

He did not anticipate any further delays and mentally set the date for his appointment at the recruiting office at February 1.

But something unexpected did come up. It would not affect his date of enlistment but would call for change in some of his other plans. It occurred on the Friday of that first of his two remaining week when Professor Morrison came into his studio. He was in the middle of his daily practise session and after exchanging brief greetings and Con chatter, his mentor spoke of the purpose of his call.

"I wonder if you would do me a favour, Patrick," he said rather seriously "and, perhaps, do yourself one at the same time," he added.

"Of course, Professor, what's on your mind?" replied the pianist.

Morrison proceeded to enlighten him. The well-known Sydney Dowager, Lady Lloyd-Randell, widow of the late iron and steel magnate, was sponsor and chair of the 'Friends of The Conservatorium' he explained, a group which did a lot to help with finances during these straitened times. She was associated with many charities in this city and seemed to be the first person called upon when a new appeal was deemed necessary. She had been landed recently with the 'Bundles for Britain' campaign which was for a movement inspired by British Red Cross reports of the plight of many thousands of needy children and elderly people in Britain who were being taken from their homes when they were deemed to be located in target areas for German bombers. There was dire shortage of warm clothing, footwear, bedding and tinned food and other items listed by the organisers who were asking for rapid response.

"Alice Lloyd-Randell is a very decent and generous soul and immediately undertook to help raise funds for this cause," explained the professor. "On the Sunday of the Australia Day long weekend she intends holding a fundraiser which she has called 'An afternoon of Classical Music' at her home in Darling Point. She has done this kind of thing before and I've organised artists from the staff and students of this place but I can't do it this time as our people will be away on leave.

"Now this is where you come in. I thought instead of the usual four or five players performing perhaps you would give a recital; not a long one, say about an hour and a half.

"Before you answer let me tell you this. She has in her ballroom, which can seat an audience of about hundred and fifty people, a superb Bechstein grand which is a delight to play and the acoustics of that place are quite wonderful. That should answer the first questions which come into your mind."

Patrick sat on the piano stool and listened to Morrison. He just nodded his head from time to time without interrupting for he had the impression he was trying to sell him a bill of goods and was getting really wound up about it. Besides, the whole idea so far was not without appeal.

"Invitations to this woman's soirees are like gold and the gentry of the Eastern Suburbs will roll up in number, quite willing to be fleeced for such a good cause. Apart from the usual Sydney social set, there will be MPs, leading business figures and the like to make up quite an impressive gathering.

"Now son, let me go on because I want you to know what is involved here. I have spoken to Alice about you and she is tremendously impressed and become excited at the prospect of you playing for her affair. I told her we would like to nominate at least twenty invitees and she has agreed. I know you may want some of these extended to your parents, Cathy Jordan, and, perhaps, her parents, Charles Jermyn and his wife and anyone else you may wish to include. The balance I suggest should go to the music critics of the Sydney dailies, Bill Lawson and his wife, the GM and Music Director of the ABC, executives of the two theatrical companies, J.C. Williamson and the Tate crowd. In other words, a selection of people who should be made aware of the very fine pianist they have in their midst.

"Now you can see what I have in mind and your recital is really a double-edged sword for me." He stopped there before concluding by asking, "what do you think?"

"I think I could do it for you, Professor," replied Patrick quite deliberately, "I did have some other plans but I think they could be changed to fit in with things. I better bounce it off the ABC first to see if they have any objection because of my commitment to them," he continued and immediately felt guilty of misleading the professor because of his intention to cancel those same commitments.

"Other than that I will be pleased to do it and I like the idea of those special guests from the concert world you spoke of. That was very thoughtful of you. I would like to invite Cathy and her parents and, of course, my mother and father. There is one other I would like to be asked, a former coach of mine, Sister Mary Annunciata, a music teacher from the Bathurst convent"

He had already formed the idea this could be a kind of farewell performance for him and a time for him to remember those who helped him on his way.

"Thanks for that Patrick. I knew you would help me out and, as you say, it will not do your career any harm to let those people hear you play. I will attend to those invitations and perhaps we can meet early in the year and discuss the works you intend to play."

"Yes, of course," said Patrick. "It's a bit of a mixed audience so perhaps the general appeal of Chopin might be the way to go. I'll put something together and see what you think," he said as the professor stood up to leave.

His last few days at the Conservatorium of New South Wales passed very quickly, or so it seemed to him. He adhered to his routine for practise but had a little more time to spare now that his orchestral opus was out of the way. Because of the students' and staff's varying schedules and lesson timetables, he started saying his goodbyes early in the piece and was touched by the genuine warmth and expressions of farewell and good wishes he received from people whom he had come to know, perhaps only slightly, over the past two years. Marion Cross gave a farewell meal at Pine Trees for him which turned into a party and attended by all current boarders and again he was struck by the sincere friendliness they displayed towards him.

He and Cathy got together whenever possible. On the days, during those last weeks, when she worked at her father's office, they met for a meal or just a cup of coffee and on two of these occasions he had taken her to recitals at the Sydney Town Hall; one by a well-known American baritone who had recently forsaken the operatic stage for the movie screen, and a most talented French violinist making a great name for herself on the world stage. Unfortunately she was to die tragically in a plane crash not long afterwards.

Parting after these meetings seemed to arouse the growing physical appeal they had for each other. The emotion she displayed during their tender goodbye kissing and embracing again brought home to him her vulnerability and that she would surrender whenever he chose, for her desire was almost palpable.

He felt exactly the same way about this beautiful, young girl and, on such occasions, it crossed his mind as to whether or not he would be able to control his own emotions given the right place and circumstances, and succumb to behaviour of a more intimate nature. He was not made of stone nor was he singularly noble but he did have a fairly strict moral code which did not countenance the final intimacy between man and woman outside of marriage. This was a deterrent but not the principal one for he felt to 'illegally' take the virtue of one he loved so much, no matter her own feelings, would be an act his conscience would not allow. Despite this, he had increasing doubts about his moral strength and was aware there were times of passion when a man's conscience deserted him entirely. In a way he was grateful he would not have to contend with this temptation for much longer as the Australian Army would allow him very little time for that kind of recreation.

It was about three on the final Saturday that they met at Circular Quay and took the ferry to Manly, then walked along the busy Corso to the ocean beach before changing in to swim suits at the bathing sheds. They enjoyed a long, playful surf late on that warm, calm summer afternoon.

They had 'tea', as he insisted on calling it, in the dining room of the rather swish Hotel Steyne which was close to the harbour waterfront. It was getting on for nine when they finished a post-dinner, rather romantic, hand-holding stroll, by the light of a half-moon, along the beach of the open swimming baths adjacent to the ferry wharf.

They had not talked a lot, for once, but there was such a comfortable, loving feeling ever present between them that day that it would make it one of those occasions, especially in light of things to come, which would live in their memories for a long time.

Back at Circular Quay and, after their usual romantic goodnight ritual, he put her into a taxi after confirming he would be at her home for dinner on the morrow, prior to him leaving the following day to return to Bathurst for the Christmas season. At his behest Irene had telephoned her mother to extend an invitation for her daughter to spend a few days at Magdalene before the New Year, giving an assurance her daughter would receive every care during her stay. Mrs. Jordan was most gracious in agreeing to the visit and said how much she was looking forward to meeting Patrick's parents.

On some occasions, when he brought Cathy home early enough, she would invite him in for coffee or similar and he had met her father and brothers on a few occasions and renewed his acquaintance with Mrs. Jordon. The invitation to dinner was, however, a first but he felt at ease about it as he had found them to be very decent, normal people. It turned out to be a very pleasant evening for him; the conversation at the dinner table was lively and intelligent and Patrick had no problem keeping up with the important man of law and his two articled clerks who were also his sons. Afterwards in the huge lounge room he accompanied her as she played her parents preferred pieces. They pressed him to do something for them as well and he graciously obliged with ten minutes or so with some of Handel's more tuneful works. He quickly lost himself in what he was doing and when he stood up it was to find his little audience somewhat in awe. Her family thanked him, wished him well for the festive season and expressed their wish to catch up with him again in the New Year.

It was less than twenty four hours after leaving the Jordan home that he found himself preparing for bed in his own room at Magdalene. Leaving Cathy behind in Sydney had been hard but the sheer joy of just being back here gave him a sense of peace and serenity he had not experienced on similar occasions. It all had to do, of course, with his awareness that he may be absent from this precious place for years; perhaps for ever, and that is why this occasion felt so special to him. He would not permit his feeling of well-being to be dampened by the knowledge that in a few days he would have to tell his parents and Cathy of his intention to enlist, and of the great consternation that would, undoubtedly, ensue.

Chapter 24

*T*om and Irene had been at the station when the train arrived in Bathurst and there was no doubting the pleasure they experienced at having him home for a few weeks. It took something special to get Tom off the property but he was beaming and most effusive, for him, in greeting his son. The brief hug he gave him was a first for them and, perhaps, an indication of how much he must have missed his son's presence at Magdalene these past two years.

Irene was full of questions about Cathy Jordan, the Con and the ABC and he was evasive with his replies about the latter. When she plied him closely, he dismissed her with "we will just have to wait and see, Mum." She was really looking forward to meeting Cathy but somehow refrained from asking the question as to how serious they were about each other.

There was much to talk about and they brought him up-to-date with events at the property. Tom's health had improved noticeably and was more active now. He enjoyed working with Ray Boundy who was doing such a good job in his overall management of the run. Molly Read his sister had been a godsend as housekeeper and she and Irene had done great things recently in refurbishing the homestead itself. As well, with the help of some of the hands, they had planted lawn and arranged flower beds to beautify the immediate vicinity.

There was additional reason for Irene to be house proud these days. Changes had taken place in the social life of the area in the past two or three years, with better 'roads', better motor cars and the party-line telephone system all helping to bring former distant neighbours much closer together. Visitors and friends now 'called in' as they passed on their way to Bathurst or Orange, and birthdays, anniversaries and other informal occasions were sufficient reason for neighbours to socialise in a way that was not possible a few years back.

The Sheridans enjoyed a pleasant family Christmas. They drove to Bathurst for midnight Mass where Patrick caught up with several friends including the Bests and, briefly, Sr. Annunciata, whom he promised to visit before returning to Sydney.

Molly Read prepared a great meal whilst they slept in the following morning and set a very festive board for them and their guests. Their good friends, the Bests, who came out from Bathurst, and Molly and her brother, as well as the new overseer, sat down with them after Tom served pre-lunch drinks, setting the right atmosphere for the most important occasion of the year. There was no sign of tension two days later when Patrick introduced Cathy to his parents after she alighted from the family car. He had met the afternoon train from Sydney and they had driven out slowly to the property. With her arm through his as it held the steering wheel on this clear, sunny evening, she laughed as she expressed her slight apprehension at the prospect of meeting Irene. With the best goodwill in the world towards their children's sweethearts, she knew how jealously mothers guarded their sons. He was, after all, an only son. After assuring her his mother was no ogre, they dismissed that subject and confined their discussion to matters seemingly important to young people in love. However, she was a little puzzled at times when he appeared dismissive of some matters normally an important part of their conversations. Before the week was much older, she would learn the reason for this.

Irene very quickly made her feel at home. She led the way inside and introduced her to Molly before showing her to the bright, airy guest room which once had been Patrick's nursery. She felt a pang when she saw the violin case and told Cathy she would put it in the drawing room for her and that she could practise to her heart's content at any time she felt like it, adding how much she was looking forward to hearing her play.

Molly joined them for the evening meal she had specially prepared for their guest, and they sat around the table afterwards and talked, with Tom holding forth to Cathy on the history of Magdalene - which seemed to have intrigued her from the start.

They retired to the drawing room for coffee where Tom, who had had one or two brandies, insisted Irene play some of his favourite Irish airs. Not long after she did so, he dropped off into a quiet and peaceful sleep in his comfortable armchair.

At breakfast the following morning they were both light-hearted and gay and the banter between them a sign of a healthy and affectionate relationship. None of this was lost on Irene who was quite taken with this young musician. As a mother, her approval of her son's companion became more apparent as the days went by. Patrick was young enough not to let his load get him down and, for these few days, he let the daunting task of telling his loved ones of his intentions slip from his mind.

It was indeed a romantic and idyllic time for them both. Each evening there was music in the drawing room, with Tom in his armchair and Irene joining in, though she was quietly emotional when notes from the girl's violin filled the room. There were long, hand-holding walks; one along the green banks of the Magdalene creek which was still running deep due to good summer rain. She commented on the beauty of seeing huge flocks of sheep grazing on the home pastures with the low purple hills rising in the background.

In the early twilight before each evening meal they took the long stride to collect mail from the box out on the side of the main road. Irene noted they took ever so much longer than she in carrying out this chore. Then on the second night she saw a spot of lipstick on her son's shirt collar and the girl appeared more rosy-cheeked than usual.

Cathy and Irene helped Molly prepare the meal each evening and she and Irene chatted about many things. A nice familiar amiability developed between them but Patrick was a little surprised when Cathy started to address Irene, respectfully, as Mother Sheridan.

In anticipation she had brought her jodhpurs and the boots she wore during her horse riding classes at the Swiss finishing school. Although the instruction had been in sidesaddle, she could also sit astride in the conventional way and in the late afternoon of the last full day of her stay at Magdalene, Tom Sheridan saddled her a suitable mount. She and Patrick set out on a long, meandering ride around the property. They walked, trotted, cantered and slow-galloped the horses before dismounting and leading them down to drink from the creek where it flowed crystal clear over a large bed of small, smooth stones.

They duly remounted and cantered some distance across undulating fields before coming to the base of a higher, wooded area, near the property's eastern boundary. Here he helped her dismount, and tethered the horses to a low branch on a gum tree. He held her arm as they ascended a short, steep rise on to an escarpment that extended out from the surrounding area, and he told her to close her eyes as led her through low scrub to a wide open area on the edge of the knoll.

"You can open them now Cath and tell me what you think."

He stood close with his arm around her waist as she took in the panorama for the first time. For a few moments she did not utter a word and then gasped, "Oh Sheridan, you didn't exaggerate a bit. It's incredible and even more sublime than I ever imagined it could be. No wonder you love this place."

They stood there together looking into the distant beauty as the sun behind them started to think about setting for the day.

"It is a great spot," he said, wistfully, in the new light of great uncertainty, "and I will build that house here one day and live in it for the rest of my life and try to write some decent music."

They sat down in the soft grass, still looking towards the purple haze of the Blue Mountains in the distance and neither spoke. He could feel there was something in her silence as she hadn't responded to his previous remarks.

Finally, she started to speak and there was a catch in her voice and he knew she was upset about something. "I've not forgotten you telling me about your plans for this spot and, if you remember, I asked you then whether I was included in that grand scheme of things. But you didn't answer me then, so I ask again. You're part of me, Pat, and I don't think life would be worth living without you, so I must know now if I'm to have a place in your life."

It was his turn to be silent and he sat there with a hand on his forehead and her face saddened as she feared the delay in his response was an unacceptable omen. Finally, he got up quite deliberately, as though he had made up his mind about something, and stood looking down at her and gently stroking her hair as he did so.

"Cathy, Cathy, Cathy," he said softly but desperately, "there is something I have to tell you that I have not told anyone else," and he took her hand as she too stood up with a look of alarm on her face.

"Before I tell you I want to clear the air on one or two matters. Let me say first of all, my dear Cathy, if I had to live my life without you it would amount to nothing more than a series of wasted years because you are already so much of what I am and what I hope to be. In answer to the question you have just asked, of course, you are the most important part of my life and always will be, if you are agreeable?

"Also you appear to doubt at times as to whether I find you attractive physically and I want to leave you in no doubt about this. If you had been aware of the number of times I've had an almost uncontrollable need to ravish you, you would have run screaming into the night. Believe me, if I didn't love you so much I would have taken advantage of you long ago. I'm not noble and not highly moral in my thoughts but I just can't bring myself to do that to you, no matter how agreeable you may appear to be. Looking at you at this very moment I find my decency is only hanging on by a thread.

"I had thought about it many times and made up my mind to propose we get married once my arrangement with the ABC was settled. I knew there would have been problems with our careers but reckoned we could work our way through those if we tried."

He was about to continue but she interrupted and looking up at him with tears of apparent joy streaming down her face, she said, "Please, Pat, don't say any more. Just kiss me and hold me tight for a while. I don't know what you are going to tell me that is so important but now I know how you feel, nothing else really matters."

"I wish it was as easy as that," he said gently, as he took her in his arms, "you know by now I feel strongly about a lot of things; Mum and Dad, Magdalene, the music and, above all, you. But, unfortunately, I'm also somewhat of a bloody patriot and love of this country is deeply embedded in me. It's in real danger, Cath, in my opinion, and I know I've got to help out because if anything happened because of the war and I didn't lift a finger, I would never be able to live with myself.

"You are the first to know this, not even Tom and Irene are aware, and it will be a hell of shock for all of you and I don't want to sound too melodramatic as thousands of young Australian blokes are doing the same thing. I'll be joining the army in a few weeks' time, Cath, and, therefore, the arrangement with the ABC is off and it also means my whole career thing now is on hold until after the war."

Her look of shock and disbelief was something he was to see on the faces of the many people he was to tell of his intention over the ensuing weeks. Her vocal anguish and reasoned protestations would also be repeated again and again by those people who were close to him and aware of his musical brilliance.

And now the time had arrived for him to tell his parents. They started back slowly to the homestead in the twilight of a benign summer day but it was completely dark by the time they reached the outer gates. Tom, who was watching out for them came down to the horse barn with a kerosene lantern and he helped her out of the saddle.

"I don't know where you two have been or what you have been doing and I can only guess," he said, "but you better leave the horses to me and get up to the house pronto because Irene has been having kittens wondering where you were all this time."

"I showed Cathy Denny's Knoll, Dad and the horses were a bit tired so we had a slow ride back. I bet Mum won't be happy about me keeping Cathy out so late."

He paused, as though he had a sudden thought, before saying, "Look, Cathy, you shoot up to the house and calm her down. I want to have a few words with Dad and we'll be up shortly."

They led the two horses into the barn and started to unsaddle them. Pat, looking across at his father, said in a deliberate matter of fact tone, "Dad, I'm going to join up," and before Tom could respond he went on, "I've told Cathy who's pretty upset but I'm a bit concerned as to how Mum will take it. What's the best way to tell her?"

The look of surprise and dismay on his father's face was almost a replica of Cath's reaction but he had also paled a little and sat down on a nearby bale of hay.

"Phew! That's a bit of a shock! Son, are you sure you've thought it through? What about your music and all that? Do you think you should give it all up just to go and fight for the bloody poms?" was the Irish-Australian's first anxious reaction to his son's news.

"Of course, I've given it a lot of thought, Dad, and I'm not thinking of the poms but of Australia because I know we are going to be in real strife here if the war goes badly in Europe and North Africa. We're defenceless and that's been realised by those thousands of blokes here who have given up jobs and careers to volunteer and I feel the same way about it. I'm sorry for you and Mum but it is something I just have to do and I've made up my mind," said Patrick staring across at Tom.

They sat there, in silence, looking at each other, whilst Tom let his son's news sink in.

"Bloody hell, Pat," he said quietly, "I don't know how you're going to tell Irene about this; she'll just explode. I think your career means more to her than it is does to you and you giving it up like this will just about kill her. I suggest you tell her somewhere on her own so that she doesn't say things in front of people she may come to regret later."

"I'll do that," said his son, "and believe me, Dad, this is the hardest thing I've ever done in my life and I'm still coming to grips with it. The only thing I can hang on to, and Mum must be made to realise this too, is that I'm not giving up any career; I'm just postponing it for a while."

They watered and fed the horses before putting them into stalls. Then side-by-side, both slightly tense, they walked slowly towards the light streaming through the homestead's kitchen window.

With the meal over that night, Cathy followed Tom out to the back porch where he was taking a late evening pipe and they started to talk quietly for they could feel what was in the air. Pat used an excuse to take his mother into the drawing room where he closed the door and broke the news to her of his intended enlistment.

There were no hysterics as she sat there without a word with her face reddening with anger as she looked at her son.

"What on earth are you talking about, Patrick? Have you gone completely mad? Of course you are not joining the army; I won't have it. We are not going to throw up years and years of training and planning for you to drop it just as your career is about to start. We are not going to sacrifice all this for a silly school boy notion about honour and patriotic duty," she said with a voice still under control but with slight crescendo in evidence. He could see he was in for the argument of his life judging from the anger he could see in his mother's eyes as she glared at him.

In low, quiet tones he tried to reason with her but she was in no mood to listen and, indeed, saw no point in doing so. Nothing could convince her there was even the slightest justification for her son to join the army. She interrupted him constantly as he tried to explain his position, until he saw there was no point in continuing. He got up and put his arms around her and placed a kiss on her forehead.

"I'm sorry you feel that way, Mum. I know it was asking a lot to expect you to understand, but that's the way it is. I don't want to be a hero, far from it, but it's one of those many times when your mind tells you one thing and your heart another. As I said to Dad, it is something I feel I have to do, whether I like to or not and I'm afraid that's the way it must be."

He left her sitting there and went to his bedroom and sat on the edge of his bed in gloomy retrospection. Irene got up shortly afterwards and went out to the porch where Tom and the girl were talking.

"I'm going down to the mail box, Tom, it hasn't been cleared today; I need the walk," she said, and gave Cathy a sad smile as she went by.

She had only taken a few steps into the enveloping darkness when Cathy called out in a subdued voice, "Do you mind if I come with you, Mother Sheridan?"

Irene waited and held out her hand for the girl to take as they made the long walk, there and back, in sympathetic silence. They kissed and held each other for an emotional moment after they got back inside and went to their bedrooms without making any attempt to wish Patrick good-night.

After Cathy left the following day the atmosphere in the Magdalene homestead was strained, to say the least, with Molly and Tom doing everything they could to make things appear normal, but to no avail. Irene was implacable and she did not address her son in any way during the two days prior to him returning to Sydney, where he was to advise all those associated with his impending career that it was to be put on hold until the end of the war. It was Patrick's intention to stay at the YMCA in Sydney as he did not want his father to finance him any longer now that there was no chance of repaying him any time in the near future. But Tom would not hear of it and insisted he use the Magdalene account at Usher's Hotel until such time as the army became responsible for his living quarters.

On the afternoon of his arrival he telephoned the ABC and arranged an appointment to see the General Manager the following morning. The Concert Manager was present also when Patrick told them he would be unable to proceed with the concert arrangements he had made with them.

They were very much put out and concerned but soon realised there was nothing they could do about it and, with great reluctance, accepted the situation. They thanked him for letting them know so promptly and wished him well and indicated they would be prepared to talk again when the war was over. As they shook hands the Concert Manager told him he and his boss had accepted invitations to attend his recital at the Lloyd-Randell mansion and would look forward to hearing him play, even though it might heighten the disappointment they already felt by his withdrawal.

In the presence of Charles Jermyn, Professor Juliann Morrison listened to what Patrick had to say and they were both shocked and aghast, but proffered only the same arguments he himself and others had used to reason why he was not obliged to enlist. But they had no option other than to accept the situation because of their former pupil's unwavering determination to stand by his decision.

Charles Jermyn seemed to sum it up when he addressed Professor Morrison directly, "He appears to have let a sense of honour and duty get in the way of his career, Julian, and I'm afraid I can't argue against that."

"If you say so, Charles," Morrison responded ruefully, "but what an almighty waste."

Then, to clear other matters on his mind, Patrick told them of his meeting with the ABC management and advised Morrison he had deferred his enlistment by a few days in order to do the Bundles for Britain recital. The professor had overlooked that possible complication and thanked him for his consideration. Patrick said he would be going back to Bathurst at the end of the week but would return in time to prepare for the recital. The professor said he had already given that matter some prior thought and asked Patrick to contact him again prior to returning home.

Whilst they had spoken on the telephone, Cathy and Patrick had not been able to get together so far during this visit. He had been busy, of course, and she had now been rehearsing with the Sydney Symphony for nearly a week and they had no opportunity to meet.

Nevertheless, he thought she may feel neglected and perhaps he should try to make it up to her in some way. When he got back to his room that evening he called her and suggested they have a late meal together at Rudolpho's which, he had been told, was Sydney's swankiest night spot. She was impressed and excited and agreed to be there for an eight-thirty booking.

"This is one of your better ideas, Pat Sheridan," she said, "so let's make a night of it; I don't suppose there will be many more of them for a while. I'll dress up a bit for you, soldier boy, so make sure you look sharp yourself," she said before they hung up.

The restaurant was one very large, crystal-chandeliered room with colourful drapes and carpeting which created a pleasant ambience in combination with softly played music coming from a five-piece orchestra located near a small dance floor. The sound of laughter and conversation was coming from the many occupied tables.

It was a night when romantic memories were made and they knew these, probably, had to last them a long time. They were to be referred to often in the loving letters they were to exchange over coming years. With waiters hovering around in attendance, Cathy ordered a Steak Dianne which was prepared at their table. Pat surprised her when a Bordeaux of good vintage was brought to the table just as her meal was being served.

"You remembered! How wonderful!" she enthused, "we could never afford this wine in Paris," and she laughed at the face he pretended to pull when the Italian waiter insisted he taste it before it was served. "You don't have to try to impress me like this, Sheridan," she continued, "because I love you enough already and I don't know what I will do when the army takes you away from me."

"Start eating before it gets cold, woman," he said. "We're not going to spoil tonight by talking about it now." He reached over and touched her hand and added softly, "but we will talk about it, soon, I promise"

They ate, and drank the wine slowly, and had long, dreamy dances between the courses when he held her ever so close in response to their love for each other, the pleasant effect of the wine and the gentle music being played by a sympathetic orchestra.

Time fled and it was well after midnight when he looked at his watch as patrons started to drift out from the restaurant. In the ride to her home in the taxi she told him it had been an unreal and wondrous evening and one she was never likely to forget. To his mind this had been a kind of a farewell occasion. He too had enjoyed it beyond all expectations and gave a thought of gratitude to a generous father who had made it possible. He told the driver to wait whilst he took her to the front door and a final kiss and embrace to wish her goodbye. He was returning on the midday train to Bathurst, he told her, and would call her from Magdalene when he arrived.

He arose late from his bed the following morning at Usher's Hotel and as soon as he came back from breakfast he telephoned Julian Morrison as requested.

"So glad you called," he said. "I've been in touch with Alice Lloyd-Randell about your recital, Patrick, and told her you would be coming down from Bathurst a few days before hand to prepare and this would include trying out her piano and checking the acoustics of the room. She agreed immediately and suggested that, if it were convenient for you, you could use one of the guest suites in her home on those few days before the soiree."

"That sounds pretty good, Professor. It's not far from the Jordan house and that is a plus for me. At the moment I don't know if my parents are coming down and if they do they, probably, would expect me to stay with them at Usher's," said Patrick.

"Well, here's her number. When you decide, give her a call and let her know what you intend to do. Make no mistake about this Dowager; she is a true music lover from way back and has a great understanding of the subject and our profession. You would be in good hands if you decide to take up her offer. She's a highly intelligent and generous woman and, as I have already told her of your exceptional ability, she is anxious to meet you. I have no doubt you will both get on, and that may be important, Patrick, as she is just the kind of person who could be of immense help when you are restarting your career after the war."

"Thank you for all that, and the compliment, Professor. Once again, I'm very much obliged to you and I'll certainly contact Lady Alice once I have spoken to my parents," said Patrick as he closed off the conversation.

To a limited extent Irene had accepted the situation with her son but her life's dream had been destroyed. Whilst she had forgiven him she would never understand exactly what motivated him to give up a career of such brilliant promise. Perhaps he could pursue it again when the war finished, "but when would that be?" she asked herself. To date nobody whom Patrick had told had had the thought he might not come back from the war or that he would be seriously injured. Irene joined that group of optimists because it was unthinkable. Australian ground forces had not yet seen action and it would take the first casualty lists to raise such fears in the minds of his relatives and friends.

He was pleased and very much relieved when she, with Molly Read, met him at the station. She pulled him to her and kissed him on the cheek and he could feel the tears from her eyes running down his own face.

On the way to Magdalene in the car he told her of the reaction of the people at the ABC, and his friends at the Conservatorium, to his news and she listened with her face set and made no comment. He mentioned also the invitation to stay with the Dowager in the lead up to the recital and that he could not answer it until he knew whether or not she and Tom were coming down to hear him play. If they were he would stay with them at Usher's.

"No, don't do that," she said, "we won't be coming down until the night before anyway, and it's important you familiarise yourself with the piano and the hall beforehand. Come back with us after the recital and we can have one or two days together before you go into the army." She stopped as her voice choked and, although she recovered quickly, there was only limited conversation until Patrick drove the car through the homestead gates.

Chapter 25

$\mathcal{L}$ady Alice Lloyd-Randell had a reputation for being a gracious, charming and hospitable hostess and these attributes were very much in evidence when she welcomed the tall, young pianist from Bathurst into her home. As arranged on the telephone the previous evening, her chauffeur had met him at Central Station and she had 'received' him in her private drawing room upon his arrival.

She was an unpretentious woman, and the sincerity of her appreciation was palpable when she thanked him for agreeing to play for her charitable appeal. Julian Morrison had told her so much about him she could hardly wait to hear him play, she said. However, she promised not to eavesdrop when he was rehearsing as she wished to reserve that pleasure at his actual performance.

They had an enjoyably long and interesting conversation over lunch in her own small dining room and he was amazed to learn of the number of renowned pianists and other superb artists she had heard over the years during frequent travels abroad with her husband.

It was smiles and amiability as they left the table and Allenby showed him to his guest suite where his suit case had been unpacked and clothes hung in the large walk-in wardrobe. The butler drew his attention to a suit and a white tuxedo which had become slightly creased, asking "would he like them taken to the housekeeper to have them pressed?"

Patrick agreed readily for he intended, at Irene's insistence, to wear the tuxedo for the recital. With him in tow she had selected this item of apparel, very carefully, several weeks before at Richards, the exclusive men's store near the Hotel Australia, with the intention of him wearing it on appropriate occasions during their now-aborted visit to Europe. Patrick was his own man in most regards but often gave way to his mother's superior dress sense for what he should wear as such things were of little interest to him.

On the day of the recital Patrick overslept and only awoke when Allenby knocked on his door with a breakfast tray in hand. He felt rested and calm, but somewhat thoughtful, not because of the pending performance but for the realisation this was the last day of his old life.

Tomorrow he would become a soldier and commencing an existence about which he knew absolutely nothing. Now everyone and everything he held dear in the past would have to be put on hold until this war was over. He was reconciled to the situation and did not feel in the least sorry for himself for he knew he was doing no more than the duty he owed to Australia. That was an obligation also being met by many thousands of his contempories.

He dismissed this from his mind as he took a leisurely walk down to Rushcutters Bay where he stopped by the impressive yacht club and watched crews as they prepared their craft for a Sunday sail. It was a sparkling Sydney summer's morning and the boats with their whiter than white sheets were a pleasant sight as they made their way through light blue water on to Sydney Harbour. It was a somewhat acceptable change of scene for this boy from the bush and he felt very much at peace with the world as he made his way back to the mansion.

On arriving, he went to the Bechstein and played music, other than that programmed for the recital, for an hour or so before asking Allenby to serve him a light lunch on the wide, marbled patio overlooking the harbour. Before going back to his room he sought out Lady Alice who was overseeing final seating arrangements for the performance. There was a kind of organised informality about what she was doing with many lounge chairs and settees being interspersed with the dozens of comfortable, straight-backed chairs hired for the occasion.

They sat together on a nearby settee for a final exchange on the procedure for the performance. Patrick told her he would make his entrance at three and go directly to the piano, unannounced, and, after the welcoming applause, if any, had ceased, he would commence the recital. He regretted he could not stay on for the fund-raising after the recital as he wanted to spend as much time as possible with his parents before they returned to Bathurst. She asked him, and he agreed, to meet briefly with a small group of prominent people whom, she said, had graced the occasion with their presence.

The programme, which had been printed in gold lettering with a copy to be placed on every seat, had been devised by them in consultation with Charles Morrison. They had decided the first half of the recital should comprise works of Beethoven, Mozart and Brahms in order to cater for the more musically-sophisticated members of the audience, with the second stanza being devoted to the better-known works of leading composers that would appeal to the gathering as a whole. Patrick had selected the actual works he would perform whilst adhering to that guideline.

Back in his room he sat down on the comfortable bedroom chair after picking a book of short stories by O. Henry which was on the bedside table, and began to read. After two of the American author's whimsical yarns he looked at his watch to find it was getting on for two, so he put the book down and went to the en suite where he shaved and had a leisurely shower before coming back into the room to dress. He was quite ready with ten or fifteen minutes to spare when there was a knock at the door which he opened to find his parents standing there in the company of Allenby, who had shown them the way to his room. "Sorry to bust in like this, son," said a slightly embarrassed Tom Sheridan, "but you know your mother, she just had to be sure you put your pants and other things on straight. She doesn't trust us jokers when it comes to clobber."

"Do be quiet, Tom, you are always going on about something!"

Patrick looked at his mother as she made the mild rebuke and noticed her expression, whilst still drawn, was slightly less intense than when he had seen her last.

"So you have learnt, Patrick. You look fine, and dressed yourself well enough to appear before that crowd down there. We've met Lady Lloyd-Randell, by the way, and are sitting with her and Cathy's parents who also introduced themselves." She looked at her watch before continuing, "we must not dally; you're nearly due. So our friend here can take us back down now," she said turning to Allenby with a smile. "Play well and we'll see you when it is all over," she said and she kissed him on the cheek as they took their leave.

Irene had been devastated by her son's decision and her dismay and sense of hopelessness had been there for all to see these past few weeks. She would never be able to accept what had happened but slowly she was learning to live with it and her mood had lightened a little by now. She did not think she could bear to come to the recital but, as she still loved her son despite what he had done to her, she decided, for his sake, to endure what could be a heartbreaking experience.

It could all have been so, so different, she thought. Instead of the long and glorious career she had hoped for him, this could be his first and only formal recital, for who knew if he would be able to resume where he left off if the war lasted any length of time. It was an almost intolerable shame his unique and remarkable talent should be lost simply because of his compelling sense of duty. The loss meant more to her as only she, and she alone, knew the potential for greatness that lay within the boy - due to his European ancestry and the generations of fine musicians in which it was steeped. So many people had been perplexed by his extraordinary ability they immediately asked the question of his heritage, to which only she had the true answer and that she could never give.

She did not let it enter her head that her son could be wounded or perhaps killed during his service, for that was something too unbearable to even contemplate. From the outset she felt confident the army, in its wisdom, would assign him duties compatible with his civilian calling and, therefore, he was unlikely to ever find himself in harm's way. Little did she know he intended to enlist as a recruit with a civilian occupation recorded as that of 'Stockman'.

These were the thoughts which traversed her mind every day from the time he had told her of his intention. Also, she could not help but lament the fact that had it not been for the war, she and Patrick would be on a passenger liner bound for Europe on the first stage of their journey to Heidelberg.

Allenby took them back to their place in the hall and she and Tom sat down together alongside Cathy, who asked "How is he?"

At her reply of "Good" they, almost automatically, took each other's hand. She was about to tell her more when the people around them started to applaud politely and they looked up to find Patrick already ascending the two steps which led to the wide, slightly elevated platform on which the gleaming Bechstein stood with lid and hood open ready for him to join it.

Before he sat down, he stood by the instrument for a few moments bowing his head ever so slightly to the audience in acknowledgement of this courtesy such gatherings usually extended to any artist, whomsoever they were.

Irene hardly recognised the young man she had seen just a few minutes earlier. He was standing tall and erect and seemingly calm and relaxed but with a mien that had completely changed. It was no longer that of a young person but of one more mature and worldly, with an inoffensive air of self-assurance that gave her a vision of her son she had never seen before. She then knew that he, without realising it, had donned the mantle of the great artist he undoubtedly was. This change in him was in some way an outward manifestation of the genius that was truly his.

This pianist had not acquired mannerisms at the keyboard. As in all things, he approached it in a normal and natural manner for that was the only way he knew of doing anything. So he seated himself at the Bechstein and after a few moments started to play in much the same way as he would in his own drawing room.

The recital drew to a close with the audience demanding a fourth encore. As the final strains of Schumann's *Traumerei* drifted away, Patrick carefully and conclusively shut the Bechstein's lid and left the platform. He walked over to Lady Alice and graciously shook her hand before kissing his mother, and then Cathy, on the cheek and after placing his hand briefly on his father's shoulder, he left the hall to return to his guest room to the accompaniment of the still generous clapping which seemed reluctant to die down.

It was half an hour or so before he returned to the hall. Now dressed in a dark-grey double-breasted suit he was ready, as promised to Lady Alice, to be introduced to her committee. He then made his final farewells before leading Cathy and his parents out to the car where the chauffeur and Allenby were waiting with his suitcase. Lady Alice with her group and many other members of the audience accompanied them to wave goodbye. Few of them, including their hostess, knowing that this young man who had held them enthralled that afternoon was about to enlist and, in all probability, would not play another serious note until the war was over.

Julian Morrison was standing alone on the patio above and watched them drive away with an expression on his face which told of the great sense of loss and extreme disappointment he was feeling. Today he had heard what he considered an incomparable pianist giving a performance the like of which he would never hear again. It seemed almost tragic to him to think such genius could be lost to the musical world, perhaps forever.

In so many ways he was just an ordinary, decent young man, Morrison thought, but blessed with a talent the extent of which was only matched by the intensity of his love for his country and all that it stood for in his own eyes. What he was sacrificing in order to serve his nation was an act of selflessness which was too extreme for him to contemplate.

Morrison thought back to the works of three immortal composers played faultlessly in the first half of today's recital. The Brahms was sublime and almost transcending in the way he released the beauty of the opus to his audience. His great love of Mozart and Beethoven was very much in evidence in their works that he performed. The professor was somewhat envious of his pupil's ability to bring to these compositions a superb interpretation of such profound tonal beauty and unwavering technical brilliance.

Strangely, it was the second half of the performance which was comprised of so called 'classical pot-boilers' which served to underline to him again his pupil's great gift. These works were performed frequently because of their sheer musical beauty and to his mind they could not be denigrated simply because they had widespread appeal. He had not heard these works performed so artistically before and this boy's rendition seemed to find another dimension to them, which other pianists seemed to be unaware. As much as anybody in that mixed audience, and unexpected as it was, he had been emotionally affected by Traumerei, *Liebestraum, Clare de Lune, the Rain Drop Prelude* of Chopin and Liszt's haunting *Consolation*. He himself had been guilty of using the word 'hackneyed' about these works and for the first time realised how wrong he was now that he had heard them played by a master.

Of the few times he had heard young Sheridan play in public, he had been quite surprised at the immediate and complete silence induced by his initial sitting at the keyboard. There seemed to be something about his 'presence' as he struck the first notes of a piece at a performance, in which time appeared to stand still and this endured to the conclusion of the work when, in stark contrast, the noise of rapturous applause flooded the auditorium.

Today, it had been no different. Lady Alice and her gathering had been entranced and carried away by a musical experience that would live in their memories for a long time. The kindly Dowager had tears in her eyes when she thanked him for suggesting Patrick for her soiree. He was aware that, apart from the music, today had also been a great social triumph for her as well. Julian Morrison turned away with a sigh and started back across the patio to the main gathering, wondering finally how someone with an Irish/Australian Bush background could be the vessel of such incredible talent. "The Minstrel Boy to the war has gone," he mused mournfully, but, please God, he would not be found in "the ranks of death."

After the Sheridans and Cathy arrived back at Usher's Hotel on that late Sunday afternoon, they went to the coffee lounge on the ground floor for afternoon tea. They were in sore need of this after what had been a long and emotional experience for them all. They had to be careful of their conversation in view of what lay ahead and deliberately steered clear of a subject which might induce a tearful reaction from the women.

When they arose from the table, agreeably refreshed, and made their way to the lift, Patrick suggested to Cathy they take a walk through Hyde Park as it was now somewhat cooler; but, he hastened to assure his parents, they would be back in time for the evening meal.

Their mood was quiet and companionable, but somewhat sombre, as they made their way towards the Park's inviting avenue of shady green trees. After contemplating the myriad antics of the Archibald Fountain, he took her arm and continued on towards the welcoming canopy of the Morton Bay Figs.

The look on her face said it all for him.

"We haven't really talked much about things and I know how you must feel, Cath, and I hate the thought of leaving you as much as you do, but it just can't be helped," he said ever so gently. "I'm going to miss a lot of things, the piano, that goes without saying, Magdalene and Mum and Dad, but I think I can cope with that. I have to tell you, the only thing that made me hesitate about enlisting was the prospect of being away from you. I know every day in the army will be sheer hell because of that alone..." and he broke off as though afraid to go on.

She stopped walking and stood looking up at him with tear-dimmed eyes. "My darling, as I've said before, I don't understand what has driven you to this but as it is Australia which is so important to you, I feel I can't compete. I respect what you are doing and admire you for it, in a way, but I will never understand why you are prepared to give up so much more than could possibly be expected of you. I know enough about music to realise what a truly great artist you could be and people of your accomplishments are not expected to go to war."

"We've been over all this before and enough is enough because I know it upsets you," he responded. "The war won't last forever and, perhaps, then, when I am free of the army, you will be foolish enough to agree to become my wife."

"That's if you ever ask me," she said almost scornfully.

"Cathy, I intended to ask you when I came back from Heidelberg," he said defensively, "and you know what has happened since then. I can't ask you to marry me now, the way things are. I may be away for years and I'm not going to tie you down with any formal engagement for that length of time. You are still a very young and beautiful kid and, even with the best of intentions now, you do not know how your feelings could change in that time. I hate the thought of it but you are entitled to your happiness. If someone else should come along whilst I'm away, I'm not going to have you burdened with my diamond ring on your finger."

"You talk a lot of hogwash for a supposedly intelligent man, Patrick Sheridan. Of course I'll be waiting; even if it takes forever. Surely you realise now that the grip I have on you is strengthened by every fibre of love and desire of my being and I will never let go. Rest assured, when those men in khaki are done with you, I'll be waiting at the wharf, bus stop, rail station or wherever you happen to get off. We're both young, remember, and there will be plenty of time for us to do all those things we want to do. So what I am saying is your old diamond ring won't make a scrape of difference one way or the other - although I would like to have it now," was her reasoned reply.

"You know how hard it is for me to refuse you anything, but my mind is made up about tying you down, so let's drop it, Cath. I love you and I can't say more than that. But I hope you will be waiting when I come back because it could be pretty good for us, I think... marry you, have a decent but short piano career and then build our house on Denny's Knoll. And then, eventually, with half-a-dozen kids running about the place disturbing me, I would try to write some worthwhile music. That's what I have in mind for us if it is alright with you," he concluded and took her tightening grip on his hand to be whole-hearted agreement of his idea.

After that exchange they were quiet and thoughtful, apparently taking on board what they had just said to each other. When they reached the War Memorial at the end of the Park near Park Street, it acted as a trigger for his memory and he began to tell her what would be happening with the Army over the next few days.

And so, in an everyday tone of voice, he laid it out for her.

Tomorrow, Monday, he was to report at ten o'clock to Victoria Barracks in Paddington for his entrance medical examination. He had been told at the Recruiting Depot this would take up most of the day. If passed he'd be sworn in late that afternoon and then ordered to present himself at eight o'clock on Tuesday morning at the Hordern Pavilion in the Sydney Show Ground, which had been taken over by the Army as an induction and transit centre. From there on he did not know what would happen but from what he had heard it would be several weeks before he got leave of any description. He would write to her at the first opportunity. They had a quiet evening meal with his parents who then retired as they were tired; it had been a busy few days for them. They were to catch the 8.35 am to Bathurst at Central Station and their son would see them off there on his way to the Barracks. They gave Cathy a fond farewell and expressed the hope she would visit them at Magdalene while Patrick was away.

He went home with Cathy in the cab in order to say goodbye to her parents, before going back to his room at Usher's for a disturbed night's sleep. Irene could not restrain her tears the following morning as, with ashen face, she kissed her son at the station and then turned without a word and got on to the train. Tom tried to shake his son's hand but it turned into a firm, long hug. Patrick heard the single sob escape from his father and realised again their relationship could only be gauged by the depth of feeling they had for each other and never by the few words they had ever exchanged on the subject. He waved to them and waited until the train pulled out of the station before making his way back to Oxford Street, where he caught a tram and arrived for his appointment at the Barracks with half an hour to spare.

III

War

Chapter 26

Pat Sheridan had already given thought as to what life in the army would be like and decided, no matter the contrast with his current mode, he would endeavour to take it in his stride. He had spent time in the company of stockmen, drovers, shearers and the like whilst growing up at Magdalene and he thought they were, probably, the most down-to-earth characters one could possibly meet. Their language was more than colourful and conversation concerning the opposite sex was totally uninhibited, more than often a more passing subject whenever they got together for a yarn. So he was not anticipating any shocks to his system with that aspect of living in a totally robust male environment.

He was aware of what he had given up to join the army. But now that the day had come he found the feeling of loss was somewhat tempered by the sense of excitement he felt for the new and unknown experiences which now lay ahead of him.

He passed the army medical with the maximum 'A1' and had been sworn into service that same afternoon whilst touching a single Bible. Several other recruits took the oath of allegiance at the same time. From that moment on he became 'Private Sheridan P.', and subject to strict Standing Orders applying to Australian Armed Services. Next morning he reported to Recruit Reception at the Showgrounds. Following a long wait, just standing around, he was allocated a bunk in the Hordern Pavilion along with fifty or more other recruits, .

It was during that 'just standing around' he thought of Cathy and the night before when they had said 'goodbye' at her tram stop. She had hinted she'd come back to his room at Usher's but, despite his own growing need of her, his will prevailed. Had she known how close he came to acceding to her, she would have persisted further. Whilst his parish priest, the Marist Brothers and his mother had done enough for him to suppress himself one more time, he knew he had a breaking point and on this occasion it had been a very close call.

His thoughts were interrupted by a fellow asking him what was going on and when were they going to do something. Patrick gave him a dismissive, "I dunno, mate," reply and left it at that. But his train of thought had been interrupted and he came 'back to earth', as the saying goes. After leaving their personal gear on their allotted unmade bunks, most of his intake just milled about outside the Pavilion, smoking and making only casual conversation. They were still strangers to each other and as much in the dark about army procedure as each other. So they just waited without demur for they had yet to learn the good old soldier's habit of whinging out loud, with due profanity, on such occasions.

An hour or so later a sergeant who appeared to be in charge of their group came to the door of the quarters. He shouted for attention before ordering them to come in and stand at attention by their bunks. He strode to the centre of the sleeping area with his orderly corporal in tow and addressed the rookies.

"Alright, stand easy you lot, and listen up to what I say because I won't be repeating it and I don't like answering silly bloody questions afterwards. It's my misfortune to have to look after you for the next few days and the prospect doesn't fill me with delight when I look at you scrawny mob. In ten minutes' time you'll fall-in outside into two columns, with you two as markers," he said pointing to two recruits standing nearest him.

"We are going to march to the other side of the Grounds to headquarters section where you'll be individually interviewed to find out that part of the army, if any, to which you're suited. You'll come back here for midday mess and this afternoon I'll take you to the Q Store, where you'll be equipped with everything you need for life in this here army.

"The first item handed you will be an identity disc (or 'dog tag' as we call it). It is light aluminium and will be stamped with your name and initials, blood group and religion. It will be attached to a leather bootlace and you will tie it around your neck immediately and not remove it, for any reason whatsoever, until you are discharged from the service.

"At ten hundred hours tomorrow morning," he went on, "there will be a short-arm inspection at the medical hut, which is known as the Regimental Aid Post or R.A.P. Whilst there you'll be injected against TB and various other complaints and inoculated for Small Pox. A lot of you big bronzed Anzacs will feel crook afterwards and the CO may give you the rest of the day off - but don't count on it because we have a lot to do before I get rid of you bastards later in the week."

Patrick had just gone with the flow and things were much as he expected them to be. He'd yarned with a few of the blokes who were friendly enough, but a bit guarded and not at the stage of exchanging names or backgrounds as yet. That would come later, he thought. He felt a little out of it as everybody seemed to smoke cigarettes. It was a habit he had not acquired simply because he didn't like the few he had smoked, on the sly, with his football mates at Marist Brothers.

Everything the sergeant had outlined took place, more or less on time, and it was only the interview which made Patrick pause for thought. It had always been his intention to join the infantry and become a foot soldier, but the interviewer, a Captain Darling, a soldier from the previous world war, put forward ideas which he had rejected. The officer pointed out he not only 'had' his Intermediate but also a BA from the University of Sydney and was somewhat taken aback by Patrick's firm "no" to his suggestion he apply for officer training school. The officer mooted he might wish to join the Army's Education Section to which his qualifications suitably equipped him or perhaps the Services Entertainment Unit because of his Conservatorium background.

"No, thank you, sir," Patrick said quietly but firmly, "I joined with the intention of fighting if necessary and that is what I think I should do."

"Well, that's up to you, young man, but I had to let you know the options. So, it's the pbi for you which, as you will learn, is an abbreviation for 'the poor bloody infantry'. Good luck to you," said the officer as he beckoned another recruit forward to take Patrick's place at the interview desk.

It was three days later when he found himself sitting back-to-back with another recruit on the tray of an army open three ton truck on its way along Parramatta Road, in convoy with four other similar vehicles. There were six other sets of troops seated back-to-back to avoid sliding about the tray, the same as Patrick and his mate, with another twenty or so men being securely seated by resting against the vehicle's sideboards. The other trucks were similarly loaded and were on their way, with spine-jarring bounces, to the Liverpool Army Barracks, where their passengers would disembark and become part of the 1st Australian Infantry Training Battalion.

As the trucks entered the barracks area the passengers were given the universal chorus of "you'll be sorry!" from troops already stationed there. A resplendently uniformed sergeant major with Sam Brown belt and shoulder strap - obviously a permanent army man - was waiting for them as they alighted with their gear. This included backpacks, sidepacks and a cumbersome, bulging duffel (or sausage) bag into which most of their recently issued army clothing had been stuffed. These also served as a pillows for a soldier's bunks, as no bedding, other than two blankets and a hessian palisade were 'on issue' from the army Q Store. A sufficiently fatigued soldier could rest his weary head peacefully on this, even if it held, amongst many other items, his boots, metal mess gear, webbing equipment, aluminium water bottle and an odd book or two.

Initially, this 'Sar'-major' seemed a little more benign than NCOs encountered at the Showgrounds. He addressed them in reasonable tone and language after they had lined up, four ranks deep, with their gear at their feet, on the parade ground.

"You are now members of C Company, 1st Infantry Training Battalion. Your training will commence tomorrow am," he told them. "Roll call will be at 0600 hours followed by mess at 0615 and you'll parade here again at 0700 in fatigues and army hat for the start of your physical training. This will be followed by a short route march of no more than ten miles in order to break in your boots and other issued gear you will be wearing.

"When I break you off here, you'll go to one of those huts behind you and find a bunk. Claim your bunk by placing your gear on it. Take the empty hessian palisade you will find on it to the area outside the far end of the hut and fill it with the fresh straw you will find there.

"The rest of the day will be yours. Make up your bunk and stow your gear and a meal will be available at the mess hut at 1230 hours. Before you start any spine bashing, I suggest you learn to find your way around the camp; where the ablution and toilet block is located, the recreation hut and Red Cross centre, the orderly room and places like that. Once you have done that you will start to feel at home, or something like that. Alright?

"Okay; that's all for now; we are being informal and a little easy on you lot today as some of you are still recovering from needles you got earlier this week. But be assured, from today on you will know you have joined the army and moments of joy will be few and very far between from then on. Don't blame me; remember you were all so-called bloody volunteers. In other words, you asked for it and believe me you will get it."

And so life in the army began for the pianist-turned-soldier. Despite realistic anticipation of what it would be like, young Patrick Sheridan had to admit the first few days had left him thoroughly washed out. In common with most new recruits he was already missing people and aspects of his civilian life, but in his case it was the absence of the piano that created the greatest void and at this time he could not imagine any way in which it could be filled.

He was not feeling sorry for himself in the least and knew he would overcome these symptoms of withdrawal but, at this initial stage, he was finding it difficult. Other matters, to which he would have to become accustomed, had not helped his mood. He found army food to be far from appetising or even edible. Its total lack of appeal could have been brought about, to some extent, by the injections and inoculation which had left him very much under the weather for some days now.

Also, his disposition was not improved by sleeping in his army underwear on a rough blanket which covered a hessian sack, partly filled with straw, on an iron cot bed, with his duffel bag for pillow. It would take getting used to, for it was not conducive for sound sleep. Even more so when he was also subject to snores and grunts from many of the fifty or so of his comrades who shared his barracks. As the WO had said, he asked for it and he was getting it, but he knew this washed out feeling was temporary and would pass once it had taken its course.

He did not know it now, but these small problems would be dismissed from his mind once his training progressed and the army assumed tighter and tighter control of his mind and body during their waking hours. Through means he had not anticipated he was able also to overcome the great sense of loss he was feeling for the piano.

Chapter 27

*L*ife in the barracks hut took on fresh dimensions as the young soldiers became better acquainted. General group conversations and behaviour became more animated and outlandish in the accepted Australian way.

Patrick found two quite different but amiable blokes about his age occupying bunks either side of him. One was Phil Ritchie, a tall, gangling youth with fair features, a ready smile and friendly manner, who had worked as a rates clerk in a Sydney suburban council. He and Patrick had got on well from the start as they talked of cricket, rugby league, politics, the army and other matters, in a slow casual way.

Matt McCallum was a different kettle of fish; also tall and well-built with a perpetually red face and a far-receded dark hairline. He appeared somewhat taciturn at first, which was really only a natural shyness, and he soon joined bunk-side conversation with the other two. He had been an apprentice boilermaker at Mort's Dock in Sydney. As was a common practice in these days of the Great Depression, he was laid off upon reaching the age of 21 and thus entitled to receive an adult wage - which was unacceptable to his employer. Patrick had already noticed there were many such unemployed young men in the ranks of the AIF.

He told his new cobbers he'd been a stockman and had worked on his family's property but it was a long time before he mentioned his musical background to them. In a short matter of time they would come to realise it was unimportant what one had done in civilian life, for nobody cared. All that mattered in the Australian Army was what kind of a soldier you were and, more importantly, what kind of a bloke.

The trio fell into a routine of doing things together; going to mess, attending roll calls, parades and pt drill, and tramping side-by-side on interminable route marches, which was the main feature of early life in the army.

Those first two weeks were taken up with getting the new recruits sufficiently physically fit to cope with the more arduous training which lay ahead. Physical 'bloody' jerks, as they were known, for hours on end each day followed by the route marches down long, dusty bush tracks which branched in every direction through miles of low scrubland adjacent to the camp. All the unaccustomed activity cured Patrick of his insomnia - in those early weeks he and most of his hutmates were sleeping soundly in their bunks before the 9pm 'lights out' bugle sounded its instruction.

The training battalion was staffed by an Establishment of experienced officers and NCOs who, as a matter of policy, appeared to treat the recruits with scant regard and little or no tolerance. This attitude was made manifest as often as possible during this stage of their training, and no opportunity was missed to belittle or upbraid them, either individually or collectively, when the occasion seemed appropriate.

The army thought it important to temporarily lower their morale in this way as it saw its job as turning boys into men as quickly as possible. This harsh approach combined with weeks of arduous training was the proven method for doing this. The aim of lowering their self-esteem was to stop them thinking for themselves and to respond only to orders from their superior officers, whether they be of commissioned or non-commissioned rank. The army had to own the recruits' minds as well as their bodies. Having them obey orders promptly, without thinking and without question, could save their lives and the lives of their comrades. When in actual combat it was important they had learnt this lesson from the outset. After a few weeks of this Patrick and his mates, after discussing this unrelenting hostility, decided they were just a pack of bastards on ego trips intent on exercising their authority by 'taking it out' on blokes who were under their thumb.

Their training went on unabated. In the fourth week they were issued with bayonets and rifles, Lee-Enfield .303s, a cumbersome old-fashioned looking weapon and a relic of the 1914-18 war. Their long hours of physical training were replaced now by similar periods of rifle drill... shoulder arms, slope arms, port arms, salute arms, stand at ease, stand easy... every morning for several days and invariably followed by route marches in the afternoon, with rifles slung on their shoulders, over inhuman distances. The voices of the NCOs in charge of these treks rang in their ears for days and nights afterwards; ... quick march, left, left, left, right, left, pick up your bloody feet, keep in step, left, right, left, had a good home and I left, left, right, left, and so it went on for mile after mile. Every hour or so the corporal or sergeant in charge would call a halt and announce "emmer emmeresses" (mms) or men may smoke and the troops would break off and rest their exhausted bodies by squatting or just lying back on the side of the track, but not before they lit a cigarette, or rolled the 'makin's'.

It was on one of these breaks that Matt McCallum offered Patrick a smoke and, not for the first time, he accepted. From that point on he joined a huge percentage of his fellow soldiers who had an addiction for nicotine. When he went to the canteen that night he bought the first of many packets of Plain Capstan he would smoke over the ensuing few years.

As the ten weeks course progressed into its second half, Pat Sheridan started to notice changes in his appearance. Apart from his longish, dark hair being cropped to the army-required short back and sides, he was leaner although his body had bulked up in parts due to the muscle building exercising it was still undergoing on a daily basis. Thanks to frequent exposure to the elements his face was sun-browned and slightly weather-beaten as were his neck and arms. With these changes superimposed on his tall straight figure he was indeed starting to take on the appearance of the traditional bronzed Anzac.

In just a few weeks the army had changed him, outwardly, in some respects, but inwardly he was pretty much the same. Part of his life still felt numb from not having a piano in it. Intermittently he yearned for his parents and Magdalene, but now being away from Cathy Jordan had become suddenly the great cross he had to bear. He had never missed anyone or anything so much in all his young life.

He wrote to her when possible and his letters became more affectionate and loving with each missive. She replied in kind and they exchanged thoughts about their feeling for each other which might not otherwise have been expressed. They both realised now they were more in love than they had ever been. He could not wait to see her again and started to count the days to the end of the course when, it had been rumoured, the battalion might be given a few days' leave before being posted to established units.

Pat Sheridan was not maudlin about these things and he knew a majority of his soldier mates experienced similar feelings of deprivation, but, like him, they felt such matters were non masculine and, therefore, never raised in military company.

It was during the seventh week of the course that it happened. The route march had been shorter that afternoon and, after a shower in the huge ablution block, he was lying on his bunk reading a Penguin edition of Grahame Green's Brighton Rock while waiting for evening mess. For some reason he put the book down and fell into a kind of reverie and, quite suddenly, interior music came from nowhere to flood his mind. He had not heard these orchestral bars before and realised they must be of his own creation; something which had lain dormant these past few months when his mind had been preoccupied with so many other matters.

He realised at once his want to compose had returned in force and it excited him for it could mean, aesthetically, a slight bridging of the gap between what he was doing now and the life he had recently left behind. He knew that there would increasingly be fewer of those quiet hours he would need to create music, but there would be occasions and he would make the most of these as they arose.

That very evening, after mess, he bought a large, blank writing pad at the canteen and, after finding a small table in The Salvation Army Hut, sat down and ruled every page into orchestral manuscript. As and when the muse came, he thought, he would be ready for it and all in all that was a needful and satisfying prospect for him.

It was after writing to Cathy a few days later and telling her of this, that the thought struck him. He now harboured an urgent need to write another symphonic work but felt, despite his own enthusiasm, he would need some additional incentive and inspiration to attempt it under his present, portended circumstances. If he were to do it for Cathy, he thought, those two requirements would be satisfied.

When possible he turned the thought over in his mind during the next few days and, finally, wrote to her and announced his intention to write a concerto for violin and orchestra. It would be dedicated to her and would be hers and hers alone to do with as she pleased, for it was to be an expression of his devotion to her. Every note he created would draw him closer to her, he wrote, and enable him to better withstand the great personal loneliness her absence had brought to his life.

He decided, he wrote, it would be a truly romantic work with the first movement embracing a pastoral setting based on his early years at Magdalene. The second and more robust movement would follow and portray musical and personal episodes of a student's life at a conservatorium of music.

The third and final stanza, he went on, would tell of the eternal and ever growing love they had for each other and include the overwhelming sense of joy and happiness they would find when they were reunited once more. His first endeavour would be to create a recurring theme for the entire work, of such musical beauty that it would enshrine the real purpose of the composition which was, simply, to expound the depth of his affection for her. She had responded promptly in a letter which expressed her unbounded pleasure and gratitude for this gift of newly created music he promised her.

"I know you will be giving an important part of yourself to me and something which derives from the very essence of your being and I will treasure it most dearly when it is done," she wrote. "It is another bond which will bind us, my dearest Sheridan, and I love you even more, if that is possible, for your profoundly loving and thoughtful undertaking."

Pat Sheridan was a man's man in all respects but the gentle side of his artistic self did escape at times. He could never have played the piano the way he did without having something of the soul of a musical poet and, therefore, the starry-eyed prose he was exchanging with the girl he loved came quite naturally to him. It would be beyond him to perceive how this could possibly reflect upon his manliness.

A slight lessening in the training schedule had allowed romantic and musical thoughts to invade his mind. This luxury and such recollections quickly came to an end a day or two later when the orderly sergeant burst through the door of the hut at 6am as usual, stamping along the line of bunks and bellowing repeatedly:

"Up up up up up, you lazy bastards, wakey, wakey, get your hands off it, roll call in five minutes."

He stopped when he reached the far door and offered them a few word in a more reasonable tone of voice.

"Now, listen up, you blokes, just a word of warning and this is just from me to you. The soft part of your training schedule is over and you'll find the next few weeks will be bloody hell in comparison. The commander of C Company, Major Burley, is taking the morning parade and he'll fill you in on the joys that lie ahead of you. He'll tell you about the four-day exercise on the use of the bayonet which starts today and, believe me, after that you will be looking for an early bunk. You'll start on the rifle range next week and learn to shoot, I hope. And then in coming days you'll be introduced to the Bren Gun, and mortar weapons. A special treat will be instruction on tossing the 36m hand grenade and if that doesn't make you shit yourselves, nothing will.

"Night exercises that will see you in the field for 72 unbroken hours will be followed a day later by full battalion manoeuvres under combat conditions and will include the use of live ammunition. Now, aren't you a lot of lucky pricks? Have fun, ha ha, but don't say I didn't warn you. Don't be late for parade this morning as our fearless major can be very nasty in his treatment of stragglers. Get yourselves out for roll call, now!" and he left the hut, slamming the door behind him.

The now-usual groaning, whinging and complaining in general, from occupants of the hut followed his departure with stock-in-trade blasphemy and irreverent diatribes used by Australian servicemen down the years in such circumstances. Patrick had got to know several of these people and found them to be, in his opinion, basically a decent bunch of young Aussie blokes from many different walks of life and he now felt drawn to them in a half-brotherly way.

Already within the ranks of C Company in general, and his hut in particular, there was a growing sense of camaraderie which was initiated by the supposedly rough deal they were getting from their so-called superior officers. It had become not an "us against them" situation but rather "we can take anything those bastards hand out" which was binding them together. Young Sheridan thought to himself that this brave attitude would be sorely tested in the concluding weeks of their training.

He also realised it would now be many a long day before he again would have time or an appropriate place in which to commence Cathy's concerto. But he reasoned if the music did start to flow, no matter where he was or what he was doing, he would be able to retain it in his mind until such time as he could commit it to his homemade manuscript.

The warning the orderly sergeant had given them came true in every respect for the men of C Company. They had expected things to be tough but nothing could have prepared them for the gruelling and unrelenting pace of arduous and demanding training to which they were now subjected. They were left totally exhausted at the end of each and every day of those final weeks and with the kind of fatigue no amount of normal sleep seemed to alleviate. They were even too tired to complain and whinge in the usual way and most hut bunks were occupied by wearied bodies when orders permitted such rest during any hour of the day or night.

Like the others, Patrick seemed to be perpetually tired and was able to write only brief, but still tender, notes to his girl. He had tried always to write regularly to his parents but of late this meant fortnightly rather than weekly. The last few weeks had seen further changes in Patrick's attitude. Being tired-out contributed to a slight bloody-mindedness developing in him and at times his temper was on a short fuse. Life in the army had proved to be a rough and tough existence and he appeared to be responding accordingly. Now there was no music to tame his savage breast.

This manifested itself on the rifle range when he fired the first shots from his.303. He had used rifles on the property and was known as a good shot because of the ducks, rabbits, dingoes and other game he had bagged there. But his first two shots at the range missed the target altogether and the markers in the pit signalled wipe out or 'Maggie's drawers' (a piece of white cloth shaped like women's bloomers hoisted in front of the target.) With his third shot he aimed slightly to the right and scored an 'outer' which meant he had hit the extreme edge of the large target area. He was lying prone to shoot as were the forty or so other trainees on either side of him and all were under the supervision of two warrant officers who were conducting the shoot. One of them had observed Patrick's results and made the suggestion to him that if that was the best he could do he might as well "fix bayonet and charge the bastard."

"I'd do a damn side better if you gave me a decent rifle!" shouted Patrick as he turned to look at his tormentor and continued "The sights on this bloody thing probably got rusted at Gallipoli."

"Watch your tongue, Private, and hold your fire for a minute," replied the WO who then called out to a sergeant marksman standing by for just this kind of thing.

"Hey Jack, there is another of these young ladies blaming his sights. Have a look at it will you and after you kick his arse see if you can teach him to shoot."

The marksman's first two trial shots were no better than Pat's, who volunteered to the sergeant he thought the weapon was shooting to the right. After several shots the sergeant agreed and called for another rifle to be passed down to him.

"You were bloody well right Sheridan. You seem to know a bit about shooting so try this, and there's nothing wrong with the sights because it's mine."

Patrick resumed his position on the mound and his first two shot scored an 'inner' just outside the bull and the next three were in the black circle.

"Don't worry about this joker, Barry, he can shoot," the sergeant told the warrant officer. "He seems a natural and a possible marksman. I'd keep an eye on him if I were you."

The WO approached him as he came off the range and told him, "I don't like your tongue, Sheridan, so show a bit of respect in future if you know what's good for you. The sergeant tells me you are not a bad shot; are you interested in specialist training? The army is always in need of snipers and we can soon find out if you are good enough for that."

The ex-pianist was in no mood to volunteer for anything and looked the WO in the eye and replied, "I'll do anything the army orders me to do Sergeant Major," he said and then added a little sarcastically, "if that's alright with you."

A lot of troops had seen and overheard what had taken place on the range and the incident was recounted by many in the huts that night. It seemed as though Sheridan was getting a name for himself in C Company for there had been one or two other incidents associated with his name. After evening mess the troops usually had a couple of free hours before lights out when they just lounged on their bunks and yarned, read books or magazines, or cleaned their boots and rifles, and some of them played cards. Through his bunk mate, Phil Ritchie, Patrick found himself, somewhat reluctantly, involved with a group who played '500' for about an hour every night. He would have preferred to read but they were short of a fourth and he had no option but to oblige his mate.

It was during one of these games the company's well-known 'bovver boy' from the next hut barged through the door with two cronies and started tipping over empty bunks, pulling blankets off troops already in bed and throwing books and magazines about the hut all in the name of 'having a bit of fun'. He was big and lumbering and Patrick had seen him intimidating smaller men when he broke into long-waiting mess queues - which he did on a regular basis. His name was Bracken and his stock retort to anyone who objected to, or disagreed with, his half-witted antics was "if you don't bloody-well like it you can see me behind the canteen any time you like."

He stopped when he came to the bunk the bottom of which was being used as a card table by Patrick and his mates who were sitting on bunks either side of it.

"Look at these bloody pansies, will you, playing 500 like nice little boys; it's about time they grew up," said Bracken to his sidekicks as he reached down and swept the cards off the blanket.

Patrick was on his feet in an instant and stood face to face with Bracken who was not much taller but certainly much heavier than he was.

"What did you want to do that for?" he asked the idiot with almost unbridled anger.

"Because I felt like it, pooftah, do you want to make something of it?"

It was with that that Patrick lost the little composure he had left and grabbed the sturdier man by the collar and pulled his face into his.

"Call me that again, you dopey bludger, and we won't wait for the back of the canteen because I'll sit you on your fat arse right here and now," he said.

Bracken waivered because he had seen something in Patrick's expression which made him realise he had bitten off a bit more than he could chew and, like most of his type, there was a bit of dingo in him and it showed in his eyes.

"Easy on, there's no need to get like that, I was just having a bit of fun," he said defensively with a decided change in tone of voice.

"Well, you've had your bloody fun, now pick the cards up off the floor and put them back on the bunk and then get the hell out of here and don't come back," said the formerly polite and gentlemanly musician turned soldier. Bracken stood his ground for a few moments looking straight at Pat before finally giving way and, stooping down, picked up the cards and placed them on the bunk. Then, without another word or look, he followed his two mates out of the hut.

Most of the occupants had gathered round and had seen what transpired and there were cries of approval from all for what Patrick had just done. Once more he had, unintentionally, drawn attention to himself and in such a way that it would not be forgotten by those who had witnessed it.

"Bloody hell, Pat, I didn't know you could swear, much less fight. I thought that big bastard would kill you," said Phil Ritchie as he shuffled the cards to restart the game.

Sheridan was still red faced and breathing heavily as he resumed his seat on the bunk and slowly allowed his anger to subside.

"He probably could have, Phil, but somebody had to put a stop to that sod and it was worth risking a bloody good hiding just to find out if he was as tough as he pretended to be," said the hero of the hut.

Sheridan thought about the fracas as he prepared for bed after the game and he was not happy about losing his temper like that. He realised he would have to watch himself as it was out-of-character and he didn't want it to go any further. He had no regrets about joining the army because, for him, it had been almost a sacred duty. But the military training process, and the apparently banal people conducting it, were getting to him and it would be some time in the future before he would appreciate in full the benefits of this harsh initial training.

It was drawing to a close now, and for the last several weeks he had been tirelessly instructed in the art of killing other human beings - at the same time how to prevent them from killing him. It was enough to change anyone's outlook on life, at least in some way, and he was no exception. He had been told that when their training finished, the life of a soldier was one of utter boredom. Unless, of course, he was in action. He welcomed the prospect of those boring days and the free, golden hours they would bring to enable him to concentrate on the concerto he had undertaken to compose for Cathy. This would also mean his intermittent return to the world of music, where his heart and spirit formerly dwelt for so long.

Chapter 28

Patrick's intake into the 1st Infantry Training Battalion concluded its twelve weeks' course amid a degree of pomp, something which had been totally absent up to that day. There was feverish activity throughout the entire camp the next morning as staff and recruits prepared for the battalion's final parade.

A saluting dais had been erected, together with seating arrangements for the staff, at the head of the large parade ground and troops had started to file in to their positions as members of the 6th Division Military Band disembarked from two buses parked near the barrack's entrance.

Full battle dress was the order of the day but with slouch hats instead of steel helmets as was customary on such occasions. The troops paraded with shouldered rifles to which their bayonets had been fixed.

When the assembly was complete an almost eerie silence came over the throng, which gave the event a special sense of occasion for the troops as the battalion's senior sergeant major took over the parade.

"PARAAAADE ... PARAAAADE ... 'HONE," he bellowed in a huge stentorian voice and, upon the entire assembly clicking to attention and ordering arms almost as one, he continued with the same penetrating force.

"REPORT..." and waited until the four company commanders had indicated back their men were 'all present and correct' before again addressing the troops.

"BATTALION WILL PREPARE TO MARCH, SIX ABREAST IN COLUMN OF ROUTE LED BY HQ COMPANY. BATTALION ... SL0000PE ARMS ...BATTALION. MARK TIME. ... HQ COMPANY, QUICK MARCH, RIGHT WHEEL ... FORWARD."

As the HQ Company swung onto the wide path leading to the barrack's entrance/exit gate, the army band moved off ahead of them and struck up a stirring military air which could not help but send a chill down the spine of all present. The entire battalion fell into step as it left the barracks and took the tarred road on the outskirts of Liverpool, with the men marching as they had never marched before - such was the affect the fine martial music had on them as it was in such contrast to the "left, right, left" ad infinitum, delivered by surly NCOs, to which they had become accustomed.

After a measured mile of this, the march wound its way back to the barracks and onto the parade ground where the salute was taken from the dais by the battalion's commanding officer, Lieutenant-Colonel Ash. The troops' heads snapped in unison on the command "eyes right" as each company passed the dais to acknowledge the Commanding Officer's presence thereon, and for the prolonged salute he was holding for the entire battalion as it paraded past his platform.

When the battalion troops had returned to the positions they had occupied earlier in the day, the senior sergeant major again took over the parade. His voice rang out once again, ordering the incredibly quiet assembly to, "Order arms. Stand at ease, stand easy," before saluting and handing the parade back to the CO who wished to address the troops.

"Congratulations, you men," said Colonel Ash. "You have been a splendid force and I and my instructors are very proud of this battalion for the standard it has achieved in such a short space of time. Your initial training as Australian infantrymen is now complete and next week you will be advised of the AIF battalions to which you will be posted. Your training will continue with those units to bring you to their requirements before being posted overseas.

"You have all made it quite clear, one way and another, of how you feel about us," he continued with a glimmer of a smile, "but we make no apologies for our training methods for they were conceived in your own best interests as soldiers who will go into action one day soon. I also realise it will be quite some time before you appreciate the truth in what I have just said. We don't give a tinker's cuss if you call us all kinds of bastards if it means every one of you march away from here as well trained as we can possibly make you. Our methods are strict but they are successful and you people are living proof of that claim.

"As I said, most of you will be posted immediately to battalions awaiting overseas posting, but some of you have displayed attributes which make you suitable for training in specialised areas of infantry warfare before being posted, and they will be notified accordingly. Recommendations have been made for many of you to be promoted to non-commissioned rank but that will be at the discretion of the commanders of units to which you are posted.

"I repeat, as your commanding officer, I am extremely proud of you men as in my opinion you are the best trained body of troops to leave this place. I wish you good fighting and the best of personal good fortune for what lies ahead.

"Just to show we do have a heart we're arranging for company wet canteen to open at 1700 hours for one hour before mess and then from 1900 to 2100 hours, for tonight only. Now, wait for it, the beer will be free for that first hour with my compliments and those of your instructors. All of us hope to share a drink with you whilst you are still sober. Good luck to you all… It's all yours, Sergeant Major," he concluded as he handed back the parade.

It was a very happy C Company hut when the troops got back that afternoon. They quickly shed their belts, gaiters and tunics and stood around their bunks smoking and talking in groups.

"Thank the gods that's bloody over and we can get on with the real stuff," said Matt McCallum, Patrick's other bunkie. "But how bloody good was that marching with the band? For the first time you bastards looked like soldiers and you, Sheridan, had your chest chucked out further than Betty Grable."

"I wouldn't go that far, you bloody twerp, but I have to say I got a kick out of it; that's a good sound and does make you stride out," said Patrick who had really enjoyed the experience, "and hundreds of pairs of bloody boots hitting the deck at the same time was pretty stirring to this boy from the bush," he offered.

It was times like this that he wondered if there had ever been that other life solely devoted to music. He had lived and breathed nothing but army for the past several weeks and had been totally engulfed. It dominated his every waking hour to the extent he began to think there was no other existence. Sometimes, due to frustration, he asked himself the question as to why he had joined up in the first place as he now knew his presence in the forces made very little difference one way or the other.

Finally, he arrived at a stock answer for his questioning-self. He had retained his love of country and felt an obligation to defend it no matter how paltry his contribution appeared to be. He had met a lot of genuine blokes in the AIF, including many of his hut mates, and this raised the other question of, "why should they fight and not him?"

It was at the conclusion of his basic training he decided that in future he would accept whatever came along in the army, be it fair or unfair, and there would be no more self-conjecture about why he enlisted. If he had not done so he would have deemed himself a fraud and he knew he could never live with that, even if he became a pianist of some renown.

From that point on he returned to being the Pat Sheridan of old… calm, at peace with the world; with frequent reflections on growing up on Magdalene and the love and affection he bore for his parents; still ambitious for a career in music when this was all over; still very much in love with his girl, Cathy.

His intention now was, in so far as his military duties would allow him, to continue on with composing the promised concerto, the central theme for which, despite all distractions, was now firmly fixed in his musician's mind.

Chapter 29

There were only a few wharf workers on the dock as the troopship and former passenger liner 'M.V. Angola' pulled away from its Darling Harbour berth. Its sailing time had been a military secret as there were rumours of a German raider marauding in the Indian Ocean. And so there were no families or friends present on the pier to farewell the diggers at 5 o'clock on a bleak winter's morning in the year of 1940. When the vessel cast off it carried a near full-strength battalion of nearly a thousand men. Conditions were cramped and the essential facilities for use in normal daily life were no more than adequate.

Corporal Pat Sheridan felt somewhat excited and at the same time a little sombre as he leant on the rail of the ship and his eyes took in the rugged scene of the Sydney Heads as the vessel made its way out to the Pacific Ocean. The ship was bound for Egypt via Perth, Port Said and then Alexandria where the battalion would disembark for intended training with British forces in Palestine prior to joining the Allied armies now fighting the Germans in Europe. At least that was the original intention but this may have changed now that Mussolini's Italy had come into the war on the side of Nazi Germany.

The deck had been crowded when the vessel set sail up Sydney Harbour but the first sitting for morning mess had seen most of the 'passengers' disappear below deck. Patrick's company had to await the second sitting and he and some of the troops from his Platoon had stayed outside to look at the last land they would see for several days. They could also make out the grey image of the lone escort, an Australian destroyer from the last war, standing off the Heads waiting for its ward.

His platoon had been allocated a series of bunks on the second deck, the whole of which was a seagoing dormitory, with a series of four bunks, one on top of the other stretching almost up to the underdeck. Occupants of the top bunks were required to step on the lower ones in order to reach their place of rest. They shared their small bunks with their personal gear, which included bayonet and rifle, kit bag, back and sidepack, and gas mask, amongst other items, which left very little space for their wearied bodies to rest.

Patrick turned out to be a good sailor and had no trouble with sea sickness. It did affect many of his cobbers though as many of them spent most of the first night at the ship's rail ridding themselves of their evening meal and everything else they had eaten in the previous several hours.

Corporal Sheridan hoisted himself on to his second-tier bunk that night and for the first time in several days had time to think about all that had happened since he finished his initial infantry training at the Liverpool Camp those several weeks back.

With most members of his training company, he was posted to 6th Division battalion being formed at Rutherford, near Newcastle, in New South Wales. After four more weeks of intensive training and full-scale manoeuvres the entire unit was posted to Ingleburn Camp, near Liverpool, for a short period to await embarkation for overseas service. On completion of their initial training all those weeks back, they had been given only three days leave - which ruled out Patrick's return to Bathurst as too much of the precious time would be taken up with train travel. Instead he and some of his friends stayed at an army leave facility at the Sydney Showgrounds. He had an emotional reunion with Cathy and on that first night they sat for hour upon hour on the sofa in her parent's drawing room indulging themselves in the pleasure of each other's company. She had rehearsals with the orchestra for most of the following day but they met for dinner that evening and he attended the orchestra's performance on the last night of his leave.

They put on a brave face when it came time to say "goodbye", but his real mood asserted itself after he had put her in a cab and started to walk to his tram. All his recent civilian past came back to him and again he was anguished at the thought of what he had left behind... most of all his own Cathy, his family and his music which had left a void in life that could never be filled. He had deliberately avoided visiting the Conservatorium during his leave as he did not want to be reminded of how much his time there had meant to him. As for the piano, he would not touch the keys again until the conflict was over but somehow he would find the time and motivation to write the romantic work he had promised his loved one.

These thoughts came to his mind but in no way did he feel anyway sorry for himself. He had to do what he felt he was obliged to do and realised there were many thousands of Australians who were making sacrifices just as great as his because they were burdened with patriotic convictions similar to his own.

On the first full morning parade at the Ingleburn Camp the battalion was advised it was officially 'on draft' for active service overseas and that five days pre-embarkation leave would commence at 0800 the following morning. They were also given a pointed reminder before breaking off that the charge for not returning to the unit on time would not be one of 'absent without leave' but of 'desertion', which was a military crime subject to dire penalties for the offender.

Among the people he had got to know well in his platoon were two teenaged Tasmanians who could not get home and back in the leave time allowed, and they jumped at his suggestion they come home with him to Magdalene for the three days he intended to spend there. Tom and Irene made them welcome and the wonderful housekeeper, Molly Read, made sure their every meal was a feast.

On the evening before they were to return to Sydney, Patrick went to his parents' bedroom as they were about to retire for the night. Irene, whilst still deeply apprehensive about her son going to war, did not recriminate about the circumstances under which he enlisted. Love, affection, and concern set the tone of this conversation on the eve of his departure. Tom did not contribute a great deal and simply spoke of what they would do when he came home from the war.

Tom drove and Irene came also when they left for the Bathurst rail station the following morning. They had left early in order for Patrick to be able to drop in and say a quick goodbye to Cathy and Harry Beck, with whom he had boarded whilst at the Marist Brothers, and to Sister Annunciata, who was quite emotionally disturbed as she bade him farewell.

Having his two friends with him had helped ease the tension at the final parting from his parents just as the train was about to leave. He took Tom's hand firmly in his before placing his arms around his shoulders in a final embrace, and then kissing and holding his mother closely for some moments before breaking away and getting on the train with his companions. He saw tears streaming down her face as he waved from the open carriage door of the departing train. And from nowhere the thought came into his head that he may never see his mother again.

He left his friends to their own devices when they got back to Sydney Central Station and caught a cab to Cathy's home at Double Bay, where her mother had invited him to spend the final two days of his leave.

The young couple spent every possible minute together and tried to be light-hearted in their companionship as always, but there were moments of silence when a pall descended and each knew what the other was thinking of what lay ahead. On the last night of his leave, after the family had retired, he knocked gently on her bedroom door with the intention, ostensibly, of saying goodnight. She opened the door and when she saw him standing there she reached out her hand and drew him into the room and quietly closed the door.

It was not surprising that this was the last of his thoughts before falling asleep that night on the troopship as it made its way down the south eastern coast of Australia.

Patrick was content throughout the voyage and accepted the conditions as they were no worse than he had expected. Importantly for him he had, after some deliberate searching, found a small retreat near one of the lifeboats at the stern of the vessel. Although 'off limits' to troops, he had taken the risk as it was tolerable for his purpose, being quiet and unfrequented by the crew and also shaded, to some extent, from the relentless rays of the Indian Ocean sun.

Between roll calls, parades, mess and periods of his platoon's physical exercising, he was able to devote two or three hours most days to working on his violin concerto. When he thought about it, it would be inconceivable to most people that a soldier on his way to war was endeavouring to compose and fully orchestrate an extensive piece of serious classical music. It was not an easy assignment he had set himself. Most times after coming to his bolt hole he would just sit and collect himself for some time in order to prepare for the task in hand. However, despite his external situation his inner inspiration was still present and the music started to flow from his soul and mind on to the manuscript. Before the ship would reach the Red Sea the first movement would be complete and the second nearly so. Being back with music to such an extent had brought out a lot of the old Patrick and the tough masculine hide he was building around himself was being somewhat tempered through his mind being associated with former times.

He could only physically write his music in daylight hours and there was still plenty of time to fill in during the tedious voyage. He was in a regular poker school with five of his Rifle Section mates and the cards usually came out after evening mess - shuffled and dealt in a sea of cigarette smoke until 'lights out'. He read often whilst in his bunk and drew on a good supply of books which had been retained from the ex-passenger ship's library. He and some of his mates occasionally visited, and had a bet, at the 24 hour a day swy game (two-up) located on the lower deck. Run by two naval petty officers, they had cockatoos posted at appropriate points in the unlikely event of a naval or army officer coming into the vicinity. If nothing else, it helped pass the time even for those who just came to watch their mates lose their money.

Patrick himself now had a little more money to spend as he had been promoted to the rank of corporal during training at Rutherford, which added three shillings a day to his army pay - quite a significant increase. Upon joining the numbered AIF Battalion, he and some of the men from his hut at Liverpool Training Camp had been posted to C Section, 2nd Platoon of B Company. A platoon, usually commanded by a Lieutenant, comprised three rifle sections of sixteen men, with each section commanded by a sergeant or a corporal. During the battalion manoeuvres at Rutherford, C Section had done well when undertaking the platoon's responsibility for frontline reconnaissance. Pat Sheridan was somewhat responsible for this because he took very easily to map reading, compass bearings and noting and illustrating the terrain of any given area.

His platoon commander, Lieutenant Jim Mailey, sent for Patrick the day before the battalion moved to Ingleburn. "Your mob did a bloody good job this week, Sheridan, and I know a lot of it was thanks to you. The company Commander wants me to give you a 'Well done'. He suggested you should take charge of C Section with the rank of corporal. How do you feel about it? You're a good shot according to your report, not bad with a bayonet and the rest of your stuff is pretty good, and you are an ideal choice in my opinion also. Do you want the job?' Patrick looked at the young officer who was not much older than he was. He had been a sergeant in the part time Australian Militia for two or three years before the war and that meant almost automatic promotion to Commissioned rank once hostilities broke out. He seemed a decent, normal young bloke to Patrick but he didn't have much time for any officer as he didn't altogether trust them as a body, so he was careful with his reply.

"Thank you, sir," he said. "I did join up to fight but I don't like the idea of accepting responsibility for other blokes. I'd prefer to leave it that way if possible and there are others in the Section who could do the job as well as I could."

"Well. That's a hell of an attitude to take," said Mailey, "I wouldn't have sent for you if I didn't think you were the right man for the job. The war won't be won by an army of private soldiers and if nobody is willing to take responsibility we might as well give up now." Patrick did not reply and they just sat in silence looking at each other. He was in no position to argue because he had no real objection to accepting minor rank but he didn't want to appear eager. He did see the reasonableness of the officer's argument, and so, at length, he responded quietly.

"I suppose when you put it that way it would be wrong to refuse and if it is still open I'd like to accept the offer."

"Good on you, Corporal, and congratulations," said Mailey, holding out his hand. "Pick up your stripes from the Q Store and I'll see you at the First Officers and NCOs parade at Ingleburn."

He was pleased in a way; it was not a great promotion nor did it entail huge responsibility and they were a good lot of blokes in the section and all got on pretty well together most of the time. He got the usual chiacking when he told them and from that moment on he was no longer known as Pat, Sheridan or Sherrie, but simply 'Corp'.

Instinctively, he started to look after them like a mother hen. He made sure they were all on the same truck for the transfer from Rutherford to Ingleburn and saw to it they were all quartered in the same hut when they got there. He didn't take too much for granted as a Section warranted a sergeant commander and he didn't think it would be too long before that posting happened. Then prime responsibility for the sixteen men would be taken from his hands.

All that transpired about three weeks ago and now that the battalion was on its way to Egypt, it was unlikely a sergeant would be appointed to his Section until after they arrived there. So the job and the responsibility was still his and he determined to do the best he could for those in his charge.

Chapter 30

*A*s was very often the case in such army situations, there was a foul-up in the battalion's arrival arrangements at Alexandria. The convoy of trucks to take it to a British transit camp just outside Cairo had not arrived and, after disembarkin from the 'Angola', it was a discontented and vocally hostile bunch of Australians who were left waiting on the wharf in sweltering conditions. It was over three hours before the transport arrived and it was not a happy introduction to a country in which they were to spend a long period of discomfort.

After a settling-in period of just a few days, the entire infantry unit was transferred to a British training camp in Palestine. It was now clear Australian troops would not be joining the war in Europe as all British forces had been withdrawn from the Continent in the recent evacuation from Dunkirk. Now they would remain in North Africa to help fend off the Italian threat to the Suez Canal which was absolutely essential to the Allies international lines of communication and supply.

Their training, therefore, would be in desert warfare, where it meant not only did troops have to fight the enemy but also contend with incredibly harsh conditions. These included absolute shortage of water; ever present heat and flies; and multitudes of other flying, sting-carrying objects; and worst of all, sand… never ending sand… with sandstorms, in which grit invades every pore of a soldier's sweaty skin.

All this was outlined to them by an Australian Army senior medical officer who gave an amplified address to a full battalion parade on their first day at the training centre. He told the battalion of ways to lessen the extent of these problems; they could never be eliminated but could be made near tolerable by taking the measures he had outlined.

This message, however, was secondary to the main purpose of the parade, which was to issue dire warning of the social diseases which could be contracted in Cairo and other Egyptian cities. Most brothels in these areas were uncontrolled and not medically supervised, and the infection rate was reaching proportions where army medical authorities were becoming alarmed. He concluded by saying he would rather enter a field of battle than one of those places for the enemy posed less risk to his life than the occupants of an Egyptian bordello. He exaggerated, of course, but it emphasised his point.

No doubt he had briefed other Australian units on this similarly but his words probably became straws in the wind as men wearing slouch hats appeared numerically prominent in the long queues which formed outside such establishments in those early days of the war in the Middle East.

With several more weeks of training behind it, the battalion was returned to Alexandria and given five days leave. As with the bulk of the unit, Patrick and three mates from his section decided to stick together and visit Cairo where the British Army provided accommodation of bunks and showers for Imperial Force members on leave. They were looking forward to visiting a city which had a population almost double that of their island continent. The Nile, the Pyramids, and the Desert itself were among the many sights they wished to behold. A cold glass of beer or two, if they could be found, were a priority, as was the meeting with any worthwhile female companionship which might come their way. Socialising only, for the latter, as those inclined otherwise restrained themselves for they feared not so much for their virtue as for their health. They had got the message.

Phil Ritchie, his original 'bunkie', was in Patrick's small leave group together with two blokes from the poker school, Rip Barlow and Jock Wearing. They were four big young men, all about the same age and despite vastly different backgrounds and temperament, they got on well together. Rip had worked in the mines at Coolgardie before joining up and possessed the dry wit and casual approach to all things, typical of those of his calling. He had somewhat surprised his cobbers by his apparent obsession to see a belly dancer in Cairo and they agreed to help in the search whilst there.

Jock Wearing who had helped run his family's wheat property on Eyre Peninsula in South Australia, was more outgoing than the others and all their light talk seemed to centre on him.

Pat Sheridan had a lot of time for these three, as he had for several others in his section. They were straight forward, plain-speaking, dinky di Aussies. Like him, they all had their faults but he liked their company and, if when the day came for them to see action, he could not think of a better bunch to have around him. Being somewhat responsible for his section, Patrick started noticing his members' character traits and although there were three or four he still didn't know that well, he was satisfied with what he saw, especially those three with him at the present time.

Nothing prepared them for the pandemonium that was Cairo. The noise, the smell, the never ending stream of thousands and thousands of people moving like a human stream up and down the streets, lanes and alleyways of the vast, poverty stricken Egyptian city was, initially, beyond their comprehension. As they made their way along densely crowded thoroughfares, with mouths almost hanging open in astonishment, they were constantly confronted by deformed beggars, road side vendors, young and old women of questionable cleanliness offering their services, along with shouting spruikers outside every kind of retail shop, bar and eating house they passed. Their initial and lasting memory of this place would be one of clogged humanity, noise, dust, heat, indescribable odour and extreme poverty. They had come from a country in the midst of a great depression but compared with the abject poverty they had witnessed here, they had come from an affluent society.

Despite everything, the place held their youthful interest as they had never seen anything like this sprawling metropolis before. But after a few hours of non-stop strolling around they needed a break and found a reasonably uncrowded bistro on a side-street away from the main human passageways. The local beer served there wasn't bad; not as cold as they would have liked, but they settled down to enjoy it. By the third round their thirsts had been somewhat slaked.

They yarned at the bar table about the many odd (for them) sights and things they had seen that morning but it was the usually quiet miner from Coolgardie who was doing most of the talking.

Their journey had taken them through one of the many red light districts where Rip Barlow noticed several cheap looking billboards advertising belly dancers. He had not said anything at the time but a few beers were enough for him to shed any shyness or residual inhibition and he told his mates at the table he wanted to walk around on his own for a bit and would catch up with them later on.

"Don't be a bloody fool, Rip," Jock Wearing told him. "We know where you're going and that's a rough looking set up down there. You're already a bit pisso, you know, and you can get into all kinds of strife. We'll take you to see one of those birds tomorrow but in a better set up than that."

"You can go to buggery, Jock, I want to see one of them sheilas and now's the time, so don't try to stop me," replied Rip in a voice that was as determined as his ale affected condition would allow. He rose to stand on his now slightly unsteady feet.

"Jock's right, Rip," interjected Pat, "you don't want to go looking for trouble. You're a bloody two pot screamer and you need someone to look after you. That fly mob down there would have you for breakfast so I suppose one of us will have to go with you."

"You know what you can do, Corp," he replied, "I don't want any bloody hangers-on and I'll be back here in an hour or so."

As he started to make his way out Patrick got up and grabbed him by the shoulder.

"All right, you drongo, if you insist on going alone, give me your wallet."

Strangely, he didn't protest and reached into the top pocket of his tunic and handed it over. Patrick extracted an English pound note and thrust it into the same pocket and did up the brass button.

"That's your lot," he said "and don't let them pinch the change."

Despite this exchange with his mates, Rip's excited state remained and he didn't turn his head when Jock shouted out, "You be back here by five or I'll kick your arse all the way back to camp if we have to come and find you."

As he had not returned by the suggested hour, Corporal Sheridan and his two friends had another beer and then set out to find their absent cobber, which they did, quite by accident, after a long, tiring search. They noticed a disturbance some distance from where they were looking and decided to investigate the excitement, only to find their friend in the middle of a fracas - surrounded by a large group of onlookers, with four very large Egyptians who were roughly trying to restrain him from re-entering the entertainment bar out of which it appeared he had just been thrown.

Rip appeared to be very tight and was resisting violently and shouting repeatedly something about "want my souvenir" whilst one of the bouncers explained to his rescuing mates, quite reasonably and in fair English, that their friend had caused a lot of trouble in their respectable establishment, where the art of traditional belly dancing could be enjoyed whilst having a few drinks.

Their friend had arrived some time before the performance started, the man explained, and to fill in time had ordered a measure of the locally distilled spirit and, by the time the performer came on the floor, he was on to his third nip of the powerful brew and apparently feeling no pain whatsoever.

He seemed fascinated by the woman's extravagant gyrations and watched every move until the performance was over. She had started to leave when Rip, jumping from his seat, confronted her and tried to wrest from her navel the shining bauble reclining therein, yelling as he grappled with her that he just wanted a souvenir. She was able to hold him off until help arrived and he was frog-marched out through the front door and on to the pavement - which was the situation when his companions-in-arms arrived.

"Thanks, mate," said Phil Ritchie, when the big Egyptian had finished his summation. "Sorry about this, he won't bother you anymore and we'll take it from here."

The big Egyptian seemed pleased to see him go. After intermittent struggling from their charge they eventually got him back to the army hostel and threw him on his bunk, leaving him sound asleep as they went to the mess hall and the evening meal.

Rip, who was normally a quiet bloke, was even quieter than usual and noticeably hung over the following morning as the quartet made its way, per favour of the driver of an empty British Army Supply truck, to see the Pyramids and other ancient architectural wonders of Egypt.

Rip gave a groan as the truck hit the many bumps on the road but received little sympathy from his cobbers.

"I hope it taught you a lesson not to drink the local firewater. It serves you bloody well right because you can't say you weren't told," shouted Pat over the noise of the truck.

"Why don't you just shut up and let me die in peace, Corp. I know what I did but if you bastards had looked after me the way you should, it wouldn't have happened," he replied in a dry, strained voice.

"That's a typical pisspot's excuse, Pat," suggested big, jovial Jock Wearing, "don't listen to the silly bastard. He'll get over his hangover but you're paying for it now, aren't you Rippo? And how you would love the hair of the dog right now," he said, giving their mate a hefty shove on the shoulder.

"You always were a bastard, Wearing. Now let a man get a bit of rest before you start dragging him around those bloody things you want to see," was his pained reply.

They enjoyed their day of sightseeing, even Rip, who picked up quickly once they started to move about. They were impressed with the ancient monuments they had been privileged to see but after several hours of it non-stop, their interest waned and they found an army shuttle bus which took them back to Cairo proper. Finding a British Services Canteen, they were able to get some reasonably cold beer and some decent cigarettes and tobacco. Egyptian fags were strong and left an awful taste and Patrick had switched to rolling his own - they were the nearest he could get to his preferred Capstan Plain. The canteen was crowded with servicemen from many nations; English, Australian, Free French, South African, Indian amongst others. Cigarette smoke hung like a heavy grey cloud over the gathering and the talk and shouting became louder and fights and altercations loomed as the time for closing the bar approached.

The leave centre was only a mile or so from the canteen and when the bar finally shut, Patrick and his friends decided to walk back to their quarters as it was a good way of offsetting the effects of the beer they had consumed.

They had not gone far before becoming aware of the strong presence of British and Australian Provosts in the streets who were stopping and talking to everyone in uniform. They learned there was a serious flap on. All leave had been cancelled and troops were ordered to return to their units without delay.

The position in the desert war was explained to them by Lt. Mailey, their platoon commander when he addressed his platoon as soon as all its members had arrived back in camp.

Apparently, the Allies (mostly Australian), after initial success against the Italian forces in Libya, were now being driven back across the desert towards the Egyptian frontier. The British Middle East Command had decided now the Allied Forces would make a stand at the Libyan port town of Tobruk using the formidable fortifications built by the Italians who were routed from it by allied troops a few weeks earlier.

It had been the lot of the Australian 9th Infantry Division, assisted by British artillery, to resist the advancing Axis forces which were no longer exclusively Italian. They were now led by a famed German general with superior troop numbers, and tanks and artillery of higher quality and quantity than those of the Allies.

9 Division had borne the brunt of the retreat and suffered severe casualties. If they were to hold Tobruk they would need to be reinforced. Patrick's battalion and other elements of the Australian 18th Brigade had been allotted this important assignment and would join the besieged garrison with all possible haste.

Chapter 31

*A*s with other normally decent Australians who endured the siege of Tobruk, Patrick's outlook on life and death was changed forever. The garrison were, in the main, composed of very young men and 'life' had yet to catch up with most of them. Their tender years could never have prepared them for the horrors they were to contend with there.

He lived through sixteen incredible weeks of incessant warfare which included isolated incidents the horror which would haunt him forevermore. He had seen close friends and other comrades die in battle and he himself had killed another human being, several in point of fact. All this had served to overwhelm his former nature and now when he reflected on his former life it seemed somewhat of an idle dream; as though it had never happened.

As the days and weeks progressed into months, all thoughts of his music had been driven from his mind and, whilst his beloved Cathy was frequently in his thoughts, he doubted now if his mind would ever allow him to write the third movement of the violin concerto he had so solemnly promised her. He now doubted if music could ever make its way back into his soul again. His muse, and his former inspiration died at Tobruk; a casualty of war.

His platoon, with the three full rifle sections intact, were stationed on the eastern perimeter of the fortress town and were responsible for night-patrolling the immediate area including that held by enemy forces. Their patrols were either for reconnaissance or straight out attack. Both were more than hazardous and, almost unfailingly, resulted in casualties.

Disaster struck his platoon when, at full strength, they were ordered to attack and wipe out an enemy forward strong post which was obviously providing intelligence for the increasing number of forays the enemy's infantry had been making on Allied lines. Patrick's section, on its own, had done the initial reconnaissance the previous night and it now led the way for Lt. Mailey and the rest of his platoon.

These raids had to be carried out in complete silence and with the use of bayonets only as any rifle fire would precipitate an immediate response from the enemy.

The assault was a success as the Australians poured into the outpost with their bayonets fixed. The silence was only disturbed by the screams of the fifteen or so occupants as they were being slain, caught unsuspecting and totally off-guard. It was a bloody and gruesome affair and Patrick was grateful for the darkness which obscured so much of the slaughter in which he took part. Nevertheless, it had an indelible effect on his inner being and gave him an irrational sense of guilt which he would never be able to shake off.

Things went wrong for the patrol as soon as they had filed out of the enemy bunker. One of the dying Germans had apparently been able to get off a shot which raised those in nearby enemy emplacements. Two parachute flares immediately lit up the entire area and the platoon was exposed almost point-blank to machine gun and mortar fire. The platoon commander, Lt. Jim Mailey, was trying to hurry his men along when he was caught in a burst of fire and died where he fell. A mortar shell landed close enough to the retreating group to kill three of those in the rear and wound several others. One of the three killed by the mortar was Patrick's friend, Rip Barlow, who would never see another belly dancer or mine again for gold in his home town of Coolgardie.

Despite almost withering fire, the retreating platoon turned back to retrieve their dead and wounded and dragged and carried them back to their own lines. It was then that Patrick discovered that the dead included Rip, Jim Mailey and Robbie Cameron, one of the young Tasmanians he had taken home to Magdalene just before they left Australia.

He would see many more die in the ensuing weeks. The constant patrolling together with daily bombardment of their line by the German panzers, regular mortar fire and the ever attacking Stuka dive bombers, took a daily death toll on those magnificent Australians who were holding out against almost impossible odds. He also killed more Germans during intermittent trench warfare and other skirmishes - he was a good shot and knew when he fired at a human target the .303 bullet would totally fulfil its bloody task. He'd now done this more often than he ever cared to remember.

His battalion was relieved in late August 1941 and sailed for Alexandria in the dead of night on elements of the navy's Scrap-Iron Flotilla which had been subject to much battering from the Luftwaffe for several months.

They were markedly different young men to those who had come to that place a few short months earlier and after all they had endured, was it any wonder? Unrelenting war and living conditions which would have undermined the wills of lesser men... lack of food, water and sleep, living with an unclean body for weeks on end and wearing unwashed tattered uniforms, were just some of their many trials. But it was the death of so many of their comrades that had the deepest effect on them. They were still young and they would get over the experience but it would take time and even then some memories would come back to haunt them.

Upon its return from the besieged town, the battalion was drafted to Palestine for more training before joining garrison forces in Syria following the defeat of the Vichy French forces there who were then loyal to Adolph Hitler. Within months of that assignment Japan entered the war and thrust south through Pacific island countries. They did this with such force and speed the Australian Government deemed it necessary to recall major elements of the 6th and 7th Australian Division to help defend their own country. This included Patrick's battalion, which sailed from Suez in the early part of February 1942 having been in the desert for one or two months short of two years. Patrick did not look for a quiet space on the ship for the voyage home; there was no need, for his musical soul had departed and he did not expect it to return. He hoped his girl, Cathy, would understand.

It was a long, boring voyage home for these men of the AIF who travelled in a convoy of four overladen troop ships with destroyer and corvette elements of the RAN and RN as its escort. A few days out of the Canal a rumour swept the ships that the convoy had been diverted to Colombo on the orders of the British Prime Minister. He thought it more important for the war effort if the Australians joined his British forces in Burma rather than return to Australia to help defend their own country, which was now in imminent danger of invasion. The rumour turned out to be true but, much to the Diggers great satisfaction, Churchill was overruled by their own Prime Minister, John Curtin, who insisted the Australians be brought home without further delay.

Because of the reported presence of German raiders and Japanese submarines in those waters of the Indian Ocean close to Australian shores, the convoy bypassed Perth, its logical first port of call. Instead it proceeded south into the Great Southern Ocean before steering north on a course which took it to its South Australian disembarking port of Outer Harbour, adjacent to the city of Adelaide.

Because the ship was overcrowded and generally uncomfortable there was little Patrick could do on the journey but read and yarn and play cards with those few of his platoon who had survived the desert war with him. He spent some time just sitting on the deck leaning against a bulkhead and thinking about the past two years and contemplating the now uncertain future which probably included fighting the Japanese.

After seeing so many of his friends die there, he had at times been convinced he himself would not survive the war in the Middle East. This had the effect of driving all thoughts of home from his mind and Magdalene and Denny's Knoll, with its sentimental attachment for him, now seemed very unreal places. He often tried to think about Cathy and, whilst he thought his love for her was undiminished, he had trouble just trying to picture her face, the beautiful features of which he had loved so dearly.

Because of the comparative peace of shipboard life, his thoughts should have turned to music. But that was not to be, for music belonged to his past life and had no relevance for the man he had become. He did feel guilty about the promised concerto but there was nothing he could do about it for his composer's block was total and immutable. Someone who had seen so much human bloodshed, and someone who had slain fellow human beings, could never hope to write sounds which reflected the essence of artistic beauty and culture for days that were lived in peace.

These were the inner and therefore secret thoughts of the young soldier from Bathurst, but they were not reflected in his day to day life with the blokes from his platoon. To them he was their immediate leader or "Sarge" in point of fact, as he was promoted after the death of Lt. Jim Mailey. His company commander had offered him a field commission at the time, which he refused as he wanted to remain with his men, but he had agreed to lead the platoon until a replacement for Mailey could be found. That was over a year ago now and no replacement had been forthcoming. Perhaps that would change when the battalion reassembled in Australia? He may have been their sergeant and their leader, but to the men of the platoon he was their mate and cobber and they thought the world of him. He was just a decent, normal soldier, totally free of bull dust, who had endured with them the very worst aspects of the rotten job that they'd been called upon to perform for their country.

The decks were crowded with troops, anxious to see the Australian mainland again, as the vessel steamed up St. Vincent's Gulf towards the Outer Harbour. Because of its limited capacity the port could only dock one vessel at a time. Theirs was the last one to do so as it was proceeding to Sydney, whereas the others three ships were returning to the Mediterranean, via Perth, as soon as they had disembarked their passengers.

The entire battalion was given twenty four hours leave with instructions to report back to the vessel no later than noon the following day. There was a regular steam-train service to the City and Patrick with one of his original good mates, Phil Richie, arrived at the Adelaide railway station in mid-afternoon of a hot summer day. First up they sought directions to the GPO to make telephone calls home. The army permitted this but they were restricted to say no more than they were back in Australia and expected to be home within a few days.

As they made their way along North Terrace and on to the main thoroughfare of King William Street they became aware this little city, one square mile in dimension, was overcrowded with troops from their convoy. They noticed a light-hearted gathering in Adelaide. At the next intersection they watched a policeman on point-duty in his full blue uniform, but with a borrowed digger's slouch hat on his head. All along the streets this kind of thing was happening. The returning soldiers were stopping to talk and laugh with groups of civilians who eagerly sought their company.

The laughter and good humour here seemed to sum up the mood of the city, and, indeed, the entire nation, for this day on which 'the boys' arrived home. This was part of a general rejoicing which was enjoined with a soundless sigh of relief throughout the land. For there had been growing national consternation about the so far unstoppable 'yellow horde' which was rapidly approaching the country's up to now undefended northern coastline. The troops' return had alleviated this anxiety to a great extent.

No one, least of all the troops themselves, appeared to be concerned with the fact that these soldiers had just taken part in a long armed conflict and were about to risk their lives again in another of equal intensity. The nation was asking and expecting a lot from men who were still barely old enough to vote.

The Australian Army had insufficient camps in the Adelaide area to quarter all the new arrivals and had arranged for hundreds of them to be temporarily billeted in private homes throughout the suburban area.

Most of those billeted had come back into town to celebrate the important day with their mates and where better to do that than in the public bar of a real Aussie pub. Adelaide was known as the city of churches but it was just as well these were, in point of fact, outnumbered by public houses. They were doing a roaring trade but there was some expressed concern as to what would happen when the publicans endeavoured to close their establishments at 6 pm. Patrick and his friend Phil, who had both seen a lot of their fighting comrades with too much beer under their belts, would feel that concern quite justified.

With only three minutes available for his GPO telephone call, Patrick finally got through to Magdalene and firstly spoke to Tom who was, understandably, quite emotional. He was though apparently forced to hand over quickly to an excited Irene who, through a tear strained but joyful voice, plied him with questions many of which he was unable to answer. Before his time ran out he was able to tell her he anticipated being with them in a week or so and asked her to ring Cathy with the news, saying he would ring her as soon as he arrived in Sydney.

Leave passes for fourteen days were issued to the men of the battalion before they disembarked at Pyrmont in Sydney. Upon expiry of their leave they were to report to Ingleburn where the unit would be brought up to strength before being posted to jungle warfare training camps in Queensland.

Irene, as he had requested, booked him in for two nights at Usher's Hotel. As soon as he dropped his pack on the bed he telephoned Cathy's home, only to find she was rehearsing with the orchestra at the Sydney Town Hall. Before she left she had told her mother she would be home "by seven."

He was waiting at the bottom of the Town Hall steps when he saw her come through the portals and stood transfixed for a few moments as she started to descend. She was even more beautiful than he remembered and her body language had a new, certain assurance which made his vision of her even more blindingly attractive. Her features tuned white when, halfway down the steps, she saw his tall spare figure looking up at her. The expression 'she threw herself into his arms' had literal truth as she launched herself at him well before reaching the lowest step.

They took no notice of the people around them as she laughed and cried as he kissed and caressed her as they clung to each other. Eventually, he started to release her but she held on and looking up at him with tear-stained eyes implored him, "Don't let me go, Pat, please. I've lived these few moments every day for the past two years and you will never know how much this means to me." She kissed him again before resting her head on his shoulder just as he, at last, became aware of the scene they were causing in the heart of George Street.

Reluctantly they drew apart and walked slowly away from a moment in their lives that would persist in their memories for a long time, particularly in the weeks and months which lay ahead when once more they would be parted from each other.

For the next hour or so, intimately arm in arm, they strolled slowly around the city just talking and getting to know each other again. To him, she was still the same Cathy and he could not see any real change in her, but she was aware he was not quite the same Patrick as the one who had gone away. Physically, he was leaner and harder with face and neck permanently browned by the hot desert sun. It was an occasional look that came into his eyes that concerned her. It was not a forlorn or desperate look or one of hopelessness but more one of resignation to something his mind had been unable to accept.

Their romantic exchanges aside, they kept the rest of their conversation as light-hearted as possible. But during the meal they had later in Usher's coffee lounge, she did ask him to tell her about what happened whilst he was overseas. He dismissed this quickly with a slight shake of his head.

"Nothing really worth talking about, Cath. Pretty boring really, most of the time except for the war, the bloody war," he said almost vehemently, "and I don't think you would want to know about that." His words seemed to her to be unnecessarily emphatic.

His message was clear and she knew what he was trying to say. Goodness knows what he had been through, she thought. He was a more serious young man than the one she remembered and if he did not want to talk about the war, she would not press it.

She succeeded in teasing him during coffee when answering a leading question. He asked as to whether she had won any hearts and she told him of the young man who had danced attendance on her during his absence. He picked her up in his car after concerts and rehearsals, she told him, and took her to the pictures and an occasional ball. Sometimes they went to dinner and, on hot weekends, for a swim at Bondi.

The surprise on his face grew with her every word, especially when she told him she would continue seeing him whilst he was here because she was very fond of him.

She watched his expression and started to laugh. He leant across the table as though to strangle her, when she told him she was referring to her brother who would use any excuse to drive the family car even if it meant 'carting' her around in the process.

Neither suggested going to his room to talk more privately and he went home with her where he received a warm welcome home from her family They spent the following day together without doing anything in particular but just immersed themselves in the luxury of each other's company. They spoke briefly about what might lie ahead of him in the Pacific war but, again, he dismissed it quickly by saying there was time enough for that when his leave drew to a close.

She had not raised the subject of the piano and his music for she felt it may be taboo as he had made no reference to it so far. However, after one of their short companionable silences, she asked how 'her concerto' was progressing. He seemed to hesitate before answering. "Sorry I haven't said anything about it before; as you might guess, army life is not ideal for musical thought, Cath, but I have finished the first two movements, which aren't bad, and the Third is coming along and I hope to finish it sometime soon."

He told the white lie quite deliberately as he did not want her to know the work would never be finished for, more than ever now, his creative block seemed to have become complete and absolute. Patrick Sheridan may not have been killed in Tobruk but there was little doubt an important part of him died there.

Patrick felt spasms of pleasant anticipation as his train made its way slowly through the Blue Mountains on its way to his home town. He hadn't been fully aware of just how much he had missed Magdalene these past three years but now realised the idea of being there again with his parents was something he had yearned for, somewhat unconsciously, for a very long time.

Irene and Tom were overjoyed to have him back, if only for a few days, and, like him, they intended to make the most of the short time they were to have together. He noticed very little change in Tom who was still reasonably active about the property but Irene had altered a little more markedly; her hair noticeably greyer and lines on her face which were not there before. There was at times a sad and worried expression on her face so common to mothers whose sons go to war.

It was a busy time for them with neighbours dropping by after they learnt he was home and insisting their visit be returned before he went back. They drove in to Bathurst so Patrick could catch up with friends, including the Becks with whom he had boarded for some years, and the family of Brian Stiller, his high school mate, who lived opposite the Becks. It was a sad occasion for, some months previously, Brian had been killed over the Ruhr whilst flying as navigator on an RAF Wellington during a bombing raid on Germany.

While his parents attended to some business in the town, he called at the convent to see his old tutor, Sister Annunciata. She was quite overcome and could not believe he was now so totally divorced from his music and experienced great disappointment when he would not play for her. She was quite a passionate woman who was obliged to keep her emotions in check but, with tears in her eyes, she kissed him goodbye when he finally took his leave of her.

Fortunately, the Sheridan's had a lot of 'family' time together, usually during and after meals at the homestead, when they talked and reminisced. But when the subject of his music or war experiences came up, they did not last very long. His parents were quick to notice this and so the subjects were avoided. Although he tried to be his old normal self, Irene had noticed a change in her son; he was slightly more withdrawn than the Patrick she knew and, like her, although for different reasons, the war had brought an occasional expression of resigned weariness to his face. It perhaps told of those things he could not talk about.

He would not play the piano for her and said there would be time enough for that after the war and he had time to resurrect his passion for the instrument he once loved. On some nights he and Tom would sit in the drawing room after dinner and listen to her play a range of music pleasing to them both. One evening she sat at the piano alone for it had been a hot day and Tom was on his chair on the front porch trying to cool off. Patrick had been helping the housekeeper with the dishes from the evening meal. She turned to look at Patrick when he finally came into the room and he was holding pieces of manuscript which he put on top of the piano.

"Mum, I've been looking through some of that stuff I wrote before I went to the Con," he said, "would you mind giving these few pieces a go for me; they've never been played before and it might be fun to hear them now and also to see what you think."

Irene took the music down and perused it before placing it on the piano rest and began to play as he sat back in an adjacent lounge chair and closed his eyes. He was quite pleased with what he heard but Irene was carried away with the musical substance and exquisite beauty of her son's romantic works. She played them as in a progressive trance but with every fibre of her musical soul so as to do justice to the inspired work of the formidable composer who was her son.

When she had finished the final work she sat there for a moment and then uttered, almost to herself, an anguished, "Oh! Patrick!" Without another word, she left him and went to her room from where, after she had closed the door, he heard a sobbing of such intensity it filled him with a great sense of guilt and one of profound sadness. He did not go in to her because there was nothing he could really do or say to alleviate her distress. Instead, he returned the music to the large drawer in his room. It contained a multitude of his other unheard compositions, including the Outback Symphony and the two movements of his long-promised violin concerto. The sobbing had stopped when he passed his mother's room again. Slowly making his way to the front porch, he sat down and eventually began yarning quietly with his father.

It was as well that Irene was able to shake off what had happened that previous evening, for Cathy Jordan was due to arrive late that afternoon and the three of them were intending to drive into Bathurst to meet her train. She gave Patrick an apologetic smile when he came in for breakfast and touched his face gently. The incident was not referred to again except when she told Cathy the following day about some beautiful music Patrick had written. She and the girl had become soulmates ever since as she had made a few short visits to Magdalene after her son had gone away. They shared reading extracts from the letters each had received from him from the war zone in Middle East.

It was an enjoyable and romantic few days for the young couple. They didn't waste any of them for they knew, from their just past experience, such moments would seem like gold in the separation that lay ahead. She did not raise the matter of their engagement as she knew he still felt the same way about it, but after dinner on her last night at Magdalene, the three of them sat there talking, and she laid a hand on the table.

"Look at that, Mother Sheridan, a girl of my years with such a naked left hand; not a ring to be seen. I'm beginning to think your boy is just leading me on but, unfortunately, I love the oaf and there is nothing I can do about. Don't you think he should make an honest woman of me?"

"Don't ask me, Cathy," replied Irene, "how his mind has worked over the past few years is quite beyond me. I'll never understand why he doesn't tie you down and it will serve him right if a gallant knight does rides into your life whilst he's away at his war."

"You two can go on all you like," responded Patrick. "I told you before, Jordan, I'm saving up to buy you a ring but it's going to take a little more time on my soldier's pay." He reached over and took her hand from the table and kissed it gently before returning it to her lap, and that was the end of that subject also.

The next day, after an affectionate goodbye from Tom and Irene, he drove her to the station and following an extended embrace and many loving words, put her on the train and watched it pull out of the station. He would not be seeing her again on this leave. He'd explained to her that he would be going directly to Ingleburn and would try to call her from there. He could have found the time to have a few hours in Sydney with her, but there had been too many farewells and they were sad occasions. He thought he should spare her the sense of finality another one could bring.

On the way home in the train, when reflecting on her stay, Catherine was puzzled and a little concerned when she realised that although they had done a lot of horse-backing around the Magdalene property, he had not once suggested they go to Denny's Knoll. It was a place which had come to mean so much to them and was often referred to in their letters to each other. She tried in vain not to read something into it but with a kind of sixth sense she knew his avoidance of the place was quite deliberate. But why?

When Pat arrived at Ingleburn Camp, he became aware of a great sense of urgency, engendered, he found out, by the Army General Staff's great concern with the rapidity of the Japanese advance through the Pacific towards Australia. Hong Kong, the Malay Peninsula and Singapore, the Philippines and the Dutch East Indies now lay in their conquering wake and Australia's next door neighbour, Papua New Guinea, was obviously next on their list. It had to be defended at all costs because if it too fell, Australia itself would be in great jeopardy.

Within two days of re-joining his unit, his battalion, with a large number of reinforcements, assembled at full strength on the huge Ingleburn parade ground. The gravity of the situation was explained to them by the commanding officer. It was therefore no surprise when on the following morning they were advised by their company commanders that they were to move out immediately to undertake a jungle training course on the Atherton Tablelands in Northern Queensland.

The contrast with the type of warfare they experienced in the desert and what they could expect in the jungle could not have been more pronounced. But they had to learn and learn quickly for the Nipponese menace grew worse by the day. After eight weeks of gruelling jungle exercises and war games, Patrick's battalion was considered ready and was moved to a camp near the Queensland port of Townsville to await orders.

These came in the middle of the night of August 25th 1942, when the lights flashed on suddenly in all huts, just after 2 am, followed by NCOs storming in and telling the inmates they had five minutes to be on parade - and to do so in whatever state of undress they happened to be in. Each company was addressed separately and advised an emergency situation had arisen in New Guinea requiring them to move out immediately and that they could expect to be in action within seventy-two hours; that's how desperate the situation appeared to be.

In less than six hours the entire battalion had embarked at Townsville on an Australian troopship which got under way immediately the gangplank was raised. For security reasons the troops had not been told of their destination but it was the common assumption it was Port Moresby and that they were to join the Australian force currently fighting the Japanese in the Kokoda area of the Owen Stanley Ranges.

They were all wrong for, just under forty hours later, the vessel anchored off Gilli Gilli and awaited the LSMs (Landing Ship Men) to pull alongside to take the troops ashore.

Gilli Gilli was a small pier suitable only for small island trading vessels and located on the northern shore of Milne Bay on the eastern tip of the island of New Guinea. The state of the battle for the area was explained to the troops by the battalion CO, through the ship's amplifying system, only an hour or so prior to them scrambling down the rope nets on the side of the ship and into the waiting LSMs.

Three days previously a Japanese invasion force landed further up the coast near the small settlement of Aihoma and had been resisted by a composite AIF-Militia force, but the Japanese, with the use of light tanks, had driven the defenders back slowly. They were steadily advancing on their intended objectives of two Australian airstrips which lay side by side not far from Gilli Gilli where the battalion had landed.

It was a critical situation for if this battle were lost the Japanese would have gained an aerodrome which would have enable them to bomb Port Moresby and parts of northern Australia at will. In addition Milne Bay would provide them with a harbour large enough to accommodate their entire naval fleet. Such a situation would have made an invasion of the Australian mainland almost certain.

When Patrick's company disembarked, it was force-marched to positions near a third airstrip which was still under construction. It consisted of a section of cleared jungle about a mile long and two hundred yards wide extending from the edge of upper jungle down to the waters of the Bay. Because of impenetrable jungle at one end and sea on the other, if the Japanese were to succeed they would have to cross the strip on the way to their intended objective.

This was the point where Milne Bay Fortress Command decided to make a stand and all men and weaponry at their disposal were deployed along the western side of the strip. When the last of the retreating Diggers had joined them, they lay in wait in natural camouflage for the next enemy attack.

The Australians were ordered to hold fire until an attempt was made to cross the wide strip and the Japanese could be half seen gathering in force at a point midway down the strip. However it was an hour or so before they made their first banzai charge across the clearing, with much yelling and shouting. They were met with withering fire from Bren Guns, .303 rifles and 3 inch mortar shells and their ranks decimated before the few survivors struggled back to their own lines, leaving their dead strewn along the strip.

Three more charges followed over the next hour resulting in the same slaughter and withdrawal. A noticeable silence then descended on the area and it became apparent to the cautious Australian defenders that the Japanese had left their positions and had in fact started to retreat.

This was Sergeant Pat Sheridan's introduction to jungle warfare and he found it just as bloody and horrendous as the desert campaigns in which he had fought. He was no longer acting Platoon commander as the CO had appointed a young lieutenant, not long out of OCTU, to the position, after again offering the appointment to Patrick. His sole charge now was one Rifle Section of the Platoon comprising himself, a corporal 2 i/c, and fourteen privates, and he was quite satisfied with that arrangement. The Section was formed in the early days of jungle training on the Atherton Tableland and it had bonded into an effective and reliable body naturally moulded in the Anzac tradition.

They got on well together for they had come to rely on each other during their rugged training in Queensland. All had seen action in the Middle-East and were quick to realise they had a decent bloke leading them; no nonsense, no bulldust and requiring them to do no more than they had to do. "Sarge", or Pat, was good value and that was important for they knew in certain situations when in action he could be an important factor in whether they lived or died. They trained, slept and messed together for a long time and, occasionally became heartily sick of each other, and so there was the usual bickering and whinging, but nothing lasting or serious. It only needed a sharp word from Sarge if things looked like getting out of hand.

On the orders of the CO theirs was one of the first body of men to cross the strip and reconnoitre the situation before taking part in the general pursuit of the fleeing Nippon, who fought a desperate rearguard action with Bushido overtones in endeavouring to slow the Australian's advance. They left snipers hidden in upper fronds of coconut trees. This accounted for many Australian casualties before the ploy was discovered. From then on the top of such suspect trees were sprayed with Bren guns before the advance continued. Patrick's Section lost two men killed and one seriously wounded from sniper fire and it was a bitter lesson he would never forget in the actions which lay ahead of his group.

The Battle of Milne Bay lasted just two weeks and the enemy defeat was the first complete rout of their land forces since the war began in December 1941. The casualty list included more than 170 killed in action. But Milne Bay had been saved and a dangerous threat to Australia's freedom had been averted, albeit with an appalling loss of young Australian lives.

After nearly three years of active service, Sgt. Pat Sheridan had become a tough and battle-hardened soldier. But despite this, sometimes with utter dismay, he found himself viewing the tragedy of the war he witnessed not through the eyes of a warrior but with the somehow retained sensitivity of a poet's soul - a poet who used musical notes instead of words to lay bare his innermost aesthetic thought. He had joined, unknowingly, a community of minds comprising ecclesiastics, scholars, writers, academics and thinking men in the street, who, throughout history, were confounded that God had allowed Mankind to impose such unspeakable horror upon itself. Patrick's Catholic mind wondered if this was part of the price which had to be paid for the Divine gift of Free Will. To his finite mind the slaughter at Tobruk and Milne Bay alone made that cost seem too high.

Shortly after the complete evacuation by remnants of the defeated enemy force at Milne Bay, his unit was transferred to the Port Moresby area, where it was held in reserve. But within a few short weeks the entire battalion was aboard another troopship, bound for the Japanese occupied area of Buna on the north eastern coast of the island, where it was to take part in some of the bloodiest battles of the New Guinea campaign.

Chapter 32

The fierce battles which took place on the north eastern coast of New Guinea between Buna to Salamaua were fought under appalling conditions. The Japanese, who had established a beachhead at Buna some months previously, were firmly entrenched and the Buna area was so extensively fortified it necessitated the Australian-Americans force to fight relentlessly for every yard of ground they took.

The soldiers did not march so much as wade into battle through foetid, shallow and never ending swamp land. In width it extended from the edge of the Owen Stanley Ranges all the way down to the sea, and in length, to the Allies' intended objective of Salamaua. The heat and humidity were ever-present and extreme, and clouds of tropical flies and mosquitoes added greatly to the troops already near-unbearable discomfort.

Apart from the conditions and formidable foe, the Allied troops suffered a chronic shortage of food and medicine. Their bodies were never dry for weeks on end for it rained hour upon hour most days and nights. They had no shelter from it other than that provided by native trees and the hooded jungle itself, and that was scant relief to say the least.

It was therefore not surprising that within a short time the force became riddled with tropical disease. The common strain of malaria and dengue fever were rife but other more exotic and serious strains, such as malignant tersian, cerebral malaria and blackwater fever, had been contracted by a number of troops.

Most symptoms of the standard malaria, BT, strain were suppressed by the yellow tablet, Atabrine, which the troops took daily. Those few who, nevertheless, did succumb to it were only rested for a few hours in an inadequately supplied Field Hospital before being sent back into action. It was however another disease which broke out among allied troops as they advanced down the impossible terrain which occasioned growing official concern.

The Japanese had not buried their dead as they retreated and they were left for days and weeks in fox holes, fortified bunkers, blockhouses and in parts of the jungle swamp. The allied troops were told that fleas from the field rats which fed on the dead bodies had infected a number of them and caused a minor outbreak of the sometimes fatal disease known as scrub typhus. Those who did not die from the complaint were known to eventually suffer body disfigurement or shortening of extremities.

Patrick's battalion was in the thick of this action for several weeks and suffered serious casualties, as did all Allied units so engaged. His section accounted for four of the thirteen men from its platoon who were killed in action in the first week of the engagement. With three others out of action from wounds, this meant his group was down to half its normal strength. When the opportunity arose, Sgt. Sheridan informed his platoon commander of the situation, who told him reinforcements were not available and his section must continue with reconnaissance and fighting patrols as required.

As the fighting approached the outskirts of the port of Gona, the Japanese resistance was more determined and the allied advance brought to a virtual standstill. This was unacceptable to the allied command and Patrick's battalion CO was ordered to mount an all-out offensive on what was a jungle fortress.

The attack was successful but again at great cost of life in a battalion of men many of whom were already tired beyond belief and hampered by minor wounds and enervating tropical disease.

Patrick's under-manned section suffered further casualties in the closing hours of the Gona clash. The Japanese were equipped with small, portable mountain cannons which were effective at short range, and the natural ground cover, from where the section was attacking an enemy machine-gun post, took a direct hit from one of the shells. Four of his men were killed outright and another two slightly wounded, including himself, with a large layer of flesh cut from the calf of his right leg by flying shrapnel.

His platoon commander, when he saw what had happened, ordered Patrick, despite his protests, to withdraw from the action and report, with the other survivors, to the nearest field medical dressing station immediately it became safe to do so.

Before they left, the survivors arranged their dead as decently as possible on the side of an embankment and covered them with their groundsheets pending the arrival of the ever vigilant graves unit, which was aware now of the importance of burying the fallen with least possible delay. Patrick looked down at the yellow, emaciated and war-wearied bodies of the youthful warriors before they were covered. Again a deep sense of loss made his heart cry with anguish for these valiant comrades who were alive and talking with him such a few short minutes before.

His leg was bleeding profusely and he dressed the wound, with the help of his Bren gunner, Len Talbot. They sprinkled generous amounts of sulphur powder on the open flesh before binding it tightly with the bandage which, like the powder, was part of every soldier's personal medical kit.

Even before he was hit, he felt decidedly unwell. He had developed a violent headache and was perspiring more than usual even though an occasional cold spasm shook his entire frame. He put it down to lack of sleep and proper food and tried to forget all about it and just hoped it would wear off. But, of course, it didn't.

The dressing station comprised a large, mildewed tent and three ancient native huts, staffed by three medical orderlies who looked as worn-out as their patients. They cleaned and dressed the wounds of the small group and provided a bucket of black tea, a tin of bully beef and a few hard biscuits, which the patients relished as only those who are truly hungry could.

In the native huts were several 'cots', some unoccupied, made of empty hessian palisade covers slung between two pieces of native timber with ends resting on coconut logs to raise them above the wet earthen floor. The men could hardly believe their luck in finding such quarters. For the first time in weeks they would have the luxury of sleeping under cover and out of the seemingly never-ending downpours, for a few hours at least.

Pat Sheridan slept but a few short hours before getting up and making his way to the medical tent for assistance. His wounded leg was hurting badly, he was trembling with fever and his headache was much worse. As he stepped into the tent he fell to the ground and within the few seconds it took the orderlies to reach him, slipped into unconsciousness.

He was conscious for only brief periods of the ensuing three weeks before finally 'coming to' in the general ward of the Base Army Hospital in Port Moresby. A passing orderly saw his slight movement and stopped by his bed.

"Bloody hell, mate, so you've finally come around. Wait 'til the Doc hears about this! You've been out to it ever since they brought you here a couple of weeks back and they've been keeping you alive with that drip in your arm ever since. How're you feeling, anyhow?"

He was unable to answer and drowsed back into a half sleep from which he was awoken a few minutes later by someone shaking him lightly on the shoulder.

"Wake up Sheridan, we want to talk to you." Patrick was barely awake as he looked up at the tall, spare man in dark horn-rimmed glasses peering at him intently and raising his eyelids with his finger the better to look into his eyes.

"You've had a nice old dose of cerebral malaria, Sergeant," the Army doctor told him. "We thought we had lost you a couple of times. When you arrived on the boat from Buna we almost put you straight into the morgue as you were so far gone and it is really a miracle you've survived. We certainly didn't expect you to."

He went down to the foot of the bed and took a medical instrument from his pocket which looked like a table fork.

"Now, tell me if you can feel this," he said as he ran the instrument down the soles of his bare feet." Patrick nodded his head. "That's great," he said, "now waggle your toes" but he had to repeat the order before the patient obliged.

He came back and looked down at Patrick again.

"This is all bloody good; you are a lucky bloke as not many people beat this thing and you appear to be over the worst of it now. Are you feeling hungry?" and when Patrick nodded he went on. "Your stomach will have shrunk and won't be able to hold much so it will be very light tucker for the next few days and we'll maintain the drip until you are stronger. We'll keep a good eye on things for the next week or so and then decide what to do with you."

His recovery was steady but slow and it was a full two weeks before he could eat normally and have the drip removed. By this time his clear articulation had resumed and his voice and speech now were the same as before his illness. However, another week was to go by before he was allowed out of bed for just a few hours each day. A hospital doctor who treated stress and war neuroses cases came to his bedside and talked with him. When he left about an hour later he assured Patrick his mind was unimpaired from the cerebral upheaval and his intellect was fully intact, so far as he could judge.

Although still weak, Pat was, at last, beginning to feel better, with his inner health seeming to improve day by day. He awoke at the hospital one morning, under the khaki mosquito net, feeling reasonably well and strangely light-hearted. He had not felt that way for some time and there was no doubt, despite his illness, the long rest in a comfortable hospital bed combined with a regular diet, had done wonders for his disposition. What had pleased him also was this sense of well-being with which he awoke that morning had been accompanied by a sound of music; not from any outside source but from within himself -

something that had not occurred since Tobruk. Could this be the end of the composer's block? "Perhaps," he thought, as his mind turned again to The Third Movement.

On the next of the ward visits by the Salvation Army officer, Patrick took the opportunity to ask if he could possibly find him several sheets of plain foolscap paper and half a dozen or so black lead pencils and a school ruler. Such ordinary items were in short supply in Port Moresby but the kindly man said he would see what he could do but it may take some time. That didn't matter to Patrick for he was not ready for the task, but it would be as well to have the items on hand when he was.

That afternoon, leaning back in his hospital bed with eyes closed, he ran the first two movements through his mind in the hope of finding inspiration for an opening to the elusive 'Third'. Whilst the response was limited, it was sufficient for him to decided he would make a dedicated effort to finish the opus. He felt a return of that sense of excitement he experienced when composing; something he not experienced since joining the service. It was some days later, after a daily medical examination that was longer than usual, the MO expressed his satisfaction with his progress.

"You've come along well, Sergeant," he said, "and apart from slight residual weaknesses here and there, I think we can say you are almost fully recovered. Next week we will be sending you to the 23rd Convalescent Depot at Sogeri and in due course the MO there will decide whether to send you home or let you re-join your unit… it will be his decision but my personal opinion is you will soon be back with your army mates. Incidentally, I heard yesterday your crowd, or what's left of it, has been relieved at Salamaua, and is due back in this area sometime soon, so you might get some visitors."

He shook Patrick's hand, wished him luck and said it would not be necessary for him to see him again, adding he should make the most of his stay at the Con Depot, which had a good reputation among former inmates.

Despite what the doctor had said, it was an unexpected surprise for him when, the day before he was to go to the Con Depot, two friends from his Section came into the ward - Phil Ritchie, his original cobber from his earliest days in the Army and Len Talbot, his Section Bren-gunner, who had been in the cot next to him at the Buna dressing station.

When people are really glad to see each other the conversation is sincere and free-flowing and this was one of those occasions. Phil had been wounded at Milne Bay and evacuated to Townsville and had just re-joined the battalion which was now stationed at a rest camp near RAAF Number Three Strip just a few miles outside Port Moresby. Len's wounds had been slight and he was back in action near Salamaua with the battalion when it was relieved two weeks' or so after his return.

They yarned casually but non-stop until an orderly came over to the bedside and told them it was time to break it up. Patrick could not believe the battalion's casualties they told him about - more than two hundred killed and double that number wounded or suffering from tropical illness. Len told him that he and three others, whom he named, were all that was left of his Section after the Buna campaign. Nine had been killed and the others evacuated by hospital ship to Australia because of wounds or sickness. Pat told him of the doctor's findings and that after the Con Depot he did not know whether he would be going home or re-joining the unit - he had reached the stage of army life not to say which he preferred. Before they left he promised to let them know the Con Depot decision. He asked them to say g'day to the blokes in the platoon and say he would be glad to see any of them if they could find their way out to Sogeri whilst he was there.

After they left he tried not to think too much about the appalling loss of life in his unit but it still dampened the more positive outlook he had recently acquired whilst recovering from his illness. He found he was able to hang on to his overall sense of optimism even though he didn't know what the army life had in store for him. He had this feeling he would not be going home yet and that he would probably see more action in New Guinea before he did so.

He had learned from an article in the Army newspaper that the Australian 9th Division had recaptured the important town of Lae. After suffering heavy losses the Japanese had retreated into the foothills of the Finisterre Ranges and the eastern reaches of the Ramu Valley. The story implied it would be the lot of the Australian soldier to rout them out of those places. Because of the vastness of this area, a long campaign was envisaged and Patrick wondered if he would be taking part in it.

In the few days since he had listened to the completed movements of the concerto, he was convinced a sterile period of his musical life was over. Now that he could 'hear' again, the chords and themes were starting to course and he felt the time may have arrived for him to attempt writing the final chapter of his opus.

The Convalescent Depot was ideal for its intended purpose. Built around an old style colonial hotel taken over by the Army, it was a series of irregular rows of tents set on a well-kept grassy area near a fast running stream and within hearing distance of a steep waterfall less than half a mile away. The peaceful atmosphere of the place isolated it from the war. The efficient and caring staff made daily life a pleasant change for men recovering from wounds caused by war and serious illnesses contracted in the line of duty.

It was hot during the day of course, but thoughtfully placed benches beneath shading trees gave respite to those who wished to get out of their tents for a time. Recruited native labour with knapsack sprays containing insect repellent on their backs were constantly at work throughout the area and therefore mosquitoes and other tropical insects were never a problem for the patients.

When an initial medical examination and the formalities of his admission were over, Patrick was left pretty much to himself. He estimated there were about thirty or so fellow inmates, who, whilst quite friendly in the main, seemed to want to take advantage of the personal privacy the place afforded them. He was the sole occupant of a comfortable tent furnished with two white-sheeted beds complete with mosquito nets.

With all circumstances considered, he could not have asked for better conditions in which to commence his creative pursuit. But on that first afternoon, after sitting for some hours at the small table in his tent on which rested writing material eventually supplied by the good 'Salvo', he found he was bereft of the inspiration his endeavour required, despite his high expectation. Apart from making some notes concerning an idea on orchestration, he did not write a single bar of music and eventually gave up and took a long, thoughtful stroll around the depot grounds.

That evening, after mess, he wrote a long letter to Cathy before starting one to his parents. As it proceeded it evoked a rush of thoughts about Magdalene and the wonderful years of his early life there, and he took those reminiscences with him to bed that night. But there was no one there to see the happy smile on his face as he dropped off to sleep.

It was hard for him to believe, but those simple recollections had solved his problem for he awoke the following morning, once again, to the 'sound' of music. He knew then, without doubt, he would be able to honour the ambitious promise he had made to his intended wife. And so he commenced to write on that very day. Wonderful notes, chords and cadences, in pursuance of the theme, flowed generously from his mind and heart on to the rough manuscript, as though they had been imprisoned and could wait no longer to break out and join that exclusive stream of immortal music which brought so much pleasure to the world.

He was in sight of his goal when a few days later he was ordered to report to the MO's office for final examination. The young doctor pronounced him fit for duty and signed his medical papers accordingly, advising him that he would be returning to his unit at the end of the current week.

The soldier-composer felt no real disappointment at not being sent home for it was more or less what he had expected. He was quite well now and only needed a little hardening-up before being ready for combat once more. He had hoped to finish the 'work' before leaving the Con Depot but now clung to the hope that, as his battalion was undergoing a period of relative rest, he would have time to complete it before being called back into action. He did not know why but there was something compelling him to set that deadline.

❦

Chapter 33

The Depot's one-tonner took him back to his unit, now located beside the noisy fighter airstrip and he reported to the company orderly room and handed in his papers. He knew the corporal clerk in charge as they had been in Tobruk together and after a brief chat he was informed he was to report to Major Burley, the company commander, who greeted him like a long lost friend.

"Great to see you back, Pat," he said. "Heard you had a tough time of it and we had little hope of seeing you again; but here you are and you look good and we can certainly do with your help. We have lost a lot of blokes, Pat, and our reinforcements are green as grass. As you know, a lot of them these days are CMF - conscript or 'chocos' as they are known. We don't knock these blokes anymore after the job they did at Kokoda and Milne Bay. A lot of ours are under nineteen and are conscripts only because they were too young to volunteer for the AIF. They have been well trained but of course aren't battle-hardened. That's why we need experienced non-coms like you to help them along when the time comes."

"Will I be getting my old Section back, sir?" asked Patrick. "I know there aren't many of them left but I would like to continue with those that are, if possible."

"Yes, you will be sergeant. I think there are six men left from your team at Buna and I have arranged with your platoon commander for you to resume as leader of the Section and assist in the training of reinforcements. From what I hear we won't be fighting in jungle next time we go in and the action will, more likely, take place in relative open country. We'll have need of that type of reconnaissance work you did for us in the desert once again. You should concentrate on that with your new men accordingly because I think it most important."

"That's fine by me and I'm glad to be taking up where I left off," responded Patrick.

"As you know all our blokes were badly knocked about in that last campaign and we are still licking our wounds but in two or three weeks we will be getting back to full training as I know Allied Command have a job in mind for us in the not too distant future. However, we must take it easy for a little while longer as these blokes need it," the Major told him.

"By the way, Pat," he continued as the sergeant stood up to take his leave, "have you given any more thought to taking a Commission? You know you could be a lot more help to us if you had one."

"No thank you, sir. I prefer where I am and would like to stay there, if possible," Patrick replied.

"Okay, I can't say I blame you for wanting to stay with your men. The Army can be bloody lonely at times when you have officer rank on your shoulder. Good luck, Sergeant, I'll be talking with you," concluded the Major as Patrick left the room.

He found his company's lines and, when it was pointed out to him, walked into the tent of his hospital visitors, Lance Corporal Len Talbot and Corporal Phil Ritchie, shouting, "Move over, you bastards, and make room for a fighting man."

They were lying on their bunks reading and jumped up to greet him. The pleasure of having him back was all over their faces. It was an NCO's tent with four bunks and they dumped his gear on one of them and started in to interrogate him, following it with a bit of chiacking.

"What did I tell you, Phil? All the crook jokers turn up back here like bad pennies. There's no getting rid of the sods, so I suppose we have to put up with this one, but I don't know why it should happen to us," said Len Talbot with a down-cast expression which could not quite hide the smile.

Patrick threw his sidepack at him.

"You buggers wouldn't know what to do unless I was here to hold your hand. They said I could go home, you know, but not me, I knocked 'em back just because you lot couldn't even find your way to a pissaphone without me to show you the way," said their sergeant.

"What a lot of bullshit, Len," said Phil Ritchie, "this bastard really does have himself on. Of course, it could be the old cerebral malaria playing up with his marbles and he's forgotten it was you and I who got him his stripes."

"Alright, let's cut the crap before I knock your blocks off, and now tell me about the new blokes in the Section. Are they any good?" he asked his tent mates, and the conversation took a different slant because it was important to know the kind of men you had around you in battle - the life they could possibly save may be yours.

With the battalion resting, Patrick found ample time to get on with his music though at first the conditions were not ideal. He was sharing quarters and there was a lot of talking and shouting around the tent lines now that the troops were recovering from the stress of action. The noise of takeoffs and landings from the nearby fighter strip were loud and constant throughout the day and the army was grateful the RAAF could not fly sorties at night.

It was whilst attending Mass on the following Sunday, at the ecumenical tent church, that the thought struck him and he stayed behind to speak to the Catholic padre after the service. Father Bob Kennedy, a MSC from Sydney, was most helpful and after Patrick explained the situation agreed to let him use the 'church' at any time it was not occupied for religious gatherings. He would advise the protestant padres of the arrangement. He showed Pat a table at the back of the altar he could use and also indicated a Tilley pressure lamp in case he needed to work after dark when the noise from the fighter base had ceased for the day.

And so it was late at night, some ten days later, that the composer got up from the church table, fully satisfied the job was done - the Third Movement had finally been written to his own critical satisfaction. The Violin Concerto was complete and he had at last fulfilled his promise to his beloved Cathy.

He wrote a loving letter the following day and told her the news, adding his insistence that when or wherever it was performed for the first time she must be the soloist. "It is so much about you and me," he wrote, "our love, our music and our dream of Denny's Knoll which will soon become a reality."

The first two movements were in his room at Magdalene, he continued, and he was not prepared to entrust the only record of the Third to the Army Postal Service and would keep it with his personal belongings until he got back. He would present her with the full score only when she had answered "yes" to the question he would have asked her years ago had it not been for the war.

It was several weeks later that Patrick stood in file, rifle on shoulder, with his platoon on the Moresby airstrip waiting to board one of seven Dakota aircraft which were lined up on the runway to transport the battalion to Nadzab. Recently constructed by the Allies, this airfield was not far from the important and recently recaptured town of Lae on the north coast of New Guinea.

Prior to leaving their rest camp, the unit had been briefed on a campaign they were to wage against Japanese forces which occupied a strategic area where the mighty Ramu and Markham Rivers merged into a long, broad valley in the Finisterre Range. The Dakotas made round trips over three days before the battalion transfer was complete. Following a full parade the next day, they set out with native guides and porters for their destination to the lower reaches of the towering mountain range. The terrain was steep at first and it was extremely hot but there was no jungle or its attendant discomforts to contend with. The Australian foot-sloggers were grateful to Mother Nature for this concession.

Patrick kept his Section together on the long march and gave help and encouragement to the younger soldiers when he felt it was needed. Going into action caused extreme tension even among veteran soldiers, who knew what to expect, but it was a much more fearsome prospect for eighteen year old boys going in for the first time. He had always been a 'mother hen' and those who had served with him before smiled to themselves as the 'decent old bastard' went about his usual caring ways.

When the calculated compass point had been reached, temporary battalion headquarters were established with the limited amount of equipment the porters had carried up along the steep native pads. Guards were posted along a designated perimeter and the first reconnaissance patrols sent out to locate the Japanese force.

What appeared to be a medium sized enemy force was finally encountered near the entrance to the two river valley. The following day Patrick's B Company, together with C Company, advanced on the area on a wide, flanking front through semi-dense undergrowth and native grass of varying height which covered the area.

The resistance was unexpectedly weak and they fell back quickly against the first Australian foray. They did regroup around a few old native huts located closer to the valley and offered stiffer resistance but broke again as the assault became more concentrated. This puzzled the Australians for this was so unlike the Japanese who usually fought to the last man, especially so in such circumstances with the area around the buildings containing trenches and foxholes obviously constructed for defensive action.

The Australians had now lost contact with the enemy, who had retreated quickly into the valley itself. The two Companies were ordered to make camp in the hut area and await further orders before resuming their offensive. The rest of the battalion moved up to the forward group during the night and the huts became a temporary command post. The CO and the company commanders were concerned with the rapidity of the enemy retreat for such timidity was unheard of. Their suspicions were aroused and discussion on how to proceed was prolonged and detailed.

They arrived at a consensus that the Japanese were trying to lure them into the valley with undue haste and the obvious question was 'why'. Even though that was the Australian's intended route, the field officers decided to suspend their attack until they had additional Intelligence about the terrain, and the possible disposition and strength of the enemy force.

Forward patrols, sent from each platoon over the next two days, brought back much of the required information, except no enemy forces had been sighted and if they had remained in the area they were either deeply entrenched or well-camouflaged, or both.

For the first mile of so the valley was narrow, no more than a thousand yards in parts. The gentle slopes rising on either side were heavily wooded on the left or northern flank whilst the southern side was clear except for a small section two miles of so from the entrance. Here a thick stand of planted trees stood out starkly from the otherwise open countryside.

Local natives had told battalion Intelligence officers it was the site of an Anglican mission station which was deserted when the Japanese came into the area at the beginning of their New Guinea campaign. They had occupied the place until recently when it was thought they had retreated further down the valley.

On the basis of this information the CO decided they would enter the valley and advance down the extreme southern flank so that if any pockets of Japanese were concealed on the northern reach, their mortars and mountain cannon would be ineffective at that range. They would not proceed immediately for he and his staff were concerned about the Anglican Mission site. The enemy would have had time and opportunity to conceal a force armed with long range artillery on that higher ground, which could devastate any force advancing down that side of the valley.

Obviously, further reconnaissance was needed and a decision was made to send a long-distance patrol to the area to determine whether the Japanese were occupying the station or if it had been abandoned in their general retreat. It would be a difficult exercise, for the approach would be through open country and, if the Mission still was manned, the patrol exposed to enemy fire. Major Burley's suggestion that he had an experienced Section in one of his platoons which could do the job was welcomed by the CO and he ordered the exercise to be launched with least possible delay.

Less than half an hour later, Lieutenant Elsome, the current leader of Patrick's platoon, came to him and said the Company Commander wanted to see them both immediately. Burley received them in his makeshift tent and, without preamble, drew their attention to a hastily drawn map lying on a camp table, enlightening them of what had transpired at the CO's staff meeting.

"I want your platoon to supply the patrol, Bill," he said to Elsome. "I know it's a rough one but I think Sergeant Sheridan here has the experience to pull it off. It's an important job they have given us and I think he's the best man for the job."

"If you say so, sir," replied the young officer, "but I think, because of its obvious importance, I should lead it and at the same time have the benefit of Pat's experience."

"I'm afraid not. Let's face it, this is hazardous and there's no guarantee they will come through unscathed. I can't risk losing one of my platoon leaders just as we are about to go into action. No, I suggest we leave it to Sheridan. I'd like to know how he feels about it."

Patrick, who had not been asked to say a word at this stage, leant over the roughly drawn map and studied it closely before asking a question.

"How long are you giving us to do the job?"

"The CO would want the information within 24 hours; 36 at the latest."

"It may take longer if we are to do it right," replied Patrick. "If we try to go straight down the valley, if the Japs are there they will see us for sure at some stage and we won't be able to get close enough to see what they are up to. I'd like to suggest we take this native pad here," he said, pointing to a place on the map, "it will be a steep climb up that slope and will add a mile or two to the trek but it would bring us out behind those trees and with luck, we could observe the Mission from there without being detected."

"I can't argue with that," said the Major "but be as quick as you can, Pat, the CO's going to be right on my arse about this and that I can do without. Lieutenant Elsome will give you the pick of the platoon but I suppose you'd like to rely on your own blokes for this job."

"Yes, I would," confirmed Patrick. "If you can give us a native guide I'd like to get going before dark and get as far as we can tonight and then hole up for a while tomorrow and then get as close to the Mission as possible in the afternoon."

"Get going then Sergeant, and good luck. I'll see you as soon as you get back," advised the Company Commander, before adding as he handed them to the sergeant, "here, you better take my field glasses. You may need them but don't forget to return the bloody things," he concluded, giving Pat a meaningful look.

There was no saluting as the two men left the tent upon receiving their orders, for such protocol had been abandoned, together with badges of rank, in New Guinea since Japanese snipers had taken advantage of it to single out important targets.

Patrick returned to the company lines and found his Section where he had left it sitting around in a grassed hollow. Some were cleaning their rifles but the rest were just lying about smoking and talking as they tried to combat a soldier's major gripe... boredom.

He asked them to gather round and told them of the patrol.

"I think eight will be enough for this one. I want you Lenno and your Bren," he said turning to his good mate, Len Talbot. "Issey, Trevor and Stork can come and you three apes if you can stop brawling long enough." This was addressed with a laugh to three languid reinforcements who had been together since Crete and even though they would die for each other, they never seemed to stop arguing. But good soldiers they were and Patrick knew their worth from what he had seen of them at Milne Bay and Buna.

"Well, you're a nice kind of a bastard to have for a mate, what about me, aren't I coming?" this from his original bunkie at initial training, Corporal Ritchie.

"No, you're not, Phil. This is no doddle in the park and someone could get hurt or worse. Our mob here are going into action tomorrow and a lot of them for the first time and, if I'm late in getting back or something, it will be your job to look after them."

"Bugger that, Pat. They can look after themselves, they're big boys now, Mum's at home, and besides there are plenty of blokes in the platoon to show 'em how. They don't need me."

"I say they do and see you do a good job otherwise I might have to kick your arse, Corporal," said Patrick, closing the subject on his friend's frustration.

It was late the following afternoon when the patrol arrived at the position at the top of the Mission which Patrick had plotted. It had been fairly easy so far. The native guide knew the area well and it had been a carefree trek, which induced the patrol leader into a light frame of mind.

He was feeling good. He could foresee an eventual end to the war now as the Japanese were in full retreat in New Guinea and the Americans were pushing them back in all parts of the South Pacific. Perhaps it would be all over within a year, he thought. His wildest dreams of returning to his music, Cathy, his parents, Magdalene and Denny's Knoll, may yet be realised. He felt very satisfied with finishing the Third Movement, not only for the work itself but because with its completion had come a realisation there was an enormous amount of music in his soul yet to be written. And so, despite the circumstances for him being there, Patrick found himself to be happy and optimistic about his future as he lay with his men in the deep grass on a ridge overlooking the old Anglican Mission Station.

He trained the major's field glasses on the building and could see no sign of life but he was not fully convinced for he knew the Japanese to be cunning bastards who knew every trick of the game of war.

"The rest of you blokes stay here and you come with me Len and bring the Bren and we'll go down for a closer look at this joint," he whispered to the patrol. Crouching low in the grass the two soldiers ran down the slope towards the buildings and stopped before the high grass cover ended about a hundred yards or so short of their objective. Patrick again peered through the field glasses for several minutes.

"There's nobody there, Len, I think we can go in," said Patrick as he started to stand up.

At that moment the vigilant lance-corporal saw a glint in a leafy corral tree at the front of the building and yelled, "Stay down Pat!"

But it was too late. The sniper's shot rang out and Pat Sheridan was dead before his body fell to the ground.

Epilogue

Irene Sheridan was helping the housekeeper clear the breakfast things at Magdalene when she heard the car drive up to the homestead. Looking from the window, she did not recognise it as one belonging to a usual caller and saw Tom, who was having his after-breakfast cigarette, walk across to it as the driver alighted.

She recognised the Bathurst postmaster, Howard Pfitzner, a longtime friend of her husband, and wondered what had brought him all the way out here. His face seemed sombre as he talked to Tom, whose head had fallen forward on to his chest, as his friend, placing a hand on his shoulder, handed him an envelope. After dejectedly walking back to the car, he got in and drove away.

She was filled with dread as she realised the purpose of the man's mission and rushed outside to her husband who was walking towards her

"He's dead Ire, our boy's dead," he said simply, in an unrecognisable, broken voice that was full of despair. The colour drained from her face as she opened and then read the telegram she had taken from his hand. She let it drop from her nerveless fingers and stood there staring straight ahead, as though transfixed, with an expression of such pain and anguish on her ashen features that Tom thought she would collapse. He put his arms around her in support.

After a few moments, she eased herself away and walked slowly back to the house. Going to her room she shut the door and fell to her knees in silent prayer. When lying on the bed later, she closed her eyes, but not in sleep, and still her tears did not come. She had not screamed or emitted a wail nor had she wept upon hearing the dreadful news, for her suffering seemed far too profound for the usual manifestations of a mother's grief for a child who had been taken from her forever.

Only for very brief periods did she leave the room for the next several days. She was not interested in food and would not have consumed the little she had during that period had it not been for the strong insistence of Tom and Molly the housekeeper.

It was not until the following day that Tom found the strength to put into words, again, what had happened to his son. He telephoned Cathy Jordan's father and told him the heartbreaking news so that she could learn of it gently and in the presence of an understanding and loving parent.

It was some months before Irene could bring herself to resume any of the activities of her former everyday life. She had no real interest in living now, but also realised she had to go on existing and would have to make the best of it. The passage of time had made her accept she had lost her son even though she knew he would live in her heart and mind forever; to her he could never be dead - her memories of him would be part of her for as long as she lived.

As much as she wanted to, her heavy heart would not allow her to touch Patrick's personal belongings when they were returned by the Army. Tom asked Molly to go through them and send all clothing and other soldier's gear to one of the charities in Bathurst and any other items should be handed to him and not Irene. The latter comprised just two books, some opened letters to Patrick from Cathy and a parcel of music which, he told Irene, "I put in that drawer with Patrick's other music."

Irene and Cathy spoke on the telephone once or twice a month now. Initially, they had been unable to share their grief with each other because of the emotional upheaval and great sense of sadness which seemed to engulf them when they tried to converse in those early days of their grief. But now that time, the great salve, had started its work, they were able to talk more comfortably. Inevitably, when her father told her the dreadful news, Cathy had been totally devastated and inconsolable for several days. The SSO management had given her four weeks compassionate leave to recover and she spent two of these, with her mother, at a quiet guest house in Bowral, a small rustic, country town not that far from Sydney. Long walks on her own, many tears and deliberately conjured up memories of him helped her to recover sufficiently to re-join the orchestra. But her grief was far from quelled and, like Irene, she had begun to wonder if life now was worthwhile.

Cathy was aware that, whilst it had been lessening, there still remained a degree of intensity about Irene's grief which required her to avoid some subjects in their telephone conversations. But in their most recent exchange she felt she now could put a question she had been wanting to ask for a long time.

"Mother, did you find a manuscript amongst the army things when you unpacked them?"

Irene hesitated for a moment before replying in a voice not quite under control.

"I couldn't bring myself to look at them, dear," she said shakily. "Tom and Molly did that and Tom told me there was some music and he put it with other music Patrick kept in his room."

Cathy's heart beat a little faster for the Concerto had come to mean so much more to her now that Patrick had gone. It was not solely for the music itself but also because she cherished the thought of the love and devotion which lay behind the composer's reason for writing the opus for her. It would provide her with a special and intimate link with him. She had secretly hoped the work would manifest the depth of loving tenderness he had expressed for her on so many occasions.

"Dear mother," she said, "I understand why you don't want to touch his things yet. The reminders would be too painful, but would you mind if I came up for a few days and went through his music? He spoke about writing a violin concerto for me and it is something I would treasure very much if it is there."

"Of course, and I'd be grateful Cathy if you could," Irene responded. "Something should be done about his music. It can't be left lying there unknown and unplayed, I know that. I did play some of his piano pieces for him and their beauty was enough to break your heart. Tom and I'll look forward to seeing you soon."

Irene took strength from Cathy's presence and together they gathered his music and took it to the drawing room and spread it on the large table in the centre. Cathy found the first two movements immediately and then, after an anxious minute or so, discovered the package of the still rolled manuscript which was the Third Movement - it was the happiest moment she had experienced since Patrick's death.

Irene brought some sort of order to the piano music by collating it in the sequence of the dates of composition which Patrick had recorded on the manuscripts. She placed the pile alongside the large folder of her son's Outback Symphony and left the room as the young girl sat herself at the table and began to study the Concerto for Violin.

It was almost two hours later that she came back to the room and Cathy looked up from where she was still sitting. With a look of awe and wonderment on her face, she pushed the music away, stood up and turned to the older woman.

"I don't know, Mother Sheridan, perhaps I've been carried away by a new sense of closeness to Patrick, but I think this is absolutely glorious music," she said, in a serious and restrained tone of voice, referring to the concerto and symphony. "I could never find words to describe what I have just experienced but its left me with a renewed sense of reverence for our Patrick's genius. Outwardly, he was such a wonderfully normal person and to think he had so much magnificence inside him just waiting to emerge is…"

She could not go on and, with tears streaming down her face, she walked across the room and put her arms around Patrick's now weeping mother. It was some minutes before their sobbing subsided.

After dinner that evening they took a walk together along the property's quietly running stream and their conversation returned to the music.

"I've been thinking about it, Cathy. I know instinctively his music is as inspired as you say it is and it should be published and performed. We can't let it be forgotten, we owe him much more than that," said his mother, whose residual grief had given way, perhaps only temporarily, to a sense of duty towards her son.

"Cathy," she continued, "I think we should approach Professor Morrison. He certainly was aware of Patrick's greatness and I'd have no hesitation in asking if he could arrange for his Conservatorium orchestra to perform my son's music."

"The same thought crossed my mind, dear," replied Cathy. "Julian is an old family friend and very approachable and I'm sure he will do all he can. If you're happy for me to do so, I could take the two works down to him and see what he has to say."

"That would be wonderful. I'll write to him tonight and tell him of your intention and express my thanks to him in anticipation for anything he can do to assist us."

Cathy returned to Sydney the following day and it was several days later that Irene received a telephone call from Julian Morrison who, after an initial exchange, told her, "I'm sorry, Mrs. Sheridan, but there is no way my orchestra could give a first performance of your son's work. Music of such magnificence cannot be born in our stable but in one of the great music auditoria of the world. I knew your son to be a pianist without peer but this orchestral music he has written could, in my opinion, rank with the greatest ever composed. I am not given to exaggeration but I have never been so impressed in all my life.

"With your permission," he went on, "I will approach the ABC and Sir William Lawson with a view to him conducting the Sydney Symphony in an initial performance of these incredible works. Bill Lawson is well aware of your son's prowess and I feel I can assure you now your wishes will be fulfilled in due course."

Irene, who had listened in silence to the professor, expressed her gratitude in heartfelt terms before concluding by saying, "There is just one other thing, Professor. Patrick dedicated the Concerto to Cathy Jordan and it was his express wish she be soloist for its first performance. I'm afraid I would have to insist upon that."

"I wouldn't have it any other way, Mrs. Sheridan, and I'm sure the conductor will agree with us. Thank you very much for allowing me to join you in launching this wonderful contribution to that small stream of really great music."

In prominent advertisements in the Sydney daily press, the ABC announced the date of a concert by the Sydney Symphony Orchestra giving the first performance of works by the Australian composer, Patrick Sheridan. These comprising his *Symphony Number 1 in F Major ("The Outback")* and *Concerto for Violin and Orchestra in C Sharp Minor* with soloist Catherine Jordan. The orchestra being under the baton of its current resident conductor, Sir William Lawler.

Although not part of the subscription series, subscribers to the ABC Season Concerts came in numbers to the Sydney Town Hall to hear this sold-out concert of works by a new Australian composer.

These music lovers lived for the works of the master composers. For many of them music was an essential part of being and the SSO supplied Beethoven, Mozart, Bach, Brahms and one or two others in generous quantity to satisfy this need. However, they did welcome an occasional change of fare and an opportunity to hear a new 'voice' could not be resisted. Tonight it was to be that of an Australian, almost unprecedented, and it brought an air of expectancy to the hall as it began to fill.

Little did these musical sophisticates and other members of the audience know they were about to embark on an emotional roller-coaster of such intensity, they would probably remember this occasion for the rest of their days.

From the opening bars of the Outback Symphony a silence fell over the auditorium. No one moved, spoke or coughed for fear of missing a note, for such was the mesmerism of the brilliant music they were hearing. This was maintained between movements when, apart from a loud gasp or two, there was hardly a sound to be heard as the audience awaited the next stanza of the totally engrossing opus.

There was a pause, and the maestro had time to lay down his baton, after the last bars of the symphony had been played, before the assembly reacted. It was as though it had taken time to catch its collective breath as a consequence of what it had just experienced. Then an explosion of applause rent the hall as the audience, almost as one, rose to its feet, clapping and cheering in a scene of frenzied excitement seldom witnessed at celebrity concerts. Sir William Lawler was recalled to the platform on five occasions and each time beckoned the orchestra to join him in acknowledging the incredible and enthusiastic expression of appreciation for what they had just performed.

At the intermission which followed, many patrons took to the large foyer where the excitement continued and all the obvious questions were being asked. So little was known about the composer and there was little or no real enlightenment in the official programme. They were impressed beyond measure, almost incredulous, that such stunningly glorious music they had just heard was composed by one of their own countrymen.

A seething excitement continued as they resumed their seats. Eagerness to hear his other work was manifest from the low-voiced chatter going on throughout the hall and it did not cease until the conductor appeared on the platform in company with the strikingly beautiful, but virtually unknown, violinist, Catherine Jordan.

The SSO was at the top of its form that night and, in communion with the soloist, gave a rendition of a work of such majestic stature and captivating beauty that it compelled the patrons to total silence, once again. In essence, this was a musically sophisticated crowd, aware of the exquisite brilliance of the work being performed for the first time and, at its conclusion they applauded it - perhaps a little less boisterously, with perhaps more enthusiasm than they had for the symphony.

The soloist had made the difference. Her beauty and the intensity and sensitivity of her playing had endeared her to most of them. This was especially so for those close enough to the platform to see the tears which spilled down her cheek and on to her instrument as she played the plaintive heart-moving theme of the sonata which was so dominant in the final Third Movement.

The audience would not let them go and they were recalled to the platform several times, including once when the conductor fell back and let the soloist take a bow on her own. This drove the acclamation up a decibel or two.

Having made what was to be a final appearance, they had turned to leave the stage when a single, strident male voice from the southern gallery started calling, "Composer, composer." He was joined by other voices and then more, until the entire hall seemed to be shouting the same word. The noise was deafening for although the concert was over, hardly a soul had left their seat.

The conductor and the girl stopped and, after exchanging a few words, returned to centre stage. As he stepped on to the podium, she took a position by its side. He held up his hands and waited for the clamour to die down before addressing the still smouldering gathering in a conversational tone of voice.

He told them how regrettable it was the composer could not be with them, for he too would have liked to thank him for writing some of the finest music he had ever been called upon to conduct. He had been fortunate enough to know this man, he said, who was an undoubted musical genius. He was a pianist without peer with a musical mind and soul of such depth it was way beyond his comprehension.

Then, with emotion creeping into his voice, he continued, "As much as I admired him as a musician I have to say I admired him more as a human being. I saw him sacrifice everything he had for the sake of his principles. He was about to embark on what would have been an illustrious career but abandoned it with his other human ambitions in order to serve his country. His voluntary enlistment in the Australian Army in the early days of the war both astounded and dismayed all those who knew of his extraordinary gift.

"You will have noticed I have been referring to him in the past tense and it is with deep sadness I tell you he made one more sacrifice for his beloved country; that of his own life, for his was killed in action at the age of twenty five. His body was never recovered and lies buried in an unmarked grave somewhere in the highlands of New Guinea."

He paused for a few moments and looked out over the sea of faces, still seated in the now unearthly silent hall before concluding...

"Here was a great patriot, here was a magnificent musician but, above all, here was a man."

He stepped down from the podium and, taking the arm of the silently weeping girl, they left the platform together, as the stunned audience, now quiet and sombre, left their seats and slowly made their way out of the auditorium.

About the Author

Gerald Buttrose was born in 1923 in the Perth suburb of Nedlands, Western Australia and grew up, with six siblings, in the seaside village of Henley Beach in South Australia.

He served with the Australian Army in New Guinea during World War II before spending the next forty years as a business man in the City of Sydney.

He is married with four children and for the length of his business life lived in the suburb of St.Ives. He and his wife, Colleen, now reside in Ballina on the north-east coast of New South Wales.

www.ingramcontent.com/pod-product-compliance
Lightning Source LLC
Chambersburg PA
CBHW070159120726
47909CB00001B/171